MW01633977

THE HARP

Other books by the author:

Shpeter I

Shpeter II

Chaimkel the Dreamer

A Face at the Window

The Amazing Lumberjack

Sparks from the Torah

The Birdsong and Other Stories

Wings and Other Stories

Meir Uri Gottesman

FELDHEIM PUBLISHERS

First published 2005

Paperback: ISBN 978-1-68025-613-0

FELDHEIM PUBLISHERS
POB 34549
Jerusalem, Israel

208 Airport Executive Park
Nanuet, NY 10954
www.feldheim.com

Distributed in Europe by:
LEHMANNS
+44-0-191-430-0333
info@lehmanns.co.uk
www.lehmanns.co.uk

Distributed in Australia by:
GOLDS WORLD OF JUDAICA
+613 95278775
info@golds.com.au
www.golds.com.au

Printed in USA

Dedication

I dedicate this book to my
beloved children and grandchildren.
May you go from strength to strength in
Torah and mitzvos,
together with all of Israel, amen!

Special thanks to my dear wife, Susan,
for being a wonderful
eishes chayil and partner.
Thank you to the Targum Press staff, particularly Rabbi Dombey, Miriam Zakon, Diane Liff, and Chaya Baila Gavant, for all your hard work on this book.

PROLOGUE

Yoseph climbed high into the stony Shomron hills, seeking his secret refuge. The warm rays of the Sivan sun beat down heavily, and the mountainsides shimmered. He beat a firm tattoo with his staff, and his flock of sheep and goats followed in step, their little neck bells tinkling plaintively.

Deep into the hills, he climbed a rise and entered a thick copse of pines, letting the sheep meander as they would, grazing among the scraggly grass and underbrush. He passed through the pines and came out to a small clearing. Before him fell a steep hollow in whose bottom grew an ancient, gnarled apple tree. Its small green fruit were just budding, perfuming the warm air with their fragrance. Nearby, a tiny brook murmured.

He climbed down to the tree and reached a small mound of stones hidden beneath its branches. He pulled away the stones, reached down to a hole he had dug out, and extracted a large leather pouch, bound tight by a thick woolen cord. He carefully undid the cord and stretched open the pouch. Carefully, he extracted a tall, graceful harp, nearly a cubit in height. He had made it himself, cutting the cedar branches, then trimming, planing, shaping, and polishing them. Over its heart-shaped frame he stretched six strings that he had twisted himself from cured sheep veins. The harp glinted in his hands, its wood as unmarked as it had been the day he polished it.

He took one last look around and began playing, his fingers flashing flawlessly over the strings. As he played, he sang *Barchi Nafshi* in honor of Rosh Chodesh, the new moon, lifting his voice sweetly, his words flitting over the notes like a bird flitting from leaf to leaf, touching here, landing there, its wings lifted toward heaven....

> *Ashirah laShem b'chayai, azamerah leilokai b'odi, ye'erav alav sichi, anochi esmach baShem* — I will sing praises to my God while I endure. May my words be sweet to Him — I will rejoice in Hashem. Sinners will cease from the earth, and the wicked will be no more. Bless Hashem, O my soul, *Hallelukah!*

He daydreamed that he stood not under a hidden apple tree in the forest, but in the Mikdash, on the *duchan*, in front of the holy altar. In just under two years he would come of age, twenty-five, and would begin training for the service in the Mikdash. But now, he stood alone under the clear blue sky and sang his heart out to Hashem.

He looked up and saw suddenly that he was not alone. A man stood atop the rise gazing down at him. He stood in the same spot that Yoseph had emerged from, as though he had followed his footsteps. How long had he been there, and what had he seen — or heard? Yoseph had no idea. He lowered his harp, trying to conceal it behind him, and waved a greeting.

The man smiled and climbed down the little hill to Yoseph. Yoseph could not determine his age. He seemed elderly, yet he had a youthful spryness. He wore simple clothing — perhaps he was also a shepherd.

"*Chodesh tov!*" the man greeted in a friendly fashion.

"*Chodesh tov!*" Yoseph responded warily.

They stood there, the stranger looking at Yoseph in an almost fatherly fashion and Yoseph looking back uneasily.

"How long have you been here?" he asked the stranger.

"Not long. I was nearby and the sound of your playing came

through the trees. I came to listen. I see you are upset. Perhaps you are frightened of me. You need not be."

"This is my private place, where I am alone with...my harp. No one knows about this place."

"Do not fear, I am the last one to tell. Do you think you are the only one who wishes to be alone with Hashem or to sing words of praise? I also have my hiding place, and I also know how to sing."

Yoseph stared at the man, and his face softened. "In truth?"

"Why would I say a falsehood? I also sing, I even know the harp — perhaps we can sing together."

"What is your name?" asked Yoseph.

"Yaakov," he answered. "And what is yours?"

"Yoseph, son of Nachum — a Levite."

"*Shalom aleichem*," the man said, sticking out his hand. This time they shook hands warmly, and Yoseph was more at ease.

"I heard you play, and I felt the *kedushah* of your words. That is why I followed your music. Please — play more."

Yoseph demurred. His music was meant for the Almighty, when he was alone with his thoughts, when he could dream of the Mikdash — not for pleasing others. "I cannot," he said firmly. "My song is for when I am alone."

Yaakov stood there, tugging reflectively at his salt-and-pepper beard. He had a unique face, thin and fine, yet rugged and of the fields. He looked like a shepherd — but where were his sheep?

He turned to Yoseph with a twinkle. "It is Rosh Chodesh, a time to celebrate the new moon. Come, do not be stubborn — that is not a holy trait. You will play, and I shall sing — do you agree?"

He had such a warm, fatherly look that Yoseph softened. "You sing," answered Yoseph, "and I will follow you on my harp."

Yaakov gave him an appreciative smile, raised his hand, and furrowed his face in reflection. He swayed back and forth, mustering up every ounce of concentration. He seemed to have forgotten that Yoseph was there. Yoseph watched him closely and began to tremble.

I am in the presence of a tzaddik, Yoseph knew.

Finally, Yaakov lowered his hand, gave Yoseph a loving look as if he had known him all his life, and began singing:

> *Halleluhu b'teika shofar, halleluhu b'neivel v'chinor. Halleluhu b'tof u'machol, halleluhu b'minim v'ugav. Halleluhu b'tziltzelei shama, halleluhu b'tziltzelei teruah. Kol haneshamah t'hallel Kah, Hallelukah. Kol haneshamah t'hallel Kah, Hallelukah!*
>
> Praise Him with the sound of the shofar, praise Him with lyre and harp. Praise Him with song and dance, praise Him with organ and flute. Praise Him with clanging cymbals, praise Him with resonant trumpets. Let all souls praise God, Hallelukah! Let all souls praise God, *Hallelukah*!

Yaakov's voice lifted high into the heavens, and a handful of birds who were hiding in the apple tree flew off in fright. His voice was very strong, and it penetrated deep into Yoseph's own dreams. His fingers raced quickly up and down the strings of his harp, trying to match the power of the singer. Finally, after singing the psalm over and over and over again, Yaakov finished his song. He turned to Yoseph, smiled, and then shook his head.

Yoseph looked at him, puzzled.

"No good," Yaakov said quietly. "The harp is missing something."

This is my reward? Yoseph wondered.

"What is it missing?" he asked, feeling affronted.

"Please," Yaakov said, "let me hold the harp for a moment...."

Yoseph said nothing, but on its own his head shook — no.

"Do not be afraid. I will not harm you or your harp. It is very beautiful and very precious. But it is still missing something. Are you afraid that I will run away with it? You are younger than I. You will easily catch me, punish me."

Still, Yoseph hesitated. *I do not want a stranger's hands on my harp*, he thought.

Yaakov did not argue. But he looked deep into Yoseph's eyes, and for a moment Yoseph thought that he was staring at the Mikdash itself. He suddenly felt very weak. He handed the harp to the stranger.

Yaakov took it and held it over his chest, over his heart. Again, that same gesture. He lifted his right hand and furrowed his forehead in concentration. He paused a long time. Finally, he lifted his head. His eyes were closed, and he seemed in another world.

"*Achat!*" he cried out softly.

Then he raised his hand to the first string and cried out: "*Achat — ve'achat*!" He plucked at the first string and listened.

"*Achat u'shtayim*!" He plucked at the second string, listening.

"*Achat veshalosh*!" He plucked the third string.

"*Achat ve'arba*!" The fourth string.

"*Achat vechameish*!" The fifth string.

He paused, swayed with great *kavanah,* and exclaimed with great fervor: "*Achat vasheish*!"

He laid his fingers on the sixth string, and strummed it over and over.

"*Achat vasheish*!" he repeated. He stood still for a moment and then shook his head. He opened his great eyes and looked at Yoseph.

"This sixth string — it is missing something."

"What is it missing?" protested Yoseph. "It is like the rest. I stretched it myself! The sound is clear, pure."

"It is clear, it is pure — but it does not have all the tone it should have. Do not be offended. I am older than you are, and I have known the sound of the harp all my life. The string that you set must have more. Here —"

He reached into a pocket of his tunic and extracted one string. "You see — God ordained that I should have just a string that you need! Come, you can put it on yourself."

He stretched out his hand with the string dangling from it. Hesitantly, Yoseph reached out and took the string from him. He ran his fingers over it and held it alongside his own strings.

"Where does it come from?" he asked.

"It is from the vein of a ram. I cured and twisted it myself. It has all the tone in it — see, put it in your harp and you will hear!"

Quickly, Yoseph loosened his own sixth string and removed it. He tried to attach Yaakov's string. It was very compact, and, as much as he struggled, he could not stretch it onto the frame. "What is this made of?" he asked.

"Here, let me do it," the old man said.

Yoseph was reluctant to hand his precious instrument to the

stranger. It was his harp — he had made it himself. But Yaakov looked at him with such warmth and authority that Yoseph quickly surrendered the instrument into his hands.

Yaakov took back the string, grasped the harp close to his chest, and with one powerful tug wrenched the string over the frame. Yoseph knew that had it been one of his strings, it would have broken. Yaakov adjusted the knot, played his fingers gently over the string, and nodded. He returned the harp to Yoseph.

"Now, play," he said, handing back the harp. As he took back the instrument, Yoseph glanced at the old man's face. His features had suddenly turned intensely sad, and he looked away.

Yoseph held the harp, no longer shy to play before this man. Part of the stranger had infused itself into the harp. Without thinking, he began his song:

> *Lo amut ki echyeh va'asaper maasei Kah* — I shall not die! But I shall live and relate the deeds of God!

He did not choose the verse, the verse chose him. The new string drew his fingers to it, demanding to be played, and he sang the holy verse over and over. Why this verse? Why this verse? The harp's music soared. It bore into his heart, and his body trembled with joy and fear.

He stared at Yaakov. The old man stood there transfixed, his hands clenched into fists, his eyes shut tight, his lips racing in intense prayer.

Finally, overcome, Yoseph stopped. He watched the tzaddik pray, until finally his eyes opened. Yaakov's smile reappeared, but the sadness still reigned, like the sun poking through a storm cloud.

"Father Yaakov, it is late and I must go now. Tomorrow at dawn we begin the journey to bring *bikkurim* to the Mikdash. I must return and make ready. When shall we meet again?"

Yaakov lifted his hands heavenward. "Yoseph, we will meet again, of that I am sure. But when? How?" He shrugged. "Hashem will decide, at the right time, for the right purpose! Go, for I, too, must leave."

"Please, give me a *berachah* before you go," Yoseph requested.

"The road to Jerusalem is fraught with danger!"

"Who am I to bless?" Yaakov answered. Even so, he raised his hand to Yoseph's head, closed his eyes, and proclaimed: " '*Bein porat Yoseph, bein porat alei ayin* — A fruitful vine is Joseph, a fruitful vine by a spring.' Like Yoseph, Hashem has made you very handsome. Like Yoseph, your brothers shall hate you and strangers shall imprison you. Like Yoseph, you shall live, and your holiness will glow like the moon at its zenith!"

Yaakov turned and climbed quickly up the hill, disappearing into the pines. It was almost as though he was afraid that Yoseph would follow him. Yoseph stood momentarily, deep in thought. The noon sun beat down warmly, and his head felt heavy. He heard again the tinkling of the sheep's bells. Had he dreamt the whole thing? He lifted his harp and plucked on the new string.

No — it was no dream.

Chapter One

Two years before the Churban

The road to Jerusalem was crowded with pilgrims. Yoseph's whole village of Tapuach was on the move, his ancient great-great-uncle, his cousins and second and third cousins, and of course his father and brothers. Behind them, in front of them were clans from Shomron and Galilee, from Levonah and Shiloh, Tzippori and Meron, Shechem, Beit El, Dotan, Har HaMelech — a crush of humanity packed into the ancient *derech ha'avot*, winding through the Binyamin hills.

The sound of flutes and drums reverberated through the air, and the lowing of oxen who enjoyed a few days of garlanded glory, their horns painted gold, before they were abruptly collared in the Temple rings and slaughtered for sacrifices. There were baskets of fruit everywhere, balanced on heads, loaded on carts, and hanging from the backs of donkeys and camels. They were laden with the seven fruits of Eretz Yisrael — piles of wheat and barley, clusters of purple grapes and golden figs, stacks of pomegranates, olives, and dates. The air was so thick with fragrance that one could become intoxicated just by breathing deeply.

The road hummed with conversation, Torah talk, family talk, Roman talk. Although the atmosphere was joyous, the people were worried. How much longer would they be able to continue this trip to the Mikdash? Would the Roman armies interfere with their ascent, Heaven forbid? And underneath it all, like the roar of a waterfall, the beat of ten thousand footsteps, marching, marching to Yerushalayim.

Yoseph walked alongside his grandfather, Elchanan. The wizened old man, whose skin had turned a deep walnut from the sun, never discussed farm business or battle news. His thoughts and his conversation focused only on words of Torah, which was why Yoseph loved to be with him. From time to time he broke into a joyous Levite melody, and Yoseph sang along. The young men with flutes and drums were inspired and began playing loudly. Soon, the whole section echoed with the holy sounds of praise and thanks.

The sun reached its zenith, and the family stopped at a grove of palms alongside of the road. Many other clans also stopped to rest, waiting for the cooler afternoon shade. Yoseph squeezed next to his grandfather, while his father and his brothers and their families gathered across the road. They washed their hands and shared a pita bread soaked in olive oil. Sabba sat silently, meditatively.

"What are you pondering, Sabba?" the young man asked.

His grandfather glanced at him but did not answer. He chewed his bread and then took a sip from a small water jug.

Finally, he broke his silence: "It is difficult getting older. Passages that I knew so clearly become confused in my head. Maybe it is the sun."

"How many times have you made this journey to Yerushalayim?" Yoseph asked.

His grandfather smiled, his dark, leathery face wrinkling. "Who knows? However many years that I am alive — even before I was born my mother made the trip riding a donkey. They carried me to Yerushalayim as an infant, and since I could walk I have always gone."

"So many steps you've walked!"

Sabba shrugged with impatience. "Steps? Walked? You talk like a heathen. Not how many steps — how many mitzvos I've accumulated! Every *pesiah* and *pesiah* — a mitzvah!"

"Still, Sabba, it must not have been easy."

Sabba gave Yoseph a hard look. "My grandson Yoseph, I am disappointed in you. A mitzvah is not hard — missing a mitzvah is hard. Are we not Levi'im? Every step brings us closer to the *Shechinah*, higher, higher. Do you think that is hard?"

The afternoon sun moved westward over the hills, and in the cooler evening the procession moved on. Like high tide, churning with wild breakers and sudden whirlpools, the people moved, some clans walking slowly, others racing ahead to find the best lodging. Yoseph's clan moved in a steady, calm, deliberate pace.

Yoseph became separated from his grandfather and moved closer to the front of his company, where a garlanded ox plodded in the lead. He looked to the right and saw his father had caught up with him, walking a step behind him. It was the first time the two had been together since dawn.

"Shalom, Abba Mori," Yoseph greeted him formally.

His father did not return his greeting. He spoke in an undertone. "Yoseph, keep walking and do not look around."

Instinctively, Yoseph turned his head.

"I say don't turn your head and you turn your head," his father hissed. "Just walk naturally, as though everything is fine."

Yoseph patted the ox distractedly. "What happened?"

"The Romans — they're close. They took Timnah last night, and now they are moving on Emmaus. They're on the hilltops above us. They're trying not to be noticed, but our scouts spotted them."

"Do you think they will attack?"

"Who can tell? So far, there are too few of them for the many that we are. If they came down, we would have the advantage. But we have to be ready, just in case."

"What shall I do?"

"What shall you do? Wake up, won't you! For once try to be a man like your brothers. What happened to Sabba?"

Without waiting for an answer, his father slowed his steps and dropped back, rejoining Yoseph's brothers. Yoseph scanned the hilltops, but he saw nothing of the Romans. Meanwhile, he pushed through the press of marchers and sought out his grandfather.

THAT NIGHT, the pilgrims encamped at Shiloh. It was cool in the Binyamin hills, and families huddled together for warmth and safety. The news of the Roman advances spread among the pilgrims, and there was a sense of danger as well as excitement. The women camped separately beneath a grove of palms, while the men gathered around the patriarch. They sang songs of Zion,

"*Samachti b'omrim*... I rejoiced when they said to me, 'Let us go to the house of Hashem,' " and played their flutes. But it could not completely drive away the icy fear.

Yoseph shared the base of a palm tree with his grandfather. He rested his head against the trunk and stared upward at the moonless, star-filled sky. The camp had finally grown quiet.

"Sabba, do you think the Romans will try to capture Yerushalayim?"

Sabba snorted impatiently. "Go to sleep and ask your father that question in the morning."

I wish, Yoseph thought. "What if, *chas veshalom*, they try to destroy our Mikdash?" he pressed.

Elchanan did not answer, so Yoseph nudged him. "Sabba?"

"Yoseph, if *chas veshalom* the walls of our Mikdash are again destroyed, it will not come from the Romans. Our own *sinah* will consume them."

"*Chas veshalom*," Yoseph answered quickly.

"*Chas veshalom, chas veshalom, chas veshalom*," murmured Elchanan.

Above, sparkling constellations circled in still, splendid majesty. Below, grandfather and grandson finally shut their eyes and slept, dreaming of olive groves and vineyards, of sweet-sounding flutes and silver baskets piled high with golden *bikkurim* fruit.

DAWN OF the second day broke gloriously, the skies radiant and pure. A fresh breeze blew from the north, and the pilgrims rose invigorated and excited. Despite little sleep, Yoseph awoke with new passion to ascend to the Mikdash. Dread of the Romans had evaporated like the morning dew. All Israel was here, thousands and more thousands, streaming like a great river towards Yerushalayim.

The pilgrims left Shiloh, past the vineyards where the Benjamites had caught wives for themselves in the days of Shaul, and set their course for Beit El. The air was electric and joyful. At midmorning, the procession halted abruptly. Yoseph's section tried to march forward, but no one moved in front of them. The pilgrims in front had all stopped and were clumped together from one end of the road to the next. There was no place to move. The marchers behind them pressed forward, so that for a moment there was a danger that they would be crushed. But a signal was quickly passed further back, and the whole procession of pilgrims came to a halt. Donkeys brayed in annoyance, camels screamed in protest. Even the docile oxen began lowing in impatience. Sabba turned in bewilderment to Yoseph.

"Why have the people stopped walking?"

Yoseph shook his head. He turned to the pilgrims near him, but they also were perplexed. He turned and forced his way back to where his three brothers stood near one of the family wagons.

He approached his oldest brother, Shimon. It was the first time they had spoken since they left Tapuach. "Do you know anything about why we have stopped?" he asked.

Shimon looked at him and shrugged, but did not answer. Yoseph turned to the two others, Levi, who was closest to him in age, and his younger brother, Binyamin.

"Who knows?" Levi finally answered. "Maybe it's just too crowded. Or the Romans have a company blocking the road."

The brothers turned away, and Yoseph returned to his grandfather. He did not want to upset the old man by sharing his brothers' conjectures about a Roman company, even though that seemed a very likely explanation. "I'm not sure, Sabba. We might as well sit down and wait."

As if by signal, the whole procession accommodated itself to the delay. The people tethered their animals and found places to sit right on the road. These delays had happened before.

"Why don't we go on?" demanded Elchanan impatiently.

"Sabba, the road is blocked," Yoseph explained.

The old man waved his arm. "So we walk through the mountains! It is almost the *chag*!"

Yoseph smiled to himself. Nothing could stop his grandfather.

The noon sun rose, the heat built mercilessly, and a miasma of disappointment and fear blanketed the pilgrims. There was no way to move, either backward or forward. Here and there was heard the sound of flutes as pilgrims tried to lift their spirits, but even they had a lonely, poignant call, like the piteous peeping of trapped birds, not the joyous lilt that had been heard earlier.

Suddenly, the great horde of pilgrims rose in alarm. From a distance could be heard a roar like distant thunder. The thunder rolled closer, growing louder and more ominous, like an approaching storm. But what was it? Yoseph was filled with dread, and all those about him screamed hysterically. Children ran to mothers, and men stood frozen in panic. Whatever it was, it was heading their way.

Suddenly, it was their turn. A cry went up, and the throngs in front of Yoseph turned and began running back, trying to escape. Yoseph grabbed his grandfather out of harm's way to prevent him from being crushed. The families in front of Yoseph pushed to the right side of the road, attempting to flee, and abruptly the road was clear. Now came a deafening thunder of hoofbeats, the piercing blast of trumpets. The crowds fell back like wheat before a scythe. A huge company of Roman cavalry descended furiously upon them, their huge black stallions whinnying wildly and frothing at the mouth, their standards whipping grandly over their heads. They were rushing north to battle, and nothing would stop them. Whoever fell under their steeds was trampled. They were armed to the teeth, and their great helmets shielded their faces so that they looked like warriors conjured from a nightmare. They rode on and on, an endless raging column, trampling underfoot everything before them. The steep hillsides magnified their thunder, and they raised a cloud of choking brown dust that stretched for miles and blotted out the sunlight.

And then — they were gone!

There was a moment of shocked silence as the stunned pilgrims absorbed what had happened. Then a huge scream went up from every side. Mothers cried for their children, husbands searched for their wives, families for their elderly parents. The whole procession was thrown into turmoil, and the animals, frightened by the huge steeds, shook with fear.

It took many minutes before order was restored. Bit by bit, things returned to normal, children were found, families were reunited. No one was really hurt — just shocked. In an hour's time, the pilgrims were eager to move on.

But the great procession did not restart. Nothing was happening, no one moved. It was already late afternoon, the sun still burned hotly. People inquired of each other, rumors abounded — but no one knew. What was happening? Towards sunset, there suddenly appeared a very disturbing sight. A line of pilgrims was marching backwards, to the north. Why were they retreating? At first it was a thin line of marchers, but soon it grew into a thick column. It looked like the march back home after the *chag*, not the *aliyat haregel* before the holiday. Heads down, they led their donkeys and oxen, still laden with *bikkurim*, back home.

Yoseph approached one of the returnees and asked what was happening.

"We cannot go," he answered resignedly. "There is half a division of Roman soldiers standing outside Motza, blocking the way. No pilgrims are allowed into Yerushalayim. Only those who live inside the city can enter the Temple." Without waiting for a reply, the dejected pilgrim continued on his backward trek.

Yoseph returned to his grandfather and reported the news. The old man was incensed. "This never happened before in all my years," he said angrily. "Why are they doing this to us now?"

Yoseph tried to calm him. "There is a battle going on in the hills around Yerushalayim. The Romans have moved on Timna and Lod. There's fighting everywhere. There's nothing we can do!"

"But it's Shavuot!" argued Sabba. "We must bring up *bikkurim* — how dare they stop us! It is our *chag*!"

Disappointed as he himself was, Yoseph tried to explain, but Sabba would not hear of it. The old man stalked off and found himself a place by the side of the road.

Night quickly descended. The stream of returnees turned into a flood. The night was lit up with their torches, a solemn procession of defeat. There was no more sound of flutes — instead, an eerie quiet reigned. But some were not ready to surrender. The villagers from Tapuach gathered for a council at the side of the road, to decide their next move.

There were almost sixty men in the Tapuach clan. Yoseph's ancient uncle, Oziel, sat silently in the wagon that bore him, surrounded by his children and grandchildren, cousins and cousins' cousins. Yoseph stood at the edge of the circle. He listened but did not speak. His father, Nachum, and his uncles did most of the talking, while the women gathered in a circle nearby, awaiting the outcome. They were frightened and wanted to return to their homes. The only one who kept to himself was Sabba. He would make his own decision. Yoseph watched him from the corner of his eye. He stood there, praying, praying.

I bet he makes a run for Yerushalayim, Yoseph thought.

But there was little need for debate. All around them was the answer — everyone was heading home. There was a real danger to proceed — and it would lead nowhere. The only question was whether to turn back immediately, or stay the night on the road. The night road was dark, clogged with people, and there was the threat of outlaws who ran free in the hills.

After much discussion, Oziel made the final decision. "We cannot risk being here alone at night. Who knows if the Romans won't attack us here tomorrow? The only safe place is back in Tapuach, in our own homes. We will rest and pray *maariv*, and then we must return home as quickly as we can."

The men prayed, and the women distributed pita and slices of dried goat cheese. There was no time to make a fire or cook. Sabba had wandered off somewhere. Yoseph sat with his cousins, listening to their discussions of what the future held for them. He was closer to them than he was to his own family. Suddenly, his brothers Shimon and Levi appeared out of the dark and approached him. He stood up and followed them to a small decline near the road. They stood out of earshot of the clan. Near them, the flood of pilgrims surged northward, exhausted and sorrowful.

Shimon spoke first. "We have a real problem," he began, "and Abba wanted you to help out."

Yoseph was incredulous — Shimon usually excluded him from any family councils. "You need *my* help?" he asked in amazement.

Shimon ignored his tone. "It is Sabba. He refuses to come back with us."

"What other choice does he have?"

"He insists on going on to Yerushalayim on his own," Shimon explained. "He says he has brought up *bikkurim* every Shavuot of his life, and the Romans won't stop him now."

"He refuses to listen to anyone, not even Oziel," added Levi.

Yoseph shook his head, but could not hide a smile. Wave after wave of pilgrims were returning in defeat — but not Sabba.

"We should be proud of him," he answered. "He has courage."

Shimon cut him short angrily. "Courage? It's foolish stubbornness. He will put us all in danger!"

"It is still courage, stubborn or not," Yoseph answered sharply.

"Sabba lives in his own dream world — just like you do! You don't know what's happening, you don't care — you just do what you want to do! Courage? It will get us all killed!"

"Calm down, Shimon," Levi advised. "It's getting late. Don't argue, just tell him what Abba wants."

Shimon drew close to his brother. They had never been close, but there was no time for that now. "Look, Yoseph," he said more calmly, "Sabba has to be your responsibility. We can't risk the lives of our wives and children because of an old man's stubbornness, even Sabba's. We're all heading back to Tapuach tonight. Stay with Sabba until he changes his mind."

"Shimon, I don't have Sabba in my hand," Yoseph answered. "He has his own ideas — but I'll try my best. Where is Abba?"

"He left already."

Yoseph did not answer. Shimon nodded curtly and turned. Levi followed silently on the heels of his brother. Only Binyamin, who had joined up with them, stayed behind.

"They don't care for you very much, do they?" he asked.

Yoseph shrugged and tried to grin. "You don't choose your brothers, Binyamin."

Binyamin shook his head and ran back to the clan.

Somewhere in the great procession was his grandfather, heading to Yerushalayim — and Yoseph set out to find him. The last time he had seen him he had been sitting on the side of the road, lost in himself. Yoseph began walking briskly south, against the human tide. He used the only tool he had — his voice.

"Sabba Elchanan! Sabba Elchanan!" he yodeled with a piercing shepherd's call.

In the somber quiet of the march home, his voice echoed off the stony hillside. But he was rewarded with only his own voice — he could not find his grandfather. He pushed his way forward, forcing himself between marchers. They were not pleased at his pushing, but there was no time for politeness. He was growing more and more desperate when, after a mile, he chanced upon one of Sabba's cronies, an old Levite from the Temple named Shalum, also heading southward.

He tapped the old man on the shoulder and pulled him aside. Shalum looked at Yoseph in bewilderment, not recognizing him in the dark.

"I am the grandson of Elchanan ben Azariah the Levite. Have you seen him, Sabba Shalum?"

The old man's face warmed into a smile. "Ah, the grandson of Elchanan ben Azariah!"

"Have you seen my grandfather?" Yoseph asked.

"A tzaddik, a true *eved Hashem*."

"Yes, yes — but have you seen him? Our family is looking for him."

The old Levite averted his eyes. Yoseph studied him closely. *Sweet as he is, he isn't telling everything*, he thought.

Yoseph lay a firm hand on his shoulder. "Please, Sabba Shalum, it is a matter of danger. We don't know where he is — if you know, you must tell me!"

Shalum kept his silence. His eyes darted here and there. Yoseph's grip became just a bit firmer. "Please," he repeated, "I am closer to him than any of his children and grandchildren. If you know, you must tell me!"

The old man sighed. Around them, the great stream of returnees hurried back to the safety of their towns. But in the darkness of this little area, a tiny drama of life and death played itself out.

"Elchanan warned me that they would come looking for him and try to make him return...."

"His family loves him."

"Good! So then they must let him do what he has to do! He is a Levite, and it is Shavuot, the time of *bikkurim*. You must let him proceed to the Mikdash!"

"And you, Sabba Shalum — are you also trying to reach the Mikdash?"

"Maybe...."

"No maybe, Sabba Shalum. You, too, are heading to Yerushalayim. Where is my grandfather? Is he with you somewhere? You must tell me!"

The old Levite stood up straight. Now that he had been revealed himself, he rose with determination.

"A few of us will go to the Mikdash, one way or the other — even if we have to climb the walls of the Temple to get in. I am going straight down the main road until Motza. But your grandfather and his *chevrah* have chosen a different route — a trail that cuts off the main road, up into the hills. It bypasses Beit El and Motza and leads to the approach of Yerushalayim."

"Where do I find it?"

"You passed it already — on your right. You will see a large round stone, and alongside a little gully. It seems to be a simple ditch, but if you follow it, it runs behind some pines up into the mountains."

"How long ago did he set out?" Yoseph asked.

"He is with his *chevrah*. They are already more than an hour ahead of you. If you will hurry, you may catch up with them. But please — do not try to dissuade him. The Mikdash, the *duchan*, it is his whole life. Do not take that from him!"

The Mikdash is your whole life also, Yoseph thought.

He had forgotten that his long, firm hand still pressed on the poor man's skinny shoulder, and he quickly removed it.

"Did I hurt you?" he asked.

Shalum smiled. "Hurt? I felt your *kedushah* flow through your fingers into my body." He paused. "And...."

The old Levite hesitated.

"And what?"

"Your grandfather told me that when they would go look for him, it would be you they would send. I was expecting you."

Yoseph embraced the holy man, received his blessing, and rushed back northward, carried swiftly by the tide of returning pilgrims. In a short while he found the turnoff, hidden behind a great moon-shaped rock. The little culvert first twisted downwards and then led him up the side of the stony hill, dipped again into a wadi, then rose and twisted even higher.

The muffled beat of the marchers was swallowed by the hills, and Yoseph wandered alone in the profound stillness. It was difficult to follow the narrow trail. The quarter moon set early, and only the pale luster of starlight lit his way. In the distance, he heard the screech of jackals and the bark of wild dogs. But his eyes adjusted, and here and there he spied a tiny stone marker or a fresh sandal print. The trail curved southward, curving around Beit El. He had never walked these hills of Eretz Yisrael before, and from time to time he reached down, picked up a stone, and kissed it.

Sabba and his friends might be old, but they were agile. The track widened and grew flatter. Yoseph made out a cluster of fresh footprints. Sabba was not alone. He picked up his pace. In the distance, he discerned a whisper of voices. He dared not call out. He ran ahead and the voices grew louder, carried on light wings of midnight winds. He cupped his ears and listened. They were singing *bikkurim* songs!

Yoseph raced ahead — they sounded like they were just over the hill. But the voices had carried farther in the night air than he had thought. The trail turned into a flat rolling path, rising and falling like a wave, curving past wild orchards and vineyards with newly ripening grapes. It was another half-hour before he glimpsed one of the group, a black shadow against the star-spangled horizon. He lifted his legs and began to run again despite his great exhaustion, panting for breath. The pounding of his footsteps must have carried, because when he was still a hilltop away the group suddenly halted and turned to monitor his approach. Were they frightened of him? Yoseph stopped and waved his arm. He gestured towards his *kippah*. There was a pause, and someone waved back. Yoseph raced forward.

Yoseph saw one short figure break out of the company and run to greet him. Even in the darkness of night, he recognized Sabba's hasty steps. Everything was with *zerizut*, excitement, enthusiasm, energy!

They hailed each other at the same instant.

"Yoseph, my dear grandson, is that you?"

"Sabba, Sabba, I finally found you!"

The two met in the middle of the deserted road and embraced.

Yoseph struggled to catch his breath. His grandfather stood, murmuring words of thanksgiving. Finally Yoseph caught his breath and broke free.

"Yoseph, how did you find me? Who told you where I went?" Sabba asked.

Yoseph lifted his hands and looked heavenward. "Hashem showed me the way!"

"Yes, but this is the middle of a forest. How did you know? You must tell me."

"What is the difference, Sabba? I found you!"

"No," Sabba persisted, "tell me his name!"

Yoseph pulled himself straight. "No, Sabba, whoever it was, it was," he said firmly.

Sabba smiled slightly. "Good boy!" He looked back to his waiting companions. "Come, we will return to my friends — they are waiting."

Yoseph grasped his grandfather's bony shoulder. "Wait, Sabba! Abba and the rest of the family have sent me to bring you back."

Sabba feigned surprise. "Back? Back where?"

"Back home, Sabba, to Tapuach. The Romans have roadblocks around Yerushalayim. There is fighting going on all over, not far even from here. There are patrols everywhere — it's too dangerous."

"Oh...."

Some of Sabba's companions began drifting in their direction, impatient to move on. Before they could approach, Sabba called to them: "My friends, continue! Do not worry, I will catch up."

At first they hesitated, not wanting to leave him alone. But he waved his hands vigorously and urged them to move on — he wanted to be alone with Yoseph. Reluctantly, they headed slowly on.

Sabba turned to his grandson. "Yoseph, what does the family want from me? Does your Abba think I am a child? I have brought up *bikkurim* all my life. Does he expect me to stop now?"

Yoseph shook his head. "That is no argument, Sabba. This is not sixty years ago. It is a great danger — the Romans are everywhere, waiting, ready to kill. How can you endanger yourself?"

Sabba shook his head angrily. "Do you think I do not know what danger is? Yoseph — it has been a danger to go to the Mikdash since the days of Yarovam ben Nevat! But it never stopped those who truly wanted to go, those who had *bitachon*. Anyway, the Romans travel the main roads. Why would they come on this back road? And if they do suddenly appear, I know all the hiding places like the back of my hand. I promise you, nothing will befall us!"

"But if they do catch you, they'll accuse you of being a spy for the zealots! They may even kill you...."

"The Romans will not catch us," Sabba insisted. "We will go where they are not, and if we see them, we will conceal ourselves."

They stood on the dark road, looking silently at each other. Elchanan would not yield, and Yoseph knew it. What more could he do? Yoseph finally took a deep breath. He was defeated.

"But what shall I tell Abba when he asks why I did not bring you back? I have a commandment of *kibbud av*."

"He told you to bring me back and you tried. That is enough. But what did he say about you?"

"Me? He did not speak about me."

"Did he tell you not to go *oleh regel*?"

"We did not speak about me at all, just you."

Sabba grasped Yoseph's arm with his thin, powerful hands. "Listen, you did your father's bidding — and I have refused. So now, my beloved grandson — come with me! Be bold! You can never fulfill this mitzvah of *bikkurim* again! Join us!"

Yoseph did not know what to say. "There is next year," he answered lamely.

"Next year is next year! But it is not this year! This year is this year — this mitzvah can never be repeated. Next year — who knows?"

He saw Yoseph's look of uncertainty and grew more impassioned. He held him at arm's length and stared him in the face. "Yoseph...ben Nachum...ben Elchanan...ben Azariah HaLevi! You are a Levi, the son of a Levi, the great-grandson of Levi'im who stood at the Mikdash *duchan* for a thousand years. We are the Levites! We are the *shomrim*, the guards! The fearless ones! The bold ones!

"When Moshe screamed: '*Mi laShem eilai* — Who is for Hashem — join me!' who came running? The Levites! When Shechem violated Dinah, who took up their swords? Shimon — and Levi! When Hashem appointed guards to protect the purity of the Temple, who did He choose? The Levites!

"My beloved grandson, we are Levi'im! We are the fearless ones! We are *mosrei nefesh*! We are mighty cedars! Now, what does your family say? Go back and hide in Tapuach? Look after the sheep and grain, and turn our backs on the Temple! No, Yoseph, no!"

Elchanan grasped his grandson's arms so tightly it hurt. Yoseph stared into his grandfather's eyes, while the holy fervor of his grandfather's faith coursed through Sabba's fingers and into Yoseph's body.

"Sabba," he answered at last, choked with feeling, "I will not let you go to Yerushalayim alone."

In a few minutes, they had caught up with Sabba's companions.

IT WAS a hard march. There was no flat ground. Uphill, downhill, on the steep, deserted, twisting road leading southward. It was long past midnight, and the sun would rise in a few hours. Yoseph was energized by the courage of these dozen old men who pressed on, no matter what. But he had been on the road since dawn the day before, and he was suddenly overcome with utter tiredness.

"Sabba," he whispered, "can we not stop awhile to rest?"

His grandfather agreed. "I am also very weary," he admitted, slowing down a bit.

"*Rabbotai*," he murmured, "we still have a long way to go. In a short while the sun will rise. We must regain our strength and our clarity of thought. Shall we not rest for an hour, and then rise at dawn for Shema?"

The men agreed eagerly. They were all weary to the bone, but only Elchanan had had the courage to call a halt. They turned off into a field of date palms, concealing themselves far from the road.

Yoseph lay down a few feet from his grandfather, and in a blink fell into a deep sleep.

"YOSEPH, YOSEPH, wake up!" Sabba shook Yoseph awake. Yoseph opened his eyes halfway and peered up. There was a pale light of dawn in the sky.

"Come, my grandson," Sabba urged. "We must move on, before the Romans catch us."

Every muscle in Yoseph's body ached from his trek the day before. His eyelids shut of their own accord. "Move on already, Sabba? I cannot. I have no energy left."

"What do you mean, 'no energy left'?" Sabba replied impatiently. "It's *shloshet y'mei hahagbalah* and we cannot waste a moment!"

Yoseph struggled to open his eyes again but could not. "Give me a few more minutes!" he pleaded.

Sabba shook harder. "Yoseph, everyone is up and ready! We must leave now!"

"So go without me, Sabba," Yoseph mumbled in defeat. "I will catch up with you. I am faster than you old men anyway."

"Are you sure you will not lose us?"

"Hashem will lead me," Yoseph responded automatically.

Sabba laid his arm on Yoseph and whispered to him, "Yoseph, can you hear me?"

"What, Sabba?" Yoseph answered from his sleep.

"Every *mil* I will drop a piece of pomegranate skin for a signal. Look for it so you know you are on the correct path. Do you hear me?"

"I hear, I hear," Yoseph mumbled.

Sabba rose, reluctant to leave his grandson asleep alone on the deserted road but, knowing his young grandson was strong and would not tarry a moment longer than necessary, he gathered his weighty basket of *bikkurim* and hoisted it on his thin shoulders. It was still a full day's trek to Jerusalem. He looked back at Yoseph one last time, murmured a prayer, and set off with his friends.

"OUCH!"

Yoseph slapped his ear, trying to kill the insect that had just bitten him. He opened his eyes. The sun had been up for several hours already. He jumped up and washed his hands and face.

Quickly he donned his tefillin and recited the Shema. There was no one else around — all the old men had mustered up the energy he had been lacking two hours earlier. But now he was refreshed and ready.

He approached the road and peered out — it was deserted. He remembered dimly his grandfather whispering something about leaving a trail of pomegranate peels for him. But he wasn't sure if it was a dream or reality.

By day the path was more imposing. What had been a rough trail before widened into a well-trodden path, bordering many orchards and olive groves. It was not as concealed as Sabba had said. Yoseph had walked two *mil* when he came upon the first, discarded piece of pomegranate. It was hard to spot, since its deep russet color blended into the red earth of the path. Besides, Sabba never wasted anything. He left behind a grudging little slice, hardly the size of a baby's finger. Still, it had not been a dream. Heartened, Yoseph quickened his steps. The piece had already dried in the hot sun, and it meant that Sabba was still far ahead.

He remembered his chutzpah, calling Sabba's friends "old men" who couldn't move fast. Now they were paying him back. They were moving faster than he was! Even as morning turned to afternoon, they were still out of sight. The shriveled pomegranate pieces grew harder to find. Some he missed altogether, others he noticed by luck. He grew more and more anxious as the sun sank westward. The band was still out of sight, and soon it would be night again.

Sabba, where are you? he asked in his mind. *Why don't you stop and wait for me?*

The path widened into a proper road and began climbing steeply towards the periphery of Jerusalem. Yoseph's pace quickened. Every time he approached the city his face reddened, his eyes sparkled, his breath came fast, and his soul sang. He was a fish returning to its spawning grounds. The very air purified him! The road dipped into a narrow hollow, hemmed in on either side by rough-hewn walls, overgrown with a wild tangle of purple vines.

Suddenly, Yoseph froze. On the road were signs of a melee. The ground was churned up with dozens of hoofprints. Shreds of garments, hastily discarded water jugs, and sacks of abandoned *bikkurim* lay scattered everywhere, and against one of the stones was a bright red smear — blood or pomegranate?

Yoseph studied the hoofprints. There must have been at least a dozen Roman horses, huge and well shod. Their riders may have been lying in wait for the pilgrims, just beyond a curve in the path, well concealed by the vines. Or maybe it was a chance encounter, taking both sides by surprise. If there were still Romans around watching, Yoseph knew it was too late to hide. He carefully searched the *bikkurim* baskets and among the debris found a pair of tefillin, still wrapped in their pouch. Yoseph placed the tefillin in his pouch and neatly arranged the abandoned *bikkurim* baskets and jugs along the wall. As he moved one of the baskets, he saw a little wedge of pomegranate. It was slyly dropped, half-hidden, meant to be discovered only by someone who knew what to find. Sabbah had left him a signal!

He hid behind the wall and closed his eyes to rest for a few minutes. He needed to restore his strength after the day's forced march. In a few minutes he awoke refreshed. Night had fallen. Where was Sabba? He climbed back up onto the road and studied the hoofprints closely. Hoofprints and footprints mingled and pointed in every direction. Up to now, there had been no hoofprints, so the riders had not headed in his direction after the encounter. They must have come, caught the marchers, and headed back in the direction they had come from.

He began to walk again, following the footprints. In just a few minutes he sensed that someone was nearby, a slightest rustle of movement. Quickly, he reached down and grabbed a fist-sized stone, holding it in the ready.

Suddenly there was a hushed cry: "Ben Elchanan, wait!"

Yoseph slowed and tried to locate the voice: "Where are you?"

"Here, by the side of the road on the right — in front of you."

Yoseph slipped into a thick grove of trees on the side of the road. He stood in the star-lit darkness and waited. Suddenly, like spirits of the woods, three of Sabba's companions sprang up from their concealment and surrounded him. The three old men were overjoyed to see Yoseph, and he them. They embraced with passion, although, in truth, they were strangers to Yoseph.

One of the old pilgrims whispered anxiously, "Young man, do you have any food? We have not eaten all day."

Yoseph extracted some fruit and cheese, whatever he had, from his pouch and shared it with the frightened men. They gulped down the food Yoseph offered them — he wished he had more. He gave them each a long drink from his water jug.

He waited for the poor men to revive themselves. When he saw that some color had come into their faces, he pressed them: "Where is my grandfather?"

One of the men, who looked like he could be Sabba's brother, introduced himself as Peretz, a long-time friend of Sabba's. Solemnly, he told Yoseph, "The Romans have taken him."

Yoseph's face grew white. "Just him? How is it that you escaped? Where are the rest?"

"The rest ran away through the woods, toward Beit El. We hid here. Perhaps we can still proceed to the Mikdash...."

"So who did they take?"

"Just your grandfather, just Elchanan!"

"Why?"

"Your grandfather..." the old man began, "your grandfather does not know when to be silent! Here is what happened, from start to finish. We had walked all day and had gotten as far as the vineyard walls. We were pleased with ourselves, since it is only a few hours' walk up to the north wall of the city. We sang songs of praise, we shared stories, we rejoiced in our stubbornness. Suddenly we heard the pounding of hoofbeats, and, before we knew it, a dozen Roman soldiers descended on us. They were going one way and we the other, and there we were, face to face.

"We thought we would be trampled. But when they saw us, they called their horses to an abrupt halt. Their captain —"

"I believe they called him the centurion," put in a second old man.

"Right, the centurion — he looked at us and laughed. He was amused to find us there, in the middle of nowhere, trying to sneak up to Yerushalayim. He shouted at us: 'Where are you ancients going?'

"One of our people, Meir, walked forward from the company. He bowed and answered humbly: 'We are a band of poor old Jews going up to Jerusalem to bring up some fruits and beg alms from our brothers — with the captain's permission.' Then he bowed again.

"The captain was in a good humor, and he appreciated all the bowing and scraping. He decided to have some fun with us. 'How do I know that you are not *sicarii* out to join the zealots at the Temple?'

"Meir bowed yet again. He threw open his cloak and showed off his chest of skin and bones. 'Your honor, do we look like a *sicarii*? I am so thin I can hardly lift my spoon to eat, much less a dagger. Our only enemy is hunger. All we seek is a mat to rest our bones, a few pennies to buy some bread, and peace for all — especially our Roman masters.'

" 'Here, now,' the captain answered, pleased. 'You were told not to come here. I could have you thrown into prison — or worse. But I am in a good disposition. You have gone far enough. If you give me your word that you will turn back the way you came, I will let you go! Otherwise, I'll put you all in chains!'

"Meir and the rest of us saw there was no choice. The captain was in good humor, but the other soldiers kept their hands on the swords and looked at us with sheer hatred. In an instant we could be cut in half.

"Meir scraped and bowed again like Yaakov before Eisav. 'Your honor, our sacred word, with our blessings and gratitude.'

"The captain nodded and stared at the rest of us. 'And what about the rest of you?' he shouted. 'What do you say, old men! Shall I let you live? Do I have your sacred word that you will go back to where you came from?'

"The rest of us cringed and nodded and bobbed our heads in submission. And then, from nowhere, Elchanan, your grandfather, shouted: 'Your eminence, I make no such pledge!'

"We all stared at him like he was a madman. He was putting all our lives in jeopardy. But the captain was amused. He turned to his lieutenant and winked: 'Come forward, old man!'

"Your grandfather stepped forward. He stood there, looking up at the captain.

"The captain asked Elchanan sternly, 'So, old man, why can you not give me your word?'

" 'Captain,' he answered, 'I am more than twice and three times your age! Since the day I was born, I have gone up to our Holy Temple for the Shavuoth festival. I was carried in a basket on my mother's head. When I was sick, I rode up on a donkey cart, with every bone in me aching! How can I turn back now?'

"The captain stared down at him and saluted respectfully. 'Old man, I respect you for your courage and your honesty. But I am just a centurion. Over me is a general, and over him a division general, and over him a tribune, and over him the commanding general, and over him the procurator in Caesarea, and over him the governor in Syria, and over him the senate in Rome, and over him our glorious Caesar — and they all say that this festival you will not go! Is that absolutely clear?'

"The captain folded his arms firmly, no longer smiling. Even so, I think he would have let us all go, but your grandfather did not know when to stop.

"He lifted his hand to heaven and shouted back: 'But we have an Almighty in Heaven who is greater than your procurator or your governor or even the mighty Caesar himself! He is the master of this holy land, not you heathens! And it is He who commanded us to appear at His Holy Temple! You must let us go!'

"The centurion's face turned scarlet. He was so furious he slapped his reins and spun his horse almost clear around. Elchanan had insulted the Caesar in front of a whole company of legionnaires, not to mention us Jews. The officer took it as a personal affront. He pulled a spear from his belt, and I think he was going to hurl it at your grandfather right then and there. But Meir ran right between Elchanan and the centurion. He held his arms up in supplication.

" 'Please, Master Centurion,' he pleaded, 'we all know this old man — he is not in his right mind. It would be bad luck even by your own gods if you killed him!'

" 'I am in my right mind!' Elchanan shouted back.

" 'You see!' Meir argued. 'He does not know what he is saying.'

"The centurion looked from Meir to Elchanan, and then turned to his lieutenant. They conferred in whispers, deciding Elchanan's fate. Finally, the centurion turned to Meir.

" 'Get back to the other men!' he ordered.

" 'But —'

" 'Go!' he screamed, lifting his spear. Meir retreated back to where we were gathered. Elchanan stood there alone before the company of legionnaires on their huge, snorting black steeds. The centurion pointed his spear at him.

" 'Old man, you are fortunate. I am on my way to Emmaus, and I have no time for you now. You have one more day to live before I return to Motza, and then I'll decide what to do with you.'

"In a flash one of the soldiers moved forward and scooped Elchanan up. He threw him over the front of his saddle like a child's toy. Your grandfather tried to lift his head, but the soldier just pushed his back. The lieutenant motioned, and suddenly most of the company spun around and headed back in the direction they had come. That just left the centurion with a few soldiers. He glared at us for a long time and then raised his hand.

" 'If I catch you going to Jerusalem, I'll hang you all from the first tree I find. Now go back home!'

"We stood there, not sure what to do. He suddenly whipped his horse, and the huge beast started racing in our direction so that we were all going to be trampled. We dropped everything we had and ran for our lives. When we were at a distance, we turned to see if they were following us. The Romans had turned and ridden straight up into the hills towards Emmaus. Meanwhile, we all scattered into the woods."

Yoseph stood silently, digesting the terrible news.

"But where did they take my grandfather?" he asked. "Where is their camp, does anyone know?"

"I know," one of the men spoke up.

Peretz would not let him continue. "What is the purpose of your going there?" he said to Yoseph. "What will you do, attack them by yourself? In the end they will grab you, too, and there will be two *kedoshim*, not one. Will that comfort your father and mother?"

"So what shall I do, Sabba Peretz," Yoseph responded emotionally, "leave my grandfather to die alone, to endure torture by himself? Is that what a grandson does?"

"Sometimes the head must rule over the heart!" Peretz answered firmly. "Young man, I love your Sabba Elchanan dearly, but he was foolhardy — and now I fear you follow in his footsteps."

Yoseph did not try to answer. He turned to the other old man. "Will you show me to the Roman camp?"

The old man glanced nervously at Peretz, but then nodded. "Peretz is not wrong, but you are also not wrong. It is not for me to decide — but if you want me to show you the Roman camp, I will. The rest is up to you."

"So let us go — quickly!" Yoseph answered. He embraced the old men and begged Peretz's forgiveness for not listening to his counsel.

I will never abandon my Sabba, he vowed.

They set off quickly down the road. The old man reminded Yoseph of his grandfather. Sabba's companions were all alike. They dressed simply, ate sparingly, raced rather than walked, were burned deep brown by the sun — and were fiercely loyal to the Mikdash. Nothing was too hard. Yoseph and the old man marched silently, watching for fallen underbrush that might give away the Romans' presence.

They walked for almost two hours before reaching the crest of a large hill. The old man stopped short.

"There it is," he whispered. "It is where this path meets the high road."

Across a steep ravine, lights came from a large building. In the courtyard a huge bonfire burned, and against its arching flames Yoseph saw the silhouettes of soldiers pacing back and forth. Everything looked peaceful.

"What are you going to do?" the old man asked.

Yoseph shook his head, but did not answer. He did not know.

"I pray, be careful. Do not risk your life."

"What is your name?" asked Yoseph.

"Yehudah."

"Sabba Yehudah, may Hashem bless you with long, long years for your kindness to me tonight. Now, go back to your friends."

The old man hesitated, and then said, "Young man, remember

what an old man tells you. Whatever happens, good or bad, you have the *neshamah* of a tzaddik!"

He embraced Yoseph one last time and ran back into the cover of the night.

Yoseph stood there alone, thinking. Somewhere in that camp his Sabba was being held. What to do? Peretz had been right. There was no way of trying to infiltrate under darkness. He could see guards marching back and forth, and torches lit the perimeter of the camp.

He was here, and his beloved Sabba was just a few feet away. He came to a decision — the best approach was the truth. What was the use of devising stratagems? He was not clever at that. Everything was in the hands of Hashem, and he had no other choice. He decided to offer himself directly to the Romans.

Yoseph climbed carefully down the ravine. He made no attempt to conceal himself. In a moment he knew the Romans would spy him and be on guard. His only fear was that they would toss a spear or shoot an arrow before they captured him. He reached the bottom of the ravine, and began the steep climb up. He could see that on top of the ridge, at the edge of the camp, a group of soldiers were watching his progress. Some held their spears, others had their hands on their swords. As he drew closer, Yoseph lifted his hands to show he was unarmed. He stopped, climbed up higher, and paused again near the top of the ridge.

"Move one more step, Jew, and you'll have this spear in your stomach!"

Yoseph froze and lifted his hands. Three guards ran down to him. Without saying a word, they pulled his arms roughly behind his back and bound his wrists with a rough rope. They ran their hands over him, looking for hidden weapons. Satisfied, they dragged him up to the top of the hill and into their camp.

The officer in charge withdrew his short sword and held it to Yoseph's neck, pricking his skin.

"What do you want in our camp?" he demanded.

Despite his fear, Yoseph spoke calmly. "I have come to speak to the commander of the camp."

The officer snorted. "Commander of the camp — no less? Who

are you, an emissary from King Agrippa? What business do you have with the commander?"

"I am here to plead for my grandfather. He is an old man. He was taken prisoner today by your soldiers and is being held here for judgment. I have come to ask for Roman mercy...."

The officer withdrew his sword by a finger's breadth. "Who else came with you?" he asked.

"No one. I am alone."

The Roman officer gave Yoseph a long, fierce look. "Are you telling me that you walked into our camp on your own?" He shook his sword in Yoseph's face and shouted, "Don't lie to me — where is the rest of your gang?"

"I am alone," Yoseph repeated.

"Then what is to stop me from slitting your throat and throwing you down the hill for the wild dogs to feast on?"

Despite his great fear, Yoseph struggled to stay calm. "Nothing — I am in your hands. I am armed with faith in my God, and made reckless by the love of my grandfather."

The soldier nodded and lowered his spear respectfully. He was pleased. "Jew, you are either brave or insane. Either way, I wish I had you in my company. I will take you to the commander myself."

Yoseph was led through the silent camp. Not many soldiers were about in the middle of the night. He tried to hold his head high with dignity, although his wrists were still bound painfully by thick ropes. The head of the guard walked ahead of him, while two soldiers, their hands on their spears, followed closely behind. He felt like a calf being led to slaughter.

Where was Sabba? His eyes darted about the grounds, hoping to magically catch a glimpse.

They entered a stone building, a khan that had been appropriated by the Romans. Torches hung from the walls, lighting the huge hall. On either side were empty stalls. The khan had been established for pilgrims and for merchants traveling from Syria to Egypt, but now it was a Roman guard post on the road to Yerushalayim.

The captain knocked discreetly on a door at the back of the hall. A young soldier opened the door a crack.

"We have caught a Jewish prisoner who wishes to speak to the commander."

The soldier surveyed Yoseph sourly. It was the middle of the night. Reluctantly, he opened the door wide, allowing in the retinue. The commander of the post was half-sitting, half-reclining on a chair, a jug of wine and some scattered papers lying on a table next to him. He looked up in annoyance at the intrusion.

The officer saluted sharply. "I am in charge of the middle watch. A half-hour ago, this Jew presented himself to our camp. He made no attempt to conceal himself and had no arms. He claims that he came by himself, without friends, and he asked to speak to you."

The commander wore an embroidered uniform, indicating his high rank. He was middle-aged, with the grizzled face of a veteran. He glanced at Yoseph with curiosity.

"Who are you?" he asked nonchalantly. "What do you want?"

"My name is Yoseph ben Nachum, a Levite from Judea. My grandfather was taken prisoner today on the road to Jerusalem, and I heard he was taken to this camp. I came here to plead for his release."

The commander turned to his young aide. "Who is that?"

"It is one of Caputo's prisoners," the aide said, a hint of derision in his voice. "He sent him here today with a dozen cavalry to watch him. He's a little old Jew he claims insulted the Caesar and Rome publicly."

"For that he had to stop a dozen of our best fighters from going to Lod?" The commander raised his eyebrows.

"What did he say?" he queried further.

"No one is really sure. Caputo will be back in a day or two, and then he will be put on trial."

"And where is the old man now?"

"In the hole."

The commander's face twisted with disgust at the mention of "the hole."

Yoseph could not contain himself. "So — he is still alive!" he exclaimed.

The aide shook his head, and the commander grimaced. "Don't

hold your breath, Jew," he advised. "If he fell into Caputo's hands, don't expect much mercy. Anyway, it is not in my hands. Caputo heard the insult, and he must pass judgment."

Yoseph stepped forward imploringly. The commander seemed human enough. "Can I not see my grandfather, to try to comfort him?"

The commander shook his head. "Now, in the middle of the night? I wouldn't send my worst enemy into that pit, much less my men."

"I'll go myself. Just show me the door and throw me in with him."

The commander slapped the table and smiled. Yoseph realized then that he was not sober. "Throw you in? You have guts. No — I respect your bravery, Jew. But it will wait until tomorrow. We have to build a wall around the camp first. Then we'll see."

He looked up at the captain who had brought Yoseph to him. "Take him out — and make sure you untie his hands. I like this Jew — he has courage!"

Yoseph's hands were released, and he was allowed to find a place to rest in one of the empty stalls in the stable. Word had spread about Yoseph's daring, and there was no attempt to guard him. Yoseph found an odorous blanket and fell asleep.

HE WOKE up the next morning to the sounds of heavy pounding and officers yelling orders. It took him a few minutes to remember where he was. He found a basin of water and washed his hands, then quickly donned his tefillin and prayed discreetly in the corner of his stall. The Mikdash was so close — but so far. Meanwhile, the shouts and hammering outside grew louder.

He stepped into the bright sunshine. The camp, almost deserted the night before, was now full of Roman legionnaires. They must have marched up in the morning. They were busy constructing a defensive wall around the camp, working like one great machine. Yoseph had never seen such a sight before. Some dug a deep moat, while others carried tree trunks that had been cut down nearby, building a high wooden palisade. Every soldier was armed with a shovel and ax, and everyone seemed to know exactly what to do and where to do it. The camp was being made secure against any surprise attack.

Yoseph wandered unmolested around the camp. Occasionally, he was eyed with curiosity by soldiers who wondered what a Jew was doing in their midst. But mainly, he was ignored. Where was Sabba?

The freedom Yoseph had been allowed gave him hope. Perhaps — perhaps his Sabba and he would stand in the Mikdash that night after all! It was already *erev Shavuot* and there was no time to waste. He decided to return to the main building and plead before the commander.

He had hardly turned when he saw a small company of soldiers heading briskly in his direction. Unlike the builders, their spears were held at the ready. Yoseph stopped and awaited their approach. The captain who had discovered him the night before led the men.

As they approached, Yoseph nodded respectfully. The captain glanced at Yoseph, but did not respond to his greeting.

"Follow me," he ordered without pausing.

Yoseph followed him across the camp to an outcrop of large rocks. A heavy wooden door, like a hatch, had been forced into a gap between two black stones. The captain signaled, and two soldiers approached the door. One opened the heavy metal lock and lifted the hatch open, while the other kept guard, his spear at the ready.

Yoseph looked at the captain, unsure how to proceed.

"You wanted to see the prisoner — he's in there."

With great trepidation, Yoseph approached the entrance.

"Wait," the captain ordered. He handed Yoseph a small earthenware lamp. "You'll need this in there."

"I thank you for your kindness," Yoseph said. *Why is the Roman doing this for me?* he wondered.

Yoseph entered, stooping low to clear the entrance. As soon as he was in, the door behind him slammed shut, and he heard the latch being dragged closed. *I am now a prisoner, too,* he thought. The lamp shone on a cave-like room, dug deep into the mountainside. The floor sloped downwards, and the roof arched just inches over his head. No wonder they called it a hole.

"Sabba Elchanan," Yoseph called in a hushed voice. He didn't want to frighten the old man.

There was no answer. He moved deeper into the cave. "Sabba Elchanan," he called more loudly.

Suddenly, a familiar voice rasped, "Who's there?"

"Sabba, it is me, Yoseph! Where are you, Sabba?"

"I am here!" Sabba called back. "At the far wall, at the back!"

The floor was uneven and carpeted with rocks, and Yoseph was forced to move carefully, holding the lamp in one hand. He stopped in shock when he glimpsed Sabba's form, locked in a sitting position to one of the stones at the far wall, huddled like another stone in the wall of the mountain.

Yoseph fell to his knees and embraced his beloved grandfather with his free arm. "Sabba!" he cried joyously. "Sabba, I found you!"

Sabba held onto his grandson, unable to answer. Yoseph knew he was weeping.

For a long time, neither one spoke. They clung to each other in the dark cavern, black except for the little pool of light spilling from the lamp. Sabba rocked back and forth, staring incredulously at his grandson. Finally, he whispered, "My dear grandson! How did you find me here in the middle of the earth?"

Yoseph told his grandfather of his pursuit to find him. He begged forgiveness for having overslept the previous morning, leaving Sabba on his own. Perhaps he could have prevented his impetuous outburst!

"Who told you about that?" Sabba asked in amazement. "How do you know everything?"

Even in the darkness of the prison cell, Yoseph had to smile. "A little bird told me," he whispered. He heard Sabba laugh, and it made him happy. He explained how he had approached the camp on his own and was taken to the commander.

His grandfather stared at him. "Yoseph, you walked into a Roman camp by yourself — in the middle of the night? How are you allowed to do such a thing?"

"And how were you allowed to humiliate a Roman officer before his men, and insult their Caesar?"

"I insulted no one!" Sabba answered heatedly. "But I could not be silent when a heathen insults our right to fulfill a mitzvah! This is Jewish land, not Roman land! The mitzvot are Hashem's mitzvot! How could I be silent?"

"But couldn't you be more...diplomatic?" Yoseph asked.

Sabba snorted. "Diplomatic — I am not a diplomat!"

Even after just a few minutes of sitting on the hard earth, Yoseph needed to shift position slightly. Yet Sabba sat motionless, chained to the wall. The poor man must be in great pain. Yoseph put his face close to his grandfather's. "Sabba, I am sorry you are trapped."

"My *neshamah* is not trapped," the old man answered.

"Sabba, have you had anything to eat, to drink?"

"Before they locked me in here, they gave me some water, and they have been here twice with a little food. I guess they don't want me to die before they have a chance to execute me."

Yoseph reached into his cloak and extracted a small fig. He passed it to Sabba, who chewed it eagerly.

"Listen, Sabba," he said, "nothing is decided yet. Look how the Romans gave me the run of the camp! Perhaps I can speak to the centurion who had you imprisoned. Just let me do the talking. We can still reach Jerusalem for Shavuot!"

Sabba shook his head. "You are a dreamer, Yoseph. Eisav is Eisav. Do you expect to find mercy here?"

"Sabba, there is a chance. We must hope!"

"Yoseph, I am older than you. I am not afraid of death. You will yet live many good years. If I survive today, then I will pass on tomorrow or the day after. But if I die now, it will be *al kiddush haShem*! I will die because I did not allow the heathens to blaspheme our holiness!"

Yoseph was exasperated. "Sabba, how do you talk? You sound like you want to die!"

"No, but I am not afraid, and I will not bend. I am a Levite! I worry more about you. What will they do with you?"

"They will not harm me. I have earned the respect of the officer who arrested me."

"They told you?"

"No, but I know."

Sabba nodded. He took Yoseph's hand in his and dozed off. Yoseph tucked his chin into his knees. He could not sleep. He was not as despairing as his grandfather was. What joy could there be in killing an old man like his grandfather?

But the heavy chains on Sabba's arms and legs did not allow him to sleep long. He awoke with a start.

"Yoseph, are you still here?"

"Yes, Sabba."

"I was afraid that it was all a dream — that you were not really there."

"It is no dream, Sabba."

Sabba pulled himself up, dragging the heavy chains that held him. They stood silently, shoulder pressed against shoulder. But there was a great difference. Yoseph was safe, and he could move. Sabba was trapped and in great pain — although he did not whisper a word about it.

"When is the *chag*?" asked Sabba.

"Tonight."

"Tonight?"

"Yes. It is the fifth of Sivan. Right now it is midmorning, and we are only a few hours from Yerushalayim. When they let us out, we will walk up to the Mikdash together."

There was silence as Sabba absorbed all he had heard.

Then he grasped Yoseph's arm. "Do you want to hear about *bikkurim*?"

"Yes — everything."

"In earlier days, after Hordus but before the terrible procurators descended on us, we could barely walk the roads, they were so full! The sound of flutes on the ascent to Yerushalayim was louder than the music of the Simchat Beit HaSho'eivah! And the beauty of the fruits, a purple and scarlet river of fruits, flowing upwards towards the Temple. The aroma of Gan Eden wafted in the air, and the silver baskets sparkled in the sunlight like a thousand shields of Solomon. When we entered the city, parades came out to meet us, the heads of the *kohanim*, the elders of the Levites, the scholars and the aristocrats, they marched out to meet us and shouted in blessing: '*Bo'achem l'shalom*! May your coming be in peace!' The silversmiths and carpenters paused from their work, the scholars stood up from their verses, and they chanted: '*Chavivah mitzvah b'shaatah!* How precious is a mitzvah in its time!'

"Yerushalayim was in her glory, like a great matron ensconced upon a golden couch, welcoming her children with broad arms and calling: 'Come home, children, there is place for you all!' "

Sabba struggled to rise. He lifted his hands heavenward and cried out: " '*Omdot hayu ragleinu bish'arayich Yerushalayim* — Our feet stood firm within your gates, O Jerusalem.' "

Yoseph rose and tried to bring him back down to his seat.

"Tonight, Sabba, with Hashem's help, we will again be in Yerushalayim. Come, be seated...."

But Sabba continued, lamenting what had been and what would not be for many long years to come. "*Yerushalayim habenuyah ke'ir shechubrah lah yachdav* — The built-up Jerusalem is like a city that is bound together!' "

"Sabba, Sabba, I even know where you dropped your *bikkurim*! Perhaps we can still collect them, bring them to the *mizbei'ach* —"

" '*Shesham alu shevatim, shivtei Kah, eidut leYisrael — l'hodot l'sheim Hashem* — For there the tribes ascended, the tribes of God, a testimony for Israel, to give thanks to the name of Hashem...."

Yoseph held his grandfather tightly. His Sabba was far away, in a beautiful world, a Jerusalem world. "Sabba," he promised, "we will stay up all night, you and I, and study Torah. We will sit at the feet of the *chachamim*...."

Finally, dragged down by the weight of the thick wooden manacles, Sabba collapsed back to his place. Yoseph held him, and in a few minutes, the old man fell asleep again.

Suddenly, there was a clatter of the latch being pulled, and with a tremendous bang the hatch was smashed open. Sabba and Yoseph blinked as sunlight flashed off the blades of the entering soldiers, burning mercilessly into their eyes.

"Prisoner, rise!" a guard screamed. "Rise! Rise!"

Disoriented, blinded by the sunlight, Yoseph jumped up. Sabba tried to stand, too, but the wooden chains pulled him down like an anchor.

The soldiers entered the cavern, filling the entrance. Mercifully, their swords no longer caught the outside light, and Yoseph could now see more fully what was going on. A milder flow of midday light came from the hatch, until a figure wearing a centurion's crest filled the hatch and stormed in. The cave was full now, Yoseph, Sabba, the burly guards, and in the middle, the centurion. Yoseph stood at attention like a soldier, but his body trembled.

"Where is the prisoner?" the centurion demanded.

"Here," Sabba answered in a croaking voice. Despite his brave words of an hour before, Yoseph could hear his fright.

"Sir," Yoseph interjected, "may I please speak?"

The centurion stared at him for a moment. Against the light of the door, Yoseph could not make out his features — his face was a black silhouette.

"Who are you?" he asked.

"I am the grandson of your prisoner," Yoseph answered. "I came here to find my grandfather and plead for his life."

"You came by yourself?"

"Yes."

"Come here — where I am standing."

Yoseph carefully made his way forward, hurrying as fast as he could without slipping on the rocks. As he drew closer to the centurion, the guards alongside placed their hands on their swords. For the first time, he could see the centurion's face. They stood almost side to side. Yoseph was amazed at how young he was, maybe even Yoseph's own age. They were the same height, except for the centurion's tall helmet.

"What is your name?" the centurion asked.

"My name is Yoseph ben Nachum from Samaria.... Sir, if I may — everything that transpired with my grandfather — I take responsibility. He is an old man, and I was sent by the family to watch over him. I fell asleep from exhaustion, and he went off on his own with his companions. He has no political ideas. He doesn't even understand what is happening in Judea. He has been a pious servant of the Temple, and all he wanted was to follow the tradition. I met his companions and they told me that he insulted you and our Caesar. I have come to abjectly apologize for him and to ask your mercy."

"So maybe I should execute you, not him."

"If it means that you let him go, I take responsibility."

"No!" Sabba screamed. "It is my doing, not his. Leave him alone!"

The centurion turned to one of the guards. "This is a fine deal. They are fighting for the privilege of dying." He smiled, and Yoseph's hopes soared.

"Look, I'm inclined to be forgiving. We just smashed your brothers in Lod. Smashed them! We're on the way south, and soon we will be marching through your Temple! But the old man insulted our generals and governors and Caesar himself — before our soldiers. I will not let that go by. If he will stand before our men and eat his words, the matter is ended. Do you hear that, old man?"

There was silence, and then Sabba croaked out, "I will not apologize. What I said is true. Our God is greater than your Caesar, than your whole army. I will not take that back!"

"Sabba!" Yoseph cut him short.

The centurion sneered. "What do you want from me, Judean? I gave him a choice, and he said no. He will die!"

He turned to leave. Yoseph grabbed his arm. Immediately, the guards pulled their swords. Yoseph fell to his knees. "Please," he begged, "let me speak!"

The centurion halted. "I don't like men on their knees. Get up! What more is there to say?"

Yoseph stood up, his knees smarting from his fall to the rocky ground. "Sir, I will apologize for my grandfather, in front of you, in front of all the camp. He is not in his right mind all the time!"

"Yoseph, don't say that," croaked Sabba.

"Everything that he did is my fault. I will be blamed by my family if any harm befalls him. Let me stand in his place!"

"And you will give a complete apology, to me, to our men, to Caesar."

"I will say whatever you want."

"Yoseph, I don't want you to do that!" cried Sabba.

"You hear him?" mocked the centurion.

"I don't hear anything. I want to save my grandfather's life."

The centurion looked at him. In a strange way, he resembled

Yoseph slightly. They had the same tall, lean figure — although the centurion's arms were more developed from his many hours of military activity. Both had strong features, except that the centurion's face was clean shaven except for his two days' stubble, while Yoseph had a full black beard and curled *pei'ot* pulled behind his ears.

"All right," he said. "Come outside, and I will arrange for your declaration."

"No! No!" Sabba screamed from the back. "Yoseph, Yoseph! You have nothing to apologize for. I am not afraid of dying!"

"Sir," Yoseph said to the centurion, "I am grateful for your generosity. One more favor. My grandfather is very upset. Leave me alone for a moment with him, and then I shall meet you."

"Granted."

The centurion turned and left the cave, followed by the two guards. They left the door open, and bright sunlight streamed into the cavern. Yoseph rushed to the back of the room. The sunlight found its way even into the deepest recesses, and he could see his Sabba's face. He looked so haggard and thin. His face was tear stained. Only Hashem knew how much he had suffered in the past twenty-four hours.

He held his Sabba in his arms. "Beloved Sabba, you are so holy, and I love you so much. What do you care what I say or how I humiliate myself? These people, death means nothing to them. What do I care what they think — I will mouth a few words, and then you will be free. Maybe they'll let us proceed to Jerusalem. There is still time!"

"Oh, Yoseph, Yoseph! We can surrender our own honor, but we cannot surrender the honor of our God! What will you apologize? Will you say that their Caesar is more powerful than Hashem? It is better to die for *kiddush haShem*."

"Look, Sabba, I will give them what they want. They want to know that they rule Judea. Let them! They want us to obey Caesar — so we obey. What does it have to do with our faith?"

"Yoseph, they are Eisav! They will deceive you, and they will make you bend! We are Levi'im! We are cedars! *Mi laShem eilai!* Do not forget!"

"I will not forget, Sabba." They embraced one last time, and Yoseph rushed out the entrance.

It was a beautiful Sivan day. A warm breeze blew from the north, and the soldiers' tunics blew around their shoulders like crimson flags. A drum summoned a company of legionnaires to the parade ground, and they stood there, fifty strong. They stood rigidly in rows, staring straight ahead as if they had been cut of stone. At the perimeter of the camp, other soldiers went about their business as though nothing was happening. A small platform was erected in front of the soldiers, and the sacred standard of the Fifth Legion fluttered high above in the breeze.

The centurion marched Yoseph up onto the platform so he could be seen by all the legionnaires. The centurion's voice rang out:

"Soldiers of Rome! Some of you were with me yesterday when an old Jew publicly insulted Caesar and Rome! Hail, Caesar!"

Like a machine, the soldiers lifted their arms and roared, "Hail, Caesar!"

"As you know, I will not tolerate rebellion; I will not tolerate irreverence to Rome or to our emperor. This Jew is the grandson of that old man. He tells me that his grandfather is a doddering old man who did not understand what he said. In honor of our victories in Lod and Emmaus I have agreed to accept his public apology and declaration of loyalty to Rome! Do you agree?"

Again, they lifted their arms in salute and shouted: "Hail, Caesar!"

The centurion placed his hands triumphantly at his side and glared at Yoseph. "Step forward and face my men."

Yoseph stepped forward. He surveyed the legionnaires. Although their heads faced rigidly forward, all eyes were on him.

"Go on," the centurion ordered.

"What should I say?"

The centurion stood near him and instructed: "I render my abject apology to this Fifth Legion for the rash words of my grandfather."

Yoseph recited the words carefully. Every word brought his Sabba's freedom closer.

"We declare our fealty to the governor of Syria and procurator of Judea —"

"We declare our fealty to the governor of Syria and procurator of Judea —"

"— our loyalty to the Roman government —"

"— our loyalty to the Roman government —"

"— and declare that Caesar is the divine ruler over Jerusalem —"

"— that Caesar is master and ruler over Jerusalem —"

"— divine ruler —" the centurion repeated.

Yoseph turned to him pleadingly. "I can't say that. Caesar is emperor, but he is not a god. There is only one God."

The centurion approached Yoseph and hissed, "I put myself out to help your grandfather. Don't affront me in front of my men. Say the word 'divine' and he is saved."

Yoseph stepped back and shook his head. "I can't. There is only one God in Heaven. I want to obey, but don't ask me to say what we are not allowed to say — or even think!"

"You are as crazy as your grandfather."

"Please, let him live!"

"I'm counting to ten in my head. Say 'divine' or he is dead!"

The two men stood there, glaring at each other.

"No," Yoseph said. He turned and stepped down from the platform. Immediately, half a dozen guards fell on him and grabbed him by the arms, pulling them behind him viciously. Meanwhile, the centurion stood stock still on the platform, stone faced and humbled.

"Take him back to the hole!" he finally screamed. "Bring me the old man!"

Yoseph did not struggle as he was dragged roughly across the hard ground. Sabba had been right.

A soldier flung open the cave door, and Yoseph was forced inside. Meanwhile, other soldiers poured into the cave, looking for his grandfather. In the darkness he looked like another stone. They finally found him and rushed to unchain him. He was carried toward the entrance, passing close enough to where Yoseph lay for them to almost touch. Yoseph reached out his arm, but Sabba was already past him at the cave door. "Sabba," he screamed, "I was strong! I did not bend! I was a Levite!"

He heard his grandfather call out his name — and then he was gone. A soldier ran to where Yoseph lay and kicked him viciously to the ground. Then he turned and slammed the cave door shut, and everything was suddenly still.

This time there was no light. Yoseph paced back and forth in the darkness like a trapped animal for who knew how long. Poor Sabba! Poor, stubborn Sabba! He tripped over the rock-strewn floor, reciting *Tehillim,* praying that his grandfather's suffering would end quickly, painlessly. Was he next? The centurion was a wild man — anything was possible. Suddenly, the door was thrown open, and a burst of sunshine flooded the cavern.

A head appeared in the door.

"Out!" a soldier screamed, his voice echoing maddeningly through the cave.

Yoseph ran to the door and stepped out. Momentarily blinded by the sunlight, he blinked furiously, trying to focus.

"Is my grandfather still alive?" he asked plaintively.

"Keep quiet and follow us," the soldier ordered. There were four guards in all, two in front and two behind. They kept their hands on their spears and marched briskly. Slowly, Yoseph's eyes adjusted and he looked out onto the parade grounds. Then he saw his Sabba. He stopped short, shocked by what he saw. A hard blow struck him in the back.

"March!" the chief guard ordered.

Yoseph walked slowly, like a man in a daze. They approached the platform where Yoseph had stood an hour before. The legionnaires had been dismissed, and now there were but a half-dozen soldiers gathered around the platform. Sabba hung on a rough pole and crossbar. His arms and legs had been pierced with crude iron spikes. The bottoms of his legs, which had been manacled, were raw and bleeding. He hung under the burning sky, his eyes fixed ahead.

"You wanted him to die," the guard hissed, "so go help him."

Yoseph climbed onto the platform unsteadily. Sabba hung there, his head drooping to the side. His swollen, parched lips moved piteously.

"Water...water..." he pleaded in a whisper. Yoseph drew closer, but two burly guards kept him back. Sabba did not seem to even notice his coming, and Yoseph could not look at anything but his suffering grandfather. Then he realized — Sabba was locked in eye contact with the officer on the platform — the centurion! The two were locked in some contest. Sabba did not take his eyes off the Roman, and the centurion did not see Yoseph.

Yoseph could not help himself. He screamed at the centurion: "What have you done to my grandfather?"

As though breaking from a trance, the centurion turned his gaze from Sabba and saw Yoseph. Sabba, released from his stare, also noticed his grandson. He cried out like a wounded animal.

The centurion turned to him, looking confused. Yoseph lifted his hands: "Why have you done this to an old man?" he screamed. "What did he do to deserve this?"

At first, the centurion did not answer. Then his look turned to pure fury. "I didn't do anything — you did it! I gave you every chance! I gave him every chance! I stood you up and let you say one word — one word — and he would have been free to go to Jerusalem! You did this!"

"Aren't you a human being?" Yoseph asked. "Do you not have a father, a mother? Let him down! He is innocent! If you want to kill him...this is not killing — you wouldn't do this to an animal! Let him down! Let him live!"

"You ignored me in front of my soldiers. You did this! Here — take my sword and kill him! End his suffering!"

Again, Sabba groaned pitifully.

Yoseph lowered his voice. He could not outshout the Roman. "I beg of you, let him live! He never harmed you!"

The centurion shook his head. He turned to the guards. "Make sure he doesn't touch his grandfather. He can stay with him until he's dead — then give him the body." The centurion turned and stalked off the platform.

Yoseph stood there, staring up at his grandfather hanging from the post. Sabba's face was drenched with sweat, and his eyes floated upward. But when he gained his strength, he stared down hard at Yoseph.

"Sabba," Yoseph cried, "I love you so much. It is my fault. Sabba! Sabba!"

Despite his pain, Sabba tried to shake his head. On their own accord, his lips murmured: "Water...water...."

Yoseph turned to the guards. "Please, give me a cup. Let me give him a small drink, show some pity."

One of the guards stepped forward. "It will only make it worse for him. I've seen plenty of crucifixions. It just stretches it out, makes the agony worse. Let him die."

"No!"

"Here." The guard took a cloth that had been soaked in water. He placed it on the tip of his spear. "Wipe his forehead with it."

Carefully, Yoseph reached out and touched his grandfather's forehead with the cloth. Sabba's eyes closed with pleasure. Discreetly, Yoseph let the cloth touch his grandfather's parched lips. When he had wiped away the perspiration, Yoseph returned the spear to the guard. Sabba's eyes had opened.

"Yoseph," he whispered, "come here."

Yoseph drew close, making sure to keep his hands at his sides. He tilted his ear next to Sabba's mouth. Sabba looked around at the guards and whispered slowly into his ear:

"*Yehei shmei rabba mevorach — le'olam ule'olmei ol'maya!* — May His great Name be blessed forever, and forever and ever!"

That was all. Yoseph stepped back and stared at his grandfather. He looked back, twitching his brows just slightly. He was smiling with his eyes!

Yoseph knew — Sabba had won. He was dying for *kiddush haShem* the way he wanted. Yoseph nodded and clenched his hand in victory.

"Sabba," he vowed, "wherever I am, you will always be with me."

Sabba tried to nod. He closed his eyes. He seemed at peace. Yoseph saw him recite Shema with his last ounce of strength, and then his head dropped. His chest stopped heaving, and he was gone.

Baruch dayan ha'emet.

"He's gone," said one of the guards.

"Someone fetch a donkey," ordered the chief guard.

Someone brought a ladder, and two of the guards wrenched the spikes out of Sabba's body, lowering him to the ground.

"Give me a blanket," Yoseph said.

Even the hardened guards were moved by the death they had witnessed and by the old man's courage. A rough brown blanket was found, and Yoseph carefully wrapped it around his grandfather's frail body. He hardly weighed anything. With the help of a guard, he lifted Sabba's body and laid it over the donkey's back.

Just then, the camp commander, who had given Yoseph free rein when he was first captured, came marching briskly towards Yoseph.

"What happened?" he asked.

"My grandfather is dead," Yoseph answered.

The commander shook his head. Yoseph was bewildered. Who were these Romans? Some were kind, some cruel.

"You can leave the camp now," the commander said. "The guards will show you to the entrance. Keep away from here, you understand? And keep from away from Caputo."

"Caputo?"

"The centurion. He did all this. Just go — and keep far away! Go back to your own town. Just go!"

Yoseph thanked him. He led the donkey bearing his grandfather's body out of the camp, surrounded by a half-dozen guards. They escorted him to the camp entrance, and he was given permission to leave.

Shavuot would begin in a few hours. In the distance, Yoseph saw the main road leading back towards Tapuach. He ignored that road and instead led the donkey into the hills toward the south. They traversed a few deep canyons, and then climbed to the crest of a great hill. In the far distance, Yoseph saw the walls of Yerushalayim.

"Look, Sabba," Yoseph announced, "we reached Yerushalayim for Shavuot!"

Gently, he lowered the bundle containing his grandfather's body from the donkey and rested it on the ground. He took the shovel the Romans had given him and dug a shallow grave, just three *tefachim* down. He laid his grandfather to rest, his head in the direction of the beloved city.

"May you celebrate Shavuot tonight under the *Kisei HaKavod*," he murmured.

He placed a stone marker on the grave, turned, and headed back towards home. There was no more to be done.

Chapter Two

Eighteen months before the Churban

M*ardu bach Yehuda'i*.... Three little words whispered by Bar Kamtza into the ears of Caesar.... *Mardu bach Yehuda'i*, the Jews have rebelled against you! It was the *makeh be'patish*, the final hammer blow that set the mighty Roman war machine against Jerusalem.

But it was more, more. A nation was squeezed until her breath was forced out of her by one rapacious, cruel procurator after another — Felix, Festus, Albinus, Florus — insults to the Temple, subjugation, torture, slavery, unspeakable massacres, crucifixions, Jews suffocated under the crushing heal of Rome.

A nation at war with itself, divided between those loyal to the Torah sages who sought compromise, and iron-willed fighters who recalled the victory of the Maccabees against the Greek tyrants and hoped for new miracles; wealthy Sadducees and royalists who sympathized with Rome, and fanatic *sicarii* who pursued their enemies among the throngs of Jerusalem and murdered them instantly with one thrust of their razor-sharp blades.

There were early victories, false dawns, Beit Choron, Yerushalayim, Roman armies defeated, Matzada and the Antonia Fortress liberated. There were heroic defenses of Gamla and Gush Chalav, hopes of reinforcements from Abidane and Babylonia, even from the Jews of Rome themselves....

Dreams...dreams.... The Roman eagle had been aroused to fury, and from every end of the empire legion upon legion stormed into Galilee and Judea. One by one, cities and towns fell to siege, surrendered, or were massacred. The war moved to its finale of fire and blood. Desperate fighters poured into Yerushalayim to defend its walls, girding it before the Roman onslaught.

The land was filled with the blast of trumpets and the thunder of hoofbeats, the rattling of spears and the whistle of catapults, the whirring of arrows and the whoosh of torches, the roaring of armies and the thunder of battering rams, the cries of the dying and the moans of the living.

BACK HOME, Yoseph's father, Nachum, faced financial ruin. He owned plentiful olive groves and vineyards, tracts of date palms and presses that produced potent wine. He oversaw scores of peasant laborers who tended his orchards, pressed his bountiful harvest into vats of wine and oil, and filled his granaries to the bursting.

He borrowed heavily and each year shared the profits with his creditors. But his bounty turned against him and sank him in debt. Roman troops were everywhere, and all roads were unsafe. There was no law and order. His wagonloads of produce were rich prey for bandits — Jews, Samaritans, Arabs, Greeks, and Roman officers. Young men drunk with rebellion used his strong wine to gain courage. Everything turned sour and bad. An evil eye befell his best wine, and hundreds of casks soured into bitter vinegar. No one in his family was there to help him, to relieve his burden. Shimon and Levi had joined the army of Shimon bar Giora, Binyamin had gone to study Torah in Yavneh. Yoseph was useless when it came to business, and so Nachum was alone to face his creditors.

It was a cool Shevat morning when he saddled his donkey and made the humiliating trek north to meet with Betzalel ben Kaspi, to whom he owed the most money. The loan had actually come due a week earlier. Hoping he could raise the money, Nachum put off going to see his creditor, but he waited in dread for the sight of the creditor knocking at his door. It was a foolish fear, for Betzalel, a very wealthy man who held the fortune of many farmers like Nachum in his hand, did not have to come begging for his money. He bided his time, but when his patience was ended, he sprang mercilessly like an iron trap, breaking his debtors in two, taking their land, their homes, their children.

Betzalel lived in the village of Dotan, amidst rich olive groves and flocks that grazed in nearby fields. Nachum did not have to come to his door. Betzalel spied him coming down the road and went to greet him grandly. He smiled and embraced Nachum, walking alongside his donkey as a show of respect.

Nachum tied his donkey to the water trough, and Betzalel himself brought out a generous bale of hay for the beast to feed on.

"Come in, come in, Master Nachum. I am honored by your visit."

Nachum followed his host into the cool, dark interior of his home. Wealth whispered from every corner, with finely crafted tables and chairs in the Greek style, silk murals adorning the walls, and the floor decorated with a beautiful, multicolored mosaic.

"Welcome to our home, Master Nachum. Please sit and join me for refreshment."

"May only blessing and peace and good health visit your home, Master Betzalel."

"*Amein!*" the other man answered piously. "May he who blesses be blessed himself!"

"*Amein!*" answered Nachum.

Servants appeared with trays of fresh pitas, cool spiced wine, cheeses, pomegranates, and cakes.

Betzalel nodded pleasantly at Nachum. "I am honored by your visit. Eat something!"

"I must discuss our business first," Nachum said shamefacedly.

"Our business will not run away. Eat, then we can speak."

The two men washed their hands and made the blessing. They ate silently. There was not much need to speak. Each knew what was on the other's mind, and they communicated with a smile and a wink and an occasional polite burp.

Finally, the repast ended. The servants removed the trays, leaving the two with fresh wine cups. Betzalel leaned contentedly back on his couch, at ease in his castle. He smiled benignly at Nachum, who sat stiffly, his head bowed.

"So how fares it, my dear friend?"

"*Baruch Hashem* for every day." He cleared his throat. "You know, Betzalel, that I have a debt to you that is already overdue."

"Yes, I know that." Betzalel's smile did not leave him.

"I have always paid you on time, to the day — year after year."

"Yes, I am aware of that."

"This year is different."

"Oh? How?" Betzalel's smile dissolved into a look of puzzlement.

"Things have turned very bad for me. My wine has turned sour. I cannot sell my stocks of oil. I used to send my best wine to Damascus and Tyre, and now the roads are full of robbers."

Betzalel lifted his eyes and looked directly at Nachum. "You owe me a considerable sum, Master Nachum. I have invested much in your harvest. What can you give on account?"

Nachum lifted his hands and shook his head. "At this moment, nothing."

Betzalel's face hardened. "Nothing, Master Nachum, nothing? I lent you ten thousand Tyrean *sela* and you have nothing to give me?"

"I am deeply saddened, Master Betzalel, but I need some more time. I hope things will turn around, improve."

Betzalel shook his head sourly and waved his hand. "Words, words, mere words. I need my loan repaid, not words of hope."

"Master Betzalel, please! I have always paid you promptly in the past."

Betzalel did not bother to answer. The two eyed each other wordlessly, Betzalel's face bitter and impatient.

Suddenly, Betzalel's face softened. He turned almost pleasantly to Nachum. "You know, Reb Nachum, I could take everything you own. Your fields, your vineyards, even your home — they are all encumbered to me. You do understand that?"

"Yes, of course." *What is he driving at?* wondered Nachum.

"And yet, your bad fortune is not your doing. I have acquired many other fields by forfeiture, fields of good, honest men just like you. It is bad for everyone — between the Romans and the bandit rebels our people are being bled white."

"Then you do understand, Master Betzalel."

"Yes, and frankly, what need do I have of another grove of date trees? I have enough barrels of unsold wine to make a lake. Better you keep your lands, work them, pay my debt off *maneh* by *maneh*...."

Nachum caught his breath, unable to believe Betzalel's sudden turn of heart. He nodded in gratitude. Then Betzalel lifted one finger. "But in turn I need a favor from you."

So there was a sting hidden in the honey.

Betzalel gazed suspiciously at Nachum. "Well, do you want to hear my proposal or not?"

Nachum nodded warily. "Please proceed, Betzalel."

"We all have problems, you know. Even with all my good fortune, I have a stone lying on my heart also...."

"Who doesn't, in these terrible times?"

Betzalel stared at him hard, then continued, "Yes. I have a daughter who long ago should have been married off, but she is still here at home."

"I am sure, with your many connections, that you will soon find a proper *zivug* for her."

Betzalel shook his head. "It is not so simple. One cannot purchase a son-in-law like one purchases a parcel of land. My daughter...Rachel...she is not a well child."

"May Hashem help."

"*Amein*, but it is not something that a doctor can remedy. She...cannot speak."

"Not a word?"

"For more than ten years, since she was a child. She was a beautiful child and then one day —" Betzalel snapped his fingers "— she suddenly stopped speaking."

"What happened? All of a sudden, she could not talk?"

Betzalel shrugged and pursed his lips. His eyes rolled upwards in real grief. "I am sure it was an *ayin hara*."

"But, Master Betzalel, what help can I be?"

"I have long sought a suitable lad who could marry her and look after her. I have the means to help, you understand. I am told that you have a son who has long passed the time that a young man takes a wife. What is his story?"

Nachum sighed with relief, leaning back in his chair. He understood everything now, and he was not displeased. "Master Betzalel, how many children are you blessed with?"

Betzalel waved away his question. "We do not count children.

Let us say that I am blessed, except for this poor child."

"Well, I am not afraid to say how many I have. I have four boys and three girls. The boys are real boys, the girls are real girls. Our *yichus* is very good, very, very pure. But even in the best families there is sometimes a weak link, a child who, shall we say...the cup is not quite filled to the top. Two of my sons are fearless fighters, one dreams of being a scholar, and one — he is neither here nor there. He is satisfied to walk the mountains with his sheep, play his harp, and daydream about standing on the *duchan* in front of the Temple altar. He has no ambition for wealth, for study, even for marriage."

"Would he marry if he was promised a comfortable settlement, a little house of his own, his own flock to tend?" asked Betzalel.

Nachum gestured vaguely. "I am not certain."

Betzalel's voice turned harsh. "Well, Nachum ben Elchanan, if I were you, I would make it my business to convince him to get married. Because here is my offer. If your son marries my Rachel, takes her off my hands, then I will erase your debt to me. Do you understand? You will not owe me a penny! You will be able to sell whatever goods you have and reestablish yourself. But if you don't convince him, then believe me, I will take every last penny you have, or will ever earn! I will leave you worse than a pauper. I will make you a homeless beggar!"

Nachum stared at Betzalel with a mixture of fear and contempt. He wanted to rebuke him, even curse him to his face, but he held himself back. Instead, he smiled pleasantly. "Perhaps I can meet your daughter, so I will be able to describe her to my Yoseph."

Betzalel knocked on his table, and a servant appeared through the door. "Tell Rachel that her father wants to see her at once."

They sat there waiting for her appearance. In the quiet, Nachum could hear children playing outside and the sound of flocks being led to midday shade, the braying of a donkey. A cool breeze swept through the shady room, and Nachum grew drowsy. He only realized that Rachel had entered the room from Betzalel's gaze. The girl had appeared behind him as silently as a spirit.

"Rachel, we have a guest who would like to meet you."

Nachum turned and looked at Rachel. He forced himself to hide his shock. The young woman was about eighteen, of moderate height. Her eyes were lively, even attractive, but her mouth was frozen into a twisted, scowling grimace that distorted her face into a repulsive mask.

She stood there staring at him. Nachum smiled politely. "I am very pleased to meet you, Rachel."

The poor creature stood there, not responding.

"Master Nachum is my friend, Rachel. Why don't you greet him?"

Rachel bowed stiffly to Nachum. Nachum responded with a nod.

"You may go now, Rachel," Betzalel said.

She left as noiselessly as she entered.

Nachum turned sympathetically to his host. "What happened to that poor child?"

"We do not know. One day she was a beautiful child, shy but happy. The next day she was the shattered vessel that you see. No doctor's medicine, no tzaddik's prayer, no healer's *kameah*s have been able to help her." He sighed. "It was the evil eye, people who were jealous of my wealth and my family."

"I am sorry for you, Master Betzalel."

There was a moment's quiet, and again Betzalel's mood changed. He poked a finger in Nachum's direction. "That is how things stand. All our sighing will not change matters. This child needs a husband to take care of her, and you can help me. The choice is yours. You will convince your son to marry my daughter, and we will both be freed from our sorrow. Or you will refuse me, and you will never lift your head as a free man again!"

Nachum tugged on his beard meditatively, then responded, "Master Betzalel, in principle I have no objection to your offer. It is time my son Yoseph wed. As for your threat, do not make threats so lightly. How do you know you will be alive tomorrow to carry them out? The cup of misfortune has passed to me, tomorrow it may pass to you. Come, let us deal as old friends! I am happy with your proposal, but it is not in my hands. I must speak to my son, and he has his own ideas. But if we do make this match, I will be honored to be bound with the Ben Kaspi household in marriage."

A smile unfolded on Betzalel's lips. He was pleased with

Nachum's defiant response. He would make a worthy *mechutan*. He lifted his cup and saluted Nachum: "*L'chayim*!"

Nachum smiled and raised his cup in response: "*L'chayim u'levrachah!* For you, for me, for our nation Israel!"

"YOSEPH! YOSEPH! Where are you?"

Yoseph turned towards the voice that hailed him. It sounded like Binyamin, but it could not be — he was in Yavneh. The voice grew stronger, and then, over a small rise, appeared the curly red head of his youngest brother. He was smiling and waving excitedly.

Yoseph ran over and embraced him. "Binyamin, what are you doing here? I thought you were studying in Yavneh!"

"If you would get your head out of the clouds, you would have heard that I was summoned here!"

"Summoned? Why?"

"Do I know?" he shrugged in his innocent way. "Abba said come, so I came!"

Despite his months of intense studying, Binyamin looked fresh and strong, as if he had spent his days in the fields.

"Anyway, *mazal tov*! I hear you may become a *chatan* soon."

Yoseph stepped back in astonishment. "Where did you hear that? It's the first I know about it!"

Binyamin retreated from his indiscreet remark. "Oh, I don't know. I thought that's why they brought me back home. Anyway, Abba told me to call you to the house. He has to speak to you."

"What about my sheep?"

"I don't think Abba wants to speak to them, just to you. I'll watch them for you. Don't worry, I'll drive away any mountain lions."

Yoseph grinned and handed him his shepherd's staff. He showed his brother where he had hidden a jug of water and some fruit, and then headed homeward.

It was almost an hour trek back to the house. Although Yoseph returned each night to his lodging, he had hardly spoken more than a few words to his father since his grandfather had died. His family blamed him for Sabba's death. They heard how he had overslept and let Sabba go off on his own. They heard every detail from

Sabba's ancient companions. But they knew nothing about Sabba's terrible death or Yoseph's attempt to save him. That remained locked in his heart. His father was cold to him, only speaking when there was a need, mostly about the flock. They were like two strangers sharing the same house.

But his father was his father. If he had summoned Yoseph from his flock, it must be something urgent. He stopped at a stream and washed away the grime from his face. When he reached the house, he entered through a side door and ran straight to his own chamber, where he removed his dusty shepherd's robes and donned a clean tunic. He doused his face one more time, then entered the main rooms. The house was empty except for the old house servant, Akiva.

"Where is my father?" he asked.

"He will be here soon," Akiva answered. The servant set some cakes and a jug of cool water before him.

Yoseph sat there, pondering the sudden turn of events and what it meant. Why had Binyamin suddenly returned? What was this nonsense about becoming a *chatan*? In a few minutes, the door opened and his father appeared.

Yoseph rose. "*Shalom aleichem,* Abba Mori," he greeted his father.

His father nodded coolly, not bothering to return the greeting. "Sit down, Yoseph. I need to speak to you."

Yoseph sat down across from his father. He noticed that his father had lost weight and his face had lines that had not been there a month before.

"I did not know that Binyamin had returned from Yavneh," he remarked.

His father looked at him and tugged at his beard. "Yes, I asked him to come, to be...available."

"Available? Is there something the matter, Abba?"

"No.... Yes.... We'll see. Yoseph, we must speak seriously."

"I have always been ready, Abba."

"What is going to be with you, Yoseph? You are almost twenty-five. Is it not time that you settled down, dedicated yourself to some useful pursuit — like your brothers?"

"I have a pursuit, Abba, you know that."

"What, to play a harp at the Temple? It is a mitzvah, I agree, but it is not a career, it is not a future. How will you get married? From where will come your *parnasah*?"

"Hashem will provide, Abba, as he provided you, and Sabba, and all of us."

Nachum shook his head forcefully. "I also have *bitachon*, Yoseph, but we have to have our feet on the ground. You are a dreamer, but we must be real."

Yoseph did not respond. His father had not summoned him from his flock to give him a lecture. Something must be afoot. Binyamin had already spilled the beans.

Nachum leaned forward, looking straight at his son. "Now listen, Yoseph. A proposal has been made that I think you should accept."

"What proposal?"

"I have a business partner, an old friend, Betzalel ben Kaspi. He is a very wealthy man, with scores of fields and granaries, many orchards and flocks. He is one of the wealthiest men in the Shomron. He has daughter, a...fine girl, respectful and...quiet. He is seeking a *chatan* for his daughter, and he heard many fine things about you."

"What fine things could he have heard?"

His father threw up his hands in impatience. "What's the difference? That you have two arms, two legs — do I know? Perhaps that you are so tall and fine-featured. Maybe that you play the harp so well. He heard of you, and he is interested. What do you say, Yoseph?"

"But I don't know if I am ready to get married yet. I have not even started my initiation on the *duchan*! I have not played my first psalm yet!"

"What does one thing have to do with the other? Did not the prophet say: '*Lo latohu v'ra'ah, lashevet yetzarah*'? The Almighty made the earth to be filled and for man to propagate! My goodness — you are twenty-four, Yoseph. It is time!"

Yoseph tugged at his black beard. He did not answer.

Nachum lowered his voice confidentially. "My son, there is

more to it also. This Ben Kaspi, he...he has me by the throat. I owe him ten thousand Tyrean *sela*. I cannot pay him back. While you were out with the flocks, all my wine went sour. He will take everything we have. We will be penniless. But if we join our houses through this match, we will be spared."

So that was the real story.

"Who is this daughter? What is her name?" Yoseph asked warily.

"Her name is Rachel, and she is a fine girl of eighteen."

"And how does she look?"

"Look...she looks like a fine young woman. Oh, yes, she does have one problem."

"A problem?"

"She cannot speak."

"The girl cannot speak? This is who you have chosen for me, Abba?"

"Yoseph, she is a wonderful young woman. She is pure, she is respectful, you will never have to worry about *parnasah* the rest of your life. You can always take a second wife later, one who talks. But this way we will all be saved, your mother, me, your brothers and sisters. It is all in your hands."

"Abba, how can you ask me this? It is like you are selling me to save the family."

"Yoseph, she is a good girl from a good family. You finally have a chance to redeem yourself — to do something for your family, not just yourself!"

"Abba —"

"Yoseph, will you not at least meet her? Perhaps she will find favor in your eyes. Please, Yoseph."

Yoseph was shocked to see that his father was begging him. So the situation was desperate. He tugged his beard and drummed the table nervously with his fingers. Finally he looked up. He had no choice.

"I will meet her, Abba. Then we shall see."

He is coming to meet me, this Yoseph. What do they want of me? Why does my father torture me, shame me? They have come now for two years, the rich, the poor, the short, the tall, the handsome, the homely, the witty ones, the dullards. I stand before them like a calf to be sold. They look, some mumble a few words, some turn away in disgust.

Let me be, let me be! Now here is a new one. His family is at my father's mercy. It has happened before. Perhaps he will spend a few minutes, maybe even try to be polite so that Father does not grab everything they have. But then he will be gone. Good! Who needs him!

They say this new one, Yoseph, is very handsome. One look at me and he will probably snicker out loud and run out laughing.

Oh, Hashem, why was I born? Why did You make me like this? I am so sad. I am so sad.

PESACH HAD passed, but still the rains fell on the Shomron hills. A veil of fog hung over the valley forests, and a chill wind blew over the mountain crests. Yoseph pulled his robe closer to him, hiding his head from the cold drizzle that pounded his face. His donkey was leery of the slippery slopes, and trod slowly and carefully.

It was a two days' trek to Ben Kaspi's home. Yoseph had much time to think. He was not really ready to get married yet. The following year he would be twenty-five and would be able to stand as a novice at the Temple *duchan*. Since a child he had heard stories from his grandfather of his great ancestors who had dedicated themselves to praying and singing before Hashem. That was all he wanted. His family mocked him for being a simple shepherd. But was King David not a shepherd, and from this he composed the holy *Tehillim*? Was Sabba not a shepherd? Sabba, like David, had entered Hashem's wilderness, alone, alone with his flock, and come out mantled in *kedushah*.

His family did not understand, and thought him strange, with his love of songs, of the harp, of lifting his voice into the purified skies of Eretz Yisrael.

He was doing what he wanted to do, what he had to do.

And now, the hand of Hashem had grabbed him and said it was time for him to take a wife. Perhaps that was what he needed to be worthy of the altar. But why a woman who could not speak? What would he say to her? He never spoke to women, except to his mother and sisters, and they did all the talking. But here, he had to speak. What would he say?

If he did not marry her, whoever she was, whether she was beautiful or plain, his family would be ruined. It was all on his shoulders. Chilled and soaked to the skin, he finally spied the village of Dotan on the mountain, and his donkey wearily climbed the muddy path to the princely domicile of Betzalel ben Kaspi.

Betzalel himself came out to greet him. He embraced him warmly as the son of his old comrade. He did not take him through the main door, but brought him to a private entrance that only the family was allowed to use.

Betzalel led him to a tall chest and showed him a dozen fresh tunics that hung along its walls. "Choose whichever you please," he said. "I want you to look dry and attractive before Rachel. Whatever happens, please accept them as a gift from me."

Yoseph did not want to accept, but he was chilled to the skin, and his own clothing clung to him like wet sheets. Betzalel left the room, and he changed into a dry, handsome change of clothing. Betzalel had even left him clean, new sandals.

Betzalel knocked a few minutes later. He smiled with satisfaction at his visitor's new garb and led Yoseph into the main room. Although Yoseph's family was not poor, he had never seen such an elegant domicile in his life.

Betzalel sat him at a table that was laden with all sorts of cakes and fruits, as well as a fine, silver pitcher filled with a spiced cold beverage and ornately carved drinking cups.

"I welcome you to our home, Yoseph. We are honored to have you here, and I hope that my daughter and you find favor in each other's eyes. God has blessed me with much, and I am prepared to share my blessing with whoever becomes Rachel's *chatan*."

Yoseph did not answer directly. He did not trust Ben Kaspi's smile and his generosity, knowing that he held a sword of ruin over his family's neck — and would wield it!

"I know that you and Rachel need your privacy. I will go summon her. I hope your meeting is pleasant. After you two have spoken, I shall escort you to the road."

Betzalel disappeared from the room. Yoseph murmured over and over, "*Im Hashem lo yivneh bayit, shav amlu vonav bo* — If Hashem will not build the house, in vain do the builders labor on it...."

There was a patter of footsteps, as light as a lamb's, and Rachel entered the room. Yoseph rose and looked at her.

He is so handsome, she gasped with astonishment.

What happened to her mouth? he wondered in shock.

They stood there, frozen. Yoseph smiled awkwardly. "I guess we can't just stand here all day. Shouldn't we sit down?"

Rachel nodded, and they found chairs across the table from each other. "Do you want a cake, a fruit?" he asked.

She shook her head. Yoseph was in a quandary. He had not eaten on the journey and he was famished. "If you don't eat anything, then I can't eat anything — and I'm starving! Can't you eat something — at least make believe you're eating?" He smiled.

She reached across the table, took a few cakes, and set them on a plate before him. She poured him a drink. She took a pomegranate and carved it into neat slices, giving him half and taking the rest for herself.

Relieved, Yoseph recited a blessing over a cake. In her heart Rachel also recited a blessing, over the fruit, and over Yoseph. Yoseph was too hungry to be polite. He gulped down the cakes, and downed his drink in one great swallow. She poured him more.

So his father had fooled him after all. He had told him that she was mute, but he had not told him that her mouth was so twisted into a grimace that it distorted her whole face.

Yoseph finally felt satisfied and refreshed. Rachel ate just one slice of the pomegranate, to be courteous.

Now what?

He turned to Rachel. "You don't speak?"

She nodded uncertainly.

"So do you mind if I speak, if I tell you a story?"

She shook her head.

"There is a young man who lives in Tapuach. He has already passed twenty-four years, and soon he will stand on the *duchan* at the Temple. He will play his harp to Hashem as the wine is being poured out on the altar. He has three brothers and three sisters, but it is like he is an only child. He goes out alone into the fields and tends his flock, and sings melodies to Hashem. He is not very learned in Torah and has no great commercial ambitions. He is not a brave freedom fighter. He just wants to be alone, to think and to dream.

"There are those who mock him for this, even his own father, even his own brothers, but that is who he is."

He studied her face. "Do you like my story? Shall I continue?"

He is so strange, this one. Is he for real?

She nodded. The twisted scowl never left her face, but her eyes spoke.

"Good. And so he has been in his own world, in his own dreams, to walk the path of his forefathers, to be a true Levi, a singer in the Holy Temple. I — I have never really met a woman to discuss marriage before, you know. You are not the fifth woman I have spoken to, or the tenth, or the twentieth. You are the first, and I am very...awkward."

Don't be awkward, please, don't be awkward! Just talk and talk and talk....

"Now, Rachel, it is your turn to speak."

She sat bolt upright in alarm. *What does he want from me?*

"Oh, yes, Rachel, you can speak. Can you say 'yes'?"

She nodded. His face scrunched up in dismay. "Are you going to sit there, nodding up and down the whole day? Your head may fall off! If you want to say yes, lift your hand up."

She lifted her hand.

"Good, that is yes. And no?"

Her hand went down.

"So you can speak. We will speak your language."

If Betzalel or Rachel's mother or the servants were eavesdropping behind closed doors (which they were), they would have thought that the couple had run out of things to talk about. There was no sound coming from the great chamber, no whispers, no laughter, no questions, no declarations. But Yoseph and Rachel spoke very well — with their hands. Yoseph acted out the story of his trek to Dotan, he described his flock, he mimicked his harp playing.

Rachel responded with her hands, asking questions by lying her hands flat before her, telling of her life of cooking and helping her mother, and even describing her immense, silent loneliness, leaning her head sadly against her own hands.

No one ever listened to me before. I could never speak to anyone.

Finally, Yoseph broke the silence. He was hungry again. "Can I have another cake?"

Her hand went up. She watched as he gobbled down his fifth pastry.

He is so beautiful and so kind. But he will say good-bye, and I will never see him again.

She is such a beautiful soul, Yoseph thought, *even if her father is Ben Kaspi. We can't pick our parents. Who will ever marry her if I don't?*

As Yoseph chewed deliberately on his sixth pastry, he pondered his whole future. Moshe Rabbeinu had been chosen to be the shepherd of Israel because he had shown mercy to one little parched lamb in his flock. This poor girl, so lonely, so locked in her silence, so hard to gaze at until one looked into her soul, she was his thirsty, lonely lamb.

He ended the pantomime and spoke directly.

"Rachel, I came here at first because my father asked me to — you know that?"

She nodded.

"He asked me to make a match with you to help our family out of its great hardship. But I told him that I could not marry someone just to please him, even to save our fields and vineyards...."

At least he is honest.... He tried to like me.

"But now I have met you, and what I ask you now is not for my father, but of my own choice. Do you truly believe that? Otherwise, I will stop."

She nodded.

"So what I am asking, I am asking for myself. Rachel — will you marry me?"

She sat there, stunned, frozen in shock and awe.

"Rachel, will you be my wife?" he repeated.

She could not lift her head, she could not answer. Her cheeks turned deep red. By themselves, her two hands rose, trembling.

Yes. Yes. Yes. Yes. Yes. Yes.... Baruch Hashem, yes!

IT WAS a rushed wedding, befitting the strange match. There was no early celebration of *tena'im*, no parade of messengers bearing gifts from the groom to his bride, no elaborate engagement feast. The land was aflame with war, resistance against Rome, siege and carnage. The roads were full of peril from Roman soldiers and bandits. Besides — each family feared the other would have a change of heart.

Just three months after Yoseph and Rachel agreed to marry, in the middle of Av, Nachum led his family to Dotan to recite the *eirusin* and *nissuin* blessings in one quick celebration. Only Nachum's closest friends escorted him on the wedding trip. They traveled by night to elude the Romans.

Yoseph and his family arrived early in the morning of the fifteenth of Av. While they rested, huge pots cooked over open fires, and a dozen ovens glowed with freshly baking bread. In the fields, sheep were slaughtered for the night's feast.

Rachel's mother tried her best to make Rachel presentable, wrapping her with layer upon layer of rich purple and scarlet silks. She painted her pretty eyes large with blue makeup and colored her cheeks a bright crimson, to distract the gaze from her misshapen mouth. She perfumed her hair with balsam and myrrh and dressed her with necklace upon necklace of fine gold.

But behind all the preparations was an incredulity that this marriage was really happening. Someone was really going to marry Rachel! Some women whispered unkindly that the marriage would only succeed if Rachel kept her wedding veil on permanently, so that the groom would not have to wake up each morning to her bitter scowl. The men wondered if the bride would have to watch the sheep while Yoseph wandered off to play his harp in the woods.

Night came, and the ceremony began. The *tena'im* were read. Betzalel obligated himself to support the couple in a simple but adequate manner. Nachum promised to provide his son with a small house, a piece of land, and a modest flock of sheep.

The young couple stood side by side under a *chupah* that had been erected in the village square. Above, the warm Shomron night glistened with the white gleaming face of the moon and a veil of a thousand silver stars. They stood trembling, hoping for a new beginning, hoping for a chance to build a holy *bayit*.

Can I make a good wife? Can Yoseph really care for me?

Is this the right thing? Am I marrying Rachel just to save my father?

In the glow of blazing torches, the families celebrated the union. The men and women headed off separately, and the feast began, with song and dance, plentiful food and drink, ear-piercing yodels of joy, and clever *badchanim* who sang humorous praises of *chatan* and *kallah*. In the early hours of the morning, the feast finally ended. The two families sighed with relief.

There was another guest at the wedding, although no one saw him.

Far away, in the hills of Ephraim, the old man climbed down the little hollow to the apple tree. Above, the glowing full moon of the fifteenth of Av shone off his face, and he saw and felt everything, their joy, their shyness, their wonder, their fear.

He saw what they could not see, and his body trembled. He clapped his hands, and swayed round and round. He wept, he laughed, he shook, he danced, he closed his eyes and watched and watched.

His lips moved in prayer:

> *Simeini kachotam al libecha, kachotam al zeroecha, ki azah chamavet ahavah, kashah chish'ol kinah. Rishafeha rishpei eish, shalhevetkah!* Set me as a seal upon your heart, as a seal on Your arm, for love is as strong as death, jealousy is hard as the grave. Its flashes are flashes of fire, the flame of God!

He stood there all night, rejoicing with the *chatan* and *kallah*. They did not see him, but he saw them. Slowly, the lustrous moon sailed to the west, and the first rays of dawn lit the eastern hilltop. Yaakov gazed one last time at the apple tree and touched one of its branches. Quickly, he disappeared into the hidden woods.

THEIR LITTLE house was so private and hidden that no travelers would come upon it except by sheer luck. It was as if both families had agreed that the best place for the couple was out of sight. It was nestled in a small decline among the Shomron hills, well north of Tapuach and a good day's ride to Dotan. They were close to everybody and nobody. They were blissfully hidden from the great battles that swept around them and saw nothing of the suffering. They lived in their own intimate world, where the days were measured by the times of Shema and prayer, leading the flock to pasture, milking the ewes and feeding the lambs.

Rachel worshiped Yoseph. How had she deserved such a husband? He was as handsome as the sun, kind and gentle to her, and bound to *avodat Hashem*. She saw how his strong rugged body trembled with *kavanah* when he recited Shema. She secretly watched him sway in prayer and heard the murmur of *Tehillim* he recited even when he performed menial jobs. She spoke to him with her hands, and even with small, chirping sounds. He watched her in puzzlement until he understood what she wanted. He never tried to speak for her or put words into her mouth before she was ready. He was so patient. She wished so much that she could speak to him — but she was afraid to break her silence.

It was a hard time for Yoseph. He dedicated himself to being kind to his wife, and knowing that he had saved his father's home and the family fortune comforted him. But what life was this for him? Poor Rachel could not utter a word, and every conversation was a struggle. He spoke, and she tried so hard to make herself understood. She tried her best to please him, but that constant, twisted scowl, so angry even when she was not angry, did not leave her for a moment — as if someone had placed a curse on her.

He lived in the Shomron, but his heart dwelt in the Holy Temple. In a few months he would reach his twenty-fifth birthday, and he could begin his initiation at the Levites' *duchan*.

He had not visited his harp once since his wedding. It was hidden an hour's ride from their home, near Tapuach. He yearned to play it, but he did not want to leave his wife alone.

"Rachel," he announced one morning, "I am going today to a special place in the hills where my harp is hidden. Do you wish to come with me?"

She quickly agreed, and the young couple gathered their flock and marched together deep into the hills, past green woods and hidden meadows. It was almost Cheshvan, but the sun still shone warmly. The sheep were not used to such long treks, but they gamboled happily, their little bells tinkling, eager for new pasture. Yoseph and Rachel walked silently, but Yoseph saw that Rachel was happy, despite her frozen scowl. The apple tree was his secret, and he wanted to share it with her.

They climbed into a copse of pines, and then they were there, looking down at the apple tree. A little stream murmured nearby, and the flock raced ahead to drink.

Yoseph swept his arm towards the apple tree. "This is where I play my harp," he told her. "You're the first person I ever brought here."

They climbed down into the hollow, and Yoseph found a large, round stone for Rachel to sit on. He reached under a pile of branches and extracted a large leather pouch. Carefully, he untied the protective string and extracted his harp. Its fine strings glistened gold in the morning sun.

Rachel watched him, her face frozen. He clasped the harp against his heart and began playing. His fingers raced over the strings like gazelles skipping through the rocks. His whole soul was in his fingers, in his voice, in his heart. He sang and sang, his head tilted upwards, his eyes shut tight.

I hope I am giving her some happiness, he thought. *She must bear such great sadness in her life that she cannot smile. I must give her joy.*

Suddenly he stopped playing and turned to his wife.

"You see this string?"

She peered over, and he plucked at the sixth string.

"It's not mine. A holy man gave it to me last year. I've been afraid to play it — it seems so thin that it'll break. Shall I try it?"

Her small hand went up.

He smiled. "If it breaks, you'll have to fix it!"

Yoseph held the harp close. He closed his eyes and let his fingers fall on all the strings, even the sixth. He started cautiously, but the harp came alive in his fingers as if it had a will of its own. He lifted his voice, but it was not his voice. He heard the tzaddik singing with him, his heart beating with him, holiness and purity surging through his body. The sixth string trembled at his fingers, and its vibrations swept through his body like an icy shiver. He forgot who he was, where he was, with whom he was. He was swept up in a world of song and praise, swept up in pure holiness and joy.

Finally, overcome, he had to stop. He sat there exhausted, his eyes closed, face awash in sweat.

"Yoseph, please play more."

Yoseph sat still and slowly opened his eyes. He gazed at his wife in astonishment.

"Yoseph," she repeated, "please sing more to Hashem."

Her voice was quiet, hesitant, sweet like honey.

Yoseph tried to speak calmly. "Rachel, you really want me to play more?"

She nodded.

"But where is your smile? If you can speak to me, you can also smile at me!"

She looked at him, and a tear fell from her eye.

"Rachel, my wife, smile at me and I will play."

Rachel rose from her seat and ran to the little brook. The lambs scurried away as she bent low, scooped up water in her hands, and washed her face. Again and again she bathed her face, finally dabbing it dry with the sleeve of her tunic. She covered her face with her hands, like a woman reciting the Sabbath blessings, and returned to Yoseph. He waited silently as she seated herself across from him on the stone.

Rachel removed her hands and smiled at Yoseph. He stared at his wife. Rachel was as beautiful as the sun. Her smile was pure radiance, and when her lips parted, her teeth glistened like a flock of ewes rising from the stream. She was so beautiful. His head dropped into his hand and he began weeping.

She rose from her seat and fell to the ground in front of him.

"Rachel, is that you?"

"Yes, Yoseph, it is I."

They sat there looking at each other in wonder. Although they had been married for two months, it was as if they were meeting for the first time.

Rachel's fingers caressed the harp. He had promised to play, but he could not. He set it down and asked in wonder, "Rachel, my

Rachel, who are you? What is this?"

So Rachel began her tale:

"I stopped speaking in my seventh year. Until then I was quiet, but happy. I had lost my mother just a year before —"

"The woman you call Imma, is she not your mother?"

"No, she is one of my father's other wives. She has looked after me well, but she is not a mother." Rachel sighed, then continued, "I saw everything that happened around me, especially how my father conducted himself with people who owed him money."

"You must not speak ill, Rachel."

She was silent for so long that Yoseph feared she had descended back to her muteness. Her smile disappeared.

"Dear Yoseph, you must let me tell my story my way," she said at last.

"There was a man who owed my father much money, but he had nothing to pay back, no land, not even children to sell. At my father's orders, two men took him out to a field, a field where I had gone to play alone, and they began beating him. They did not see me, for I was hiding.

"The poor man cried, begging them to stop. 'I have nothing! I have nothing!' he pleaded over and over. But they kept beating him until suddenly he grew still and fell to the ground. They lifted him up and tried to stir him awake, but he fell down again.

" 'He is dead!' one said to the other. 'We have killed him!'

" 'Why did you strike him so hard?' the other reproached him.

"When I heard they had killed him, I screamed from my hiding place. The two men ran over to me and lifted me up.

" 'It is Betzalel's daughter!' They were shocked when they realized that I had seen everything. 'She will tell someone.'

" 'What can we do?' the other asked.

"The other man turned to me. He was very large and strong, and so angry that I had seen them! 'Rachel, if you tell anyone about this they will take revenge against your father! And we will come after you! Do you understand? It was an accident, no more. You must be silent or your father will pay dearly — and you will be hurt! Do you understand?'

"I nodded my head and looked down. Suddenly, he struck me

with a terrible blow across my mouth. His hand was so heavy it twisted up my whole face like a fig. Then he let me go and I ran away.

"I knew those men, Yoseph! They were murderers, but even afterwards they strutted about freely in my father's house!

"I decided then that I would not speak again. I would not let my face smile falsely where people are so evil, so deceitful and so wicked and so mean! I cannot abide meanness, Yoseph — it makes me ill! My head spins, my brain bursts with pain! I am sorry, but I am weak. How can I smile when the very air sparks with hatred and lies? I searched for love and kindness, forgiveness and sincerity — and it had vanished!"

"And now?"

"Today, when you played the harp, you began playing that — other string —"

"The sixth string."

"I heard a new sound, a voice, a voice of honesty...a voice of...*chesed*...."

"It was his voice, Rachel, the voice of the tzaddik. I heard it also — he was singing with me."

Rachel beamed, and they rose from the ground together in honor of the wondrous, precious moment.

Yoseph looked at her in worry. "But this is it, Rachel, this is the world that you described. I have also known hate and rejection. But I cannot play the harp and sing all day! I must return the harp to its hiding place, and we must go back to Tapuach. I am afraid that you will grow sad and silent again."

She rested her hand on the harp and looked up at him. "No, my dear Yoseph. I have heard your voice, and your voice is the sweetness of the harp. All that I seek — I find with you."

CHESHVAN PASSED, and Kislev swept in softly. The almond trees slept, but the sun warmed the fields. Migrating birds whistled and twittered overhead, while caressing winds, pregnant with life-giving rains, swept in curtains over the Shomron hills. The young couple, who had been unloved in their own families, found happiness with each other.

Remote in their little home, forsaken by brothers and sisters, they were blissfully unaware of the terrible battles that swirled in Beit El and Gofna, Chevron and Yericho. Powerful Roman armies, laden with engines of war, stormed into Eretz Yisrael from Syria, Egypt, and the sea. They gathered their legions to crush the Judean rebellion before it ignited the whole empire.

But Yoseph and Rachel's little home was a blessed island of peace. Rachel had never been so happy in her life. Hashem had blessed her with a special husband. He was tender with her, he was gentle and patient with the sheep. He was happy with whatever she did and whatever she set before him. Although her father was very wealthy, Yoseph refused to ask for more. He craved simplicity and the freedom to commune with Hashem. He counted the days when he would play before the altar. Once they returned to the harp's hiding place, and Yoseph sang his heart out, words that soared like birds in flight, and she was filled with joy.

And yet — something was missing. There was one secret she had hidden from Yoseph. In those lonely years, when she had been shunned by her own brothers and sisters, her father took pity on a strange man who dwelt alone in the hills. It was rumored that he was one of the thirty-six hidden tzaddikim of the generation. Her father gave him a room, and from time to time he stayed for a few days. He gazed on her with great kindness and told her stories of Sarah and Rivkah and, above all, Mother Rachel. She could not answer, but he read her eyes and kept talking.

"You, too, will become a great woman like them!" he promised.

And when she looked back piteously with her twisted face and cried, he looked at her fiercely. "Rachel, Rachel, someday your face will shine like the moon! And your husband will be a tzaddik — and a *talmid chacham*!"

But now Rachel watched her husband and was troubled. He kept the mitzvos simply, with a pure heart. When he prayed, his whole soul poured out into the words — nothing could distract him, not even a lion's roar.

But where was the Torah? He did not study, and he had no teacher to learn from, and that saddened her. Twice she dreamt that the holy man appeared to her and asked: "Rachel, *Torah mah t'hei aleha*? Rachel, when will he study Torah?"

Should she speak to him, should she not speak? He was such a good husband, and they were so happy together. Should she be silent? The third time the tzaddik appeared in her dream, he was impatient:

"Rachel, *Torah mah t'hei aleha*? Is it not time?"

ONE SABBATH, after the morning *seudah*, when the holiness of Shabbat glistened off every rain-soaked leaf, she broached the subject.

"Yoseph, when do you study Torah?"

He smiled dreamily at her. It had been a good meal.

"Rachel, you married a simple shepherd, not a scholar. Binyamin will be the *talmid chacham* of our family."

He rose and stretched. "I am going to go and rest."

She waggled her hand downwards. "No, wait, Yoseph, don't go away. Please — sit back down...."

He collapsed wearily down to the carpet.

"I know that you are not a scholar, but you are not a plain shepherd, either. Plain shepherds don't sing to Hashem like you do. They do not pray with the *kavanah* you do. You have a special *neshamah*."

"You also have a special *neshamah*, Rachel."

"If I were a man, I would not waste my *neshamah*. I would find a master to teach me Torah. I would want to become a *talmid chacham*, Yoseph. I would not give away my portion of Torah to others."

There was a silence. *Are we having an argument?* he asked himself.

Yoseph looked at his wife and saw that something was bothering her. Was she was disappointed in him? He was perplexed — he was so used to doing what his heart told him.

He tried to reason. "Listen, Rachel, there are all sorts of ways to serve Hashem. There are those who have good minds and iron memories, like my Sabba had — like Binyamin. But some of us are born with broken hearts, with a need to cry out to Hashem in *tefillah*.

"Look — look, even King David wrote: '*Rachash libi davar tov*. My heart stirs with a good thing!' His harp hung over his bed, and he rose each night at midnight to sing *Tehillim*. His heart made him sing!"

"But didn't he spend the first half of the night studying Torah?" she answered quickly. "Then he played his harp — right?"

For a formerly silent woman, she is catching up fast, thought Yoseph.

She saw he was hurt, and she had not meant to hurt him. "My beloved husband, I don't mean to hurt you. You are my whole life. But...think about it! As it is the holy Shabbat, think about it."

She dropped the subject and let the seed ripen.

But now a little misty cloud hung over their marriage. She said nothing, but when he sat, or went out on some task, or stood lazily watching the sheep, or recited yet more *Tehillim*, their eyes caught and held.

She's wondering why I do not study, he thought.

Is he making a decision? she wondered.

They lived in two worlds, the world of speech and deed, where they were like two halves of one soul, and the silent world of unspoken questions and hopes, and eyes that spoke in flickers and frowns.

Will you become a talmid chacham?

Shall I become a talmid chacham?

Two weeks passed. Once more the holy man appeared in her dreams:

"Did he say yes?"

"I have done what I can. You must help me!"

"I will," he promised. "I will...."

YOSEPH'S SOUL was a harp that vibrated with every holy thought, crying out in longing for truth. Rachel's words took seed in him, and he struggled as it took root. *What shall I do? How shall I do? When? With whom? And what of my song?*

The second morning of Chanukah, Yoseph turned to his wife.

"Rachel, I have been thinking a lot about what you said — about learning Torah."

"I know, Yoseph."

"I need to be by myself for a little while. Just alone — not even for a whole day."

"Are you going to the hiding place?"

"You know?"

"I know you. You cannot do anything that is not straight from the heart. I will wait, and when you return this evening we will light the menorah."

She gave him some provisions and a jug of water for his trek, and he set off southwards. She watched him disappear and turned to mind the sheep.

She prayed, he prayed, and far away the tzaddik also prayed — and prepared himself.

THE EARTH around his hiding place had turned muddy, and Yoseph's clothing was soon splattered. Since he had no shovel, he used the edge of a fallen branch to extricate the leather bag from where earth had sucked it down. Perhaps it was not such a good place. But when he pulled the harp from its leather case, it was clean and unharmed.

The skies turned leaden, and it began drizzling. Yoseph hid under the tree and held the harp protectively, like a baby. He had not been here alone for many months, and he cherished the silence.

His fingers called to the strings, and they responded. He looked up to the gray, drizzly skies and pleaded with Hashem: "What do You want from me? I finally found someone with whom I can share my life. My heart is so full of happiness with her, and now I sing with real joy. But now she wants me to become a *talmid chacham*. What do I know of the Torah? I know the Tanach, but that is not very much. I have seen the sages of the Sanhedrin who can speak seventy languages and know all the law backwards and forwards. How can I compare to them? I am a donkey and they are angels!

"And where do I start? Where do I go? Where do I find a teacher? Does Torah grow on trees like apples, so that I can a pick a *pasuk* like you pluck an apple? And yet Rachel says I must learn Torah — and she's right!"

He held the harp close to his heart and sang:

> *Nichsefah v'gam kaltah nafshi l'chatzrot Hashem, libi uv'sari yeranenu el Keil chai* — My soul yearns, yea, it pines for the courtyards of Hashem. My heart and my flesh pray fervently to the Living God.
>
> *Gam tzipor matz'ah bayit ud'ror kein lah asher shatah efrocheha* — Even a bird finds her nest and the free bird her nest where she laid her young.

"Hashem, I am a bird who has built a nest, but now I don't know where to fly! Where shall I turn? Who will teach me? What do You want from me?"

He pulled his hand over the harp and cried out: " '*Ashrei* —' "

"*Shalom aleichem*," a voice spoke behind him.

Yoseph almost jumped up into the tree. He turned, and just a few feet behind him stood the tzaddik, Yaakov. He was leaning against the tree, watching and smiling.

"How — how long have you been there?" asked Yoseph.

"A while," Yaakov answered.

"You heard everything I said?"

"I heard everything you said with your lips, but I do not know what you said in your heart."

"What do you mean?"

"Did you mean in your heart what you said with your lips?"

"Yes, why else would I say it?"

"Oh, many times people say one thing with their mouth and mean something else in their heart of hearts. But if you mean it, I will help you. By the way, has my string been of any use?"

Yoseph rang a note on it. "It caused my wife to start speaking again."

"*Baruch Hashem* — not bad," Yaakov murmured. He didn't ask for any further — as if he knew everything already.

"Yoseph, I did not disappoint you with my string, and now I will not disappoint you with my advice. You have a *neshamah* that has descended from the highest realm. But a *neshamah* without Torah is like a candle without a flame. Go to the great tzaddik Rabbi Tzaddok, and he will teach you where to start. He is in

Yerushalayim, and he will kindle the flame in you."

"Yerushalayim? How can I bring my wife to Yerushalayim?"

"It is not for your wife to go there. Romans surround the walls, but Rabbi Tzaddok is just outside the city, recovering from his fasting. It is very dangerous, not for a woman. You will find him, he will instruct you — and then you will return."

Yoseph's face turned pale. "Father Yaakov, you are telling me to leave my wife of just a few months! And I don't know even where to find Rabbi Tzaddok."

"Hashem will guide you. Then — you will return and begin truly learning Torah."

"But I don't want to leave Rachel!" he cried.

"You will not leave her."

"But you said I should go alone."

"She will be with you wherever you are, and you with her. Did not my one little string help you?"

"Yes...."

"Then believe me that my words will help you even more."

Yoseph did not answer, but his fingers ran fiercely over the harp and it snarled back.

"No, Yoseph, not with anger, but with *bitachon*. If you want to seek Torah, it must be with joy. Come, play a little for me, make me joyous, and I will sing to you about the Torah you will study."

Yoseph took a deep breath to calm himself and began playing. The tzaddik waved his arm in a great curve heavenwards, and began, part in words, part in song —

"Before there was a world, when the Holy One was One and Only, He chose to burst His light into our world — *tzimtzum b'tzimtzum*, contraction after contraction. He made a place for His holiness to descend, from so high, from the *kutzo shel yud*, from the very point of the *yud*, from His Heavenly Throne, down, down into the world — *sefirah* after *sefirah* descending into our material world and yet attached above!

"All this was Hashem's will, and that will is His intellect, and all this is in the Torah. When you study His word, you unite yourself with Hashem's thoughts. You are embracing the King! It is a unity beyond any unity; your soul soars to the highest realms!"

He turned to Yoseph and shouted: "And this you are sad about? You should be joyous!"

Yoseph stopped playing. "But what about my wife — what about Rachel? How shall I tell her?"

"Yoseph, tonight is the third night of Chanukah. When you light the lamps, both of you gaze into the flame — and then you will know what to say."

The rain had stopped, but still drops of water dripped down from the branches onto the holy man's face. Bathed in utter purity, he had the face of an angel.

Yoseph wept. "Father Yaakov, I am so afraid."

The old man smiled sadly and nodded. "I, too, am afraid, my beloved Yoseph. But be strong — be strong! *Chazak*! And Hashem will lead you."

"What of my harp?" he asked. "Shall I leave it hidden here for safekeeping?"

Abruptly, Yaakov's face reddened like a flame. "No, no, no! Take it, take it! You will need it — I promise!"

IT WAS late evening when he finally returned home. The skies had cleared, and a thin crescent moon rose over the eastern horizon. He saw Rachel through the window, bathed in candlelight. She hovered over the menorah, straightening its wicks, readying it for him. Before he rushed in he gazed at her, feeling sad.

He knocked on the door, and she greeted him with the blinding smile that only he knew existed. She looked at him in surprise.

"You brought home your harp," she said.

He nodded. "I'll explain...later. Come, it is late, let's light the menorah."

He carried the unlit lamp outside, placing it on a shelf near his door. A little breeze blew, and the *shammash* flame danced back and forth, struggling to stay alive. He closed his eyes and recited the blessings, then carefully lit the lamps, one, two, three.

They stood there, watching as the candles did a little mitzvah dance, bowing and tipping to each other, flaming up and twisting sideways, like dancers at a wedding.

"Why don't you sing?" she asked.

"Rachel, I met a tzaddik, Yaakov. He told me that we should stare at the flames of the lamps, and then I will tell you what he said."

They stood there staring, peering deep into the flames, the fiery bursts of Chanukah, letters of the Torah dancing towards them, *alef*s and *bet*s, *daled*s, *shin*s, and *yud*s shining into the pupils of their eyes, into their souls, into the roots of their existence, igniting a love for Torah, a love for their Creator....

> *Nichsefah v'gam kaltah nafshi l'chatzrot Hashem, libi uv'sari yeranenu el Keil chai....*

They stood there, remolding in holiness, their whole lives transformed.

Yoseph sang quietly:

> *Lo tirah mipachad lailah* — Thou shalt not fear the terror of night, nor the arrow that flies by day; nor the pestilence that walks in gloom, nor the destroyer who lays waste at noon.... *Ki mal'achav....* For He will charge His angels for you, to protect you in all your ways....

"Rachel," he whispered, "I went to my secret place, but I was not alone. I met the tzaddik whose harp string caused you to smile again. He told me I must go to Yerushalayim — to Rabbi Tzaddok, who will set me on the way of Torah...."

She did not answer. She nodded, but looked very sad.

"I cannot take you, Rachel, it is too dangerous. But Yerushalayim is only a two-day walk, three days at most. I will find this Rabbi Tzaddok, and then return straight away to you."

"I will be very lonely without you. Three days there, three days back, who knows how long until you find him...."

"I know — but that is what I must do, Rachel. I will take you back to your father's home until I return."

"No!" she cried.

"What other place is there? I cannot leave you here alone. I will take you back home for a short while, I will find Rabbi Tzaddok, and then I will run back, with God's help...."

She took a deep breath and looked at him. "Yoseph, if I must return home, I will cover my face! When I was unable to speak and my face was distorted, they mocked me and looked away. Now my face is only for you."

They gazed at the candles intently, lost in thought. The letters were beautiful, the menorah was beautiful, the Torah was beautiful — but the world was not so beautiful. She turned to Yoseph. "Now I must tell you a secret. Yoseph, we are going to have a baby."

He looked at her in shock. "What? Are you sure?"

"I am sure, my dear husband. I knew for a few days. That is why I had dreams....."

"Dreams?"

"It does not matter."

He looked at her, absorbing the startling news. "Rachel, I shall wait till after Chanukah, then I will bring you to your father's house. I will do what I have to, and then hurry home."

"Wherever you will be, I will be with you," she said.

He looked at her, perplexed.

She pointed to the white crescent above. "You see, when the moon rises over the mountains of the east, you will see it in Yerushalayim, and I will see it in Dotan. The face of the moon is your face, it is my face. You will see me and I will see you, and we shall tell each other all that is in our hearts. The silver glow that touches you will touch me."

"Then I shall see you every night the moon rises," he said.

"And I shall know you are there when the moon glows over me," she answered.

"And we shall greet the dawn together when the moon departs into the sea," they said together, in chorus.

They smiled at each other — with such fondness, such fierceness, such *bitachon*, such oneness of heart!

The tzaddik had been right — they would never be apart.

Chapter Three

Five months before the Churban

It was a long and treacherous walk to Jerusalem, a walk that involved twisting through the Binyamin hills, skirting Samaritan villages, and making the final steep ascent to Yerushalayim. There were Romans everywhere, in addition to bandits, bears, wolves, and wild dogs. Yoseph and Rachel's parting was not simple. Heavy rains fell in Tevet and early Shevat, making travel impossible. After Tu BeShvat, Yoseph took Rachel back up to Dotan and settled her in her parents' house. Ben Kaspi was not pleased, but grudgingly agreed when he heard she would be there for just a few weeks. Then the rain fell in torrents, and Yoseph was forced to stay until Purim. Rachel hid her face behind a veil and spoke to no one except him.

At last, Yoseph set out southward, traveling through the hills that skirted the main roads. At dusk, he descended to the ancient *derech ha'avot*. The last time he had walked here, the road was full of pilgrims, and he had walked shoulder to shoulder with his beloved Sabba. Now even the Romans had disappeared.

He walked briskly, his bag slung over his shoulder. He was anxious to find Rabbi Tzaddok, do what he had to, and return home. The road seemed familiar, and his whole body prickled like that of a child playing hide-and-seek who knows he is close to his prey. He walked to the side of the road and inspected the terrain. New underbrush had grown, but he pushed back a branch and found what he knew was there — the moon-shaped rock where Sabba had turned off for Yerushalayim.

He heard animals barking in the distance, and the dark stillness of the woods frightened him. But he felt Sabba's soul calling him:

"Come my way, my dear grandson!" Impelled by his deep loneliness for his grandfather, even it meant just touching his grave, Yoseph squeezed by the stone and entered the narrow, twisting trail. Soon his eyes adjusted to the darkness of the hills, and he felt his grandfather's soul hovering near him.

The trail widened into a path, and he came upon a small clearing, bordered by a cluster of date trees. He stopped and studied the trees. This was the place! He and Sabba and the rest of the group had slept here that night, and he had slept in, abandoning Sabba to his fate. He went over to the tree and kicked it angrily.

He turned to walk off, then returned quickly to the tree. "It was me, not you — forgive me."

It was all there, the same road, the same widening path, the same meandering fields and vineyards. Yoseph dreaded what lay ahead. He descended a steep dip in the road. Rough stone walls lay on either side, crowned by thick vines that had been pruned for the winter. This was the place! Here the Romans had encountered Sabba and taken him prisoner.

He searched the ground carefully — could there still be a relic left? Too many travelers had passed since then, and they scavenged the area, removing every tiny jug, every scrap of cloth. There was nothing except his grandfather's holy soul, hovering close by.

Yoseph stood in the dark and silent path and swayed back and forth, his eyes closed. He was absolutely alone, alone with Hashem, alone with the soul of his grandfather.

Here I will recite the Shema, he thought. *Here I will pray the amidah, and Sabba will be with me.*

He faced Jerusalem, standing rigid like a stone. In the deep silence of the night, in the heart of the deserted road, he began the silent *amidah*. He clasped his hands over his breast, like a slave pleading before his master. He sensed that he was at the edge of great things — but what, where, when? Word by word, blessing by blessing, he poured out his fears, his hopes, his praise.

Suddenly he stopped and listened. He heard a low rumble. He assured himself that it was the wind rustling the branches, no more. He continued praying — but the rumble grew louder, approaching from behind. Hoofbeats!

They were approaching quickly, now about a *mil* away. Romans! He stood in the middle of the road and would be trampled in a few minutes. His life was suddenly in mortal danger. Should he flee? He turned back stubbornly to his prayers, reciting the words slowly, carefully, deliberately. Here his Sabba had met his fate, and he was ready.

The ground shook as the steeds crested the hill and bore down furiously upon him. He braced himself.

Baruch atah Hashem — go'eil Yisrael!

They were almost atop him when he heard a shout: "Halt!"

There was a sound of reins against flanks, horses wheeling wildly and pounding their hooves in protest. He was in the center of a circle of huge mounts, so close he could feel their warm, moist breath against his neck.

Yoseph steeled himself and continued to pray, eyes shut, utterly focused on the great God before him.

He felt the sharp prick of a spear against his neck.

"Jew, what are you doing here?" a soldier screamed.

Yoseph bowed for *Modim*. The spear followed him down and pierced him sharply as he lifted his head. But he continued praying.

He heard one of the soldiers dismount and step towards him. He felt the edge of a sword across his neck.

He paused, waiting for death.

"Stop there!" a voice commanded. "Step away until he finishes his prayers."

Abruptly the blade was removed and the soldier retreated. Yoseph's body shook, but he clung to his *kavanah* right down to the final blessing, to the final three paces back.

He opened his eyes, turned, and gazed at the intruders. The horses were even larger than he had imagined, two dozen huge black stallions mounted by soldiers. He could not make out their faces, and they huddled like black shapes against the dark sky.

One of the riders dismounted from his horse and approached Yoseph. His uniform was decorated, indicating that he was an officer of rank.

He approached Yoseph and put a hand on his shoulder, drawing him away from the others. He spoke almost familiarly.

"Why did you choose to pray in the middle of a road?" he asked.

Yoseph could still not discern his face, but he responded in the same matter-of-fact way. "A few minutes ago this road was absolutely deserted. I have been walking here for hours without seeing any sign of life. I never expected the Roman army to come crashing in on me!"

The officer laughed. And then he said the strangest thing.

"You have not yet said *Aleinu.*"

Yoseph looked at him in astonishment, but responded simply, "For *Aleinu,* I can get off the road, out of the way."

Yoseph walked to the stone wall and the officer accompanied him. The legionnaires sat on their mounts, waiting respectfully. It was obvious that the officer was in charge, and he was a Jew.

Quickly Yoseph began *Aleinu.* His amazement increased when the Roman officer recited it quietly with him, word for word. But again, Yoseph was discreet and did not ask anything.

When they had finished, the officer addressed him. "I was extremely impressed by your courage on the road. What is your name?"

"Yoseph ben Nachum, from the town of Tapuach."

"I am Yoseph ben Matityahu, a *kohein.* You can call me Josephus. What were you doing here all by yourself?"

"I am going to Jerusalem to study."

Josephus stepped back. "Are you completely mad? Study in Jerusalem? Don't you know that people are dying in the streets there? The city is under siege. Are you living in a dream?"

"I'm not going to Jerusalem itself, but somewhere outside its walls. There is a sage who I must find."

"A sage?"

Yoseph hesitated to reveal his name.

"The holy sage Rabbi Tzaddok," he finally said.

Josephus was silent, then shook his head. "Unbelievable."

Yoseph did not ask what was unbelievable, nor why a Jew was an officer with the Romans, no less.

"And how exactly were you going to reach Jerusalem, on golden wings? The roads are full of soldiers who would sell you into slavery in a moment. How did you expect to get to Rabbi Tzaddok?"

"By staying on the back trails, out of sight."

"And when you got to Jerusalem? There is nothing but cleared land for miles around. What then?"

"I don't know. I will put my trust in God."

Josephus lowered his head and drummed his fingers against the stone wall. "You're foolish, but you are sincere. You will ride with me and I'll take you straightaway to Jerusalem."

"I prefer to walk," Yoseph answered firmly.

Josephus raised his head and stared through the darkness. "No, you are coming with us," he said firmly. "Follow me!" He walked back to his horse.

Yoseph wanted to argue, but two soldiers rode up to him on horseback. In the darkness they looked like dark, faceless apparitions. One of them was so huge that Yoseph thought he was really a machine mounted on a horse. But the machine suddenly spoke up. "Get up on the general's horse now — that's an order!" He cracked his reins sharply, and Yoseph hurried towards Josephus.

Yoseph had never mounted a horse before, and he struggled to climb up. He heard laughter. Josephus reached down and lifted his leather pouch, holding it until he was seated. Then he signaled, and the horses thundered ahead. Josephus turned and shouted to Yoseph, but Yoseph could not hear him over the hoofbeats. He leaned forward, and Josephus shouted in his ear.

"What are you carrying in that bag?"

Yoseph was startled at his interest. "A harp. I am a Levite, and I brought it to play in the Temple."

Josephus shook his head, but did not respond. Yoseph was baffled by his captor. Who was this Jew who claimed to be a *kohein*, and was a Roman general? As for himself, he didn't know if he was prisoner or guest. He was exhausted and hungry, but the risk of being hurtled down the next precipice or smashing his head against the next branch were too great for him to relax his grip.

DAWN BROKE as they crossed Motza. Somewhere nearby was his Sabba's grave. He heard a rumble rising from the capital, like low thunder. As they neared Jerusalem, the rumbling intensified.

Yoseph leaned forward. "Is that a thunderstorm?"

Josephus looked back impatiently. "Don't ask so many questions!"

They neared the outskirts of Yerushalayim, having turned onto the main road. The rumbling had increased to loud pounding, like giant hammers against stone, so fierce that Yoseph's head throbbed. The road was swarming with humanity, Romans, Arab traders, gangs of Jewish slaves dragging siege towers towards the city. The ascent was brutal, and the towers tilted and threatened to crush them.

Josephus's company slowed, weaving its way through the human tide. Soon the road became even more crowded. A crowd of prisoners, perhaps two hundred, was marching towards them. Josephus's company moved to the side of the road. Yoseph stared at the captives in shock. They marched before him, frightened men, women, and children. Their faces were sunken from hunger, burned from the sun. They marched barefoot, sinking into the mud to their ankles, stumbling as they walked. Their arms were fettered in shackles, and the younger men had yokes about their necks, choking them. Guards walked alongside, screaming and prodding them with their spears. As they passed, the captives lifted their heads pitifully to the Romans, mounted proudly on their powerful steeds. Many stared at Yoseph. His head was covered with a *kippah*, tzitzit dangled from his tunic, and he was hale and hearty, clinging to the back of a Roman general. He looked away, ashamed.

Josephus pointed at them. "They are surrendering by the hundreds! Is this the Jerusalem you were rushing to?"

"Where are they being taken?" Yoseph asked.

"Some will work the mines, others will be put on ships and thrown overboard. They won't last long."

The pitiful parade of captives finally passed, and the company climbed back onto the road towards Jerusalem. From a distance, a band of horsemen appeared, racing in their direction. They stopped for no one, and people scattered frantically before them. As soon as Josephus's commander spied them, he signaled his men and they began racing to meet them. The riders carried the imperial standard of the Fifteenth Legion.

They saluted the commander quickly, but rode directly to Josephus.

"General, greetings from Commander Titus. He welcomes you back to Jerusalem and summons you to meet with him tomorrow evening."

Josephus saluted smartly. "Tell the general that I am honored by his invitation, and extend my deepest loyalty! Where will he be?"

"He is surveying the siege walls today, and tomorrow he will be reviewing the Tenth Legion. He will see you in his headquarters tomorrow evening."

Josephus lifted his hand in salute again. "I will be there and await his orders."

The messenger saluted, wheeled his horse, and raced back to Jerusalem. The commander approached Josephus deferentially, awed by Titus's special summons.

"Where do you wish us to escort you to, General?" he asked.

"I am tired," Josephus answered. "We will head straight to the Fifth Legion camp."

They climbed the final ascent and suddenly the walls of the city rose before them. Soldiers patrolled everywhere, searching for escapees from the city, ready to sling arrows at any defenders who showed their heads. In the distance, siege towers rolled toward the walls, and the unceasing pounding of the battering rams against stone created a deafening sound.

Josephus skirted the west wall and rode westward towards the Roman camp. He entered the Fifth Legion camp like a triumphant warrior, head lifted defiantly. Wherever he turned, he was treated deferentially. If anyone thought it strange that a simple Jew was riding with him, he kept his eyes and thoughts to himself.

Yoseph had never felt more at Hashem's mercy. Here he was, in the heart of the huge Roman headquarters, legionnaires everywhere — marching in strict formation, relaxing, sparring like children at mock combat, sharpening their swords. The camp was laid out precisely, with rows upon rows of barracks, craftsmen's shops, blacksmiths, hospitals, storehouses. Guards patrolled the perimeter walls, and there were watchtowers at every corner.

Josephus dismissed his company and rode through the camp

with just two escorts. One was the huge legionnaire that Yoseph had encountered in the darkness of night. His huge size unsettled Yoseph, and he avoided looking straight at him. The giant rode behind him silently, but Yoseph felt his stare boring into his back.

Josephus reached a large tent and stopped. An aide rushed out and helped him dismount. Yoseph slid off the horse so rapidly he almost injured himself.

Josephus turned to the remaining legionnaires. "Get some sleep and report to me tonight!"

They rode off, and he turned to Yoseph. "Follow me."

Yoseph threw his bag over his shoulder and followed Josephus into the tent.

"You will stay here for the time being," he said.

Yoseph summoned up his nerve. "General, you saved my life on the road last night and brought me to Jerusalem faster than I ever hoped! I thank you for that. But I have to go on my way now and do what I have to do."

"What is that?" Josephus asked quizzically.

"Find the holy man."

"Who, Rabbi Tzaddok?"

Yoseph was surprised he remembered his name. "Yes."

"Who do you think is protecting Rabbi Tzaddok? I am! You'll go to him when I am ready to send you."

Yoseph's eyes widened with astonishment. "You know Rabbi Tzaddok? You know where he is?"

"I am his protector, I tell you — or else he wouldn't have survived a day. You'll go to him when I am ready to send you."

"But why do you need me here?" Yoseph argued. "I am just a simple Tapuach shepherd. What do you want from me?"

Josephus stared at him. He wagged a finger in rebuttal. "You're no simple shepherd. You're something else, but you won't tell me. You have a power!"

Yoseph looked at him in amazement. "Power? I? What power?"

"Listen — anyone who can stop a company of charging legion horses without moving a finger has a power! I saw you pray — you pray with holiness. Now you are going to stay with me and bring me good *mazla*!"

Yoseph felt as if he had been struck by lightning. What was Josephus talking about? "But I have no power — nothing! I'm just a shepherd!"

"Look, immediately after I saved you, Titus himself sent a delegation to summon me. I hadn't even reached Jerusalem! Who ever received such recognition from the Flavians? It was you — you brought me good *mazla*!"

Yoseph wanted to argue, but Josephus turned away. He pointed off-handedly to a servant's cot in the back of the tent, under the low slope of the roof.

"That'll be your bed — make yourself at home."

The memory of the Jewish prisoners on the way to captivity still haunted him, but his need for sleep was even stronger. Yoseph fell on the bed and fell into a deep sleep. It was not until late afternoon that he opened his eyes and looked across the tent at Josephus, who was sitting at his desk, writing furiously.

He washed his hands and slipped on his sandals, then walked over to Josephus. "What are you writing, General?" he asked.

Josephus lay down his pen and turned to him. Without his helmet, he looked different — and very Jewish. His large nose twitched in anger.

"Listen, Levite, you see me writing? When I am writing, I am writing — don't disturb me. Go about your business, and when I am ready for you I will summon you."

Go about his business — he had no business!

Yoseph stepped out of the tent into the raw evening. A thin, cold rain fell, chilling him to the bone. The battering rams had stilled, and he set out to explore his surroundings. The hope of escape lurked in his brain. The camp was set up like a small, neat town, with barracks, a central marshaling ground, earthen walls, and towers. Although he was a Jew, no one seemed wary of him. There were Jewish slaves and traders everywhere. He walked down the short avenues, watched the smiths beating their weapons, soldiers gathered in small groups at leisure, even doctors treating wounded soldiers. In the middle flew the Fifth Legion banner.

Yoseph tried to orient himself. He meandered through the camp eyeing the walls and the towers, looking for an opening. Everyone made mistakes, even Romans. He wanted to slip away, find Rabbi Tzadok, and head back to Rachel even by tomorrow. There were no gaps in the walls, but as no one seemed to be guarding him, he drew closer and closer to the main gate. The day grew dark as a thick layer of clouds blew overhead. The gray curtain of rain grew heavier, making visibility harder, and he whispered a prayer as he reached the exit. He was almost parallel with the gateposts when a voice rang out:

"Halt!"

Yoseph kept walking.

"One more step and I'll jam this spear right through you!"

Yoseph stopped. Two legionnaires approached him quickly. One had his spear out; the other had his hand on his sword handle.

"Where do you think you're going?" the soldier holding the spear shouted.

Yoseph was prepared. "General Josephus told me there is a Pharisee camp nearby. I was going to visit it and return."

"By whose leave?"

"General Josephus. He said I could wander on my own."

"He never said you could wander out of the camp."

"He never said I couldn't."

The guard lifted his spear and waved it in front of Yoseph's face. "I know who you are. You're the general's prisoner. You were trying to escape."

"No...."

"One more time you try to walk out of here, and I will report it to General Josephus. He'll have you whipped until you cry for mercy. Get back into the camp and stay away from this gate!"

Yoseph wanted to argue, but his courage crumbled. He nodded sullenly and returned to Josephus's tent under the soldiers' watch ful gaze.

It was already night when Yoseph entered Josephus's tent. Josephus was in a jovial mood. He had finished writing and his table was laden with fine foods and wine. A bright lamp hung from the roof, filling the tent with a cheerful light. Servants slipped discreetly in and out, filling his every need.

"Sit down, Levite," he called, gesturing to a couch across from him. Yoseph was not sure whether it was an invitation or an order. Either way, he sat down.

"Will you eat nothing?" Josephus asked.

"I have my own food in my pouch."

Josephus clapped his hands and a servant appeared. "Bring our guest's bag over here."

The servant ran to Yoseph's cot, retrieved the bag, and began opening it.

Yoseph reached out his hand and stopped him. "I'll do it myself," he said.

He took the bag, rummaged about in it, and extracted a small container of dried cheese. He closed the pouch carefully and set it alongside his chair. Josephus eyed him closely.

"Why are you so protective of your old traveling bag? Do you have jewels in there?" he asked humorously.

Yoseph looked at him straight on. "I told you last night, I have a harp that I made with my own hands — to play before the holy altar."

Josephus did not answer. "Levite, how old are you?"

"Twenty-four."

"I'm only eight years older than you. You are not a fool. I don't understand you. Do you not know that we are in the middle of a war, that no one can enter Jerusalem and no one can leave? Do you really expect to play that harp in the Temple?"

Yoseph stared at him, fear and anger fighting in him. "How shall I answer you, General? Shall I answer you as a prisoner to a Roman general, or as one Jew to another, a Levite to a *kohein*?"

"Answer me honestly, and don't worry about the uniform. You are not my prisoner, you are my guest."

"Are you really a *kohein*?"

"My mother was a Hasmonean."

"And you studied some Torah?"

"I spent three years in the desert studying with the Essenes, and then I joined the Pharisees."

"Did you never learn about *emunah* and *bitachon* and *mesirut nefesh*?"

In the long night, with the booming of the battering rams rumbling in the distance, Yoseph told Josephus his peculiar story. Of his family who lived in Tapuach who had dismissed him, his marriage to a wounded, mute woman who was suddenly transformed into a beautiful wife who demanded that he study Torah. He told of the tzaddik Yaakov who told him to go to Jerusalem and find Rabbi Tzadok. He even told of his Sabba and how he had come to pray on the back road where he was found.

Josephus listened patiently, and then he smiled.

"So that is your story — you're here because a holy man sent you, is that it?" His voice was mocking.

Yoseph was very angry. "Why do you laugh?" he shouted. "Do the words of a tzaddik mean nothing to you? Are you not a Jew? Don't you believe in anything?"

Josephus raised a finger, brushing away his outburst. His smile did not leave him. "Listen, Levite, I don't need your lecture about being a Jew. I also had my holy man. He led me out to the desert, and we immersed in *mikveh*s and fasted and had dreams. But it was a waste. I am as much a Jew as you are — I am a *kohein*! But you are naïve. You have seen nothing, know nothing. Tell me, have you ever been in Tyre?"

What business did he have in Tyre? "No."

"I have. Have you been in Antioch, in Alexandria, in Athens, in Rome?"

"No."

"Have you seen the senate, visited the empress, traversed the length of the Appian Way?"

"What is the Appian Way?"

"I have! The world is united under Rome, it is peaceful, Pax Romana! Don't preach to me about being a Jew! I am a *kohein*! But I am a realist — is it a sin to be a realist? I tell you, Levite — Yoseph — you will never play your harp at the altar!"

"General, if I am as naïve as you say, then let me go! What do you want from me? Let me go, please!"

Josephus slammed his cup on the table. "Never!"

He is drunk, Yoseph knew. He realized that the best thing he could do was to be quiet.

They sat for a while in moody silence. Suddenly, Josephus

spoke: "Levite, play me something from *Tehillim*."

It was such an abrupt request, Yoseph thought he hadn't heard clearly. Josephus turned to him, a dazed look on his face. "Did you not hear me the first time? Play something — something holy!"

Yoseph reluctantly reached down to his pouch and extracted his harp. *I hate this*, he thought. But he knew it was not the time to refuse Josephus. He held the harp over his heart.

"What do you want me to play, General?"

Josephus glared at him. "Don't call me general. My name is Yoseph, just like yours. Play...*Eich nashir*."

A strange request from a Roman general. Slowly, he began strumming the strings and lifted his voice. Josephus lifted his hand and put a finger over his mouth. "Quietly," he whispered, "discreetly. No one outside must hear."

In a hushed voice, Yoseph began singing:

> *Eich nashir...et shir Hashem...al admat neichar* — How shall we sing the songs of Hashem on foreign land? If I forget thee, O Jerusalem, let my right arm wither.... May my tongue cleave to my mouth, if I do not remember you, if I do not raise Jerusalem upon the chief of my joy....

As Yoseph sang, he thought of the holy Mikdash just a short distance away from him that he could not visit, and the executioners at the gates, and the shackled slaves being led away, and he wept as he sang, his strings mewing like little kittens. Josephus sobbed drunkenly next to him. They were two Jews trapped in a sea of Edom. He sang for a long while, until he had no more voice and no more breath. He halted and slipped the harp away.

The two Yosephs looked at each for a long time — the general and his guest. Then Josephus announced: "I promise you — you will get to see Rabbi Tzaddok!"

YOSEPH AWOKE the next morning to the sight of a nightmare standing in front of him.

The giant legionnaire, his head almost touching the roof of the tent, straddled the bed in front of him, glaring down. "We ride out in one half-hour. General Josephus's orders — be there, ready!"

For good measure, he gave the bed a sharp kick, almost spilling Yoseph over the side. Yoseph stared after his visitor speechlessly as he strode out of the tent. He had never seen such a huge man in his life.

Yoseph sat up quickly and washed his hands. There was little time, and he didn't want a second visit from the colossus. He donned his tallit and tefillin and prayed quickly, trying to concentrate. But he was not quick enough. Before he wrapped up his tallit, the giant was back in, shouting angrily.

"Josephus is waiting! Why aren't you there?" His voice sounded like it came out of a wine barrel.

Yoseph was too awestruck to answer. This man was like a force of nature. He followed him quickly to the marshaling field. Josephus was mounted, surrounded by his escort of heavily armed cavalry. They stared at Yoseph coldly as though they resented his presence.

Josephus glanced at Yoseph. Gone was the soft-hearted Jew who wept for Jerusalem. Now he was all general. Yoseph was given a huge stallion to ride alongside Josephus. Maybe they wanted him to fall and break his neck. Determined not to show weakness or inadequacy, Yoseph mounted the stallion handily, clearing the saddle like a born rider.

The captain signaled and the company sallied forth from the camp, heading southward. There was a deceptive tranquility as they followed the road along the west wall of the city. Yoseph heard spring birds twittering from the bushes, and even the rumble of battering rams was gone.

Yoseph nudged his horse towards Josephus. "Where are we going?" he asked.

"Today you get your first lesson in Roman power."

They reached the southern corner of the wall and turned sharply eastward, descending into the Hinnom Valley, past the lower city. The day turned warm, and the legionnaires' faces flushed red under their helmets.

Josephus uttered not a word. He carefully surveyed every foot of the wall and the surrounding landscape that they passed, looking for tunnels or other escape routes. They traversed the Shiloach and reached the foot of the Mount of Olives. Josephus's lieutenant lifted his hand, and the riders halted and rallied in preparation for the steep ascent to the top.

Josephus broke his silence. "Levite, you remember our talk last night? I told you you would never enter the Temple. You thought I was exaggerating — now you'll see for yourself."

Josephus crouched low over his horse and signaled, and the company began its dash to the top. As they climbed, the city revealed itself before them like a giant stage. Yoseph kept one eye on the road and with the other gazed upon his beloved Mikdash. It was overrun with defenders — on the Temple Mount, the colonnades, the women's court, even peering down from the steps of the Sanctuary. All around, Yerushalayim looked like a city under construction. Great towers and scaffolding concealed her walls, and Roman soldiers scurried up and down her sides like workmen. Above, Jewish defenders faced off against them, hurling stones and arrows. Yet despite the thousands of soldiers and defenders, there was an odd stillness, like two wrestlers locked in exhausted embrace.

Where is the battle? Yoseph wondered.

Midway up the mountain, Josephus called a halt. He turned to Yoseph. "Do you have your harp ready, Levite?" he taunted. "Look at your Temple — it is a battlefield, not a place of holiness."

He pointed his hand towards Jerusalem. "They are starving there, literally starving! The zealots burned down twenty years of grain! There is nothing left to eat — nothing! They're eating their own children. Once the summer comes, they'll die of thirst!"

Josephus pointed out a camp in the Kidron Valley. "That's King Agrippa's army — three thousand Jewish soldiers!"

"Fighting with Rome — against the Temple?"

"They're fighting the bandits who kidnaped the Temple! He is the king of the Jews, isn't he? The defenders are the ones who are rebelling!"

He snapped his reins and they rode on to the crest of Har HaZeitim. Across the Kidron Valley, the Temple lay revealed before them in all its helplessness and agony. Yoseph gazed longingly at the beloved altar glowing faintly with hot embers of the *ma'arachah.* There was his *duchan* — he was so close! He longed for his harp. It was well past the morning *tamid*, yet the altar looked deserted. *Kohanim* in their white sacramental garments scurried about among the fighters, but there were no *korbanot.*

Josephus followed his gaze. "I tried to warn you! The Temple is sealed up, in shambles! The zealots are warring against each other, and the Romans watch them and laugh! The Romans have gathered four legions, sixty thousand men, and tens of thousands of auxiliaries from the provinces! The whole might of the empire is here! How long will they hold out? This is your Temple, Levite! Look at it and weep!"

Yoseph was crushed. Was this the holy Mikdash of his Sabba?

Josephus turned and saw his own Roman escort eyeing him oddly. He stared them down and barked commands: "We'll ride up to Mount Scopus. Titus has changed his plans — there will be an attack on the north wall at midday!"

They crossed the ridge and raced to the top of Mount Scopus. Then they halted and turned towards the city. Many other units had gathered, too. They sat on the mountains surrounding Jerusalem, watching the battle about to commence like spectators at a sporting match.

Below them stretched the Twelfth Legion, aligned in great, orderly divisions, archers, infantry, cavalry, drummers, ensigns, auxiliaries, a rainbow of uniforms and native garb, all prepared for the combat ahead. Hardened veterans all, they had been rushed to Judea to crush the rebellion once and for all. High up on the wall, the Jewish defenders had gathered like a swarm of ants to defend their nest.

"This is Titus's surprise," Josephus said grimly. "He rushed the Twelfth down from the hills overnight to break into the New City."

Yoseph rose on his horse and watched helplessly. The battle was so far away that the soldiers looked like toys. Even as they watched, more attack towers were wheeled forward, crowded with archers and soldiers with their swords drawn. But there was no attack. Then, out of the ranks of the legions, a strange, wide machine, close to the earth, began squirming its way towards the base of the wall. It consisted of gleaming shields, joined like the scales of a fish, and it slithered forward slowly like an enormous serpent.

"What is that?" Yoseph asked.

"It is the testudo. There are thousands of soldiers under there, the toughest fighters. They'll be the first over the wall with their knives drawn. Nothing can stop them!"

The scent of impending battle wafted towards them on the slight breeze. Even on Mount Scopus the Romans smelled blood. The warhorses, sensing the coming attack, snorted and skipped in their places, eager to charge into the fray.

All at once, the battering rams began pounding against the wall with a deafening thunder. The Romans unleashed their terrible catapults, hurling massive stones and flaming arrows at the heads of the defenders. One huge, ragged stone found its mark, smashing a column of defenders in one instant of horror. Flaming arrows fell into the city. Flames sprang up in a dozen places in fountains of fire. Yoseph saw desperate Jerusalemites rushing to quench the flames.

The drums beat a tattoo, the trumpets sounded, shields clanged. A deep shout of death and blood arose as horses screamed wildly, anxious for the charge. The disciplined ranks moved slowly forward like a great machine. On the walls, the defenders fought back furiously, beating back the attackers on the siege towers with their long poles, unleashing a torrent of arrows, like black rain, against the enemy below them. But the testudo undulated forward, like a great beast, an unstoppable vanguard of slaughter, its long, narrow ladders hidden, the soldiers beneath it ready to mount the walls and swamp the defenders.

The whole attack hinged on the testudo's assault.

One of the men in Josephus's company suddenly screamed out: "Oil! They have oil!"

But for the attackers below there was no warning. Bands of defenders suddenly appeared on the wall above the testudo with huge vats of boiling oil. They bent over the wall, took their measure, and then skillfully poured the liquid over the advancing testudo below. At first there was nothing, but in a few seconds the searing oil flowed between the shields, spilled onto the backs of the attackers, and seeped under their uniforms. The testudo fissured and broke apart in an agony of pitiful screams, as the soldiers' skin and flesh burned away under the blazing liquid. There was no escape. The stricken soldiers lay writhing and helpless below the wall while a rain of black arrows struck them down. High up on the wall, the heartened defenders rushed out against the archers, while yet other fighters ran recklessly across the wall and torched the siege towers. The dry timbers exploded in flames, and desperate Romans leapt to their deaths.

A retreat was sounded, and the legion began retreating from the wall, fearing attack. The Jewish defenders watched the Romans fall back like a giant ebb tide and roared in triumph. They waved their spears and bows, taunting the defeated enemy.

Outnumbered and outarmed, they had beaten off a mighty Roman legion!

IT WAS a silent, sullen ride back to Josephus's camp. Although his company had not participated in the battle — it had not even been their legion fighting — they all felt the sting and shame of defeat. The sight of the stricken soldiers turning over and over in a desperate attempt to prevent the burning oil from eating into their flesh was seared into their memories forever. Even Josephus, protected by Titus himself, felt the fury of his men. They returned the way they had come, descending back through the Hinnom Valley and returning to the camp slowly. The triumphant dash was forgotten. There was no question of meeting Titus anymore — the defeat had changed everything.

It was night when Josephus and Yoseph were finally back in their tent. All this time, Josephus had said hardly a word. There was no more boasting of the helpless Jerusalem. The tent flap was closed, and a servant set a platter of food before him and disappeared. Josephus tasted the food and downed some wine. Abruptly his attitude changed. His face relaxed, and he looked almost...pleased.

"So what did you think of today's battle?" he asked.

Yoseph was not sure how to answer — he did not trust Josephus. "It was awful suffering on both sides!"

Josephus leaned forward animatedly. "But look at the chutzpah, look at the cunning!" he whispered. "Outnumbered, no chance of winning, catapults ready to tear off their heads in an instant, and they stood their ground — our men stood their ground!"

Yoseph was shocked at his duplicity. " 'Our men,' General? I thought you were on the Roman side! You said the Jewish fighters are mad, bandits, rebels. Now they are 'our men'?"

"And what are you and I? Are we Romans? Do you think those legionnaires who rode with me today think me Roman? I am a Jew, a *kohein*! Even as I fight the zealots, I am still proud of them."

"How can you be on one side and also on the other?"

"Why not? One has to know when to be here and when to be there."

Yoseph stared at him. "I don't understand you, Josephus." It was the first time he used the other man's name, without his title.

Josephus, who had drunk some more wine, waved his hand dismissively. "It does not matter what you understand, Levite. You think like a naïve child! Where is your harp?"

His request was a surprise. Reluctantly, Yoseph rose, went to his couch, and extracted the harp from his bag. He uncovered it carefully and let his fingers feel the purity and holiness of the strings. Josephus watched him closely.

"Do you still think you will play your harp in the Mikdash?" he taunted.

Yoseph nodded. "If Hashem wants, yes. Everything is possible."

Josephus snickered in derision. He was drunk.

"Play!" he commanded.

Yoseph fingered his harp and considered what to play. He rejoiced inwardly at the Jewish victory he had witnessed. His fingers swooped down the strings in a rousing tune.

"Shhh!" Josephus hissed. "Play quietly — be discreet! If they hear you outside celebrating they'll come in and kill us both!"

Yoseph moved closer to Josephus and played more lightly. But there was no mistaking the joy and thanksgiving.

> *Ashrei tivchar ut'kareiv yishkon chatzeirecha* — Happy is the one whom You choose and draw near to dwell in Your courts.

> May we be sated with the goodness of Your House, the holiest part of your Sanctuary!

Josephus did not sing, afraid that he would be overheard. But a smile graced his lips, and he swung the cup back and forth in rhythm.

Who is this man? wondered Yoseph. *He has one face for the Romans, another face for me — how many more faces? And what is his real face?*

After he had played a long time, Yoseph resolved to seize the moment. He abruptly raised his hands from the harp. Josephus looked up. "Why did you stop?" he demanded.

"Josephus — Yoseph — listen! You are a *kohein*, and I am a Levite. We have One Almighty we worship, and one Torah we follow. I ask you a favor as a Levite who serves in the Temple from a *kohein* who stands at the holy altar —"

Josephus waved his hand. "Oh, what now? Your freedom? Never!"

"No — I will be loyal to you. I will be your servant. But I traveled to Jerusalem to find the holy sage, Rabbi Tzaddok. I want you to allow me to study Torah with him."

"Yes, and then disappear in a flash."

"No, I will return."

Josephus laughed. "Why should I believe you?"

"I give you my word."

"Your word? Oh, great deal! And how do I know your word is worth a *perutah*?"

Yoseph paused, struggling for a response. His fingers ran up and down softly over the harp, and they whispered messages to him.

"Josephus, don't you like my music? I know you do — I can see it in your face. It is not I, it is the harp! You see, one of the strings was given to me by a holy man named Yaakov. There is no sound like it because it rises from the holiness of his soul. I feel his *neshamah* in me, his voice in my voice, his fingers on mine. General Josephus, I will leave my harp here as a security. If I were to part with it, I would be ripping my own soul out! Does that assure you?"

Josephus lay down his cup. "Let me see the harp."

Reluctantly, Yoseph handed the instrument to Josephus, who dragged his fingers over the strings and studied its burnished frame. Every finger he touched to the harp was like a dart in Yoseph's soul, like the Mikdash itself being violated. But he had no choice. Finally, Josephus returned the harp and clapped his hands loudly, summoning a servant.

"Get me Rufus!" he ordered.

In a moment the tent flap flung open, and Yoseph cringed. It was the huge Og who had woken him in the morning. His huge frame filled the tent, and his face was set like an iron mask.

"Rufus, this man is my prisoner, but I am giving him certain privileges. There is a Pharisee camp an hour's walk north of us, the one with the holy man. I am allowing him freedom to visit there during daylight — only. He will leave the harp he is holding here as a security. Make sure he leaves it, and if he does not return by sunset, smash it to pieces, no questions asked! You understand clearly?"

The giant nodded, turned, and gave Yoseph a withering look that shook him.

Josephus turned to Yoseph, smiling pleasantly. He saw the effect that Rufus had on Yoseph. "Levite, you accept these conditions? Your harp will be in Rufus's hands!"

Yoseph had no time to ponder. It was yes or no if he wanted to meet Rabbi Tzaddok.

He assented quickly, all the time feeling the giant's gaze on him.

"Good, very good," said Josephus. "So we all know the rules of the game."

Rufus was dismissed, and Josephus was soon asleep. Yoseph lay awake on his couch, awaiting his moment, for his night still held other mysteries.

And Rachel Called

RACHEL MOVED like a shadow through the darkness of the house, sweeping past her sisters' chambers, then her mother's, until she slipped outdoors. In the distance, a guard dog barked, caught her scent, and grew silent. Her shadow stretched and shrank in the moonlight like liquid. She ran into the concealment of a small hollow and slipped behind a tree, out of sight of the great house. She gasped as the gleaming half-moon suddenly disappeared behind a cloud, but then it reemerged, radiant and untouchable.

She dropped her veil, looked heavenward, and whispered:

Yoseph, my Yoseph, where are you? I pray for the day that I can run off and speak to you face to face. How I long for you!

I cannot see the splendor of your countenance, for it is partly concealed from me. Why do you look away? Have you forgotten me? How can I exist without you, my foundation stone and my light?

I am unwanted here, Yoseph, even among my own family. They mock me: "Where is your loving husband? Where has he fled? Has he grown weary of your twisted face, so that you always hide behind a veil?"

They mock me with their songs: "Anah halach dodeich.... Where has your beloved gone, O fairest among women?"

They think you have abandoned me and that I am alone. They do not know that I greet you with each rising and setting of the moon, and glimpse you in the silver moonlight....

"Dodi yarad legano.... My beloved has gone down to his garden, to the beds of spices to graze in the garden and to pick roses...." For you have gone to study Hashem's Torah!

I have a secret that I was afraid to tell you about face to face, my Yoseph! I have a power — the ability to sense feelings. As a fox can scent his prey and an eagle discerns her nest, so my heart is a silken thread that moves to every slight instance of love and hate.

Oh, Yoseph, what I see, what I feel! It is in the very air! Our land is aflame with hatred! I feel it in the air! There is so much anger, so much jealousy, so much vengeance everywhere!

I am so afraid, Yoseph! Will Hashem not remove His Shechinah from us and escape to the highest throne of heaven?

I had a terrible dream, Yoseph! I saw the Beit HaMikdash empty, the chambers and the courtyards abandoned! The menorah was dark, and the great altar had grown cold.

I wept and I cried: "Where is the Shechinah?"

And a voice called back: "Dodi yarad legano.... My beloved has gone down to His garden!"

All our hatred had driven the Shechinah away! And then I thought of your harp, my beloved Yoseph HaTzaddik! I heard its sound of ahavah, love for every Jew, love for every creature that Hashem made in the world, the sound of forgiveness!

I dreamed you played your harp on the roof of the Mikdash, and all the sparks of holiness flew back like birds to their nest, and the menorah shone, and the altar was aflame with holy sacrifices!

Rachel's voice rose in her great longing and was answered by every forest beast of the night. Frightened, Rachel turned and ran back to the safety of the house.

And Yoseph Answered

YOSEPH LEFT his bed, pulled on his tunic to protect himself from the Jerusalem cold, and softly crept out of the tent. The grounds were quiet except for the guards posted at the gates and the watchtowers above the walls. He saw curious eyes on him, but as he headed towards the interior of the camp, they lost interest. He sought some concealment from the enemy, but there was none. Barracks and storehouses filled the whole camp, and there was no way to seclude himself among the pagan soldiers. He found a small niche behind one of the storehouses, and his face radiated splendor and purity to the ivory face of the moon.

Rachel, Rachel, if only I could hear the words you whisper! You are my queen for whom I shine — without you what purpose do I have? Do I not hear your longing for me and the suffering that you endure? Do they think I would ever abandon you — is that how they taunt you? My sole desire is to be with you, so that together we can draw the Shechinah back into the world.

I long for you, Rachel, but it is not yet time for me to return. I have not even begun to learn. I must find the tzaddik, Rabbi Tzaddok, and he will teach me. They have taken my harp as a security, but they cannot take my neshamah! Rachel, pray for me, for us! Those who torment you do not know the beauty of your words or the glory of your countenance. Conceal it from them until I return!

Suddenly, a sentry's voice rang out: "Who is hiding behind the storehouse?"

Quickly, Yoseph turned and fled to his tent.

Chapter Four

Four-and-a-half months before the Churban

Yoseph awoke and looked across the tent. Josephus still lay fast asleep. He prayed quickly and then walked outside to find the whole camp in motion. The cheerful greetings and bantering the soldiers had shared the day before were no more. A grim determination, a sullen silence, gripped the camp. The legionnaires had awoken with the bitter taste of defeat in their mouths and set about to avenge their humiliated brethren. Although they knew Yoseph's protected status, they looked at him with undisguised hatred.

He walked cautiously towards the guarded camp entrance. He expected to be challenged and then to explain himself. But Josephus had not wasted any time. The commander of the guards nodded at his approach, and the soldiers at the gate waved him out. It was almost like an honor guard, escorting his release. Yoseph nodded a silent thank you, stepped forward — and he was out.

He gazed around, incredulous. He was free! He was alone, unguarded, unchained! Part of him wanted to run away, to escape from Jerusalem and Josephus and the Romans and return to Rachel and the safety of their little castle. He could simply walk away from the nightmare that trapped him. But no...he had come to find Rabbi Tzaddok, to receive direction in studying Torah. Besides, he had given his word to Josephus, and his precious harp hung in the balance!

He walked northward through a depressing forest of stumps, every tree having been felled by the Romans for siege towers and catapults. The wall of the city rose to his right. By some miracle, a thick bramble bush had survived unscathed along the road, an island of shade against the morning sun.

Yoseph stopped momentarily alongside the bush to rest. Suddenly he heard a strange stirring, like an animal in hiding, and then the branches parted roughly. Like a chick emerging from its shell, the huge form of Rufus rose up from the bush, towering over him imposingly.

Yoseph was too shocked to be afraid. "Rufus, what are you doing here? General Josephus gave me permission to leave the camp, you heard him yourself!"

Rufus glared at him, then spoke deliberately. "I know Josephus gave you permission. But I have a message for you."

"From Josephus?"

"No, from me, from Rufus!"

He raised his two great arms. "You see these hands? They're twice as thick as any man's in the Roman legions. Josephus said that if you don't come back we would smash your harp. But I am warning you — Josephus is my commander and I am sworn to him! If you try to escape, I will follow you to the end of the empire and break your neck with these hands! Do you understand that, Levite?"

Yoseph stared at the giant. "Did Josephus send you to tell me this?"

The question infuriated the giant. He drew closer like a wild beast and stood over Yoseph.

"Don't ask me about Josephus!" he exploded. "I am talking to you, not Josephus. Josephus will smash your harp, but I will smash you! Do you understand?"

Yoseph, shaken, nodded angrily.

"I didn't hear you!" Rufus screamed in his face. "Did you understand me or not?" He raised his fist, ready to strike.

"I — I understand!" Yoseph answered miserably, ashamed and humiliated.

The giant smirked victoriously. He waved his huge arm in contempt. "Now go look for your holy man!"

Yoseph rushed off as quickly as his legs could take him. The road disappeared into a small wadi, and Yoseph escaped the giant's gaze. His whole body shook. Who was this monster and what did he want from Yoseph? He no longer felt free. An invisible cord bound him to the Roman camp, to Josephus, to — Rufus!

He stopped and took a deep breath. *I must have bitachon*, he told himself.

But where was the camp of the Perushim? A band of old women huddled at the side of the road, begging for food. They had escaped the city, but had no place to run. Apparently even the Romans didn't want them. Yoseph broke off a section from his own bread and shared it with them.

"May you live to see the redemption," he consoled them. "Good women, do you know where I could find the camp of the Pharisees and Rabbi Tzaddok?"

At the mention of his name, a great wail went up from the wretched group. "It is not far!" one of them cried, pointing further up the road.

One of the weathered crones laid her two hands against her face and rocked her head from side to side: "He is a holy man, a holy man!"

Yoseph blessed them and rushed on. The road rose slightly and curved towards the east, and then Yoseph caught his first glimpse of Rabbi Tzaddok's encampment. It was set up neatly on a hilltop, west of the road. The Romans wanted everyone on the walls of Jerusalem to see how those who surrendered to the Romans were treated — especially the Perushim, the followers of the rabbis. A half-dozen tents surrounded a larger tent set in the middle, and there was much activity in the camp. Clusters of students sat together, discussing Torah. On the edges, women bent over clay ovens, preparing meals. The camp was surrounded by a low stone fence, keeping intruders out, but making the grounds visible to all who passed. The path leading up to the gate was guarded by Roman sentries. They appeared relaxed, but they kept a sharp eye for anyone approaching the grounds.

Yoseph had grown accustomed to dealing with the Roman soldiers. As a lot, they were not bad, but aroused, or under orders, they were capable of the worst barbarities, torturing and murdering without a drop of pity or remorse. As he approached the camp, guards rushed their hands to their swords. He did not know what to expect.

Three soldiers, their swords drawn, went out to meet him. Behind them, other Romans held their spears at the ready. Yoseph withdrew a small sheet of paper, given to him by Josephus, from his cloak and dangled it in front of him like a shield. He raised both hands to show he held no weapons.

The captain approached him.

"Stand where you are," he ordered. "Don't move a step."

Yoseph froze in place, waving the paper in front of him.

The captain grabbed the sheet from him, not bothering to look at it. He glared at Yoseph. "Who are you? What do you want?"

"My name is Yoseph, from Samaria. I have come here to seek the master, Rabbi Tzaddok. I bear a letter of permission from General Josephus."

The captain stared at him. "You're not a student. Where is your scholar's robe? Why is your head not covered with a turban?"

Yoseph nodded agreement. "You are correct, Captain. I am not like those in the camp. I am a novice who has arrived to commence studying."

The captain surveyed him again and finally peered at the letter. He could not read, but he recognized the imperial seal. He gave one last hard glance at Yoseph and returned the sheet.

"Go on," he said. "You may pass."

Yoseph rushed quickly towards the camp, whispering thanks to Hashem under his breath. He had done it — he had reached Rabbi Tzaddok's camp!

He entered the narrow gateway and surveyed the camp. There were about thirty students sitting there, huddled in small teams of twos and threes, chanting passages of Torah to each other and debating their meaning. They appeared to be Yoseph's age, but some were much older. At one end of the camp, a group of women stood near a tent, baking bread in small ovens and tending to boiling kettles. There were other men, servants who tended the grounds and mended breaks in the fence. A few hens marched about, clucking contentedly. Were it not for the Roman sentries outside and the heavily defended walls of Jerusalem that rose nearby, it would have looked like a little country settlement.

No one looked up when Yoseph entered, and no one approached him. Where was Rabbi Tzaddok? From the layout of the camp, he surmised that the large tent was his dwelling. There was no time for subtleties — he had to return by sunset. Trying not to be too obvious, he ambled towards the entrance of the tent. He was just a few feet away from the door when one of the workmen saw him and shook his hand in warning, ordering him away. Yoseph stopped abruptly, nodded, and headed towards two students who were engaged intensely in their studies.

They spoke with heavy Babylonian accents, and it was hard for him to decipher their language. They were arguing some law concerning the menorah. He sat down beside them, trying to understand their discussion. As though he was not there, they continued their debate, not once looking in his direction.

Finally, their arguments exhausted, they fell silent. Yoseph saw his chance.

"Excuse me, my masters, but I am seeking Rabbi Tzaddok...."

The two students sat up in shock. They looked at each other and then stared at Yoseph, but did not respond to his question.

This was not the welcome Yoseph had expected. Still, he persisted, "I do not mean to disrupt your learning, my masters, but I have walked all the way from Dotan to study with Rabbi Tzaddok. Can you not at least tell me where he is?"

One of the scholars finally turned to him, his finger raised to his lips. He gestured to Yoseph with a raised hand — *wait!* Then he twirled his finger further and further ahead — *I will tell you later, when we are finished.* Without acknowledging him, the other scholar began arguing again.

Yoseph sat for almost two hours, growing more and more impatient. The two students turned to him from time to time, as though inviting him into their discussion to express an opinion. But all he could do was grasp a word here and there of their Babylonian dialect.

How long am I going to sit here? he wondered.

Suddenly, just past midday, an older man emerged from the large tent and clapped his hands loudly for attention. When everyone grew silent, he announced in a powerful voice, "*Rabbotai*, God willing, our teacher will give a *shiur* after *minchah gedolah*. Prepare yourselves speedily, and pray well that he has the strength to be with us!"

He disappeared back into the tent. There was an immediate excitement as the scholars dispersed to prepare for their rabbi's lecture. Yoseph's two companions rose quickly. One glanced briefly at Yoseph, nodded, and wandered off. But the scholar who had gestured to Yoseph earlier now welcomed him warmly. He smiled, his face radiating friendliness.

"I am sorry we could not answer. When we are in learning, we do not interrupt for worldly matters, however pressing. Every moment of Torah is precious — especially since we don't know when our Roman friends out there will suddenly walk in and cut our throats."

Yoseph apologized for his obvious impatience. "I am here to speak to Rabbi Tzaddok. Where can I find him?"

"Why do you want to speak to him?" the scholar asked.

"He will guide me to study Torah. I was sent to him by a certain tzaddik."

"And where did you study until now?"

Why is he asking me all these questions? Yoseph wondered. But he had no choice but answer him. "I have not studied before, just this and that, here and there. But I was sent by a tzaddik Master Yaakov to speak to Rabbi Tzaddok."

A troubled look clouded the scholar's face. "You never studied before, and now you wish to study with Rabbi Tzaddok, no one less?"

"That is what I was told, and that is what I will do," answered Yoseph heatedly.

The scholar looked at Yoseph sympathetically.

"I admire your determination, young man. But...." He shook his head.

"But what?"

"Rabbi Tzaddok is the greatest tzaddik of this generation, a *tanna*, a holy sage who has fasted forty years to save the Mikdash. He is a teacher for scholars, for the chosen few, the *yechidim* — not for beginners, neophytes. Find yourself an experienced *melamed* and learn to your heart's content!"

Yoseph was near tears. He had just met this scholar, but the glow of his serene visage drew him like a holy flame. He could not let him drive him away.

He pleaded with him, "Master, I have spent my whole life preparing to serve Hashem in the Mikdash. No one taught me to play the harp, but I learned to play it from my own heart — and I play well! Twice the Romans took me captive, but that did not stop me. They crucified my grandfather and I was blamed wrongly for his death, and that did not stop me! A holy tzaddik commanded me to find Rabbi Tzaddok. I left my wife and the child she is carrying, and I did not let even that stop me! Now that I am at the very entrance to Rabbi Tzaddok's tent, you tell me I cannot see him? No! You must not stop me! *Hashem li velo ira*!"

Yoseph's voice rose, and he was near tears.

The scholar stared at Yoseph a minute, then kindly rested his hand on his shoulder. "Come, I will take you to the *meturgeman*. He will decide."

He led Yoseph to the large tent and knocked against a post.

"Yes?" a voice responded.

"Rabbeinu Yitzchak, may I enter?"

"Who is there?"

"I, your least student, Aharon."

There was a sort of grunt, which Aharon interpreted as a yes. He lifted the tent flap and led Yoseph inside. Despite the bright sun outside, the large room was cold and empty, except for an oil lamp that hung from a ceiling post. The *meturgeman* sat cross-legged on a carpet, stroking his long white beard, deep in meditation. He did not look up at his visitors.

"Please forgive me, master," Aharon apologized, "I know this is an awkward time to disturb you on the day that our master is to give a *shiur*. But we have a visitor in our camp who wishes to speak with you."

The man turned to Yoseph and eyed him wordlessly. Then he turned away, staring straight ahead.

"What do you want?"

But Yoseph could not answer, so awed was he by the holy countenance of the *meturgeman*. He looked helplessly to Aharon, who intervened.

"He wishes to study with us, Rabbeinu HaMeturgeman, and to study Torah from Rabbi Tzaddok. He has traveled a long distance through dangerous roads."

"What is your name?" the *meturgeman* asked.

"Yoseph ben Nachum HaLevi, from Tapuach.... Rabbeinu HaMeturgeman, perhaps you have heard of a certain tzaddik who dwells in the Shomron by the name of Yaakov?"

The *meturgeman* did not answer, but his brows knitted into a deep furrow, so Yoseph knew that he had heard of him.

"He is the one who told me to come to Yerushalayim and study with Rabbi Tzaddok. I have exerted great effort to reach this camp. I beg you to let me stay."

The *meturgeman* tugged reflectively at his beard, not speaking. He addressed Aharon. "How do we know that he is as he claims to be — that he is not an apostate who will take our holy teacher's words and distort them?"

"My master, he is not an apostate. I know him just a little while, but he has a lofty *neshamah* that craves Torah. His difficulty is that he has little learning, and our master's teaching will be difficult. But I will help him...."

"Young man, if I would allow all those students who wish to gaze upon the holy countenance of Rabbi Tzaddok to enter, there would be line up from here to the Mikdash. The Romans would object! Our master is very weak, fragile like a flickering wick in the wind. Every new student is an extra burden on his shoulders."

"I will not be a burden, Rabbeinu HaMeturgeman!" Yoseph interrupted. "I shall sit in a corner with my mouth closed and my ears open, and my heart will be open wide like the entrance of a ballroom to swallow every word."

What might pass for a smile swept over the *meturgeman*'s face. He turned to Yoseph. "Our beloved brother Aharon has taken responsibility for you. I will permit you to stay for a few days, and then I shall judge your progress and decide further."

Rabbi Yitzchak fell back silently to his meditations. Aharon tugged Yoseph's sleeve, and the two backed out of the tent.

Aharon turned to Yoseph, his face beaming in the noon sun. "*Mazal tov*, the *meturgeman* has let you stay! I did not think he would, but he did!"

"Why is he so severe?" asked Yoseph. "All I want is to study Torah with the holy tzaddik."

Aharon lifted his hands heavenwards. "Because he is Rabbi Yitzchak, that's all! He is fearful that someone will take Rabbi Tzaddok's teachings and abuse them. It has happened with others! Yet he let you stay! May you be worthy to sit at our master's feet."

Aharon was a gift from Heaven sent to Yoseph. He immediately took him under his wing. He led him to the *mikveh* that had been dug discreetly in the back of a tent. Yoseph purified himself, and then Aharon dressed him in dark scholar's robes so that he immediately fit in among the students. The turban was reserved for the advanced *tzurvah d'rabbanan*, but Yoseph's robe had a hood to cover his head for *yirat Shamayim*.

At the start of the seventh hour, the *meturgeman* suddenly appeared and clapped his hands briskly: "*Minchah! Minchah!*"

The students stopped their studies and flocked towards the large tent. The room had been set up as a *beit midrash*, with carpets, and a small *aron kodesh* that faced east towards the Mikdash. One of the students approached the *amud*.

Yoseph whispered to Aharon. "Where is Rabbi Tzaddok?"

Aharon raised his finger to his lips and pointed toward a curtain that closed off the back of the tent.

Minchah was very intense. The students swayed almost violently, raising their fists to their chests, bowing and rising on their toes with emotion. Their faces contorted with pain, and their sighs and sobs filled the room. The camp was an island of safety, but the whole of Yerushalayim was under the enemy's sword, and all the misery passed through their bodies.

The prayer ended, and the students dropped to the carpeted floor, sitting cross-legged in utter silence, awaiting Rabbi Tzaddok. Suddenly Rabbi Yitzchak emerged from behind the curtain and gave the slightest nod. The students rose silently as one. There was a pause, the curtain flap opened, and Rabbi Tzaddok was led to his pillow, escorted by one of the students. Yoseph could not see Rabbi Tzaddok's face. He looked as fragile as a reed.

The tzaddik was short, his head bowed low, and a hood concealed his face. He settled into his raised pillow, the *meturgeman* nodded, and the students dropped to their places in a swoop. Yoseph sat at the far back, hiding behind the younger scholars. Rabbi Tzaddok touched his skeletal fingers to each other and began speaking.

Yoseph leaned forward, but all he could hear was a low singsong drone, no words. Rabbi Tzaddok paused every few minutes, and the *meturgeman* repeated his words in a strong, clear voice. He not only repeated, but also elaborated and interpreted. Rabbi Tzaddok spoke a few phrases, while Rabbi Yitzchak's recitation took much longer. From time to time a student rose and challenged a point, and Rabbi Yitzchak responded almost vehemently. He was more patient when a student was unclear of a meaning and begged him to repeat.

Yoseph struggled to hear Rabbi Tzaddok himself, even one word, but all he heard was a buzzing. The *meturgeman*'s swift and complex explanations flew over his head — he couldn't understand anything. He could not even see Rabbi Tzaddok's face. A phalanx of students sat before him, blocking his vision.

The *shiur* was lengthy, almost two hours. Yoseph sat silent like a stone, deeply disappointed. This was not what he had expected. He had understood nothing. It was all beyond him. Just at the last few moments of the *shiur*, as the *meturgeman* recited the final teachings, Rabbi Tzaddok raised his head slightly and his hood slipped back.

He surveyed his pupils, looking from one to the other, and for an instant his eyes locked on Yoseph. Yoseph stared at his holy countenance, and his whole body began shaking. He grabbed his arms to control his trembling. A burning heat swept through him, a searing flame, so that he almost cried out.

He knew — he had seen the countenance of the *Shechinah*.

"SO HOW are the Pharisees faring at Rabbi Tzaddok's camp?"

Josephus hovered over his table, scattered with sheets of fine papyrus. He seemed to be in an especially jovial mood.

"*Baruch Hashem*, they are doing well."

"And the holy man?"

"*Baruch Hashem*," Yoseph said faintly. He did not like even mentioning Rabbi Tzaddok's name in this place.

Josephus put down his pen and looked up sharply. "*Baruch Hashem, Baruch Hashem* — is that all you can say? Weren't you at their camp? Didn't you see how well they live? My soldiers protect them! They have plenty to eat and drink when the rest of Jerusalem is starving — I did it!"

"If so, the great mitzvah is yours," Yoseph answered.

Josephus sneered at the word *mitzvah*. Yet he was in a high mood and turned back busily to his writing.

He looked up again. "And so — did you see the holy man?"

Yoseph paused, then finally answered. "Yes."

"Then you are one of the rare few. Since he began eating again, no one is allowed into the camp. They claim he has been fasting for years — a lot of good that has done anyone.... And what did he have to say?"

"He gave a *shiur*, a Torah *shiur*. I...I did not really understand it."

Again, Josephus sneered contemptuously. Yoseph grew angrier, but held his peace. Josephus returned to his papers.

"General Josephus, may I ask — what is all this writing you are doing? Is it commands to your troops?"

He looked up, pleased at Yoseph's interest. "No, what I am writing is more important than that. Do you see what is going on outside, against the walls of Jerusalem? What we are seeing, Levite, is history! Whatever happens, this war will be remembered for a thousand years. Never has Rome gathered such great forces against one city! And the Romans will win, believe me!"

"Is it not in Hashem's hands?" Yoseph challenged. "Did they not suffer a bad defeat just yesterday?"

Josephus waved his hand contemptuously. "That was a pinprick, the bite of an ant. Today, twice as many siege towers went up, and a score of catapults. Just listen!"

He grew silent. In the distance was the booming thunder of the iron-headed battering rams pounding against the walls of the city, unceasing pressure of metal against stone until the stones crumbled and the city lay exposed.

Josephus's eyes sparkled, and there was a glorious smile on his face. He rose. "Listen — do you hear that, Levite? That is the sound of Rome, of victory pounding at the gates! A hundred thousand soldiers stand at the ready, like a great machine. They are waiting for the walls to shatter, and then they will sweep in like the sea and it will be over. This is what Hashem has ordained, do you not see? I also studied Torah, Levite, I also studied! The voice of Jacob and the hands of Esau! This is the time for Esau's hands — whether you like it or not!"

"But Josephus, you are a Jew, a *kohein*! Why do you smile when you say this?"

Josephus grew angry. "Yoseph, do you want me to have you thrown to the lions? Watch your words!"

"So throw me to the lions!" Yoseph responded sharply. "Let them choke on me! But you are still a Jew! How dare you smile when Jerusalem suffers so?"

Josephus rose and approached Yoseph, who did not flinch. He stared at him momentarily, and then spoke calmly. "Levite, we should have known each other when I was younger, and I also cherished holiness like you. Perhaps you would have inspired me with your purity, and I would have been a servant in the Mikdash. You are right, Yoseph, but it is too late. I am spoiled — by power, by pleasure, by honor. But I shall try to guard my feelings before you. Do you understand? Come, don't look so angrily at me, and I shall return your harp to you."

Josephus clapped his hands, and a servant appeared. "Summon Rufus! Tell him to bring the Levite's harp!"

The giant appeared shortly, holding Yoseph's harp. Yoseph stared at the precious instrument in the hands of the Roman Goliath and felt violated. The legionnaire appeared wearing his huge helmet, and in the tent he looked more like a golem than a man.

"Return to him his harp," Josephus commanded.

Rufus handed the harp to Yoseph, who grasped it eagerly. But Rufus did not release his hold. Instead, he laid his massive hand over Yoseph's and pressed down, just enough to remind him of the warning given so long ago — just that morning! He glared at Yoseph for an instant, released his fingers, and left the tent.

Josephus saw everything and smiled. "Take care, Yoseph. Do not make Rufus your enemy. He is my loyal dog, sworn to me from Yodafat. If you will be true to me, you will find great advantage. But if you try to escape, Rufus will pounce on you like a wild beast.... Now, Levite, take up your harp. I have written enough for tonight — play me your songs of Zion!"

THE NEXT weeks were strange indeed. Yoseph traveled in two worlds. Each morning he rose before dawn and, under the watchful gaze of Rufus, set off for Rabbi Tzaddok's camp. He spent each morning listening to Aharon review halachot with his colleague, Avigdor. From time to time Aharon interrupted his discussion and tried to explain some point to Yoseph. Avigdor waited impatiently through these digressions, closing his eyes and disappearing into his thoughts, waving his thumb and mumbling to himself.

Even as he listened to Aharon, Yoseph watched Avigdor's displeasure. *He doesn't like me*, he thought. Avigdor had not said one word to him since his arrival.

After the morning study session ended, Aharon took Yoseph aside and began teaching him Mishnah, repeating lines over and over until he memorized them — even if he did not understand them fully. It all dealt with Temple laws, the rams and lambs, the spices, the meal offerings, the great showbreads. It gnawed at Yoseph's soul. Here were the Temple laws, and here was the Temple just a short distance away — and it was sealed to him!

Rabbi Tzaddok was too weak to lecture every day. He gave his next *shiur* a few days later. His voice was very faint, and even the *meturgeman* struggled to understand him. The years of fasting had taken their toll. Yoseph understood a glimmer more now, but the tzaddik's deep thoughts passed high over his head, and he sat gloomily, impatient and frustrated.

Again, towards the end of the *shiur*, Rabbi Tzaddok lifted his head and surveyed his students. Briefly, his holy countenance was visible. Yoseph raised himself slightly off the floor and drank in his visage, begging the tzaddik for help. When his eyes met Rabbi

Tzaddok's, he did not tremble with fear. He felt the tzaddik's gaze linger on him, even a twinkle of recognition, of greeting.

He knows I am here, he thought. *I must speak with him.*

JOSEPHUS WAS right — the Roman legions streamed to Jerusalem, and the smell of approaching battle hung in the air like the heaviness before a thunderstorm. There was no end to the Roman army — legions, cohorts, and centuries of warriors, archers, cavalry, engineers, and medical corps, every color, every uniform and tongue, prepared for the great assault. They had every weapon of war, great and small; every nature of sword and spear, every make of shield and armor. They swept over the hills towards the city in a human tide, grim faced, primed, lusting for blood, honor, and wealth, seventy hungry wolves fallen upon a lamb. The thunder of battering rams against the north walls did not cease, day and night. Newly positioned catapults stood near the Pharisee camp, hurling stones and flaming spears against the city, blazing crimson flashes against the glorious blue sky.

Yoseph attracted more and more interest as he walked to and from Rabbi Tzaddok's camp. He walked in the ravines and hillocks, avoiding the crowded road. He kept his head down, his eyes averted. But he could not avoid the road forever, and as he approached the Fifth Legion camp or the entrance to Rabbi Tzaddok's enclosure, he encountered the soldiers of many armies. He was stopped over and over, questioned, threatened, even spat on, and over and over had to produce Josephus's worn official permission.

One night, he discussed his plight with Josephus, who seemed pleased with him, especially after he played the harp.

"I need something so that I will be recognized as under Roman protection."

Josephus considered the request.

"I can send Rufus to escort you," he offered, half seriously.

"I am more frightened of him than the Roman legions," Yoseph answered, causing Josephus to smile.

"Then there is only one other mark I can give you, short of you wearing a legion uniform."

"Never."

Josephus approached a chest in a corner of the tent. He rummaged through it and then extracted a small blue medallion. He passed it to Yoseph. On the medallion were inscribed a few Latin words.

"What is it?" Yoseph asked.

"It is a slave's medallion. It says that the bearer of this medallion is a slave to Josephus ben Matthias. If they see you wearing this, no one will challenge you."

Yoseph turned white. "A slave's medallion? For me? I am a Levite the son of a Levite who has stood at the Temple since the days of King Solomon! How can I wear a slave medallion?" He was near tears.

Josephus shrugged. "It is your choice, Levite. No one you care about needs to see it. You can walk out of this camp a free man and enter Rabbi Tzaddok's camp a free man, a student. But on the road...." He shook his head. "Don't be a fool! Do you know who is coming down the roads these days? The whole world! Titus has called out everyone, Greeks and Arabs, Franks and Barbarians — even Mongols. They have no rules, these auxiliaries — they're wild men, undisciplined. They will grab you one day and no one will ever hear from you again. Maybe they'll cut your throat for sport or sell you off for a few dinars. Look at you — what a handsome slave you'll make! So do what you want!"

He threw the medallion down on the table and stalked off.

Yoseph looked at the medallion and shuddered with shame. Perhaps he should just stay here in the Roman camp, safe? No, that was impossible. He must go to Rabbi Tzaddok. Gingerly, as if he was touching something impure, he reached down and lifted the medallion. He owned a farm north of Tapuach, he had a beautiful wife, Rachel, and yet he had to wear a slave's medallion!

If that was what was necessary to study Torah with Rabbi Tzaddok — so be it. Softly, he slipped the medallion into his cloak.

It was a strange, humiliating feeling. As soon as he was a distance from the Roman camp, he slipped on his slave's badge. His head automatically bent with shame. The Roman soldiers and auxiliaries — even other slaves — looked past him as though he did not exist. He was no longer a man, but a chattel, like a cow or a dog. Yet he accomplished his goal — no one approached him, no one threatened him. He was property belonging to some master, and that was sufficient.

The moment he spied Rabbi Tzaddok's encampment, he slipped off the badge. He raised his head, stood tall, and took a deep, manly breath, trying to cleanse away his humiliation. Perhaps it wasn't worth it — his precious harp and maintaining his ties to Josephus. He should just run away and hide in Rabbi Tzaddok's tent. But Rufus would pursue him!

He greeted Aharon, who met him near the entrance. "Our teacher Rabbi Tzaddok will give a *shiur* today," he announced happily. "It will be on a very difficult subject, *machshavah pesulah* — forbidden intent during the altar sacrifices — and we must prepare carefully."

Avigdor, Aharon's study partner, was already in his place, twirling his thumb and murmuring. Aharon and Yoseph could see him from afar. Watching him, Yoseph could not contain his feelings.

"I don't think Avigdor cares for me much," he confided in Aharon. "He not only doesn't say a *shalom aleichem*, he also doesn't even turn in my direction." He shook his head in vexation and began walking towards their place.

Aharon grabbed him abruptly by the sleeve and held him back. "Yoseph, don't be so quick to criticize Avigdor."

"I'm not criticizing, but how hard is it to say a *shalom aleichem*?"

"Would you believe, Yoseph, that my brother Avigdor is locked in a great battle with himself? His Torah is his only weapon against his own impulses, against his *yetzer hara*. Only with Torah can he keep himself pure. Believe me, he is a kind person, and he is proud of you — but he is caught in a battle."

"I don't understand. What kind of battle? Why is he different from you or me?"

"Levite, do you not sing the Psalms? Some start with the word *mizmor*, some start with *shir*, and some start with *laminatzei'ach* — a song of victory! Let him be who he is, as you are who you are!"

The three sat for many hours, preparing for Rabbi Tzaddok's

lecture. Then all the students gathered in the large tent, recited *minchah*, and waited silently and expectantly for Rabbi Tzaddok to appear. Everyone rose at his entrance. He was so frail and stooped, Yoseph could barely see the top of his head. His voice, too, was very faint. His singsong lecture was hardly audible, and Rabbi Yitzchak the *meturgeman* bent low, hesitating before repeating his words, as though not sure himself. Yoseph could not understand a word of it, and after an hour, his eyes drooped. *Was this the Torah I left Rachel for?* he thought despairingly.

Rabbi Tzaddok stopped speaking abruptly and was led out. The disciples, who usually argued noisily after their master's departure, exited quickly and wordlessly. They seemed subdued. Their beloved teacher was clearly failing.

Yoseph sought out Aharon. The whole mood of the camp had turned somber. Aharon sat at his usual place, looking especially distant. Something was wrong. Had Yoseph misspoken when he complained about Avigdor? Perhaps he should apologize. He stared down at his own feet, waiting for his teacher to speak, but Aharon remained ominously silent.

Finally Aharon raised his head and stared at Yoseph. His look was cold.

It was too much. Yoseph fell before his mentor. "My teacher, what have I done? Tell me!"

Aharon reached into his robe and extracted a small blue medallion. He showed it to Yoseph. "Is this yours?"

Yoseph stared at it in disbelief and struck his head in fury. How could he have been so stupid! It was Josephus's slave medallion. He had been so quick to hide it when he approached the camp that he had not tucked it in properly. It must have fallen out of his robe when he sat with Aharon and Avigdor.

"Yes, I must have dropped it."

"You are a slave to Josephus ben Matthias? You never told me that!"

Yoseph tried to explain. "Please listen, Rabbi Aharon! I am not a slave to Josephus — or anyone else. I am his prisoner, under his special protection. I came all the way from my home in the Shomron to study with Rabbi Tzaddok — just as I said. I met General Josephus on the road here by Hashem's providence. He liked me because I was sincere — it reminded him of his own youth. So he kept me because he believed I brought him good *mazla*. Each night, I return to his camp among the Romans. But it has become dangerous, so yesterday he gave me this medallion to wear on the road, for protection."

Aharon stared at him. "Do you know who this Josephus is?"

"Just that he was appointed a general by the Romans."

For the first time since they met, Aharon raised his voice. "He is the greatest traitor of the Jewish people! The Sanhedrin appointed him commander of all the Jewish armies in the Galilee. Instead of leading, he betrayed his own people and lied to them again and again, until they fell like helpless sheep before the Romans. He could have stopped the Romans before they came here — in Tiveriah, Tzippori, Gamla, Acco, Gush Chalav, Yodafat! Instead he deceived his own people, he betrayed his comrades and brought the Romans to Yerushalayim's doorstep!"

Yoseph listened open mouthed. "I did not know!"

"Why did you not know? Where have you been? Our people is at the edge of destruction — where have you been?"

"I did not know..." Yoseph repeated lamely.

"Where is Josephus now?"

Yoseph pointed southward. "In the Fifth Legion camp — that is where I sleep at night."

Aharon's face softened. He handed back the medallion and Yoseph tucked it away very carefully, deep into his cloak.

Yoseph fell before his teacher's feet. "Rabbi Aharon," he cried, "I am sorry for my naïveté. I have dreamt too long, too long about my harp, about the *duchan*. I have not cared enough about what is happening in the world...."

Aharon cut him short. "Listen to me, Yoseph. You must return soon, so I will speak quickly. You must be very careful! Tell him nothing, no secrets, no plans, for he will turn your sincerity against you. See if you can run away. He has destroyed whole cities, so why not you? Do you understand me, Yoseph?"

Yoseph, ashen faced, nodded: "I understand."

But what could he do? He was trapped!

HE LIVED in two worlds, the world of Torah and the world of the enemy. Josephus grew more agitated as the campaign entered a new climax. He described the Roman plans, the divisions and generals, and even knew the names of the Jewish defenders on the walls. There was no regret in his voice when he discussed the situation with Yoseph. It was a contest with winners and losers, and Josephus wanted to be with the winners.

And yet...Josephus had a strange fascination with Yoseph's harp. It was like a talisman because it had been designated for the Holy Temple. Even as he made his plans with the Romans, he made Yoseph play each night, after his writing. If Yoseph demurred, he threatened to refuse him permission to go Rabbi Tzaddok's camp. Josephus spoke calmly, familiarly, but always the menacing shadow of Rufus hovered nearby, watching his every inflection, as though he relished the chance to lay his great hands on Yoseph.

Each morning, when Yoseph slipped his badge of slavery around his neck, he knew it was no longer a token — he was Josephus's slave. Like the Jews in Egypt, he had been lured into slavery with sweet words and a smile.

A week before Pesach the gates to Rabbi Tzaddok's encampment were abruptly barred to Yoseph. Rabbi Tzaddok would give no more *shiurim* until after the *chag*, and Yoseph remained confined to the Roman camp. Josephus arranged the matzah baking for Yoseph, as well as for the other Jews who dealt among the Romans — even some legionnaires. Yoseph dreamed of returning to Rachel, even to his father-in-law's home in Dotan, but all the roads were filled with soldiers on the march, and any Jew caught was killed or sold away.

On *erev Pesach*, Yoseph awoke with deep sadness. This was the day he had gone up with his grandfather and family to offer the *korban Pesach*. Sabba had stood proudly on the *duchan* singing the Hallel as the long lines of *kohanim* offered the blood on the altar. The crowds were immense, but even among the multitudes, Yoseph could distinguish Sabba's voice. It had such fervor, such a love of God and the Temple, that it rose up like a bird and stood on the shoulders of the other singers.

He did not know what to do with himself. There was no place to go, so he wandered restlessly around the camp. He wore the slave's medallion so that no one molest him. He had grown accustomed to it. It was a badge of protection, and he no longer cared that people looked right through him. He watched the sun move overhead towards high noon and knew that close by the people who remained in Yerushalayim were crowding into the Mikdash, from which he was barred.

Suddenly he heard his name called. "Hey, Levite! Levite!"

He turned and saw Rufus running towards him. Yoseph had grown used to his immense size, but seeing the giant running reminded Yoseph of a horse on two legs. He stood and awaited his approach.

"General Josephus wants you back at the tent right now."

"What happened?" Yoseph asked.

The giant glared at him. "Right now!" he repeated.

Yoseph followed Rufus. He was surprised to see three saddled horses held by servants outside the tent. He entered the tent, where Josephus stood waiting impatiently. Rufus waited at attention, but Josephus ordered him out. Yoseph rarely saw Josephus during the day. When they were alone, Josephus turned to him.

"Do you know what time it is?"

"Almost *chatzot*."

"They are lining up in the Temple to bring the *korban Pesach*. Do you not miss that?"

"General, what do you think?"

"Yoseph, go bring your harp."

Yoseph was mystified, but he did not ask questions. He ran to his corner and began lifting the harp from its pouch.

"No," Josephus said, "keep it hidden. Just bring it along."

They walked out of the tent. Rufus was already mounted. Josephus pointed to the horses. "Jump up," he ordered. "We're going riding."

Yoseph had not ridden for many weeks, but he swiftly mounted the steed, throwing his pouch over his shoulder. Josephus snapped his reins, and the horses raced for the camp entrance. It was a beautiful day in Nissan, and a cool breeze blew off the western hills. The smell of fresh grain wafted in from as far away as Michmas, and they rode quickly past Pompeii's camp and the Lower City, down into the Hinnom Valley and finally up to the Mount of Olives. For a moment a glimmer of hope flashed in Yoseph's head that they would set foot into the Temple. Perhaps Josephus had bribed someone. But he knew it was a pipe dream. If Josephus appeared in the Mikdash, he would be pulled apart, limb by limb.

Instead, they rode up the road towards the crest of the mountain. When they were halfway up, Josephus ordered a halt and turned to Rufus. "You remain here. I and the Levite are going to the top."

Rufus looked quizzically at Josephus and then glared moodily at Yoseph, clearly incensed at being left out.

Josephus and Yoseph proceeded until they found a small plateau near the top. They dismounted, and the horses stood patiently, forming a barrier between them and the cohorts of legionnaires who stood on the ridge. They stood at the edge of the little platform, looking down on the Temple. Despite war and famine, the Mikdash was crowded with worshipers. Somehow, hundreds of starving Jerusalemites had managed to find lambs for the sacrifice. It was like the old days, but in miniature. The rows of priests stood at the altar, the slaughterers gathered at the Beit HaMitbachayim, the Levites crowded on the *duchan*, reciting Hallel, their voices inaudible to Yoseph. Around them swelled the voices of thousands of troops and their livestock, the clash of trumpets, the thunder of battering rams. Even as the blood of the offerings was sprinkled upon the altar, the business of war continued and the defenders manned the walls, ready for an attack.

"I wish I was in the *azarah*," Yoseph said.

"I once stood in those lines, among the *kohanim*, passing the chalices of blood to the altar," Josephus murmured.

"Then you saw my grandfather at the *duchan*," said Yoseph.

"And your grandfather saw me." They glanced at each other, and the general and his slave were suddenly just two Jews, bonded by their faith.

"Play from Hallel," Josephus commanded abruptly.

Yoseph hesitated. Josephus looked at him. "Play from Hallel," he repeated.

Reluctantly, Yoseph removed the harp from its pouch. He held it against his chest and looked around. Everywhere were Roman soldiers. The walls of the city were draped with scaffolding and siege towers like giant, black shrouds. The catapults aimed their stones into the Temple courtyards even as the paschal lambs were being offered. The rams' heads battered thunderously at the gates. He touched his fingers to the harp and began singing.

One word escaped his mouth and then his throat caught. He could not speak. He began crying, sobbing like a child.

His beloved Mikdash — what were they doing to it? What was happening to his glorious Yerushalayim?

He put down his harp and wept inconsolably. Josephus wept with him.

He couldn't believe it was really happening.

PESACH ENDED, but still Yoseph could not return to Rabbi Tzaddok's camp. The *shiurim* did not begin until Iyar, but when the new month arrived, the roads were overrun with fresh divisions of Romans, marching to the western wall of the city. Josephus did not let Yoseph leave the camp until he practically fell to his feet and pleaded.

Finally, Josephus relented. "I smell battle in the air," he warned. "If you are harmed, your blood is on your own head."

Yoseph approached the camp with uneasiness. He had been gone almost a month, and he felt like a stranger again. He entered the camp and spied Aharon. His friend beamed with surprise when he saw him and ran over to embrace him warmly. But there was a worried look on his face.

Yoseph stepped back and studied his mentor. "What is the matter?" he asked.

"I was approached by the *meturgeman*, Rabbi Yitzchak, soon after Rosh Chodesh. He asked if you were going to return, and I said I thought yes, but I did not know when. He said that when you do return, he needs to meet with you."

Yoseph looked Rabbi Aharon straight in the eye. "Did you tell him about Josephus — about the slave badge?"

"Not a word!"

Yoseph sighed with relief. "Then — what is it?"

"I think he wants to examine you."

"Examine me? About what?"

"Things have not gone well here. Rabbi Tzaddok has grown very weak. There is talk that the Romans will close our camp and our holy teacher will join Rabban Yochanan ben Zakai in Yavneh. Rabbi Yitzchak is very strict about who may stay in the camp."

But I left my wife just to be able to meet Rabbi Tzaddok — how can they not let me stay? Yoseph thought in despair.

Just then Rabbi Yitzchak himself appeared and strode quickly towards them. *He must have been watching the gate all along*, Yoseph thought. Aharon stood at attention, and Yoseph greeted the *meturgeman* respectfully.

Rabbi Yitzchak barely acknowledged the greeting. He lifted his hand and signaled Yoseph to follow him. Rabbi Yitzchak walked briskly, and Yoseph followed nervously at his heels, feeling like a little child. The *meturgeman* brought him to his small, Spartan quarters, furnished with a narrow cot, a low table, and a lamp.

"Young man, I allowed you to attend Rabbi Tzaddok's *shiurim* at Rabbi Aharon's request. But we cannot allow any more visitors unless they truly understand our master. This is a new *zeman*. I will ask you about the *shiurim* you attended."

Yoseph was gripped with panic. Although he'd spent the last month reviewing the *mishnayos* that Aharon had taught him, he knew only the basics and would never be able to answer the questions on Rabbi Tzaddok's *shiur*. Surely Rabbi Yitzchak knew that.

"Here is my first question: Does *zerikah* make a *chatat* unfit after the first application? What about after the second application?"

"*Zerikah*?" repeated Yoseph dumbly.

"Does *machshavah l'haniach* cause *pigul* or not?"

Yoseph looked at the *meturgeman* helplessly.

"Is *chutz limkomo* like *mekomo* or not?"

"*Chutz limkomo*...outside of which place?" asked Yoseph.

Rabbi Yitzchak stood up impatiently. "I've had enough," he declared. "You don't know anything!"

He turned to leave the tent. Yoseph seized him impetuously by the sleeve. The *meturgeman* glared at him furiously, but when he saw Yoseph had tears in his eyes, he softened.

"Please, Rabbeinu HaMeturgeman, let me speak to you for a moment."

The *meturgeman* nodded grimly.

"I — I am sorry that I could not answer your questions, my master. I did not realize how difficult the *shiurim* of Rabbi Tzaddok would be. But I am new here, new to studying. Can you not give me a little more time? I will study harder with Rabbi Aharon!"

Rabbi Yitzchak spoke with unaccustomed warmth. "Listen, Yoseph, I do not doubt your sincerity. You are a fine young man. But I must protect our holy teacher! He has grown very frail. He has hardly eaten in days. Every student is part of his soul. He sees everyone, his *neshamah* goes out to everyone. Rabban Yochanan extracted a promise from Emperor Vespasian that Rabbi Tzaddok would be protected and nursed back to health. Soon he will travel to Yavneh. We cannot have one extra student in the *shiur* — only the most learned."

"But a great tzaddik named Rabbi Yaakov sent me specially to speak to Rabbi Tzaddok — was that a mistake?"

"I know Rabbi Yaakov well, but he is in the north, and he does not know how terrible things have become in Jerusalem. He does not know how frail Rabbi Tzaddok is. Go back to him, tell him you tried your best, and he will send you elsewhere."

But Yoseph persisted. "I don't want to go to back! Rabbi Yaakov sent me here, to Rabbi Tzaddok — no one else. Please, let me stay!"

He pleaded like a child, but he did not care.

Rabbi Yitzchak tugged thoughtfully at his long white beard. Finally, he sighed and placed his hands firmly on his knees.

"This is my final offer to you. You will not attend Rabbi Tzaddok's *shiur* — is that clear? If you try to enter, I will have you thrown out of the camp. But if you agree to remain as a simple laborer, helping us maintain the camp and studying sometimes with your friend Rabbi Aharon — then you may stay. That is my offer — accept it, or leave our camp immediately."

Had he left Rachel to become a laborer? But did he have a

choice? How else would he ever reach Rabbi Tzaddok?

Yoseph put out his hand. "I accept," he answered.

Without taking Yoseph's hand, Rabbi Yitzchak rose and departed.

Yoseph returned to Aharon and Avigdor. Aharon looked up, but if he noticed the dejection on Yoseph's face he did not show it. The two scholars continued their studies, and from time to time Aharon turned to Yoseph, drawing him into the discussion. Yoseph stared back silently, too shaken to respond.

Just before noon, Rabbi Yitzchak appeared and clapped loudly for attention.

"*Rabbotai*," he announced, "our teacher Rabbi Tzaddok will study with us earlier than usual today. I warn you that he is quite weak and is teaching only with the greatest *mesirut nefesh*. He has hardly eaten anything for two days. If you have questions, ask me afterwards. Let our master deliver his *shiur* quickly, so he can rest!"

The students gazed at one another with great concern. They shook their heads, wrung their hands, and murmured hurried prayers. Aharon and Avigdor sat silently, lost in contemplation.

It was Avigdor who pulled Aharon back to their studies. "Come," he urged, "we still have a few minutes before the *shiur*. Let us continue."

Instead of agreeing, Aharon turned to Yoseph. "What happened with the *meturgeman*?"

Yoseph shook his head. "He asked me some questions, and I could not answer them."

"And?"

"I am forbidden to attend Rabbi Tzaddok's *shiur* anymore."

Aharon's face clouded. "So what will you do?"

"I agreed to stay as a worker. That way I can remain in the camp. Perhaps you will still study with me — if you can find time."

"One does not find time, one makes time. *Bli neder*, I will make time for you. Do not despair, you will yet become a *ben Torah*."

Yes, he thought bitterly, *but I will never get to speak to Rabbi Tzaddok for a hundred years*.

One of Rabbi Yitzchak's assistants appeared before the great tent. "*Shiur*! *Shiur*!" he announced loudly. "Please assemble quickly!"

Yoseph stood on the side and watched the chosen ones, the learned scholars, file into the tent. Once he had been among them. Now he watched them enviously, an outsider, forbidden to enter.

He felt someone approach him. He turned and was startled to see Aharon's learning partner, Avigdor, standing next to him. He had always been aloof, but now he seemed to want to talk.

"They said you may not enter the *shiur*?" he asked.

"Yes. I can only stay as a worker — otherwise I must leave the camp."

"And what will you do?"

"What choice do I have? I will stay as a simple worker."

Suddenly, the usually cool scholar raised his voice with feeling. "No, Yoseph! I tell you — go back into the tent with the students!"

Yoseph stared at him. "What do you mean? Rabbi Yitzchak said I am forbidden —"

Avigdor shook his head. "Go in there anyway! It is a test! Run in!"

Yoseph raised his hands in dismay. "But they will throw me out!"

"If they throw you out, then go back in a second time!"

"How can you say that, Rabbi Avigdor? They'll pick me up and throw me out again! They'll put guards at the door...."

"Then run around to the back door, and sneak back in!"

Yoseph could not understand the change in Avigdor. He was a different person, a man on fire. "Why are you saying this to me, Rabbi Avigdor? You never took interest in me before."

The scholar's face hardened. "Because there are no bars to Torah. If they tell you no — you must smash all the bars. To become a *ben Torah* you must battle. In battle there is either victory or defeat. You must be a victor, not a defeatist! Come, walk into the *shiur* with me — do not be afraid. They can throw you out forty times, but still you must persist!"

Yoseph stood frozen, paralyzed with uncertainty. Avigdor began walking towards the study tent. He turned one last time and stared at Yoseph, then disappeared into the tent.

Should he follow? Before he could decide, his ruminations were interrupted by a little old man in a dusty robe.

"Pardon me," he said politely, "but are you the new helper that Rabbi Yitzchak arranged?"

Yoseph broke from his reverie and nodded. "Yes, I am he!"

"Ah, *shalom aleichem, shalom aleichem*! My name is Zerach. I do all the odd jobs around here. Is it possible that you could help me?"

He was so humble in asking Yoseph's help, Yoseph could not help but smile at him. He had a truly kindly face, and a tiny Adam's apple that bobbed up and down when he spoke.

"I can try," he responded. The old man's simple sweetness made him momentarily forget Avigdor's fiery words.

"Do you know how to cook, perchance?"

"Cook? Cook what?"

"Ah...ah...a soup."

Yoseph's face creased with uncertainty. "I don't know, Sabba Zerach. What kind of soup?"

"Ah...ah...thin soup. A very, very thin soup."

Yoseph shrugged. "I'll try...."

"Good!" he exclaimed, beaming as though all the problems in the world had been solved. "*Yasher koach*! Come!"

Yoseph followed the little man, who was a full two heads shorter than he, to the cooking area. Zerach continued to chatter, every word out of his mouth a blessing and a thank you, like a bubbling fountain of kindness.

"Here we are," he said grandly, pointing to the small iron kettle sitting on some coals like it was a royal cooking pot.

"What kind of soup shall I cook, Sabba Zerach?" Yoseph asked.

The little man turned to him. "What do you cook? Here, here is what you cook. I need a soup — so thin! You see these roasted kernels? In a few minutes, just as the water boils, place this cup of kernels into the soup, and let them cook for a few minutes. And then when you see that the kernels have dissolved into the soup...just like that —" He lifted his fingers like a magician "— you take off the kettle and slowly, slowly pour out the broth, just clear broth, without even a drop of the grain mixed in."

Yoseph laughed in amusement. "You call that soup? That is just hot water!"

Reb Zerach did not answer, just ran on with his thank yous and *yasher koachs*.

He looked up at the sun. "I shall be back soon, maybe a half-hour. You will have it ready for me, yes, young man? Thank you! *Yasher koach*!"

He rushed off as abruptly as he appeared, and Yoseph smiled to himself. In the intense, earnest world of Rabbi Tzaddok's camp, he was a funny, sweet little man.

For the first time, Yoseph was by himself. The other workers had vanished, and Yoseph had time to think.

Had he made a mistake in coming here?

What had he gained, and what had he lost? He had heeded Rabbi Yaakov and pleased Rachel by going off to study Torah. But where was the Torah, and what had he learned? Before, he had gone into the fields and forests and sung out his soul to Hashem. He had created beautiful music with his harp — the holy letters sprang off the strings and flew heavenward. Even the gentle sheep sang as they grazed, and the olive-scented Shomron winds blew in his face. He had been free, he had been close to God. Now he was caught in the maelstrom, no Torah, no joy, no wife, no freedom, his holy harp defiled by the hands of an overgrown pagan....

Was this why he had come to Jerusalem?

Avigdor was right — you were either victorious or beaten. Here he was beaten. This was not his place — the *meturgeman* had said so himself. He would finish this day, pour the silly pot of watery soup into a bowl, and then — go!

He peered into the kettle. The roasted grains had dissolved into the water, and the old man would be back soon to collect his bowl. Zerach had told him to strain the broth so that all the kernels stayed back. But it was not so easily done. He found a rag to wrap around the handle of the kettle and lifted it with one hand, holding the bowl steady with his other hand. But the kettle was heavier than he had thought, and he struggled to keep it balanced. He had filled the bowl halfway when the cloth slipped. The exposed handle scorched his hand, and the hot liquid poured out, scalding his thumb.

He cried out in pain and dropped the pot back onto the coals, holding the half-filled bowl in one hand as he nursed his blistered thumb. It was too much, too much.

Who needed this? Had he walked from Tapuach to Jerusalem to burn his harp fingers?

He dropped his head onto his injured hand and began crying, crying for himself, for his thumb, for everything. He didn't notice that his tears dropped like raindrops into the bowl.

"Young man!" Zerach appeared from nowhere. "Where is...ah...our soup?"

He was so amusing, this little man, so cheery in this bleak world that Yoseph laughed even as he cried. He lifted the bowl carefully and held it out.

"Be careful," he warned. "It's very hot!"

Zerach accepted it as if it were a holy offering and peered down at the gray liquid. His eyes lit up.

"Perfect!" he exclaimed. "*Yasher koach*!"

He began walking cautiously towards the great tent. The students had already left the *shiur*, and there was great excitement as they argued over what they had studied. Yoseph sighed deeply, watching them from afar. After a while he took a handful of water from a bucket nearby and washed his face. He had done it all — he had studied Torah, he had been a cook — and now it was time to leave.

He sought out Aharon, who was finishing his noon meal.

"Aharon, I have decided to leave the camp for good."

Aharon's mind seemed elsewhere. He looked at Yoseph distractedly. "Yoseph, are you sure?"

"Aharon, this is not for me. I was not meant to be a cook or sweep the grounds or be Josephus's slave. I am a Levite, a *meyuchas* — I'm going home."

Aharon shrugged half-heartedly.

"Rabbi Aharon, what is the matter?"

Aharon shook himself out of his reverie. He tried to smile. "I am sorry, Yoseph. My mind is elsewhere. But we are all very frightened. Our beloved teacher looked so ill today. He cannot eat. His complexion is pale, his eyes sunken. All he lives on is *mesirut nefesh*. What will be, Yoseph?"

Yoseph felt embarrassed at his own selfish concerns. He gazed around and saw the same distress on the faces of the other students. He felt like an intruder. He embraced his teacher. "May Hashem bless you for the kindness you showed me!"

"Yoseph, may you find all that you seek."

Yoseph embraced him again and backed away, bowing. He knew they would never meet again. Aharon watched him, smiled sadly, and turned back.

Yoseph fingered the medallion hidden in his robe. He surveyed the camp one last time, turned, and headed for the gate. Already the sounds of study faded, and he could discern the rigid faces of the Roman guards outside. He was almost past the gate when he heard voices shouting behind him.

"Yoseph! Yoseph ben Nachum HaLevi! Wait! Wait!"

He turned. Rabbi Yitzchak, the austere *meturgeman*, was hurrying toward him, followed by a huffing, puffing Zerach. They made such an odd pair, the dignified Rabbi Yitzchak and the sweet-natured little man, that he stopped and stared in astonishment.

"Master Yoseph, where are you going?" the *meturgeman* demanded.

Yoseph was shocked to hear the great scholar call him "Master." He responded without prevarication. "I am sorry I did not say good-bye. I considered your offer, Rabbeinu HaMeturgeman, and I decided that this is not my place. Forgive me, dear Sabba Zerach!"

"Oh, no!" wailed little Zerach, "you cannot leave!"

"Why not?" asked Yoseph, astonished.

Rabbi Yitzchak interrupted. "Master Yoseph, you prepared a soup a few minutes ago?"

"Yes." Yoseph nodded, puzzled.

"Do you know who it was for?"

Yoseph shook his head.

"It was for our holy teacher, Moreinu v'Rabbeinu Rabbi Tzaddok!" Zerach blurted out excitedly.

Rabbi Yitzchak motioned for him to be silent and explained, more calmly, "Rabbi Tzaddok has not eaten for a few days. When he sipped your soup, his eyes suddenly lit up. He asked me: 'Where did this food come from?'

" 'Why, Master?' I asked. 'Is something wrong?'

"But a look of pleasure lit his holy face. 'I taste the holy Mikdash in this food! Bring me the person who prepared this!' "

Yoseph gaped at Rabbi Yitzchak, hardly comprehending.

The *meturgeman* looked at him impatiently. "Yoseph, why are you hesitating? The holy Rabbi Tzaddok wants to speak to you! Come!"

Yoseph returned to Rabbi Tzaddok's tent in a daze. He raced past all the astonished scholars on Rabbi Yitzchak and Zerach's heels. The three entered the empty *beit midrash*, where the *meturgeman* grasped Yoseph by the arm and lifted his finger to his lips. He spoke in just above a whisper.

"Our holy teacher is very frail. Speak very softly and do not say anything that will upset him. Stick to the point. Listen to what he has to say, and when you leave, do not turn your back, *chas veshalom*. When you hear me clap my hands outside, it means you have tarried too long — leave quickly! Do you understand?"

Yoseph nodded. While Zerach busied himself with his duties, Rabbi Yitzchak indicated to a curtain in the back of the tent that led to Rabbi Tzaddok's chamber.

Nervously, Yoseph approached the curtain and pulled it aside. Rabbi Tzaddok sat on a pillow, near a corner of the room. His head was concealed by his dark hood, and he was locked deeply in his thoughts. Yoseph stood there, uncertain what to do. Instinctively, he cleared his throat.

The holy tzaddik did not look up, but gestured for him to sit near him. Yoseph walked over and knelt down, facing Rabbi Tzaddok. Rabbi Tzaddok lifted his small, clear eyes and smiled warmly at him.

Yoseph tried to stay strong, but he could not. Tears welled in his eyes and he soon began sobbing.

He dropped his head like a child into the tzaddik's bosom. "Rebbe," he sobbed, "Rebbe, I found you, I found you!"

"*Baruch Hashem*," Rabbi Tzaddok whispered. "*Baruch Hashem*, you have finally come to me."

After a few minutes, Yoseph calmed himself. He lifted his head, wiped his eyes, and sat up, embarrassed by his behavior.

"Who are you, my son?" Rabbi Tzaddok asked.

Yoseph remembered the *meturgeman*'s instruction and spoke in almost a whisper. "My name is Yoseph ben Nachum HaLevi, from Tapuach. I came to study Torah from the Rebbe. It has been so hard for me...."

Rabbi Tzaddok waved his words aside. "But there is more, there is more to you! I tasted your tears in my food, and they taste of the salt of the altar. Who taught you this?"

Yoseph shook his head. He could not believe that he was disputing the holy Rabbi Tzaddok! "No, Rebbe, I am just a simple shepherd, unlearned, unknown, and unloved. But all my life I have prayed for the day that I would stand on the *duchan* and play my harp before the altar. I wander among the hills of Binyamin singing simple praises to Hashem, nothing more...."

The holy man shut his eyes and swayed back and forth. He shook his head. "Yoseph HaTzaddik, a spark of the Mikdash entered your soul. Your tears have the taste of the altar."

Yoseph shook his head violently. "Rebbe, I am a simple shepherd, no more!"

Rabbi Tzaddok raised his voice suddenly: "Yoseph HaTzaddik — nothing less!"

Immediately, there was a sharp clap from outside — the signal from Rabbi Yitzchak.

"Rebbe, I came here from Tapuach to study Torah. I left my wife who is with child, I faced great troubles, and even now I am held captive by the enemy — but they have let me come to you."

"Who sent you to me?" asked Rabbi Tzaddok.

"Rabbi Yaakov."

The tzaddik's face lit up with pleasure. "Ah, Yaakov." He opened his eyes and glanced at Yoseph. "Now I understand everything."

Yoseph bowed his head and waited. Finally, Rabbi Tzaddok spoke. "The tzaddik sent you to us for many things. You have all the good *middot*, but now they have become complete."

"Rabbi Yaakov sent me to learn Torah from you. I have sat in your *shiurim*, but I understood so little."

"Someday you will understand everything I teach. But if you

want to be a *ben Torah*, you must acquire one thing —"

The clap outside was repeated, more insistently.

"You have the love of Hashem, the power of *shirah*, the purity of heart. But you are missing one thing if you wish to study Torah —"

Yoseph waited, dreading another warning clap from outside.

"*Yegiah baTorah*. You must struggle with all your soul to grow in Torah."

"I will study hard," Yoseph vowed.

"No, *yegiah*! *Yegiah* is not just study. It is to cast your whole being into Torah. It means by day and by night, when you are well and when you suffer pain. It means when you are fresh, and when you are so weary that you must hold up your eyelids with your fingers. Say it: '*Yegiah baTorah*.' "

"*Yegiah baTorah*."

"Again, louder: '*Yegiah baTorah*!' "

"*Yegiah baTorah*!" Yoseph shouted. There was a loud round of clapping from outside. The clapping stopped, and there was intense stillness.

"Rebbe," Yoseph asked, "what should I learn?"

The teacher pulled his hood low over his eyes and murmured, " '*Uv'chol makom muktar u'mugash lishmi* — In every place offerings are made to My name!'

"Know, my beloved Yoseph, that someday there will be no Beit HaMikdash! Someday our only offerings will be the words of our mouths. Learn *kodashim*, Yoseph HaTzaddik! Learn of the *korbanot* and the wine pouring, the spice offering and the *menachot*, study so well that you can feel them in your hand, smell them in your nostrils. For our only Mikdash will be the Mikdash of Torah!"

The tzaddik fell back onto his pillow. Yoseph had not meant to excite the holy man.

"Rebbe," he whispered, "bless me!"

Rabbi Tzaddok opened his eyes and smiled sadly. "Yoseph, may you know the sweetness of Torah, the *yegiah*, the sweet *yegiah*...."

Yoseph kissed the tzaddik's hand and rose. He backed slowly towards the curtain. Rabbi Tzaddok's eyes dropped, but just as he was about to exit, he lifted them one final time.

"Yoseph HaTzaddik," he said, "know that you are not alone."

And Rachel Called

RACHEL STOOD under a glistening half-moon. Its silver radiance transformed her into a shimmering spirit of the night. Her neshamah reached upward to the heavens, and she felt Yoseph's presence so far away, and yet so close.

Yoseph, how brightly you shine down upon me — your face is not turned away! I see you but cannot touch you. Have you left me behind? Have you studied with the holy teacher and soared to higher worlds, away from me? Perhaps you have forgotten me altogether?

Ki hinei hastav avar.... Behold the winter is past, the rain is over and gone — the blossoms have appeared in the land!

But you are not here, my husband, and I am frightened.

The Romans have returned. When they besieged Beit El and Emmaus, they ignored our little village and passed by to Jerusalem. But now they have returned like pickers in the field! They are seeking slaves to sell to market, more gold, more plunder. They are camped just a few miles from our home and have cast a great net to find us. My father wants us to flee, to hide — but where? Your family in Tapuach is also in great danger. How shall we save ourselves when our enemy is so relentless?

Yoseph, please come back — do not forget us! I have nothing of my own but that you shine upon me! I fear I will never speak again without you. Now I hide behind so many veils and am scorned by all.

Yoseph, I hear someone coming! They are searching for me. I must go until next time, when once more I will gaze up and emerge in your holy glow....

And Yoseph Answered

ALONE ON a small hillock outside of Rabbi Tzaddok's camp, Yoseph answered....

Rachel, Rachel, look at the shimmering moon. It is such a beautiful Iyar night, such a star-spangled sky. Why must there be so much suffering in the world?

I dream that you stand in a Shomron valley, gazing at the moon and whispering to me. It is our moon, yours and mine, to carry our words, so that I am always beside you.

Do you think, Rachel, that I have forgotten you? Can a harp forget its strings? Without you, what am I but a lifeless star flung far from its constellation?

My life has become so strange. Normally I travel back and forth between the Roman camp and Rabbi Tzaddok's group, but today the Romans would not let me return home. A great battle is taking place at the Third Wall of the city close by, and for me to set out now is certain death. They know if harm befalls me, Josephus will hold them accountable.

But, Rachel, I have met Rabbi Tzaddok! Rabbi Yaakov's prophecy has come true. Rabbi Tzaddok has set me on the road of Torah, a hard, uphill path, a road of struggle and yegiah. But why else are we alive? I have learned from other teachers as well. I had met two scholars named Aharon and Avigdor, the meturgeman Rabbi Yitzchak, and the sweetest little man named Zerach. Each one poured his soul into me.

And what is mine is yours.

I must go now, Rachel, for the first rays of morning are lighting from the east — barkai! Soon I will set out for Josephus's camp. I shall find my harp and plead for us, and for the city and the Temple.

Good-bye, my wife, good-bye....

Chapter Five

Three months before the Churban

The next morning was the most harrowing morning of Yoseph's life.

The Romans had finally smashed open Yerushalayim's outer wall, and the legions flooded in with fury. The whole northern half of the city collapsed like an overripe fruit, the defenders overrun. All that was left — the Mikdash and the Upper and Lower Cities — was as packed as three compact acorn shells. The Romans knew they just had to squeeze and squeeze until the shell shattered and its contents could be consumed. The legionnaires celebrated with wild frenzy.

The Romans had forced him to camp on a lonely rise of ground just outside of Rabbi Tzaddok's camp. Yoseph had pleaded that Josephus had ordered him to return by nightfall, but his pleas fell on deaf ears. All night he heard the roar of battle and the thundering cheers of the legions as the fiery missiles arched against the black sky. Then there was a strange stillness as the battering rams did their job and grew silent — the great wall had been breached.

Just before dawn he rose to warn Rachel of what was happening. Weariness overcame him, and he fell briefly into a fitful, dream-plagued sleep. He awoke at sunrise, peered down at the road, and was overcome by what he saw.

It was a great victory parade, a triumph. Thousands of legionnaires moved about, some heading for the battle, others streaming out laden with booty, dragging victims, drunk with joy. All discipline was forgotten. The battle had been transformed into a celebration, a feast of slaughter. Among the soldiers were hundreds of captives, men, women, and children, all bound up like cattle, only their legs free so they could shuffle along. Their heads were bowed low, and some bled from blade wounds. When they lifted their heads to plead for water, the soldiers beat them with thick wooden clubs. Soldiers on horseback rode among the infantry, heads raised in triumph, honed spears jabbing the backs of the Jewish prisoners.

The ranks of victorious legionnaires stretched as far as the eye could see. It was through this line that Yoseph had to pass to return to the safety of the Fifth Legion camp. Without hesitation he took his slave's medallion and hung it prominently around his neck. In truth, he wanted to kiss it. It was his only protection against the bloodthirsty soldiers.

Slowly, he descended to the crowded road, looking desperately for legionnaires that he knew. But many of them still wore their helmets lowered, so their faces were concealed. Some had even left their helmet masks closed, so they looked like angels of death, rather than human beings.

He kept his head down and tried to hide among the foot soldiers, away from the merciless cavalry. But in his Perushi garb, with his tzitzit hanging so bravely from his cloak, his *kippah* standing so straight on his head, he was a red flag of defiance to the enemy. Legionnaires walking past him delivered vicious blows to his side or slammed the back of his neck with their hands. He forced himself to move on as fast as he could despite the numbing pain.

One time a horseman suddenly swept forward on his mount and jabbed him with the side of his spear, knocking him off the road. He fell to his knees, and other soldiers kicked him with their boots. When he tried to rise, they howled with laughter.

He faced his tormentors and lifted his medallion in their faces. "I am a slave to General Josephus! Please do not harm me!"

At this display, a legionnaire drew his dagger and began pursuing him. Yoseph sped away, weaving desperately among the ranks of legionnaires. He turned to find his pursuer, and saw that the legionnaire had long since given up the chase and stood laughing where Yoseph had left him.

The only way Yoseph survived the pain, the humiliation, and the fear was by seeing Rabbi Tzaddok's face in front of him. All the humiliation and the pain he endured, he endured because of him, and it was worth it.

Finally, he reached his "home" — the Fifth Legion camp.

But if he thought he could find relief and safety in the camp, he was sorely mistaken. The camp, which was always a model of strict discipline, was wild with joy. The Romans had spent months trying to breach the Third Wall. They had paid dearly with losses, and now they had finally smashed in. Revenge and celebration was uppermost on the soldiers' minds.

A pungent, unpleasant smell filled the air. Yoseph didn't recognize it at first, but a look around at the legionnaires' uniforms made it clear: It was the smell of human blood. The soldier's uniforms were dark with the blood of their victims. The blood had dried and stained their uniforms, but they wore them like badges of honor, proof that they had taken part in the slaughter.

Yoseph kept toward the edge of the pathway, huddling against the tents, to escape notice. At last he spied Josephus's tent and sighed with relief. But his relief was premature. A huge crowd of soldiers had gathered outside Josephus's tent, cheering and screaming wildly.

His eyes growing wide, Yoseph stopped walking to observe the spectacle. Amidst the crowd of soldiers stood the great Rufus. The giant held a hapless captive aloft in his two great hands, tossing him up and down like a plaything. He banged his victim hard against a tent pole, shook him like a jug of liquid that needed mixing, and then cast him to the ground so violently that the prisoner never rose.

"Give me two more!" he shouted.

Two more hapless prisoners were thrust before him. He lifted one in each hand and smashed their heads together until they stopped struggling. Finally, Rufus threw them down.

How was he going to get into Josephus's tent? Yoseph knew he had to make a run for it. As Rufus lifted a new victim high over his head, Yoseph, his breath coming in short gasps, raced through the crowd to the entrance of the tent. He was almost past Rufus when the giant caught sight of him. For an instant their eyes met. Yoseph knew Rufus would make him his next victim, slave's badge or not.

He cast down the prisoner in his hands and swooped down to catch him. Yoseph twirled artfully, bent low, stopped, and then raced past the lumbering giant. Rufus lunged for him with a snarl, but it was too late. Yoseph snapped the tent flap open and was in. He was safe!

Inside, he saw Josephus standing hunched over his table, conferring with a half-dozen centurions. They peered into documents, pointing and commenting. Around them stood younger officers, listening and writing notes — in all more than a dozen men. They didn't mark his entrance, and Yoseph slunk to his own corner, trying to make himself invisible. At least the raucous celebration outside was muffled.

Yoseph took water from his basin and carefully washed his face and hands. He ached everywhere, and, to make matters worse, his thumb was still blistered and painful.

There was nothing to do but wait on Josephus. He dared not leave the tent. He reached behind his narrow couch and felt for the leather pouch that held his harp — fortunately, it was still there. Josephus had not confiscated it for not returning.

The company of officers burst into laughter. Josephus slapped one of the men's shoulders in good humor. Yoseph could not discern their words, but victory shone from their faces.

Yoseph fell down on his couch in desolation, knowing their smiles equaled Jewish suffering.

Finally, the meeting ended and the officers filed out boisterously. There was a sudden quiet, a blessed stillness. Yoseph rose from his place and glared at Josephus. He said nothing, but the anger in the air was palpable.

Josephus stared back at him. He pointed his finger like an accuser, and shouted, "Don't look at me with such hatred!"

Yoseph could not hold back. "You are a Jew. You are a *kohein*. You rejoice with our enemies? You laugh with them?"

Josephus shook his head. "You are a fool — an idiot! I, rejoice? I, rejoice? I did everything I could to prevent this from happening!"

"I do not believe you."

"I don't care what you believe! Ben Nachum, come here — I want to show you something."

Yoseph stood motionless. If he moved he would be betraying his own people.

"Come here!" Josephus shouted. "I command you!"

With no choice Yoseph approached the table, his face set in a deep scowl. Josephus snickered bitterly. "Don't worry, Levite, I won't make you carry a sword for us. I want to show you something."

He laid a map before him. "Do you know what this is?"

Yoseph shook his head. He knew but would not answer.

"This is a map of Jerusalem. You see here on the edge — this is the outer wall, the Third Wall. This was where the defenders were strongest — along the western perimeter. Titus sent his best soldiers and his strongest battering rams to break the walls. But they held out! Those starving, outnumbered defenders, warring among themselves — they held out! Levite, they are madmen! They are not heroes!"

He turned with great emotion to Yoseph and almost pleaded, "Yoseph, do you know what I did? I went for seven days — without armor — just on my horse! I paraded before them alone as one Jew to another and cried out: 'Madmen, why are you fighting a war you can't win? Today, tomorrow, you will be defeated! Give up! Save your women and children!'

"They screamed curses at me, Yoseph! They spat and shot arrows, hurled stones. 'Traitor! Murderer!' They even ran out of the city to attack me, and I escaped by a hair! So now, when you see the price they paid — you glare at me as though I am to blame?" He stared at Yoseph, his raised hand trembling with anger.

"What happened yesterday?" Yoseph asked.

"It was terrible to behold. I don't think the Romans themselves believed their luck. The walls finally broke. The defenders held out for a while, but the Romans just overran them. The horsemen ran right over the defenders, trampling them to death. It was not a battle — it was a slaughter, pure butchery. How could our God allow this? Oh!"

He threw the map down on the table and walked away, overcome. He took a gulp of wine and, cup in hand, returned to the table, looking calmer. Standing shoulder to shoulder with Yoseph, he studied the battle lines on the map. The Romans had reached the gates of the Antonia Fortress — the Mikdash was next.

Tears welled in Yoseph's eyes. He did not look up from the table. "But a few minutes ago you laughed and joked with your Roman friends. You even discussed strategy with them."

Josephus pointed his cup at Yoseph. "I told you, Yoseph, I told you! I do what I must do. The first commandment is to survive. If you survive, then there is a tomorrow. That — and to record what is happening, so that even a thousand years from now they shall remember — and maybe learn!"

He grew quiet and slumped into his chair. His eyes were glazed — with weariness, triumph, guilt? Who could understand this man?

Yoseph knew it was time for him to withdraw. He needed sleep desperately. "General, would you mind if I go rest?" he asked cautiously. "The march back from Rabbi Tzaddok was a nightmare this morning...."

Josephus nodded without looking up. "Yes, remain in the tent today. There are things happening in this camp that are not for your pious eyes!"

Yoseph slept many hours that day, his sleep visited by fantastic, tortured dreams. He finally rose near sunset, washed his hands and prayed *minchah*. Rabbi Tzaddok's holy face was fixed in his mind's eye. How he longed for the tzaddik!

Night fell, and Josephus was nowhere to be seen. Yoseph grew restless. He stuck his head out of the tent and looked around. All was quiet again. After allowing the jubilant legionnaires to rejoice, the Roman commanders had reined in their troops. The camp streets were swept clean, the usual sentries stood at their watch. Yoseph slipped out and wandered aimlessly about the camp. Without thinking, he had put on his slave medallion. It was part of him now, and he was no longer mortified by it.

On their own, his feet gravitated to the deepest environs of the camp, where the Jewish captives were being held. He wanted to see them, to talk to them, to find out what had really transpired.

The captives were guarded by a company of heavily armed soldiers holding their spears in readiness, which was unusual in the security of the camp. When he approached, they suddenly gathered like a barrier to stop him. The captain of the guard told him, "This is the prisoner area. You may not go further."

Yoseph wasn't about to give up so fast. "I am a protégé of General Josephus. He has given me permission to pass through the camp as I wish."

"You are not a protégé, you are a slave. Go back to your duties."

Yoseph had forgotten his medallion. "I — I wear this only to protect myself. Is there no one here who recognizes me?"

He scanned the faces of the soldiers and spied a familiar face. The guard broke rank, approached the captain, and whispered in his ear. The captain nodded, never removing his eyes from Yoseph.

He approached Yoseph. "If you're not a slave, don't wear the badge of a slave. It is against the law! What business do you have here?"

Yoseph did not hesitate. "Those prisoners are my brothers. I want to see how they fare."

The captain responded sympathetically but directly. "Those people are desperate. If you enter, a Jew walking free, they'll spit in your face as a traitor. What good can you do them?"

"If they spit, they spit. I must see them."

"Look, Jew! The tents to the left are for the women. Don't go near them, you understand? I will let you into one tent —" he pointed to the tent closest to where they stood "— where the children are. But if they fall on you, don't blame us."

Yoseph nodded his thanks and passed through the guards. The only light was from the setting half-moon above. He approached the large tent, which was guarded by a half dozen legionnaires. They let him pass. Nervously, not even sure what he was doing or why, he opened the flap and entered.

The overpowering smell of the sweating young bodies crowded into the tent was a blow to his senses. They were not sleeping as he had expected, but were all huddled together in the pitch darkness. One young voice rang out: "*Ve'emunah kol zot....*"

They were praying *maariv*! He could tell from the *shaliach tzibbur*'s high-pitched voice that he was young, barely a bar mitzvah.

Although Yoseph had not yet recited *maariv*, they were too far along in the prayers for him to join in. He listened to their young voices with his heart full of a mixture of pain, love, and pride for them. There were no adults in the tent leading them, no teachers, no rabbis, yet they knew the words of the prayer by heart and recited them with great sincerity.

The children completed the blessings of Shema and struggled to stand up for the *amidah*. Bound up together in a great network of ropes, they groaned and cried with pain as they struggled to their feet. Finally, they all rose and began swaying in prayer. Yoseph felt the holiness of their words ascending like a flame heavenwards. He felt as if he were standing in the Mikdash and peering into the Heichal — ascending, being swooped upward. The *mesirut nefesh* overwhelmed him, and he saw the *Shechinah* smiling with joy.

Maariv ended, and, like a great wave, all the children, weak from fatigue and hunger, collapsed back to the ground. Here and there, Yoseph hear sobs. "Abba! Imma!"

Yoseph, who was tall and unchained, stood out in the throng. The children who were closest to him noticed his presence.

One of the children asked, "Who are you?" His throat parched from thirst, he hardly spoke above a whisper.

"My name is Yoseph ben Nachum HaLevi. I am a prisoner of the Romans just like you," Yoseph explained.

"Do you have something to drink?"

"No, not with me." Yoseph regretted his lack of foresight. "Next time I come, *bli neder*." Then he asked, "Who are you children? Where are you from?"

"We are Perushim from the New City," the boy responded with a half-sob. "The Romans broke into our houses this morning and killed our parents. Then they separated the boys and girls and brought us here in chains."

"And what will they do with you?"

Suddenly, one of the other children broke in. "Why do you ask all these questions?" he demanded. "Are you with the Romans? Why are you not in chains?"

"I am fortunate. I am from Shomron, and I am not a prisoner of war as you are," Yoseph explained.

A very young boy called out, like a child calling his mother, "We have not had a rebbe since our capture. Can you teach us some Torah?"

"What can I teach you?"

"Teach us some mishnah, teach us some halachah?" He asked it like a child begging for a candy.

Embarrassed, Yoseph admitted, "I am not a scholar. I do not know *mishnayot* by heart."

The older child, the one who had asked why he wasn't in chains, spoke up. "You are a grown man, and you cannot recite a mishnah by heart?"

"I cannot."

"Come," the boy urged his young comrades. "Why waste more time? We will each say over what we know — we will teach each other until Hashem shows us mercy from our enemies!"

He sounds just like a little Avigdor, Yoseph thought.

They turned away from Yoseph and began singing *mishnayot* together in a singsong, just like the scholars in Rabbi Tzaddok's yeshivah. Their voices were parched and cracked, yet they persisted, raising their voices in Torah.

Yoseph remained a few minutes, and then could not listen anymore. Silently, he rose and left the tent.

BACK IN Josephus's tent, Yoseph lay on his couch staring at the ceiling. Josephus slept a few feet away, snoring tranquilly, at peace because he had picked the winning team. Yoseph thought for a long time about the brave Yerushalmi children. He pictured the beautiful face of Rabbi Tzaddok. At last, he came to a hard decision.

Next to his bed lay his harp, the most precious thing in his life after Rachel. But now it was almost an impediment. What was his fear of Josephus — that if he deserted the camp, Rufus would destroy it. He reached over and caressed the worn leather pouch that held his harp. He loved it so dearly — but he could not let it stop him from living. He had to escape, to flee from Rufus's grasp, find Rachel, and become a *ben Torah*!

Walking the hills and playing melodies was very sweet — but it wasn't Torah.

He lay his hand on the pouch and whispered: "*Kinor*, I love you, but I must abandon you. Forgive me."

He closed his eyes and slept fitfully, waking every few minutes to see if the first light had seeped through the curtains. Finally he saw the faintest glimmer of daylight. It was time to escape. As Josephus slept on, he quickly washed, donned his tallis and *tefillin* and prayed, and then silently slipped out of the tent. The camp was still, almost deserted. He slipped on the medallion of servitude and approached the camp entrance. Freedom was just steps away.

To Yoseph's surprise, the guards who usually waved him on at the gate quickly ran to block his way.

"Why are you stopping me?" he asked.

Without looking at him directly, the sentry answered stonily, "Orders from General Josephus. You are no longer allowed to leave this camp."

"But why?" Yoseph asked in bewilderment.

The burly officer in charge of the guard came forward and yelled, "Slave boy! Get back to your tent and stay there!" He put his hand on the hilt of his sword menacingly.

Tears of disappointment welled in Yoseph's eyes and obscured his vision. He was left with no choice but to return to Josephus's tent.

Josephus was still asleep at midday. Yoseph sat glumly on his couch, trying to chant *mishnayot* he had learned from Aharon and scraps he had heard from Rabbi Tzaddok's *shiur*, but he was so depressed about his new situation that he could not concentrate.

At last he reached over and retrieved his harp. He held it to his chest guiltily, feeling like a runaway husband who had tried to run away and now was back with his tail between his legs. He kissed the harp and begged it for forgiveness. How could he have left it? It was his heart, it was his soul, it was his joy, it was his *avodat Hashem*!

Gently, he plucked the strings, five of his own making and the sixth from Rabbi Yaakov. He hadn't thought about Rabbi Yaakov for a long time, so fixated had he become upon Rabbi Tzaddok. But Rabbi Yaakov had been a father to him, and the purity of his one harp cord flowed through Yoseph's body.

He strummed lightly and whispered his longing. He didn't

want Josephus to hear him; he just wanted to sing to Hashem.

> *Ana eileich meiruchecha v'ana mipanecha evrach* — Where can I go from Your spirit, and where can I flee from Your presence? *Im esak shamayim....* If I ascend to heaven, You are there. If I make my bed in the lowest depth, behold You are there!

His soul ascended with his whispered words. Everything he had experienced over the last day — the bound-up children begging for water, the stench of dried blood on Roman uniforms, the immense Rufus happily crushing heads between his arms, his own badge of shame, all his pain — all evaporated and blew off like a mist in the heat of his *bitachon*, of his yearning for Hashem. He closed his eyes and poured out his love for everything holy, and his soul filled with peace. He played for a long time, unaware that Josephus had awoken and was listening intently.

Finally, Josephus called to him. "Yoseph, you never played for me as beautifully as you are playing now, for yourself alone."

Infuriated at the interruption, Yoseph almost dropped his harp. "I am not playing for myself alone. I play for Hashem alone!"

"They told me that you visited the children last night."

"Yes."

"How did you find them? What were they doing?"

"They were praying *maariv*, reciting the Shema with all their hearts. But they were suffering terribly. They were so thirsty that their voices were dry like dust."

"Could you help them?"

"No. What could I do?"

"So, too, I cannot do anything. The Romans will finish them today."

"Finish them? Sell them?"

"Finish them."

Yoseph ran his fingers angrily over the strings, and the harp screeched with pain. He laid it down on the couch.

"I tried to leave the camp this morning to go to Rabbi Tzaddok. They would not let me, at your orders. I thought we had an understanding."

Josephus swung out of his bed. He washed his hands and ran them, still moist, over his eyes. The sentimentality he had shown a few minutes before vanished. He pulled himself together forcefully, his face set.

"Maybe some day you can go back, but not today. Titus has invited me to a celebration marking the victory over the Third Wall. You will accompany me."

"I do not wish to go to our enemy's celebration!" Yoseph answered sharply.

Josephus jumped up and shouted back, "You will accompany me as my slave! If you disobey me I will have you crucified!"

Without another word, he strode out of the tent.

YOSEPH HAD never seen Josephus dressed so immaculately. His armor was buffed to a luster, and every hair on his head was brushed and pomaded. His crested helmet completed an outfit fit for royalty. Although he was still civil to Yoseph, there was no mistaking the new tone he used — one of master to slave. He ordered his servants to find a fine robe and new boots for Yoseph. He made Yoseph trim his hair neatly, although he did not touch his *pei'ot*, and even found him a fresh, embroidered *kippah*.

They rode out in the early evening, Josephus at the head of two dozen horsemen. The steeds were picked for strength and beauty, and the procession made an imposing sight. Titus's camp lay straight to the north, on the same road that Yoseph had trudged to reached Rabbi Tzaddok's settlement. As they rode grandly up the road, Yoseph turned to look at the camp of his beloved teacher. He scanned the hillock he had known so well — the whole camp had disappeared!

The closer they came to Titus's camp, the more guards and checkpoints they encountered. At each sentry post, Josephus reined his horse, saluted, and was recognized by the guards. When they passed the final checkpoint before Titus's camp, Josephus pulled his steed to an abrupt halt and spoke to his aide, who whirled his mount around and approached Yoseph.

"The general wants you to ride next to him."

Yoseph snapped his reins smartly and rode up to Josephus.

Josephus turned to his lieutenant. "We will ride ahead. Follow behind apace!"

From a distance Yoseph spied Titus's camp, festooned with splendid banners and ensigns.

Josephus spoke in an undertone, not to be overheard by his men. "Levite, do you know why I made you be part of this?"

"No."

"I am giving you an opportunity. Tonight you will come face-to-face with the second most powerful man in the world. Someday he will be Caesar of the whole Roman empire! He will have the power to decree life or death for whole countries — just as he has today over Jerusalem. I want you to see him and not reproach me so hastily. If we conduct ourselves judiciously, some good might come out for our people. Watch silently, and do what you are told! Do you understand?"

Yoseph did not answer. Josephus lashed at his horse's flank and the company charged forward, banners flying, heads raised arrogantly, a cloud of golden dust billowing in the orange sunset. Josephus made his grand entrance!

The camp was extremely well guarded. Even as they marched on foot to the huge tent where the feast was to take place, they were carefully questioned by fierce sentries of the Praetorian Guard — Caesar's personal army. Only three of Josephus's personal aides were allowed to accompany him, and he had to plead with the centurion at the tent entrance to gain admission for Yoseph. The officer listened to Josephus's imploration, scanned Yoseph closely, and finally nodded. The truth was that Yoseph was pleased — his curiosity to see the great enemy commander Titus had been keenly whetted.

The tent flap was opened and Yoseph's eyes widened with amazement. It took a hard push from Josephus's lieutenant to send him off to the rear of the tent. The great room was ablaze with lights, so that night was turned to day. Its walls were festooned with colorful banners and ensigns of various legions. Tribunes, generals, centurions all milled about in animated conversation. A company of musicians played celebratory marches, the sound of flutes, lyres, and drums filling the tent. On the front platform, jugglers threw flaming torches high into the air and caught them on the tips of their noses, and tumblers flew back and forth, cartwheeling in the air right over the heads of generals. No one cared. There was no room for chairs on the floor, and everyone stood.

Servants passed among the guests, carrying trays laden with all manners of delicacies and fine wines. The only chairs in the room were arrayed on two platforms in the front of the tent, one higher than the next. They stood empty, as Caesar had not yet arrived with his entourage.

Josephus was given a place near the very front, among the highest dignitaries.

Yoseph drank in all the pageantry and tumult, his eye wide with naïve wonder. He had never dreamed a world of such wealth and beauty and pleasure could exist. Even as he listened, spellbound, to the music and watched the garish entertainment in fascination, a voice inside whispered: "Yoseph, this is not for you."

But he could not run away — even if he wished to.

IT WAS well into the night, and Yoseph grew restless. There were only so many torches and colored balls that could be tossed back and forth. Tumblers gave way to magicians and singers, but that too grew tiresome. Some officers became intoxicated and staggered around even as they shouted and joked. Yoseph watched Josephus closely. He stood in the front, near the highest-ranking generals, and yet he was somewhat aloof. One time he saw Josephus turn and look towards him. Their eyes met for a second. *What is he thinking?* Yoseph wondered. He recalled the *Tehillim* they had sung together — was he remembering that?

Suddenly, a hush descended on the room. A half-dozen trumpeters entered the tent, their instruments decorated with a legion insignia. A legionnaire attired in a brilliant parade uniform strode to the lower platform and stood at the lectern near the end. Despite his slight build, he had a commanding voice that filled the room.

"Tribunes and generals of Rome, officers of the legions, auxiliaries and allies of Rome, welcome!

"Caesar welcomes you to this victory celebration, the harbinger of many to come! We welcome Commander Titus's victorious generals."

There was a pause, and the trumpets blew a fanfare.

"We welcome Sextus Cerealis, commander, Fifth Legion!"

The trumpets blew a fanfare, the musicians beat a lilting march, and the general marched in smartly, helmet in hand. There was polite applause. He took a place on the lower platform, standing and acknowledging the crowd.

"General Larcius Lapidus, commander, Tenth Legion!"

There was a smattering of applause. The Tenth had done some of the fiercest fighting in the breakthrough into the walled city.

"General Titus Frigius, commander, Fifteenth Legion!"

The applause grew louder. The Fifteenth had suffered greatly from the defenders, and word was that they had inflicted an unforgettable vengeance on the Jews.

More commanders and procurators were introduced, and they filled the lower stage, standing triumphantly and acknowledging the cheers and salutes of their lieutenants. They were the powerful fists of Roman might, unstoppable, invincible, dedicated to victory.

More trumpeters entered, and they blew a deafening fanfare. Drums beat attention. Absolute silence descended on the packed room.

The master of ceremonies began his introductions: "Honored tribunes, generals, officers! We welcome his esteemed honor, governor of Alexandria, commander of the legions under Titus — Tiberius Alexander!"

There was a blast of trumpets, and the apostate Jew Tiberius entered, escorted by his aides. Unlike the other generals, he took his place on the upper stage. He was not dressed in legion uniform, but rather in the exalted purple robes of a Roman governor. He was a tall, gaunt-faced man, clean shaved, with a thin-lipped smile on his face. He nodded to the assembled officers and received polite applause. He bowed regally, rubbing his hands together with delight.

Yoseph stared at him and shivered instinctively with repulsion.

Again, there was a pause as excitement mounted. "Mighty Roman legions! We are honored with the presence with his royal highness — King Agrippa of Judea!"

There was a long flourish of trumpets, and finally King Agrippa

— descendant of the Herodian line — entered regally, head held high, followed by his entourage. He did not look once at the assemblage but briskly ascended the steps to the upper platform. He stood regally, coldly, on the end opposite Tiberius. He was a handsome man, tall, clean-shaven in the Roman fashion. Yoseph stared at him, trying to understand.

There was absolute silence. Even the legates and tribunes looked apprehensive. A sentry stood at the entrance, ready to give the signal. Everyone stood absolutely still, hardly breathing.

The sentry turned and signaled the master of ceremonies. The trumpets sounded, and outside could be heard the loud tattoo of drums announcing Titus's arrival.

The tent flap opened, and the master of ceremonies shouted excitedly: "Brave warriors of Rome — hail Caesar! Hail Commander Titus!"

As one, the tribunes, generals, and procurators raised their arms in royal salute: "Hail Caesar! Hail Commander Titus Flavius!"

Titus sauntered in, beaming, a dozen guards around him and a woman at his side. He ascended the platform and stood in front of the chairs. He surveyed his officers, looking from face to face, totally in control.

The master of ceremonies screamed out: "All hail, our victorious divine commander, heir of Caesar, Titus Flavius!"

The room responded with a roar: "Hail Caesar!"

"And her royal highness, consort to Commander Titus, Princess Berenice of Judea!"

There was loud applause. The woman, who was very beautiful, was adorned modestly but regally. She smiled momentarily at the crowd and then returned her gaze to Titus. Titus seemed more interested in her than in all of his guests.

To the accompaniment of the military music, Caesar and his guests seated themselves. The musicians played a victory melody, and Caesar looked relaxed. But despite the festive mood, the generals and officers stood at formal attention before their commander.

Yoseph moved a step forward so that he could see Caesar

clearly. So this was the great enemy who had wrought such suffering on Jerusalem! Yoseph was astonished to see Titus was so young — perhaps only a few years older than himself! Yet he was the great conqueror! He looked so…human. If Yoseph had seen the terrible Titus on the road, he would find him almost pleasant looking, with his broad, open face, even features, firm jaw, and good-humored self-confidence.

Something unsettled Yoseph, but he did not know what or why. When Titus entered, he had been escorted by a special guard of a dozen officers. Some arrayed themselves along the walls of the tent to observe the guests. Four others followed Titus and stood at either side of the platform as bodyguards. Yoseph hardly paid attention to them at first, but after a few minutes one of the guards caught his eye. He looked somehow familiar, yet Yoseph did not know from where. He wore a Praetorian uniform, and his face was partially concealed by the side wings of his helmet. Yoseph gazed about the room, from Titus to King Agrippa to Josephus...but he was drawn back to that one soldier.

What Roman guard did he know? Yet he knew him — well. Who was he?

He searched the depths of his memory, staring again into the face that drew him like a powerful magnet, until at last he knew. It was the face of Caputo — the officer who had crucified his grandfather.

Caputo stood a few steps from Titus, resplendent in his Praetorian uniform, his face set arrogantly. Yoseph stood at the opposite end of the great hall, a slave medallion hanging from his neck. He was helpless — there was absolutely nothing he could do but stare and hate.

The musicians stopped playing, leaving the room in silence. Caesar rose from his couch and smiled. Immediately a roar of applause and cheers filled the room, each guest vying with the other to exhibit his admiration. The shouts of adulation grew louder, like a huge wave. Finally satisfied with the welcome, Titus signaled for quiet. A hush descended instantly.

"Your Majesty, King Agrippa, Your Highness, Princess Berenice, honored procurators, loyal legates, loyal tribunes, brave generals, commanders, centurions — we have triumphed!"

He smiled, and there was a roar of applause.

"It was a long and bitter fight, and we paid a heavy price — but we have prevailed! We have entered Jerusalem, and the northern precincts are ours!"

More applause.

"Rome owes its thanks to you and to our courageous legions, the greatest fighting machine the world has ever known. Nothing will stop us!"

The audience, warming to his speech, cheered, "Hail Caesar! Hail Caesar! Hail Titus!"

"But the war is not over yet. We will prevail, but there will be bitter fighting to come. More strong walls await us, and then the Fortress of Antonia, and then the Sanctuary itself."

One of the officers whistled shrilly at the mention of the Temple. There was a gale of laughter, and Caesar smiled.

"Whistle all you want, but the Jews will fight to the death for it. And I vow to you — we will let them die! Rome is invincible! Our Caesar is divine! Our gods will prevail, our generals, our legions! The rebels will be crushed, the Temple smashed to dust! Hail Caesar, hail Rome!"

The room exploded with a thunder of "Hail Caesar's" and "Hail Titus's." Titus stood before the crowd, arms folded, chin raised aggressively, in total command. He turned to Princess Berenice and smirked, as if to say, "I am top dog here!" She smiled back modestly, but with warmth.

Caesar returned to his couch and was handed a goblet of wine. The master of ceremonies returned to his podium and addressed his most distinguished royal patrons.

"Your Royal Highnesses, we have brought you a fitting tribute from this most recent victory. We wish to show you what beauty and power we have vanquished. These are the most beautiful youth of Jerusalem, once so defiant, and now our slaves."

The tent flap was drawn, and a squad of burly guards led in a procession of Hebrew prisoners. They entered in a long file. There were a dozen young men, exceptionally handsome, all the same height. Unlike the starving, broken prisoners Yoseph had seen, the captives were dressed in fine white linen tunics, their hair finely combed and curled, and their faces shining with perfumed oils. The room radiated with their combined beauty.

The only sign of their captivity was a fine silver wire wound tightly around their necks that bound them to each other. One misstep, one attempt to flee by any captive, and they all would be instantly strangled.

The master of ceremonies was effusive in his praise. "Mark, O great Commander Titus, the finest of pearls of Jerusalem, who will someday grace your great triumph in Rome!"

Titus leaned reflectively on his chin, appraising the young men like prize sheep. He sipped from his cup and looked from one to the other, sometimes whispering to Princess Berenice. The captives stood tall and absolutely motionless.

Tiberius Alexander leaned toward Titus. "It'll make a proud trophy for your triumph, Commander," he proclaimed loudly.

Suddenly, one of the young captives lifted his hand and pointed at Tiberius.

"Tiberius Alexander, you are an apostate and a traitor to your own people! You are the dregs of our people! Traitor! Serpent! Betrayer of Israel!"

Tiberius rose out of his chair, white faced. He looked in a panic around the room. All eyes were upon him, and they were not very sympathetic eyes. The bold prisoner had given voice to the repulsion that everyone secretly felt for a traitor to his own people. Even Caesar did not rush to silence the prisoner.

His face full of fury, Tiberius looked around the room — these were his allies, but now they looked at him coldly. He needed to take immediate revenge to maintain his honor.

He addressed Titus. "I insist this prisoner's throat be cut right now and here, in front of everyone who witnessed his insult! I will do it myself!"

Titus seemed to enjoy this little show. He turned to Berenice and smiled. Then he turned to her brother, King Agrippa. "Your Majesty, I let you decide — shall we let Tiberius wreak his vengeance now, or shall we take them out and strangle the prisoner on his own cord?"

King Agrippa saw the trap. Some of the mud that had been cast at Tiberius had also splattered on him. He, too, was called a traitor.

"Procurator Tiberius has been disgraced in public. He was the first to support your father Vespasian against the other rival generals! His honor demands that he exact vengeance right here before this audience."

Caesar nodded in agreement. "Give Tiberius a dagger!"

One of the guards handed Tiberius a long, thin dagger. He rose, fury burning in his eyes, and approached the young man. The captive showed no fear. He held his head high and stared into the eyes of his executioner.

Suddenly, another voice called out, smooth and patrician. Everyone turned to look. Josephus stepped forward and bowed low before Titus, and then quickly towards Tiberius.

"With profoundest honor to General Titus, and no slight to the esteemed governor of Egypt, Tiberius Alexander, may I have permission to speak!"

"General Josephus, who can ever stop you from speaking?" Titus answered good-humoredly, with obvious affection.

"As you may have heard, Commander Titus, I have prepared a special entertainment in your honor tonight. It is my way of showing my great joy at your victory. But I must also honor my ancestral faith, or else I, too, will be labeled an apostate and a traitor."

Although he held the dagger, it was Tiberius who looked like he had been stabbed as Josephus repeated the insulting word *traitor*. Unlike Josephus, who still called himself a loyal Jew, Tiberius had adopted the religion of Rome.

"General Titus, I am a *kohein*, of the priestly class. I am enjoined from being under the same roof as a dead man. If this prisoner is to be executed, I will be forced to leave this great celebration even before it has begun and before I can properly entertain you. Perhaps our esteemed Tiberius can postpone his revenge until the captives are removed — or even forgo what is rightfully his so that this beautiful captive can be shown off for the glory of Titus!"

Caesar turned to Tiberius Alexander. His look was cryptic, double edged — dangerous.

"How do you respond, Governor Tiberius? Josephus is a loyal

commander. He was the first one to prophesy that my father would become Caesar. Will you oblige him so he can proceed with his entertainment?"

There was a sharp tone in Titus's voice. Tiberius, caught in Josephus's trap, had no choice. He bowed to Titus and cast a sharp, hate-filled look at Josephus.

"It is my privilege to accommodate General Josephus," he finally responded with a forced smile. He lowered the dagger and slunk back to his place. His public humiliation, compounded by Josephus's action, could never be erased.

There was a hum of excitement that even Caesar's presence could not quell. The Jewish apostate had been brought down a peg, and everyone had witnessed it. The master of ceremonies was distressed that his carefully constructed program had been shattered. He looked helplessly at Titus, fearing the worst, but Titus seemed very pleased at the high drama. The master of ceremonies signaled, and the captives were led out again.

Titus himself raised his hand for quiet.

"General Josephus," he said formally, "I don't believe that you have given Governor Tiberius much pleasure tonight. That handsome youth he proposed to slaughter was a sacrifice worthy of Jupiter himself. What do you have in his place for our amusement?"

Josephus bowed gracefully and smiled. "Our glorious commander, I will offer you an even greater presentation, representing the might and the beauty of Caesar's great empire. All roads lead to Rome, and all Rome bows before Emperor Vespasian and Commander Titus. In honor of your great victory, behold, the colossus of Rome!"

He stretched out his arm like a showman, pointing at the entrance. His lieutenant, who stood at the ready, drew back the tent flap. There was a momentary pause, and then a huge figure appeared. He was immense, standing over seven feet, broad-shouldered like an ox. He marched in slowly and heavily, and the canary red crest of his helmet brushed the roof, like some mythological god come to pay Titus homage. Adding to his fearsome appearance, he wore an uncanny death's head visor. His arms, thick as tree trunks, were bare to the shoulder. The room quaked in his presence.

It was Rufus in all his terrible glory. Although Yoseph was well-acquainted with him, he shuddered in fright at the sight of the powerful giant. At Josephus's command, Rufus marched ponderously to the front of the room. The generals fled from his side, and even Titus looked uneasy. Josephus stood alongside his giant.

"General Titus, I bring you the champion of our Roman lines, my own personal hero whom I rescued from a certain death! He represents our great Roman legions — invincible might, perfect discipline, utter loyalty to the emperor, to Titus, to holy Rome!"

There was a burst of applause at Josephus's flowery oratory.

"And now, Commander Titus, you and your distinguished guests will witness power that you have never seen before — with your permission, Titus!"

Titus nodded, a little uneasily. Yoseph craned his neck to watch the spectacle. The Praetorian guards kept their swords at the ready, ready to pounce on the monster in case he suddenly sprang at Titus.

Josephus signaled with his hand. The tent flap parted, and three men entered, carrying a thick iron bar almost five feet in length. It was obviously heavy, and they struggled to carry it through the packed room without striking anyone. They stood before Titus, straining under its immense weight.

"Behold, Caesar," Josephus announced grandly, "they bear an iron ingot that weighs more than three men, which has been cast into an indestructible bar. If any guest here wishes to test its mettle, let him grasp it himself."

Titus waved his hand impatiently. "Your word is sufficient, Josephus. Proceed."

"Colossus of Rome, take hold of the iron bar!" Josephus ordered.

Rufus turned stiffly, took hold of the ingot, and with a scream lifted it out of the legionnaires' hands. Suddenly relieved of their burden, they fell back, nearly knocking over the dignitaries behind them. Rufus stood with his back to the crowd, facing the platform. He shouted fiercely and, with one great heave, lifted the huge piece over his head, holding it aloft triumphantly. His whole body trembled under its weight. Yoseph was reminded of the poor prisoners

Rufus had raised aloft and beaten together mercilessly.

Josephus bowed to Titus and Princess Berenice, then turned and swept his arm towards the crowd.

"Now, General Titus, honored guests, all Rome, behold the power!"

At his signal, Rufus lowered the ingot and held it chest high. He grasped it tightly at each end, took a huge breath, and began squeezing. The veins of his neck protruded, his shoulders turned bright crimson, and sweat poured down his back. He screamed again and again, pulling the bar against his chest. Slowly the bar began bending, at first imperceptibly, and then surrendering to his pull and bending in upon itself. With one final scream from Rufus, the bar bent neatly into a crescent. Rufus raised the ingot over his head, and the guests thundered their applause.

Over the tumult, Josephus shouted again and again, "Behold the might of Titus and Rome!"

Rufus lowered the bar gently and placed it at Titus's feet. He bowed, saluted sharply, and walked out of the tent in the same robotic, superhuman manner that he had entered.

Titus smiled with pleasure, and Josephus was triumphant!

The room was electric with excitement. Even the insult to Tiberius had been forgotten. Yoseph, also caught in the excitement, strained to see what would happen next.

Caesar raised his hand for quiet.

"Well done, Josephus, well done! You will bestow a prize to your champion — in my name!"

Josephus bowed and smiled, then turned to the assemblage and lifted his hand dramatically. "The giant is a champion fit for a mighty hero like our noble commander, Titus Flavius! But —" he bowed again towards the stage "— there is more."

An expectant hush fell over the room.

What more after Rufus? wondered Yoseph.

Josephus gave a dramatic sweep of his arm, half-addressing Titus, Berenice, and King Agrippa, half-addressing the assembled generals and tribunes.

"Soldiers of Rome! I am a Judean, a descendant of Abraham, while you are the sons of Romulus! But we have one common forefather, Noah. He blessed his children Shem and Jafeth with an immortal blessing: 'May the beauty of Jafeth dwell in the tents of Shem...."

"Greece and Rome were blessed with beauty and art, and we, the children of Shem, were given the tents of worship and law. But there is no more glorious marriage than when the grandeur of Rome and the piety of Judea are joined by music, which is both enchanting and holy."

Josephus paused for effect. Caesar watched him closely, curious as to where all this was leading. Yoseph heard Josephus's words, but he did not realize their meaning.

"Honored General Titus Flavius, Your Highness King Agrippa, Princess Berenice, commanders of the Roman legions! I have made a rare discovery, a musical wonder who puts all the artists of Athens and Rome to shame. His voice is pure beauty, his fingers are angel's fingers!"

Josephus's lieutenant stepped forward, holding a harp high. Recognizing the harp in an instant, Yoseph's face turned white with shock. Josephus lifted the harp triumphantly.

"Heroes of Rome! I call forward an artist blessed by God — Joseph, son of Nachum, Levite of Samaria!"

Looking straight at Yoseph, Josephus stretched out his hand: "Joseph the Levite, step forward!"

In an instant, a long passage opened before Yoseph, like the parting of the Red Sea. It led straight from his lowly place at the very back of the great tent to the stage before the mighty Titus! Yoseph stood frozen. Was he dreaming all this? Was this real? He looked dazedly at the faces staring at him, all the might of Rome waiting for him. He was frightened.

But like a sleepwalker, he had to respond. He slowly began walking forward. He saw Josephus, beaming at his surprise; the mighty Titus sitting on his throne; and his harp, his beloved harp, the gleaming harp that he had made himself in far-off Tapuach, now on display before Caesar. And as he walked forward, he felt the spirit of holy Rabbi Yaakov floating at his side, whispering in his ear what he must do.

Still in a dream, Yoseph arrived at the front of the stage.

Josephus placed the harp in his hands and signaled to him to begin playing. Automatically, he laid his fingers on the strings. Suddenly he heard Rabbi Yaakov's voice, as clear as a shofar blast: "This harp is only for Hashem!"

Yoseph took his hands off the strings and held the harp over his heart. Josephus moved close and hissed: "Levite, play now!"

Yoseph did not look at him. He bowed before Titus and called out forcefully: "Master, I cannot play my harp before you!"

There was a moment's stunned silence, and then a stir rose from the guests. The master of ceremonies' face turned ashen.

It was Caesar who demanded silence. He addressed Yoseph sternly. "Why will you not play before us?"

"Mighty Titus! Last night I heard innocent children praying to God, and today they were executed by your soldiers. How can I play? How can I sing? How can I rejoice with the killers of our people?"

The apostate Jew, Tiberius Alexander, was the first to rise up in righteous wrath. "Josephus, did you bring this lad to insult Titus? Caesar, he should be crucified!"

A stony-faced Caesar pointed at Yoseph. Every eye was riveted to him. "Jew, play before us, or I will have you scourged and crucified before the walls of the Temple before the sun rises."

"My grandfather was crucified, and he died courageously. The children I spoke to last night went to their deaths with Torah on their lips." Yoseph lifted his arms as if he was already on the Roman cross. "I made my harp to serve the Almighty — I cannot use it to betray my own people!"

King Agrippa, who had been silent until now, leaned over to Titus. "His mouth should be sealed tight, before he insults Rome further!"

Yoseph stood there unflinchingly, no longer in a dream. He had awoken. He was no longer a slave. He had given himself over to *kiddush haShem*, and he had found his freedom and his soul.

All conversation in the great hall had ceased. Everyone waited for the drama to play itself out. And then Princess Berenice suddenly intervened.

"Titus, I plead with you to spare this young man."

Titus smiled wickedly. "You fancy his handsome face, then?"

"No, Titus, I fancy his courage! Who dares stand before the mighty Titus, someday Caesar of all the world, and refuse to obey? He must contain a very great soul. It will be ill fortune for all of us if you harm him."

"Do you hear that, singer! Princess Berenice urges that I spare you. Josephus, what do you say?"

"I say that Caesar's wish is my wish!"

"King Agrippa, what do you say?"

"My sister has a sixth sense for the sacred. I would heed her...."

With great sarcasm, Titus turned to Tiberius. "Do you still wish me to crucify him, Governor Tiberius Alexander?"

Tiberius, once again outnumbered, bowed and shook his head in humiliating defeat.

Titus rose from his throne. He stared hard at Yoseph. He looked agitated and awed at the same instant. His beloved consort, Princess Berenice, had sensed a holy power in this Temple musician. It was a force he needed to use and to understand.

He turned, somber-faced, to Josephus. "General Josephus, this Temple singer is of great interest to us. I wish to interrogate him further, at my leisure. Will you cede your slave to me?"

Josephus, who loved being in the center of attention, bowed happily. "He is my gift to our noble Titus."

Titus turned to Yoseph. "Levite, do you understand? You are now Titus's own property, answerable to no one else. Rome honors courage, even of our enemies. We shall meet again soon. Take your leave — now!"

Yoseph stood bewildered. What did they all want from him? *I am dead already — what more do they want?*

Josephus squeezed his arm fiercely, to draw him away. Harp still clutched to his chest, Yoseph followed Josephus out of the tent, into the dark night. A dozen Praetorian guards stood at rigid attention. Hovering over them, like a huge black shadow, was the giant figure of Rufus.

Josephus drew Yoseph away from the guards, so he could not be overheard.

"You fool, what did you do!" he whispered furiously. "Don't

you know what an opportunity I put in your lap? Titus loves music and art! If he had heard you play, he would have made you his own personal musician. The whole Roman court would have been at your feet. How could you throw away such an opportunity?"

"Why didn't you warn me? You took me completely by surprise!"

"Because I know you are a fool. You would have turned me down! But to turn me down right before Caesar — even from you I didn't expect such recklessness! And you pulled it off! You won Caesar's heart — I can see that!"

"I don't want Caesar's heart! I don't want anyone's heart! I just want to be left alone to go back to Tapuach!"

Josephus laughed derisively. "Left alone? You will never know again what it means to be left alone! You are now under Caesar's own private guard. Every step you take will be monitored. You can never escape, never be free — you are Caesar's."

"I am Hashem's — now and always! When He wants, I shall be free!"

"You think so?" sneered Josephus. "You don't know Titus!"

And Rachel Called…

THERE WAS still a faint glimmer of light in the western sky, but Rachel had no time to wait. She peered out of her hiding place, afraid of being spotted by soldiers or bandits roaming about, and was relieved when she saw no one.

There was a new moon that night and it would soon vanish into the sea. If she did not rush out now, she could never speak to him. Signaling her companion to wait behind, she scurried out into the concealment of the tiny hollow.

She had so much to share, to tell.... She dropped her veil and lifted her eyes to the thin moon.

Yoseph, dear Yoseph, how I miss you, how I long to see your face again! The world has turned upside down for us. I have not even been able to run out and speak to you! The Romans have come, how they have come! They came by the thousands, endless rows of soldiers and horsemen. They came like the tide, sweeping away everything before them!

They are all gone, my father, our family, our wealth! My father was made a prisoner, forced to cut trees for the Roman stockades. My brothers and sisters — they were all taken away! Our home is now occupied by our enemies. And your family, Yoseph, your father and mother, they have been killed by the Romans.

All those who were so cruel to me, who mocked my twisted mouth and my muteness, have been swept away, taken to be sold as slaves, silenced forever, never to raise their heads again. The evil man who struck me — he will never speak again. The Romans placed a seal about his lips and led him away to his fate.

I do not rejoice, I must not rejoice! But there is justice in the world, and the cruelty of those who are cruel sweeps back to torment them.

How I wish I could gaze upon you once more, my dear husband Yoseph! Where are you? Are you safe? Are you studying Torah with Rabbi Tzaddok? I know you are alive, I feel your radiance flowing upon me! But how shall we meet again, Yoseph, when you don't even know where I am? I am hiding here, in our secret place, beside the apple tree. I take shelter beneath the tree and forage for berries and roots that I can chew on. Already our baby knows hunger, and he kicks so hard, so hard for more!

But, Yoseph, I finally found kindness in my own family. She is one of my half-sisters, a girl named Leah. Before our marriage, she was like a child, far removed from me, but now she has grown into a young woman. She, too, suffered — she also understands what cruelty is. One day we were alone together in the field, and she said to me, "Rachel, why do you cover your face? Why are you ashamed to show what Hashem has made you? Do you think He makes mistakes?"

I just shook my head. I was afraid to share our secret.

"I am your sister," she said. "You can show me your face. I will not turn away or mock it."

I felt her love, and I knew she was a true sister. I drew away my veil and smiled, the smile that only you know. Her eyes opened wide with wonder: "You are beautiful, Rachel!"

"Now I am!" I answered. "I can talk now, and Hashem has

blessed me with a wonderful husband who has gone to learn Torah. But it is our secret — will you go now and tell it to the others?"

She embraced me, kissed my cheek, and put my veil back over my face. "It is our secret now," she said, "and I will never tell."

When the Romans neared our village, Leah came to summon me. "Come!" she said. "We must run now, or we will be caught." She took me by the hand and led me away into the fields. I brought her here, to our secret place, and she shares it with me. Do you mind? And now she even knows the secret of our moon whispers.

How I miss you, my Yoseph, how I need you! I am getting so big, and soon my time will come. But when our child is born, what shall he be — free to serve Hashem, or yet another slave to the Roman masters?

Oh, Yoseph, please return and find me! Hashem, help us!

And Yoseph Answered…

YOSEPH STOOD on a small, rocky mound near his new tent. A half-dozen Praetorians watched him suspiciously, and in the distance loomed the ever-present shadow of Rufus. He barely glimpsed the pale crescent moon, hair thin, sinking towards the Elah Valley, and he spoke in hurried whispers.

Oh, Rachel, Rachel, how I miss you! How empty I am without you. How I dream that I could be with you again under our apple tree, and I could play my harp to Hashem, and the whole world would leave us alone.

But this is not what Hashem has chosen for us. You will not believe what suffering I have witnessed, or where the hand of God has led me. I long for righteous teachers, for Rabbi Tzaddok, for Father Yaakov, for others that I have learned from. But instead I have been cast with General Josephus, betrayer of the Galilee! I have met Titus, son of the emperor, commander of all the Roman legions! And Rachel — they are frightened of me! Isn't that mad? They are afraid to touch me! The more stubbornly I stand for Hashem, the more they protect me!

Why are wicked men so drawn to holiness? They are hypnotized by me! A fearsome giant named Rufus follows me day and night — he watches that no harm comes to a hair on my head! God has grabbed me by both pei'ot and dragged me to the front stage of our people's destiny. But why? Why me? I am not worthy.

I hope, I hope — but all of me shivers.

Oh, Rachel, do not forget me, I beg of you — as I have not forgotten you even for an instant! Pray, Rachel, pray! One day, Rachel, we will stand under the apple tree and lift our baby high up to the sun. We shall sing zemirot and tishbachot to the Almighty, and there will be peace, and there will joy, and we will never be apart again!

Yoseph sighed as the moon sank into oblivion. He slunk quickly back to his new quarters.

What will tomorrow bring? he wondered.

Chapter Six

Two months before the Churban

Titus's headquarters was no army camp — Yoseph had been thrown into distinguished company.

The inmates of Titus's special prison were men of stature, members of the Sanhedrin, Torah scholars, priests of the Temple, Sadducee aristocrats who bribed their way into Titus's protection. They all were being held there for Titus's pleasure — and he played with them like puppets. They formed their own minyans, studied, prayed, argued — all under the unblinking stare of Titus's personal Praetorian guard.

On the third day, Yoseph returned to his large tent from *shacharit* to find he had company. Three new prisoners had been brought in, an elderly man and two younger men. The young men huddled over the old one and were just settling him on his couch when Yoseph entered. The old man seemed bewildered, and they kept offering him water. They completely ignored Yoseph.

Yoseph sat and watched them from his couch on the other side of the tent, waiting for them to greet him. But when they continued to ignore him, he rose and approached them.

"*Shalom aleichem,*" he said. "Do you need help? Can I bring you something?"

They stopped fussing over the old man momentarily, looked at him, and shook their heads coldly — still not uttering a word. The old man lifted his head, peered at Yoseph, and looked back down again. *Not a friendly lot*, thought Yoseph. He returned to his corner, but he could still hear them whispering among themselves, careful not to be overheard. What could be the matter? It wasn't like they were learning Torah, as Aharon and Avigdor had been the first time he was in Rabbi Tzaddok's camp.

The Romans had laid out the couches in the tent evenly, allowing a quarter of the tent for each prisoner. To Yoseph's chagrin, the young men dragged their beds close to the old man's, so that he was shielded on each side. Yoseph was left with two thirds of the room to himself, separated from the others by a great stretch of open floor — as if he was a leper.

It was bad enough that he was imprisoned by Titus when he longed to be home. Did he also have to be ostracized by his fellow Jews? Yoseph sat there miserably, coughing every now and then, strumming a few sweet notes on his harp — anything to break the silence. He couldn't even see the old man, who was deliberately shielded from him by the two younger men.

Finally, after almost two hours of silence passed, Yoseph had had enough. He stood up angrily, stalked over to the little circle, and rolled up his sleeves. He stuck his two bare arms in their faces, practically under the nose of the old man.

"Look, *rabbotai*, see my arms! They are clear — I am not a *metzora*!"

Withdrawing his arms roughly, he turned and stormed out of the tent. This was not how he was going to spend his time waiting for Titus!

Yoseph meandered aimlessly through the prisoner area. Groups of scholars had gathered to hear *shiurim* from the *rabbanim*. He knew he should join them, find a place in their midst, but he was too shaken with righteous indignation — and angry at his own rash outburst. The Sivan sun beat fiercely on his head, and at last, tired, he wandered back to his tent.

He fell down on his bed and washed his face. The little clique in the corner still did not acknowledge him, but he saw them watching him and whispering among themselves. He lay back on his couch, lifted his harp to his chest, and strummed to himself quietly. He wanted to sleep.

Presently, one of the younger men rose and approached him. Yoseph sat up glumly.

"My grandfather sent me here. He wants to know why you waved your arms in our faces earlier?"

Yoseph sat up. "Tell him I apologize, but it was very unpleasant for me to have you huddled there not saying a word, as though I were a leper."

"What is your name?"

"Yoseph ben Nachum HaLevi — from Tapuach."

The young man nodded. "My name is Nadav. My cousin is Elazar, and our grandfather's name is Ezra, of the *mishmar* of Malkiah."

He spoke formally, without much warmth. "I will return to look after my grandfather."

He slipped back to his corner. Yoseph lay on his bed, strumming quietly on his harp, thinking. Through the corner of his eye, he watched the little family group. Although they had spoken, he felt like a glass wall stood between them.

Outside, the afternoon sun beat mercilessly. Yoseph wanted to escape, but it was a *chamsin* and it was impossible to leave the tent. Finally, he washed his hands and stood up to pray *minchah*. Bewildered by his new surroundings, feeling isolated and unwanted by his own people, he prayed his heart out, swaying with all his might. He had nowhere to go, nothing to rush for, so he spent a good half-hour pouring out his heart. He finished the *amidah*, stepped three paces back, and bowed left and right. Only then did he realize that Nadav was back, stationed alongside him.

Yoseph acknowledged him with a nod, but continued reciting *Aleinu*. He was surprised that Nadav had returned, but he was determined to recite the final prayer precisely and clearly. Finally, he concluded and nodded to his visitor.

"My grandfather would like to meet you. Could you come over and speak to him?"

There was a touch more warmth in his voice than there had been before.

Still cautious, Yoseph followed him across the room. Elazar saw him approach and rose to offer him his chair. Yoseph sat down across from Ezra. He extended his hand, but the old man did not take it.

Yoseph studied him closely. He was thin and bronzed from the sun. He reminded Yoseph of his grandfather. He appeared ancient, but his gaze was sharp, and his eyes scanned Yoseph carefully.

"*Shalom aleichem,*" Yoseph greeted him respectfully.

"*Aleichem shalom,*" he answered politely. Despite his age, he had the clear voice of someone younger. He continued to gaze at Yoseph and seemed to weigh his words carefully.

"My name is Ezra ben Todrus HaKohein. What is your name?'

"Yoseph ben Nachum, a Levite from Tapuach."

"How did you reach the camp of Titus? It is a special prison for members of the Sanhedrin, *kohanim* in charge of the Temple — how did one as young as you are come here?"

Yoseph smiled. "My master, you do not want to know my story. It is a long one that would take us all night. It was *ratzon Hashem* — God's will."

"Everything is *ratzon Hashem,*" Ezra answered impatiently. "We know that! But that doesn't answer my question."

Yoseph grew uncomfortable. What did the old man want from him? He didn't owe him an explanation.

"What does it matter, Father Ezra? I am a prisoner, is that not sufficient?"

Finally, Elazar, the elder of the two grandsons, intervened. "Don't be offended, Yoseph. Our grandfather has a reason for questioning you. Sabba Ezra served in the Temple for many years. He was in charge of all the wooden markers for those who purchased *menachot* for the sacrifices. The Romans captured him, and they want him to reveal the layout of the Mikdash so they can plan their attack. How do we know that you were not placed here by the Romans to extract information from Sabba?"

Yoseph did not know whether to laugh or cry. "Are you accusing me of being a spy?" he asked hotly. "After all I have gone through, all I have suffered, now I am a spy?"

The old man laid his thin hand on his arm. "Calm yourself — anger rests in the laps of fools. We all know what suffering is. We just fled yesterday from Yerushalayim. There is no reason to be upset."

Yoseph took a deep breath and regained his composure.

"Our grandfather was impressed by your prayers," said Nadav.

"We do think you are a pious person. But tomorrow or the next day, they will take Sabba out to be questioned, and if he does not answer as they want, they will torture him to the bone. How do we know that you were not sent to extract information from us?"

Yoseph did not know how to answer. He turned to the old man. "Sabba," he said simply, "there is nothing I can do to prove my innocence. Until Shevat I dwelt safely with my wife in the hills of Tapuach. I left it all to come to Yerushalayim to study with Rabbi Tzaddok. I brought my only companion, my harp, which I hope to play in the Mikdash. We have been Temple singers generation after generation. My own grandfather was caught by the Romans when he came up to Yerushalayim two years ago for Shavuot. They crucified him!"

"What was your grandfather's name?" Ezra asked.

"Elchanan."

"And his father?"

"Azaryah."

The old man raised his hand to his brow. He dropped his head and shook it mournfully. "You are the grandson of Elchanan — the holy Elchanan of Tapuach?"

"Yes."

The old man rose from his seat. Everyone stood with him. He looked up at Yoseph, who was a head taller than he, and embraced him with startling vigor.

"Elchanan, the holy Elchanan of Tapuach! The Temple lit up when he walked into the *azarah*! You are truly his grandson? *Baruch Hashem* that I lived to meet you!"

He stood there, still embracing Yoseph and weeping. After a while, his grandsons gently pulled him away and sat him back down on the couch.

What Sabba could not do for him in his life, he accomplished in his death. Like a heavy cloud being pushed away instantly by a mighty gust of wind, all the distance and suspicion vanished, and in its place was the sunshine of warmth, trust, and love.

THE NEXT morning, Yoseph left for the *shacharit* minyan that had been organized by the captives. For the first time since meeting

Titus, he had a glimmer of hope. He remained after the *tefillot* and listened to the *shiur*. It was about the Temple and its altar. Titus's captives, so near the Mikdash but so cut off, longed for its holy glow, and dwelled on its laws with a passion.

And he understood what was being said! Not every word, not every halachah, but sparks of the Torah ignited his soul. He was delighted.

When he returned to his tent in late morning, a pleasant surprise awaited him. His bed had been moved by Ezra's grandsons so that now all four beds were on one side of the tent, leaving a great empty space in the rest. He was no longer an outcast!

After breakfast, he brought a chair next to Sabba Ezra's couch. The old man sat swaying, reciting psalms in a beautiful singsong. Yoseph did not interrupt him, but recited his own psalms, humming his family's Levite melody.

Finally Ezra finished. He gazed at Yoseph lovingly, even as his grandsons served him a simple meal of bread and goat cheese. Yoseph spoke as the old man ate.

"Sabba Ezra, I ask forgiveness for my actions yesterday — putting my bare arms in front of your face. It was chutzpah on my part."

Ezra smiled and shook his head. "I was not insulted. In my day I saw many arms, and passed judgment on many *tzara'at* cases. I thought you really had a question."

Yoseph shuddered at the thought. He addressed the old man with great respect. "May I ask...how old is Sabba Ezra?"

"What does it matter?" Elazar interrupted abruptly, upset at the question.

Yoseph knew he had made an error — the family was afraid of an evil eye.

But Ezra shooed him off. He was not perturbed.

"One hundred and three years old!" he answered proudly.

Yoseph fell back in amazement. One hundred and three! No wonder his grandsons were upset!

"How did you merit to live such a long life?" he asked. "You must have seen so much!"

Ezra shook his head. "Why are you surprised? I am not the only ancient left from the Temple! Were it not for the famine, many would be alive, even older than I! Why not? From the time I was a child, I stood in the *azarah* and heard the high priest bless the people with Hashem's Ineffable Name! Do you think those *berachot* did not take hold? I am alive from his blessings!"

"How long did you know my Sabba?"

Ezra's face lit up with a smile. "I knew your Sabba from the time he first stood on the *duchan* as a young man. He was always pure, always hidden. He dressed simply and looked to all like a folk person. But when he raised his voice to sing, every holy *kavanah* was woven into the words of the song!"

"*Kavanah*? What *kavanah*?"

"He did not teach you?" Ezra asked in astonishment.

Yoseph remembered his last few minutes alone with his Sabba, in the "hole" — and the secrets he had tried to tell him. But it was too late.

"There was no time," he said. "The Romans took him out to be killed." A wave of bitterness swept over him, and he suddenly saw in his mind's eye the Roman officer who had executed his Sabba.

"How terrible," Ezra sobbed, "how terrible! You would have been a worthy successor to your grandfather."

He began to weep, and Yoseph felt a hand on his arm. Elazar was signaling — he must stop.

TITUS HAD created a bizarre prison. The inmates were well fed and allowed to pray and study, but it was slow, deliberate torture. The prison was Titus's playground, his pleasure chamber.

Every day, ceremonial trumpets sounded and drums thundered, announcing Titus's return to his headquarters. After he had rested for a few minutes from the burden of battle, some prisoners were summoned to appear before him. No one knew when he would be chosen, or why, or what the outcome would be. Sometimes the prisoners — high-ranking *kohanim*, aristocrats, even captured commanders from the zealot side — would return beaming. Titus was pleased by what they had said, and they received gifts, even medals. The next day, the same ones were called and beheaded. There was no rhyme, no reason for the murders other than the whim of Titus. Often prisoners entered Titus's tent whole and returned bloodied and crippled. Titus enjoyed the sport.

The inmates were always summoned by a special squad of Praetorians, headed by their commander, Caputo. Yoseph could not see him without remembering how the man had crucified his holy Sabba. If he had been courageous, he would have jumped out and strangled him with his bare hands. But he was too afraid. When he saw Titus's invitation committee coming, he hid — like the rest.

He dreamt of escaping. But great, unblinking eyes watched him ceaselessly. Not only those of Titus's fierce Praetorian guards, sworn to guard him, but also those of Rufus! Josephus had assigned him to Titus as a gift. Rufus dedicated his life to watching Yoseph — always from a distance, but Yoseph knew he was there.

SIVAN PASSED, and the days of Tammuz moved with painful slowness. The heat radiated down like a furnace, and the pleased faces of the Praetorian guards indicated new victories for Rome. Titus's camp lay outside the northwest corner of the city. The roar of the battering rams came from the distance now, for the legions had penetrated deep into the heart of Yerushalayim. Outside the camp, column upon column of newly captured prisoners was led away for execution.

Yerushalayim lived in a nightmare from which it could not awaken. The sages had warned, the sages had begged, but the zealots would not hearken — and Jerusalem paid the dreadful price. And yet the zealots fought against all hope — with unbelievable courage, with unending love for Jerusalem, with raw self-sacrifice that had no bounds.

From time to time, special prisoners were brought to the camp. They were leaders of the aristocracy, high officials of the Temple, Jewish collaborators who were being protected. They described to the other prisoners the latest fighting in the city, house by house, lane by lane. The Tenth and Fifteenth Legions had taken the Phaesal and Hippicus Towers in the west and were hacking their way deeper and deeper into the Mishneh neighborhood, trying to reach the Temple's west gate. The Antonia Fortress was in the hands of the Fifth and Twelfth Legions, and they could shoot their arrows right down into the Temple courtyard. The fighting was brutal. Yochanan of Gush Chalav burned down the colonnade between Antonia and the north Temple wall, and when the Romans tried to build a bridge, his men defended every handbreadth with their bare hands.

Yerushalayim suffered horribly from hunger and thirst. Children gathered around their *melamdim* in the city's hundreds of synagogues, slaking their thirst with their Torah. They sat and studied, trembling with fear, until the legionnaires broke through and their time came. The Romans slaughtered them one by one, even as they recited their *pesukim*. The Romans wearied of taking more slaves. There were no more buyers even for the thousands who had been led away earlier. Famine stalked the streets. Mothers made meals of their own dead infants and wept miserably even as they gulped down their terrible food.

As Eisav danced and Yaakov wept, the heavens and the angels wept, and the Almighty watched and set His great clock....

AND WHILE Jerusalem writhed in agony, the prisoners in Titus's camp dwelt like garden peacocks, well fed, safe, looked after. Yoseph, ashamed of his good fortune, ate his meals guiltily. But he did eat, and he attended minyanim and *shiurim*, because Josephus had been right — someone had to live to tell the story.

Many in the camp knew of ancient Ezra and longed to speak to him and receive his blessing. His grandchildren guarded him jealously. Elazar was nearly fifty, reserved and dignified. Nadav was younger and more emotional. But both were dedicated to serving their grandfather. Despite his age, Ezra was spry and clear minded. He remembered everything and knew everyone. He had a thousand stories, and if his grandsons had not stopped him, he could have regaled visitors day and night. But it was too much for him. Suddenly, even in midsentence, he would grow weary and would have to stop.

Yoseph was privileged. Ezra took a great liking to him, and he was allowed to sit next to him and hear his tales.

"How does it feel to be a hundred years old?" he asked one day.

Ezra leaned back in feigned surprise. "I — a hundred years old?

What are you saying? I am just a young man! Listen —" he leaned forward and whispered in confidence, "a hundred years — it goes by — flit!" He snapped his fingers. "Like nothing! Like a dream!

"The first day I stood on the altar — it is like yesterday! Herod was king, before the great tragedies! Hillel and Shammai were still alive. You could get a *berachah* from Yonatan ben Uziel! I saw them with my own eyes!

"It was a few months after my bar mitzvah. Our *mishmar*'s first turn came in Tevet. It rained in sheets, and the cold of the Temple floor went right into your bones. The first night I slept on the floor of the Beit HaMoked, with a big fire burning in the middle of the chamber to keep us warm. My father and grandfather slept on the benches. I could not sleep for excitement.

"It was nearly morning when I finally dozed off. Suddenly, there was a tremendous scream: '*Imdu kohanim la'avodatchem*! Rise up, O priests, to your service!'

"If I hadn't stood up in an instant, they would have all trampled me. I went down to the tunnel, immersed in the *mikveh*, and donned the new *begadim* my mother had sewn."

Ezra leaned forward, his eyes glowing with youthful zeal. He wasn't a hundred and three, but thirteen years old again.

"Matityahu, the captain, entered the chamber. He was always rushed. He opened the door into the *azarah*. It was still pitch black, the Temple floor was cold and slippery from the night's rain. I followed my father. We lit candles and walked around the courtyard, checking that all was in order. The altar pyre glowed over our heads, and we could smell yesterday's sacrifices smoldering on the coals. The *ulam* loomed in the darkness over us, its windows like great eyes that watched our every move.

"The first *kohein* disappeared behind the *mizbei'ach* to wash his hands. Suddenly he reappeared at the base of the great ramp. I saw he was an old man. He lifted up a silver shovel from the bottom of the ramp and tried to walk up. He was very slow — he was afraid of falling. You could just make out his white garments glowing red against the coals. Finally, he reached the top of the *mizbei'ach* and began shoveling into the coals. He had a lot of trouble digging deep into the bottom of the pyre.

" 'I'll go up and help him,' I told my father eagerly. My father clamped his hand over my mouth in response.

"Finally, he climbed down, balancing the shovel so the coals wouldn't spill out. I was afraid he was going to slide right down. He took tiny little steps — he was so nervous, poor man. But Hashem helped and he made it down. He turned, walked along the side of the ramp, and deposited the coals in the *deshen* place.

"Suddenly, all the *kohanim* started racing towards the *ulam*. My father grabbed my hand. 'Hurry, Ezra, run!'

"All the *kohanim* gathered at the other side of the ramp, where the *kiyor* was. We lined up to wash our hands and feet. Meanwhile, the old *kohein* was back, climbing the ramp, but this time a whole group of *kohanim* ran up with him, to move aside yesterday's sacrifices and make room for a new fire.

"My father turned to me. 'Ezra, this is your chance. Go quickly to the Lishkat HaEitz and bring wood for the altar.' I was so excited that I ran like a child. I went to the room where they checked the logs and grabbed a huge piece of olivewood. It was so heavy I almost dropped it. Someone helped me prop it on my shoulder. It weighed so much that it almost crushed my shoulder — Yoseph, I can still feel it pressing into me ninety years later!

"I reached the *kevesh* and looked up. I never realized how long and steep it was! It was three stories high! There were no railings, and everything was wet and slippery. Even with the salt they scattered on it, you could fall right over the side. I walked very slowly up — I didn't want to fall on my first time. My father held me. I saw he was crying, and I started sniffling, too. I was so happy. I was a *kohein*, a proper *kohein*! I reached the roof of the *mizbei'ach* and walked towards the east, where the old *kohein* stood. The old man was trying to build the wood stack neatly, but it was too heavy for him. The other *kohanim* helped him and stuck smaller kindling sticks between the big logs. Someone lifted the log off my shoulder, and together we set it on the *ma'arachah*. My shoulder felt broken.

"Someone brought up a flaming twig and handed it to the *kohein*. He stood there with his whole body shaking — he was praying so hard! Finally, he touched the flame to the kindling sticks. Little tongues of red flame started sprouting. A wind blew between the logs, and the whole pile ignited. Smoke poured in our faces, and I had to shut my eyes.

"My first time, Yoseph — and it is like yesterday! I stood atop the *mizbei'ach* and I was so proud. Later, my father made a *seudat hodaah*.

"And now —" Ezra waved his hand in anguish. "Look what has happened! Look what has happened to us!"

All the youthfulness suddenly drained from his face, and he was an old, old man. He fell back into his bed and stared silently at the ceiling. Yoseph took his hoary hand, kissed it, and slipped away wordlessly.

IN THE morning and evening Yoseph prayed together with the minyan the prisoners had formed. He listened to a *shiur* every day, picked up what he could. He forgot the world he came from. He went days without once thinking about Rachel. What was there to think about, dream about? She lived on the moon, in another world. And yet, when he did think about her, he pined so much for her he thought his heart would stop. She was his whole life. Where was she? Did she remember him? Did she ever think of him? Had she been true to her word and spoken to the moon as he had? Was she still free? Was she alive? And the baby?

Who knew? Only Hashem, only Hashem — everything was in His hands.

His one joy in the world was his harp — his one connection with the world that once was. But now, amid all the loneliness and pain, he would not touch it — he could not even bear to look at it.

Scraps of news continued to reach the camp. The battle was going badly. The zealot general, Yochanan of Gush Chalav, massed all his men along the north wall of the *azarah*, behind the Holy of Holies. They fought frantically to keep the Romans back, making desperate sorties to set fire to the Roman siege towers. Their surprise attacks drove back the enemy for a day, but the Romans had endless forces. The Jews were outnumbered ten to one. In the camp, the prisoners recited *Tehillim* day and night and prayed for the Mikdash. The Praetorians watched their efforts and sneered.

On the morning of the seventeenth of Tammuz, Yoseph felt an

odd foreboding when he awoke. The heat in the tent was terrible, and he ran out to escape. The sun was not up yet, and the waning moon floated above the western hills.

Ihu lo chazai, mazleih chazai — he could not see, but his *mazal* saw!

He immersed himself in the cistern that had been dug in one corner of the camp and then entered the *beit midrash*. Many elders were already there, studying. Gloom hung on every face.

Yoseph approached one of the men. "My master, has something happened?"

The man rolled his eyes heavenward. "May Hashem watch over *klal Yisrael*!"

Yoseph's anxiety subsided. Every day brought a new curse — was this day any different? He prayed *shacharit* but did not stay for learning. He wanted to talk to Ezra. The wise old man might understand something.

He returned to his tent and found that it was empty. Where was Ezra? Both he and his grandsons were gone. Was the old man sick? Had the invitation committee summoned him? Was that the dread that had overcome him? He thought of going out and asking a guard. But the Praetorians were a close-mouthed bunch. He sat and waited.

He heard footsteps outside, and the rustle of the tent flap. He stood up in anticipation of Ezra's return. The flap opened and a huge face appeared, grinning. It was Rufus. The giant squeezed himself into the tent sideways, carrying all sorts of gear. He looked around and dropped his load on one of the empty beds, then sat down heavily. Yoseph was sure the bed would break.

"Rufus, why are you here?" Yoseph asked, his heart in his throat.

"What's the matter, Levite, you don't care to have me around?"

"Oh, it's a pleasure having you around," answered Yoseph ingenuously, "but at a distance, where you can't break my neck."

"Behave yourself, and Rufus will make sure that no harm befalls you. I am here to protect you — at Josephus's orders."

Yoseph had a sharp answer ready, but he bit his tongue. "Really, why have you come here, Rufus?"

"I came to show you my new armor." He pointed to a polished

breastplate that lay on the couch. It was an evil work of sheer beauty. Dozens of burnished metal pieces, the size of large coins, were sewn tightly together with leather thongs. It was impenetrable, but it could move easily with his huge body.

"Very nice," said Yoseph.

"Lift it, Levite!"

"It's all right, Rufus, I believe you."

"Lift it!" he ordered. The smile had vanished from his face. Yoseph hurriedly tried to lift it — but he could hardly raise it more than an inch. It was massive.

Rufus laughed in delight. "You see. You can't even lift it up! Look here!"

The huge Roman sprang up from the couch. He swooped up the armored vest and slipped it over himself. Then he grabbed his huge spear with its razor-sharp tip and donned a new helmet with a blood-red crest. He was mammoth, a terrible force of nature created for destruction. He lifted his great arms proudly and waved his spear like a savage.

"Look at me, Levite! Dressed in my armor, I can crush any soldier in this camp!"

He lowered his spear and pointed it threateningly at Yoseph.

"I can hurl this spear from a hundred yards and hit a leaf. And I can cut you in two in a blink! Whenever I want!" He roared with laughter.

Yoseph looked at him, perplexed at his sudden hostility. Rufus lowered his spear and spoke intimately.

"Remember what Rufus tells you. Behave yourself, and I will be your best friend! Try to sneak away from me — anywhere — and I will come after you with my baby here."

He caressed the spear tenderly. Yoseph shook his head and smiled.

Rufus stared at him suspiciously. "What is so funny?"

"I was thinking. You have your baby, your spear. I have my baby, my harp."

Rufus stared at him, then snorted with a mixture of contempt and affection. "Anytime you want to have a duel — I am ready!"

He sprang up like a great cat and stormed out of the tent.

Yoseph scratched his head in perplexity, not sure whether to tremble or laugh.

But where was Ezra? The dread that Yoseph felt earlier returned to him. Seeking solace, he reached behind his bed, retrieved his harp from its leather pouch, and kissed it. Why had he neglected it so long? It was his own heart. Holding it to his bosom, he fingered its strings. His whole old life flooded through his fingers. He so much wanted to live. He so much wanted to survive this nightmare.

> *Ana eileich mei'ruchecha v'ana mipanecha evrach*? Where can I go from Your spirit, and where can I flee from Your presence? If I ascend to heaven, You are there. If I make my bed in the lowest depth, behold You are there! Were I to take up wings of dawn, were I to dwell in the distant west, There, too, Your hand would guide me, and Your right hand would grasp me!

He knew that whatever happened, he was not alone, for Hashem was with him. He played with tenderness, with passionate love of everything holy. His harp drew back his own *neshamah*, and he knew he must never neglect his precious instrument again. Everything he did, all his Torah, must contain Hashem at its heart, as his harp was his heart.

Soon after, the tent flap flew open. Two Roman soldiers stood at the entrance as Elazar and Nadav entered and gently led Ezra to his couch. Outside, Yoseph saw that other prisoners had gathered in concern. He ran to Ezra's side and helped his grandsons lower him to his couch. Satisfied that he was settled, the Praetorians closed the door and left. Yoseph took some water and washed the old man's sweaty face. He offered him a drink, but Ezra waved it away. He looked up at his grandsons and then at Yoseph, grasping his hands fiercely.

He shook his head in anguish, barely audible. "The *tamid* — stopped!"

He held onto Yoseph's hand tightly, like a child. Finally, his eyes glazed over and he released his grip, turning to the wall and dozing off. Elazar raised his finger to his lips and ordered Yoseph to move aside while his cousin kept watch over Ezra.

"What happened?" Yoseph whispered.

"This morning they came for Sabba, right after sunup. He was brought to Titus's tent, where his lieutenants were waiting. When the guards carried Sabba in, the officers were very respectful and rose in his honor.

" 'Which of you is Titus?' Sabba asked.

"They laughed at him. 'He is too busy fighting to see you, grandfather. He sends you his regrets.'

" 'What do you want from an old man?' Sabba asked. 'I am one hundred and three years old. What do you need from me?'

" 'We heard that you have been in the Temple longer than any priest,' one of the officers said. 'We wish to know about your Temple.'

" 'What do I know of the Temple?' Sabba answered. 'No more, no less than anyone....'

"The interrogator shook his head.

" 'No, no, grandfather, you are too modest. You know everything! We hear you know every office and hiding place.'

" 'I am an old, old man, over a hundred. I don't remember....'

"The interrogator lost his patience. 'We can make you remember, grandfather.'

"I could see that Sabba was thinking about what to answer, when the other officer — the commander — interrupted. 'No threats, Vitellus. Titus ordered — no threats for the old man.'

"The interrogator did not like his meddling. 'Caputo, when did you become a Judeophile? Do you have more sympathy for this old Jew than you have for our boys who have to fight their way into the Temple?'

"This little argument gave Sabba time to think. 'Why do you want to know about the Temple?' he asked.

" 'Listen,' the officer said, 'we are getting closer and closer to the Temple. You know that! It is just a matter of days — weeks at the most. It is up to you. Rome respects every deity — even our enemies'. Don't the Greeks serve their gods and the Egyptians theirs? As long as they are loyal to Caesar, who cares? There is place in the Forum for everyone, even your illogical religion. Show me a god that you can make into a statue — Zeus, Jupiter, Hercules, Mithras

— that's a god! Your God — where is He? Who ever saw Him? What mountain does he live on? What do you worship — thin air?

" 'But that is not my business. We are going into your Temple, and we want to do as little damage to the structure as we can. You must tell us how to get in and how to find our way about inside — all the secret places!'

"Sabba was insulted. He shook his head. 'God will never let you put a finger on our Mikdash.'

" 'Ha!' the officer laughed in Sabba's face. 'We broke through the last Antonia wall today! There is nothing between us and the Temple. Nothing will stop us! Bar Giora's men are trapped in the Upper City. Yochanan's fighters are starving; they can hardly lift their bows. What will stop us, grandfather?'

"Sabba shouted back, 'The merit of our holy altar! The heavenly fire that consumes our daily sacrifice, that will protect us! The merit of Abraham and the ashes of Isaac will defend us!'

"The officer answered with contempt. 'Sacrifices, what sacrifices? There are no more sacrifices on the altar! The fire is out, the altar is stone cold!'

" 'You are lying!'

" 'Shall I carry you on my back up to the Antonia, old man? See for yourself! The altar is deserted! Titus can dance a jig on your altar! Abraham and Isaac have turned their backs on you!'

"Sabba's face turned white. He turned to the commander, the one called Caputo, and begged him, 'On your mother's honor, is it true? Is the altar cold?'

"He nodded. 'It is true. They have run out of sacrifices.'

"Sabba looked up at us, dumbfounded. He whispered something and tried to rip his robe, but the cloth wouldn't tear. He wanted me to help him, but I would not. I think if he had made the rip, he would have died right there from grief. I pleaded with the commander, Caputo, 'We are your prisoners. We are not going away. Please, let me bring him back to his tent.'

"He assented. But as we lifted Sabba to bring him back, the interrogator held us back. 'Remember, this is just a reprieve. We will bring him back — and I swear to you he will tell us everything!' "

Elazar finished his narrative and went back to watch over his grandfather. Yoseph slipped out of the tent, only to be accosted by the other prisoners, anxious about Ezra. He had no desire to recount the tale. It was not his job to be the bearer of terrible news.

He paced about the camp restlessly. It all happened so fast, the walls of Antonia fortress undermined, the *tamid* stopped. But something else was bothering him, like a piece of indigestible food. It was Elazar's mention of the kindness of Caputo.

Was it the same Caputo who ordered the crucifixion of his Sabba? How could such a murderer show kindness? It did not make sense.

THE ROMANS were true to their word. The very next morning they were back, a squad of heavily armed Praetorians. They brought a chair to carry Ezra, but when his grandsons tried to accompany him they were told not to leave the tent. The poor old man was taken alone into the maw of the Roman beast.

A delegation of prisoners forced their way into Ezra's tent. They insisted on keeping watch with Elazar and Nadav — and Yoseph. They poured out their hearts in prayer all morning. At midday the sound of approaching Romans was heard at last. The anxious group ran to the tent flap. This time, the Romans carried Ezra right into the tent, delivering him straight to his couch. The old man looked very pale.

Without a word, the stone-faced guards set him down and left. Elazar and Nadav forced the guests to leave, and each bowed to the old *kohein* in turn.

When Ezra saw he was alone with his grandsons and Yoseph, he pulled himself briskly up on his couch.

"*Baruch Hashem*, it is over," he murmured. He asked for something to drink.

"Sabba, what happened?" Nadav asked.

Ezra looked at him, a tiny gleam in his eye. He made a *berachah* and took a slice of pomegranate. Gesturing to them to lean close, he spoke in such a low whisper that even a bird flying overhead would not have been able to hear him.

"They brought me back to Titus's tent and left me alone for a long time. I know their Roman games. They wanted me to become disquieted, to imagine what torture they could inflict on me. So the more I waited, the more *bitachon* I had in Hashem. I summoned the *neshamos* of the righteous *kohanim gedolim* to protect me, the great sages, even Hillel and Shammai! They stood there before me, and Choni HaMe'agel drew a circle of protection around me.

"Finally, the Romans marched in. I looked for the centurion who had shown me some respect, but he was not there. This time they were not polite, but showed their real faces.

" 'Old man,' the interrogator shouted at me, 'you wasted too much of our time. Tell us what we want to know.'

" 'What do you want to know?' I asked.

" 'We want to know every room in the Temple. What is its purpose? Where is located? How do you go in? Where are the secret passages?'

"A soldier stood next to him, ready to write everything down.

" 'I am one hundred and three years old,' I cried. 'How do you expect me to remember anything?'

" 'Tell us!' he shouted.

" 'I don't remember!' I shouted back.

"Then he ordered: 'Call in Rufus!'

"I thought to myself, *Who is this Rufus?* And then into the tent came...Og Melech HaBashan, a monster! With a spear ten feet high! He stared at me with such a look that every part of me shook. I could not help being afraid! Even Choni would have lifted up his circle and run away!

"I began talking — and they began writing. I told them the name of every door and every *lishkah*...where we kept the wood, the silver of the *machatzit hashekel*, the Lishkat HaGazit, the tunnels to the Beit HaMoked, the windows, the little rooms, the big rooms — everything! I had no choice!"

He pulled them closer, winked, and whispered into their ears, "But I told them everything backwards! What was east I told them west, what was north I told them south. Every door I put in the wrong place. All the tunnels I told them about lead to unclean places. If they follow my directions, they will never find their way!" Triumph gleamed in his eyes.

"And they believed you?" asked Elazar.

"No, of course not! So they asked me the same questions again and again — over and over in different words. They tried to trap me, but they couldn't! I made a sign in my head for everything I told them, so even if they asked ask me a hundred times I could remember my story!"

Ezra grew silent. He was pleased — but weary. The three watched in awe as the old man took another slice of fruit, closed his eyes, and murmured "*baruch Hashem*" over and over.

He was so ancient, so holy, so invincible — he was the Mikdash!

ALL HOPE was running out. The Mikdash without its holy sacrifice was like a body whose soul had departed. The faces of the prisoners grew thin and waxen from grief, while the faces of the Romans grew ruddier and more cheerful. Their victory was near. In the camp, the pious prisoners fasted, recited *Tehillim*, pleaded Heaven for mercy, and exhorted each other to *teshuvah*.

The walls of Yerushalayim, though heavily guarded, had numerous secret tunnels and escape routes. Deserters escaped daily and threw themselves upon the mercy of the Romans. The lucky ones who made it into Titus's prison told of terrible starvation, the unending crash of battering rams, siege towers, giant catapult stones hurtling at their heads — and unbelievable acts of *chesed* and *mesirut nefesh*. The Romans were at the gates of the Mikdash, with nothing to stop them.

Yoseph did not even think of Rachel. She was like a dream, a mirage of another world, a world of peace, of happiness, of normalcy. He was trapped in the nightmare of Yerushalayim. No one had a right to think of himself anymore. No one dared trust, nor rejoice, nor smile. The only security was *bitachon* in Hashem, prayer, and precious moments of Torah. Only one hope flickered in Yoseph's mind. Perhaps Titus had forgotten about him. In this terrible war, perhaps he had been just a passing fancy.

He soon discovered he was wrong.

A week after the *tamid* stopped, Yoseph entered his tent after *maariv* and found he had guests. Four legionnaires were crowded into his corner of the room. Poor Ezra and his grandsons cowered on the other side.

"You have been summoned by General Titus."

Just like that, no explanations. Caught by surprise, Yoseph's blood turned cold. If he had been warned, he would have prepared himself, prayed to Hashem, steeled himself with faith. But he was caught off guard.

The smirking guards started to form a circle around him, but Yoseph managed to stall them.

"Give me a half a minute," he begged the captain.

Without waiting for an answer, he raced across the room to Ezra and bent low before him. "Please, give me your *berachah*."

Ezra laid his thin hands on his head and murmured his blessing. Fortified, Yoseph rose and returned to his escort. By now, the color had returned to his cheeks, and he held his head up proudly.

He knew that Titus's invitees were brought to his closely guarded tent situated in the center of the camp. Indeed, they marched in that direction. But just as Yoseph was steeling himself to meet Titus, they walked past his tent towards the camp entrance.

"Where are we going?" asked Yoseph. The night was dark, since the moon had not yet risen.

"Keep quiet!" the captain ordered, and Yoseph could feel the tip of a spear jabbing at his spine. He kept quiet.

As they approached the entrance, Yoseph saw by the light of a torch a company of mounted legionnaires. Their shapes were outlined against the flames, but he could make out no faces.

The captain of the legionnaires saluted respectfully. "Do you have the musician?"

Yoseph thought it might be Titus himself, but he would not be so lightly guarded. A voice called down to him. "Jew, can you ride a horse?"

"Yes," Yoseph answered. The voice was faintly familiar.

A horse was brought up to him. "Get on," the commander ordered.

Although he had not ridden a horse for weeks, since arriving at the camp with Josephus, Yoseph mounted smoothly. The commander turned to him. "You'll ride alongside me. You are to keep absolute silence — is that clear?"

"Yes."

"You will answer me, 'Yes, Centurion.' You understand?"

"Yes, Centurion."

The commander raised his arm to whip his horse forward, when suddenly out of the darkness came the sound of heavy running. Everyone turned. Out of the night appeared a great, shadowy form, almost as tall as the horses. It was Rufus.

"What are you doing with the prisoner?" he demanded of the centurion, breathing hard.

"What business is it of yours, legionnaire?" the centurion answered. "He is under my control now. Go back to your quarters!"

Rufus was undeterred. He approached the mounted centurion and stood almost face-to-face with him.

"I have orders from General Josephus himself! This prisoner is under his special protection, and I am to watch over him — to the death. Where are you taking him?"

"Your orders? Who cares a drop about your orders, or that Jew Josephus! Our orders come from Titus himself, so go back to your tent, you overgrown ox!"

There was a muffled wave of laughter. Rufus glared at the other legionnaires and they grew silent quickly.

"Tell me where you are taking him — it is my orders to know what happens to him."

"Well, if you must know, Titus has ordered him to the Antonia Fortress. This Jew claims his God is all-powerful — tonight he will see our army run right through his God's Temple. It's the final attack!"

Rufus nodded, satisfied. "About time! Just make sure that you take good care of my boy here."

Rufus approached Yoseph, his huge head just inches from him. He spoke in an almost intimate undertone. "Don't get clever, Levite. Don't forget — you try to run away, I'll track you down to Hades itself!"

The centurion whipped his horse forward, leaving Rufus standing in the dust.

There were a dozen riders, and they headed northeast, skirting the newly erected siege wall. They reached an opening in the outer Third Wall and entered the north neighborhood of the city. They slowed their pace as they rode through the empty streets. Yoseph had never seen this part of Yerushalayim before. It was the New City, sparsely populated and furthest from the Mikdash. A thin crescent moon rose in the eastern sky, casting a ghostly light over the deserted houses. No one was left.

They traversed the New City and entered the old Mishneh district past the Second Wall. The great outer wall of the Temple Mount loomed in the distance. A terrible stench hit Yoseph's nostrils. The centurion signaled to the men to dismount. As soon as they had done so, he called them into a huddle.

"Absolute silence from here on," he whispered.

He turned to Yoseph, his face just inches away. "Jew, you understand?"

Yoseph stared back, unable to speak. It was the first time he had seen the centurion's face. Staring at him was his grandfather's executioner, Caputo.

"Jew — understood?" he repeated.

Yoseph shook himself awake and nodded.

They marched through the narrow streets of the Mishneh district, a neighborhood Yoseph knew well. He could not believe the horror before him. Bodies lay everywhere, sprawled on the ground, leaning open eyed against doorways, sitting with arms outstretched like beggars. Golden Yerushalayim, the city which never kept a dead person in its walls overnight, was flooded with corpses. Some were bloodied from their death wounds. Others were skeleton-like, their oversized clothing flapping in the warm night air — dead from starvation and thirst. Ever-silent mothers tried to nurse ever-silent babies, and old men lifted their arms in one final, endless *tefillah*. The stench was unbearable, and Yoseph covered his face with his tunic.

He wanted to cry out, but he was afraid his sobs would bring immediate punishment. Was this Yerushalayim, the city of purity, now a graveyard without graves?

He shook with horror the first time he had to step over a body as they marched. He wanted to walk around, to avoid this final ignominy to the dead. But there was no place to go. As they drew close to the Temple, the streets were carpeted with bodies, with no space for walking.

He felt shame, for after a few minutes of this he no longer shook. He had become hardened to the horror around him. The Fortress of Antonia stood on the northwest corner of the Temple's outer wall, behind the Heichal. The great fortress overlooked the Temple Mount so that the Romans could watch everything that was taking place in the Mikdash. The zealots had captured it, but now the Romans had returned. A great hole had been smashed in one of its towers, and a mountain of rubble separated between the city and the Temple Mount.

Caputo signaled, and his men halted. He pulled them close and whispered, "We attack at the ninth hour. The defenders can't stay awake forever. Their sentries are usually drowsing then, so we have the advantage of surprise. Our men are waiting for Titus's signal, and then they will rush in. There's just a narrow opening, and we should smash right through them.

"Titus is on top of the parapet, and I am going up there with the Jew. Half of you meet up with the Fifth, and the rest come with me! Absolute silence!"

The company divided, and Caputo began scaling the mountain of rubble leading up to Titus. In the pale moonlight, Yoseph could see thousands of soldiers crouching silently, at the ready. They were a human wall, squeezed side by side on the side of the mountain that faced the city. Yoseph recognized Titus's ensign on the high parapet above. Titus stood with a small squad of officers on the northern side of the parapet, hidden from anyone on the Temple Mount.

They reached Titus's position. Yoseph could not see the general's face, but the cocky tilt of his head was unmistakable. Titus had his hands clenched behind his back, pacing. The attack was imminent.

Yoseph and Caputo stood only ten feet from the general himself. From time to time, Titus turned and glanced at Caputo and then at Yoseph. A glint of satisfaction crossed his face at the sight of his Jewish captive there as a witness.

Suddenly, a shudder went through the Roman ranks. There was a quickening, an electric charge in the air. A centurion ran up noiselessly to Titus and whispered in his ear. Titus nodded. In the pale moonlight, Yoseph watched as twenty soldiers climbed the mound and crawled stealthily over to the enemy's side. They were the legion's toughest shock troops, sent to silently dispatch the sleeping sentries. Yoseph wanted desperately to shout a warning, but he remained silent, afraid.

The massed ranks of Roman troops rose, ready to rush in behind the first troops. Suddenly, there was a great roar from the far side. Warning shofars sounded, and flame-tipped arrows lit up the sky. Even from a distance the screams of battle could be heard, Roman legionnaires yelling for reinforcements, Jewish defenders shouting to each other, the crash of missiles and arrows.

Titus turned and screamed at his lieutenants, "Why are you waiting, fools! Our men have been discovered — send in the troops now — now!"

There was a thunder of drums, a blast of trumpets, a rattle of spears against shields. Like a thunderclap, the whole Roman army bellowed: "For Rome! For Caesar!"

First over were the ensigns, bearing the sacred Roman emblems. Following them, like some huge, crawling black creature, were the legionnaires, surging forward by the thousands. Caputo followed Caesar as he ran around to the other side of the parapet, where he could look almost straight down at the battle raging in the dark passageway leading from Antonia to the Mikdash. The narrow passage had become a cauldron of war, from which emerged the clash of weapons, the desperate screams of the wounded and dying. The Roman forces were all but trapped between the walls, while shadowy figures of the zealot defenders ran into the fray from the other side. All that Yoseph could see was a swirling sea of heads, caught in the frenzy of killing. Which were Romans, which were Jews, who was killing whom, who was prevailing? Darkness veiled all.

The plan for a surprise attack had failed utterly — the defenders had clearly been expecting the attack. First the Romans pushed forward, then they were cut down. Then the defenders attacked and were stopped in their tracks by the overwhelming Roman forces. Runners ran back and forth and reported to Titus. The numerical superiority of Romans was no help. With no room to maneuver, the legionnaires trampled each other. The Jews were suffering also. No one could see who was friend and who was foe. They attacked, ran back for cover, and were then killed by their own comrades by mistake.

The fighting raged all night, until the first light of dawn. All this time, Caputo stayed near Titus's side, ready for orders — which never came. Titus shook his head with dismay and fury.

"Fools!" he raged. "I should never have listened to their plans!"

At first light, the terrible carnage became clear. The alley between the fortress and the Mikdash was littered with bodies, Romans and Jews all tangled together in one great heap. Both sides were exhausted, and the survivors stood at either end of the passage, awaiting the next round.

Titus, ashen faced, turned and glared at Yoseph. "You! You brought me bad fortune!"

Yoseph's eyes widened with shock. He shook his head in vehement denial.

Yet all eyes were upon him with hatred — and fear.

As if by agreement, both sides held back from further combat. First the Romans retrieved their dead and wounded. Then the Jews sallied out to drag their dead and wounded one by one to the other side. The Roman soldiers, well fed and heavily armored, had to be carried away by a few comrades. The Jewish fighters, thin from starvation and dressed in rags, were dragged away like feathers.

The Roman troops who had borne the worst of the night's fighting were relieved, and fresh, battle-hardened legionnaires took their place, eager for battle.

Like a serpent awakening, the Romans began moving forward cautiously to renew their attack. At first the Jews held their place, but now it was clear daylight. The Roman column advanced, protected by a wall of shields, bristling with swords and javelins. Slowly, the defenders fell back. Emboldened, the Romans moved faster, nearly running.

Titus stood above, trembling with excitement.

"Careful, boys, careful," he mumbled to himself, "not too fast! Not too fast! Cut the throats of every one of them!"

They advanced faster, and Titus was unable to contain himself. He began shouting, "Slit their throats! Slit their throats! Cut every one of them to pieces!" He was almost dancing with exultation.

As though they heard his screams, the Romans broke into a full trot after the defenders, who seemed to panic. They retreated towards the Heichal, climbing the north balcony of the *azarah*.

One of Titus's lieutenants murmured. "General, I don't like this. It looks too easy!"

But Titus did not even hear him. He jumped with naked glee as his soldiers began scaling the ladders abandoned by the defenders. The legionnaires mounted the high colonnade behind the Holy of Holies and stood there, awaiting reinforcements. The Jews had retreated to the sides of the colonnade, and more ladders were brought. The Romans piled onto the colonnade until it was overrun with soldiers like ants over an abandoned fruit. The Jews were crying in despair — their precious Temple was being overrun! They shot a few futile arrows, but the Romans flung their honed javelins in response, silencing the archers.

Just as the colonnade was completely overrun with hundreds of legionnaires, a dozen defenders suddenly raced towards the Romans with torches in their hands. They appeared from nowhere, yet they came from everywhere. The Romans, caught off guard, watched them in puzzlement. They looked bent on suicide. But instead of running straight at the Romans, the defenders ran to certain prearranged locations. They took their torches and set their piles aflame. For a second there was a small billow of black smoke, and then the whole colonnade burst into flames.

"It is a trap!" screamed Caputo in despair. "Commander Titus, they've laid a trap!"

The zealots had set barrels of pitch and dry tinder all around, and flames raced madly on all sides. The soldiers began screaming in panic as the flames spread to their own bodies. There was no escape — the fire was everywhere. Soldiers, many of them on fire, leapt to their deaths. Others stood on the colonnade burning like candles, dancing a frenzied death jig in their agony. On the colonnade walls, the sacred Roman ensigns burned in full view. It was an utter, shameful defeat.

Titus, white faced, turned away from the scene. He could not watch the defeat anymore. He headed down the ramp, followed by his lieutenants. Suddenly he stopped and pointed a trembling finger at Yoseph: "You — you with your harp! You cursed us! You did this — with your harp!"

IT WAS a sullen ride back to Titus's camp. The horses had been brought straightaway to the Antonia wall. Caputo and Yoseph made their way carefully through the Mishneh neighborhood, horses treading nervously over the pitiful corpses. Overwhelmed by the events of the battle, Yoseph did not even think about the desecration. He tried to understand why they were looking at him with such hatred, as though he was responsible for their calamity.

Caputo rode alongside silently. From time to time, their horses brushed against each other. Yoseph glanced at Caputo, who returned his look with a mixture of anger, curiosity — and fear.

Does he know who I am? wondered Yoseph. *Does he remember me?*

Yoseph would not have been surprised if Caputo did not remember him. Caputo had matured in the two years since Sabba's death. His face had grown harder, darker. He looked ten years older.

I, too, have aged, Yoseph thought. *He does not know me.*

They exited the city, past the Third Wall, and turned south towards Titus's camp. The stench of death was gone. The camp came into sight, and Caputo signaled his squadron to halt.

"Ride ahead of me back to the camp," he ordered. "I will ride behind with the prisoner."

His aide rode up to him. "Centurion Caputo, isn't that risky? The prisoner can break away from you."

"What's the matter, Marcellus?" Caputo snapped back impatiently. "You don't think I can outride this Jew if I have to? Ride ahead with the men!"

The aide retreated and signaled to the legionnaires. They rushed ahead, leaving Caputo and Yoseph in a cloud of brown dust.

There was still a kilometer to the camp entrance. "Ride slowly," Caputo told Yoseph. "I want to talk to you."

They rode awhile in silence. Exhausted and dazed, Yoseph wondered what he wanted.

When Caputo said nothing, Yoseph finally broke the strained silence himself. "You know, Centurion, I had nothing to do with Titus's defeat."

Caputo nodded. "Of course I know. It was our own stupidity."

"So why does everyone blame me? I never wanted to go to the battle. It was Titus's orders."

Caputo suddenly reined his horse to a halt.

"Haven't you figured it out yet?" he asked. "Titus is crazy! He is the second most powerful man in the world after his father — someday he will be Caesar of Rome. He thinks he is a god and only a divine power can defeat him.

"By the way — what dealings have you ever had with Princess Berenice?"

"Dealings?" asked Yoseph in astonishment. "What dealing does a Tapuach shepherd have with a Jerusalem princess? I never saw her in my life until that celebration, when Josephus tried to make me play my harp."

"Well, something you did charmed her. She has spoken to Titus about you many times. She thinks that harp has special power — because you are a Levite. She says it contains the power of the holy altar. That is why Titus is holding you — until he will be ready to challenge you."

Yoseph could not help but cry out with frustration. "What does everyone want from me? Titus, Berenice, you — everyone! That crazy giant Rufus, why does he shadow me? I am just a simple shepherd from Samaria. I didn't even plan to come to Jerusalem, but was sent here to hear the holy word. Why can't Titus just send me home to my wife and forget all about me?"

Caputo sneered. "The moon will fall into the sea before you're ever set free."

All this time, their conversation had been almost casual, as if they were two old acquaintances. Caputo had been almost likable. Yoseph felt it was a disgrace to Sabba's memory if he did not finally speak up. Caputo began trotting slowly again, signaling to Yoseph to follow him.

"Wait, Centurion," Yoseph said quickly, "wait one second. I have to tell you something."

"What?" Caputo asked warily, reining in again and wheeling his horse to face Yoseph.

"Do you know who I am? Do you remember me?"

"Remember you — from where?" He looked carefully at Yoseph, suspecting a trick. "Maybe...who are you?"

"You crucified my grandfather."

Caputo stared at him, a deep look of alarm descending on his face. He shook his head so violently that Yoseph grew frightened.

"No!" he shouted.

"Yes, Caputo — the poor old man in the Motza camp who would not declare Caesar a god."

"And you wouldn't, either!"

"No! He would not betray our faith, and for that you made him die a horrible death!"

Caputo grew very distraught. He stared wildly at Yoseph and wheeled his horse this way and that as if he wanted to escape but could not. His face was ashen. It was Yoseph who calmed him.

"Why are you so agitated?" he asked with real curiosity. "Is my grandfather the only Jew you ever executed?"

Caputo lifted his trembling finger, pointed at Yoseph, and shook his head vehemently.

"I dreamt this moment over and over! I dreamt that I would be sitting next to you on a horse, and that you would tell me about your grandfather. Your grandfather kept on appearing in my dreams, warning me that he would send his grandson after me!"

Now Yoseph shook his head. "I don't understand you, Caputo."

"Didn't you hear me? I dreamt the very words you are saying. Your grandfather came to me in my dreams and warned me, 'I will send my grandson back to you, you will be riding together, and he will say, "Do you remember me? You executed my grandfather!" ' And it's happened! It's happening right now!

"What do you want from me, Jew? Leave me alone! They are right — you do have special power. Titus is right!"

Yoseph shook his head and shouted, "I have no special power! I am just reminding you of the terrible deed you did, and that there is a God in this world who remembers everything — everything! That doesn't take a wizard!"

But Caputo was having nothing of that. He stared at Yoseph wildly like he was bewitched.

"We ride back to the camp — now!" he ordered.

He whipped his horse around and, making sure that Yoseph was following, raced madly back to Titus's camp. Yoseph struggled to keep up, unable to comprehend the sudden turn of events.

Who is the prisoner and who is the warden? he wondered.

And Rachel Called...

SHE STOOD beneath the apple tree and gazed up at the thin new moon. It was difficult for her to walk now. Leah begged Rachel not to reveal herself when there was still light in the sky. But it was Rosh Chodesh Av and the only chance she had to gaze upon the hair-thin crescent moon was at dusk, when the purple sunset still lit the tops of the pine trees.

Yoseph, Yoseph, why do you conceal your face from me when I long for you so much? How can I speak to you when I can barely see your beautiful countenance? Have you forgotten me? For if not, where is the warm breath of your whispering, the flicker of your holy radiance? Now all I see is darkness and a crescent moon as cold and honed as a scimitar!

Have you forgotten me, my Yoseph? Are you even in this world? Will our baby ever see your face?

Speak to me, Yoseph, whisper, whisper!

I am all by myself, except for my sister Leah. They have all been swept away, Abba and all his wives, our brothers and sisters, our servants — scattered to the four winds. Why did Hashem spare me? Only because of you, Yoseph, for I was not with them in Dotan, but my soul fled to you in Yerushalayim. I hover each day at your side, your Torah my Torah, your mitzvot my mitzvot, you are my well — and I your wall.

Look, the moon sinks into the trees — you are leaving me so soon! But Yoseph, soon the day of birth will come, and then I shall seek you out.

If you do not return to me, I shall climb the hills of Yerushalayim! I shall bring my kinnim to the altar, and I shall not rest until I set my eyes upon you again!

Chodesh tov, my beloved Yoseph, chodesh tov. We will meet again when the moon is full, and your face shines bright with holy luminescence....

And Yoseph Answered...

YOSEPH FOUND a place to hide just as the thin moon grazed the tops of Jerusalem's hills. He stood on a little stone bench deep in the confinement of Titus's camp, hidden from the watchful gaze of the Praetorian sentries. It was his last whispered good-bye before the unknown suffering that lay ahead.

Rachel, my Rachel, how pale your face is, a tiny white tear on the rose-colored face of dusk! Do you still remember me? Were we really once husband and wife, or was it some dream I had? No, it was real, for if not for you I would not be here.

So much has happened so fast. The battle is almost over. The last defenders have retreated into the Mikdash, together with thousands of poor Jews who think they will be spared miraculously at the last moment. I hear the grinders honing their swords for the coming slaughter. The Romans will do what they want, as Hashem has decreed. An ancient kohein named Ezra told me that it was foretold — the doors of the Heichal have swung open by themselves to admit the enemy.

Rachel, the Romans have a mad idea in their heads. They think I have a power to curse them. They were defeated twice when I witnessed their battles. Now they have taken away my harp. I plead with them for its return, but they refuse. General Titus plays with me like a puppet on a string. He hates me, he fears me, he does not know what to do with me. Every day I await his summons — but it does not come.

Have I told you about the giant Rufus? He blots out the moon with his shoulders; his strength is not human. And he does not take his eyes off me. He watches over me, protects me — and yet in a second he would destroy me. He comes to my tent and taunts me, warns that Titus will crucify me on the walls of Jerusalem. Then he laughs!

Rachel, I fear we will never see each other again. Even now your thin form turns away and disappears from sight. You are so far, but in my heart you are all around me, like a wall draped in roses.

Bitachon, Rachel, bitachon!

Chapter Seven

Nine days before the Churban

Rosh Chodesh Av arrived, bright and blazing. An orange sun plowed across the morning sky, its rays bleaching every stone and tent sheet white. The camp roads were deserted, except for the Roman guards who stood silent watch. All the guests of Titus's privileged prison sought shelter in their tents. The battle had reached the Temple walls, and all day the iron battering rams thundered against the Mikdash gates.

Yoseph rose to go to the synagogue, but Elazar approached him with a special request. "Sabba wishes to make his own minyan today. Please stay to help us."

Yoseph did not know why this day should be different from any other, except that it was Rosh Chodesh. Elazar and Nadav made every effort to shield their Sabba from guests. Otherwise, the tent would have been filled day and night with people seeking his blessing. But today Nadav was dispatched to collect six more men, absolutely no more, to form a minyan.

At first no one appeared, and Yoseph recited psalms. Why was it so hard to find six men for a minyan? he wondered. Ezra sat impatiently at the edge of his couch, wrapped in his tallit and tefillin.

Presently, there was a commotion outside — a crowd had gathered. Yoseph heard Nadav's voice arguing — begging someone to enter? Suddenly, the tent flap flew open. Nadav raced in, looking exasperated. It was soon clear why. Rushing in behind him were two dozen men, all wrapped in tallit and tefillin. They all wanted to pray with Ezra! Some of the men were great sages; others were young scholars eager to gaze at Ezra. When the tent could hold no more, Nadav ran to the door and sealed the flap closed.

Ezra rose from his couch and hobbled to the eastern wall, facing the Mikdash. He began *Pesukei D'Zimrah* in a singsong chant. It was a melody that Yoseph had never heard before, but some of the older men were familiar with it and chanted along, word by word. Soon everyone picked up the chant, and the tent came alive with holy verses.

As the prayers progressed, Ezra's whole body began swaying vigorously. He bent low for *Barechu* like a young man, and when he pronounced the Shema the whole room caught on fire. A wind from Eden swept through the tent, a scented gust from the Mikdash. Reciting *Shemoneh Esrei*, Yoseph shut his eyes and whispered *Yaaleh V'Yavo* with such a passion, a yearning he had never known before. He felt he was standing again in the Mikdash, standing with Hillel, standing with Shammai, aflame!

Finally, the prayers ended, and a quiet descended on the room. The men stood about uncertainly, dropping their tallitot from their heads. Some hoped for a Rosh Chodesh blessing from Ezra, who still stood with his head buried in the wall of the tent.

"*Chodesh tov, rabbotai.*" Elazar waved his hands to shoo them out, politely but firmly.

Suddenly, Ezra turned around. "No! No!" he cried. He waved his arm broadly, gesturing for them to stay.

"We will make a *l'chayim* together!"

His grandsons looked at him with consternation and surprise, but the old man was firm. The visitors were surprised — but delighted.

But how could they make a *l'chayim* without wine? As the older men seated themselves cross-legged at Ezra's feet, Elazar and Nadav searched the tent for refreshments. A few younger visitors ran out and were soon back with wine jugs. In a few minutes, a half-dozen jugs of wine, some full, some half empty, stood on the small table in front of Ezra's couch. The old man poured the wine himself, and Nadav and Elazar, together with Yoseph, distributed the cups to the men. All this was done in almost complete silence. No one wanted to speak before Ezra or to break the holy spell that had spread over the gathering.

Although he did not look up, Ezra saw everything. Only when the very last one of the assembled received his drink did he raise his cup.

In a strong voice, he recited the *berachah*: "*Baruch atah...borei peri hagafen!*"

He lifted the cup to his lips and took a large swallow. It was strong wine, and Elazar tried to take the cup from him. But Ezra shooed him away.

"*Rabbotai, l'chayim!*"

"*L'chayim!*" they responded.

"*Chodesh tov!*"

"*U'mevorach!*"

Ezra lowered his cup to the table, and Elazar discreetly reached to remove it. Ezra pushed his hand away, and the cup stayed.

"*Rabbotai*," Ezra began, his voice made robust from the wine, "do you know why I asked you to join me today, to pray and drink *l'chayim*?"

He paused dramatically. All were silent, waiting.

"It is my birthday today, my *yom huledet*!"

There was an instant of stunned silence, and then an outburst of shouts: "*Mazal tov! Ad meah v'esrim! Chazak u'baruch!*"

Ezra lifted his cup: "*L'chayim! L'chayim!*"

He directed his blessings in every direction, telling each guest, "*L'chayim! L'chayim!*"

He took another deep gulp of wine. Again Elazar tried to remove the cup, and this time he received a firm slap on his hand.

Ezra was taking too much wine.

"Today, the birthday of Aharon the High Priest, is also my birthday! I am one hundred and four years old! *Hodu laShem ki tov!*"

There was a momentary silence, and someone shouted, "May you soon offer the holy *temidim* on the altar!"

Another voiced echoed, "May you merit to stand next to the high priest on the steps of the *ulam*!"

"May we all soon stand in the courtyards of the Holy Temple," cried a third.

Ezra smashed his cup down on the table, and wine splashed over its side. "Enough!" he shouted angrily, "Enough! How can you mention our holy Mikdash? What do you know of it? Did you see it in its glory, in its golden splendor?"

He ran his hand over his face, overcome with feeling. Elazar saw his chance and slipped away the cup. But it was too late. When Ezra looked up again, his face was flushed fiery red and his eyes gleamed. He spoke passionately, the passion of age, of wine, of an intemperate *kohein*.

Ezra waved his arm in a great arc before him, as if he was drawing a painting.

" '*Shinayich k'eider ha'recheilim she'alu min harachtzah* — Your teeth are like a flock of ewes that have come up from the washing....'

"Pesach, *rabbotai*, Pesach! They covered the hills of Jerusalem like snow, tens of thousands of snow-white lambs that had just passed through the pools for cleansing. By the tenth of Nissan, Yerushalayim was one great animal market. Hundreds of thousand of *olei regel* picked and chose among the sheep, seeking the fairest, most perfect animal.

"By midday of *erev Pesach*, they were gathered at the gates of the Temple, as far as the eye could see. In the days of King Agrippa, they counted the pilgrims — there were millions! *Am Hashem*, a nation of Hashem! There were no rich, no poor, no aristocrats, no kings. All were equal, all waited their turn. No one complained, no one pushed ahead. High up on the Temple wall, three silver *chatzotzrot* were sounded — the time for the *korban Pesach* had come!

"The great crowd of pilgrims marched forward like a huge wave. They climbed the steps to the *azarah*...."

Ezra paused and reached for his cup. It was gone. "Where is my wine?" he demanded.

"Go on, Sabba," Elazar urged. "We'll get you more soon."

Ezra rose in his seat. "Now, can you see this — you young men who never knew the Mikdash its glory? Millions and millions of Jews, brothers all, from all corners, from all lands, all manner of tongues, rich and poor, *parush* and *am ha'aretz*, all squeezing into the *azarah*. How was it possible? But they did it.

"The Leviim kept order — they were strict! They were a stern bunch, twelve outside and twelve inside the *azarah*. They held silver and gold staves, and woe to the person who tried to push ahead or cause disorder! Otherwise, it would have been a *churban*!

"And the sacrifice of the *korban Pesach*! What commotion, what *simchah*, what excitement! Line after line of *kohanim*, stretching from every corner of the courtyard to the *mizbei'ach*. There were rows of gold vessels and rows of silver ones. We passed the chalices up to the *mizbei'ach* like lightning —"

Ezra rose in his excitement. He passed one arm over the other swiftly, like a juggler passing his torches. He stared straight ahead, lost in his memories.

"Fast! Fast! Fast! No time to talk! Pass the full chalice, take back the empty.... Fast! Fast! Fast! Don't drop anything! Don't break the chain....

"Blood! Blood! Blood! Everywhere blood, pouring down the altar wall, all over the floor, up to our ankles. This was the blood of Pesach, the blood of our *cheirut*! The Levites chanted Hallel on the *duchan*, while the musicians played flutes and harps and drums and lyres on the Temple steps!

"The whole Temple shone with *simchah shel mitzvah*!

"And Yerushalayim, O holy Yerushalayim on the night of the seder, that holy night under the silver stars! The aroma of thousands and thousands of *korban Pesach* lambs roasting, the sweetness of *matzot mitzvah* on our lips, the tang of *maror* on our tongues, the Hallel, the Hallel!

"Tell me, did you ever hear a million Jews singing Hallel in one great breath, holy song pouring out from every door and window and rooftop? A city alive with *kedushah*! With *taharah*! With *shirah*! With *zimrah*! That was Yerushalayim! That was Yerushalayim! What do you know, you youngsters, what did you ever see? Who did you ever see? Who did you know?"

The old man stood there, oblivious to everyone, swept up in his memories. The men looked at him with awe and fear, and Elazar rose to calm him. He wrapped his arm lovingly about Ezra's shoulder.

"Come, dear Sabba, calm yourself. Come sit down."

Ezra looked at his grandson numbly. He gazed around the room and peered at his guests, then lowered himself to his couch.

He closed his eyes and ran his hand over his face. Then he looked up, an amused smile on his face. He seemed pleased at his own outburst.

"*Rabbotai*, perhaps you are tired of hearing an old man's stories? Do you want to hear more?"

"Sabba, you are tired," Elazar protested.

"Who says I am tired?" Ezra answered impatiently. "And if I am tired, I assure you that I will soon have all of eternity to rest." He turned to his company. "*Rabbotai*, do you wish to hear more?"

One of the men rose. "Holy Sabba Ezra, every word you utter is precious. We wish to hear more and more."

Ezra turned to Nadav. "Where is my wine?"

With no choice, Nadav returned Sabba's cup, filling it halfway.

The old man lifted the cup to his guests. "*L'chayim! L'chayim*!" he murmured, and drank from it gratefully.

As he was drinking, one of the guests called out, "Rabbeinu Ezra, tell us about Yom Kippur in the old days!"

The old man ignored him and quaffed his drink. Perhaps he did not hear. Finally, he put down his cup. An expectant silence filled the tent. Ezra's cheeks flushed bright red, and his eyes sparkled.

"Yom Kippur? How can I tell about Yom Kippur? Do you know the *kedushah* that filled the Mikdash? When it came time to slaughter the morning offering, the courtyards were so filled with worshipers that there was not an inch to move! But who was in that courtyard? What great men filled that courtyard! What *talmidei chachamim*! What tzaddikim! Men who spent their whole lives serving Hashem! They squeezed cheek by jowl just to glimpse the *kohein gadol* at his *avodah*! I was young and foolish, I did not realize my good fortune. Because my father was one of the wardens of the Mikdash, I was right there, right up front, scurrying here and there to assist. I looked down on the courtyard of the Israelites and it was a sea of faces, staring up at the *kohein gadol*. Many had not slept all night, they were trapped like fish in a net, yet they stood with awe, fear, and respect."

A mischievous smile crossed Ezra's lips.

"I know — you look at me, a man from the old days, from back when, a man from the days of Hillel, of Yonatan ben Uziel — you say, that Ezra, he looks like a righteous *kohein*!"

He waved his hand in disgust. "You don't know what a holy face is if you did not see the face of High Priest Yishmael ben Elisha! He was so handsome, so perfect, his features like those of a *malach* that you could not even gaze at for their holiness, a soul as pure as melted snow...."

He looked around and searched the tent for intruders. Then he lowered his voice confidentially.

"Now I will tell you a secret. You see, my grandsons tried to stop me, but I have not drunk wine for no reason. *Nichnas yayin, yatza sod* — wine enters, and the secret spills out! It is time to share secrets. For if I do not share them with you before I die, how will you ever know?"

Ezra rose up and lifted his arm in a great arc, drawing another scene.

"*V'hakohamin v'ha'am* — the priests and the people, when they heard Hashem's glorious, awesome Name — *Hasheim hanichbad v'hanora meforash yotzei mipi kohein gadol be'kedushah uv'taharah* — emanating from the *kohein gadol*'s mouth in holiness and purity...they fell to their knees and bowed in awe!"

Ezra dropped his voice even lower. "Now, I ask you, why were they in such awe?"

He pointed a challenging finger at his guests. "You say, Ezra, because they heard Hashem's holy name the way it is written — *kichsavah*! Yes? No! They heard that name every day! Every day, Hashem's name was mentioned in the Mikdash the way it is written! So why such awe, such trembling now? I will tell you a secret —"

Ezra lowered his voice to a whisper, and the visitors leaned forward to hear.

"On Yom Kippur Hashem's holy name emanated from the *kohein gadol*'s mouth on its own! Do you hear me — from *Shamayim*! They fell in awe because the *kohein gadol* had reached such holiness that Hashem spoke through his throat! A human being became a *malach*!"

Ezra gazed at the men staring open mouthed at him, and a smile lit his ancient, weathered face. He lifted his finger and pointed at them. "You like my secrets, don't you? Do you want to hear more?"

They sat there, spellbound. No one spoke. Finally one of the men said, "Yes, we want to hear more, Sabba Ezra! We want to hear everything."

"Everything? Everything you will not hear, for I do not know it all. But —" he lifted his cup, "*nichnas yayin, yatza sod*! Fill my cup, and I will tell you one more secret —"

Elazar grew very alarmed. "Sabba, enough! It is not safe!"

Ezra looked at him blankly and then turned to the visitors. "What say you, *rabbotai*? Do you want to hear more or not?"

"Elazar, let your grandfather speak."

Elazar turned and scowled fiercely at the man, but he was unapologetic. "What your grandfather can teach us, no one else can. When he passes from this world, who will tell us?"

An older guest raised his voice gently. "Perhaps, Ezra, we can compromise. Elazar is correct to worry. Perhaps your grandson will serve just a little more wine, and you will tell us a bit more."

The others nodded their agreement. Reluctantly, Elazar filled the cup to a third, and then firmly removed the wine jug. Ezra raised the cup to his prominent visitors.

"*L'chayim, rabbotai, chodesh tov!* May we be worthy to sit in the shade of Leviathan's skin and feast from the flesh of the Great Ox! *L'chayim tovim*!"

Ezra drank from the wine, wiping away the droplets that had spilled on his beard. If Elazar feared the strong drink would make his grandfather foolish, he was mistaken. The playful smile left his face, and his brow furrowed. He closed his eyes in concentration and began swaying fervently, summoning up all his memories and all the sparks of *kedushah* of a hundred years of Temple service. He spoke in a whisper, his eyes shut, and the visitors drew close to hear each word.

"He entered the Kodesh HaKodashim on Yom Kippur, and he held the chalice containing the blood of the sin offering in his hand. He had not eaten, he had not drunk, he had not slept, he had purified himself with immersion after immersion. He dipped his finger into the sacred blood and sprinkled upward before the Holy Ark and he sang: '*Achat*!' "

Ezra paused, and there was silence.

"*Rabbotai*," he cried, "you must sing with me — '*Achat*!' "

"*Achat*!" they sang back.

"Quickly, he dipped his finger again into the blood, and sprinkled downward towards the ark, and he sang: '*Achat, ve'achat*!' "

Ezra paused, waiting for an answer.

"*Achat ve'achat*!" they responded.

" '*Achat u'shtayim!*' "

"*Achat u'shtayim!*"

" '*Achat veshalosh*!' "

"*Achat veshalosh*!"

" '*Achat ve'arba*!' "

"*Achat ve'arba!*"

" '*Achat vechameish*!' "

"*Achat vechameish!*"

" '*Achat vasheish*!' "

"*Achat vasheish!*"

" '*Achat vasheva*!' "

"*Achat vasheva!*"

Ezra sang in a whisper, his eyes squeezed tight, his thoughts entering deeper and deeper into the mysteries of the Kodesh HaKodashim, the profound *kavanot* of the high priest, the union with the holiest of holy.

"One plus one, one plus two, one plus three, one plus four, one plus five, one plus six, one plus seven...."

"Again, *rabbotai*, again, again!"

He lifted his arms and squeezed his hands into two fists, shaking them with powerful emotion. His eyes were shut tightly, and he sang again: " '*Achat!*' "

Together, the ancient *kohein* and his visitors repeated the holy counting. Many of the men had closed their eyes like Ezra, transported out of their prison, out of their suffering, to a higher world. Suddenly, Ezra stopped abruptly and opened his eyes. He lifted his voice.

"Children, do you know the secret of the high priest's count? *Achat*! There is one *achat* above, one Holy One who is unknowable and unseeable, an *Ein Sof* who we cannot comprehend or even understand! One, just one, alone and incomprehensible!"

He paused, leaned forward, and murmured almost to himself, "Look to the *yud*...."

Suddenly, he sat up straight and raised his voice. "This is not what Hashem wanted, but to allow His *kedushah* to come down, down into our bitter world, through the seven *sefirot*, down into the world of *Asiyah*.

"*Achat*! One Above, the *Ein Sof*.

"*Achat ve'achat* — one plus one into the world of *chesed*.

"*Achat u'shtayim* — one plus two into the world of *gevurah*.

"*Achat veshalosh* — one plus three into the world of *tiferet*.

"*Achat ve'arba* — one plus four into the world of *netzach*.

"*Achat vechamesh* — one plus five into the world of *hod*.

"*Achat vasheish* — one plus six into the world of *yesod*.

"*Achat vasheva* — one plus seven into the world of *malchut*."

Ezra began shouting. "Do you understand me, *rabbotai*? From the highest realms, realms we cannot comprehend, *malchut* descended into our dark world. Every blade of grass, every stone shines with Godliness! And the *kohein gadol* raised it all up, raised it up — raised it up — raised up the whole world and united above and below!

"*Achat*! There is nothing but Hashem — do you hear? Listen to me! Listen to an old man who has lived one hundred and four years and has seen all — there is nothing but Godliness!

"Do not be afraid! Even at the last moment, do not run! Lift your hand Heavenward and you will prevail!"

Ezra rose in his agitation, his face beet red. Elazar and Nadav leaped up to calm him, grasping his arms and gently lowering him back to the couch. The visitors, shaken by the old man's outburst, rose as one to leave.

Suddenly the tent flap flew open. The visitors were pushed out the entrance as a half-dozen Roman soldiers flooded into the room. Ezra, his grandsons, and Yoseph froze in place, but the soldiers did not approach them. They remained stiffly at attention near the door.

Presently, the door opened again, and Caputo entered. His eyes fell on Yoseph, and a small smile crossed his face. He said nothing, only nodded. Yoseph ran quickly to Ezra, who lay wearily on his couch. He grasped the old man's hands and fell before him. "Master, they have come for me, bless me!"

Ezra raised his hand and placed it on Yoseph's head: "*Bein porat Yoseph, bein porat alei ayin* — a fruitful vine is Joseph, a fruitful vine upon the wall...."

Yoseph kissed his hand and rose. His eyes met Caputo's. The centurion nodded, turned, and exited the tent. Yoseph followed him out, the guards were right behind him. Caputo called him to his side, and the soldiers grouped around them.

"Titus wants you," he said. "Prepare yourself."

What he meant by "prepare yourself" Yoseph could not fathom. Surrounded by a half-dozen guards, summoned without warning, there was not much he could do to prepare. His fate was in Hashem's hands.

Titus's tent was in the center of the camp, and Yoseph tried to collect his thoughts. But their orderly march was suddenly interrupted by none other than...Rufus. Nothing passed his scrutiny! Even when he seemed to have disappeared, he was somewhere, watching. Seeing the procession heading to Titus's headquarters, he came flying to intercept it. He dashed straight at Caputo, and even the centurion looked frightened.

Caputo, not wanting to be overrun, ordered his men to halt.

"Where are you going with the Levite?" Rufus demanded.

"He is going to be interviewed by Titus," Caputo answered impatiently. "Do not hold us up with your questions. The commander is waiting."

"And when will he return?" Rufus demanded.

"Don't be impertinent — he'll return when and if Titus is ready to send him back."

Rufus would not back down. "Make sure he returns," he warned. "You're bringing him there, you make sure to bring him back."

He gave Caputo a withering look, and the centurion looked genuinely alarmed. Then the giant turned to Yoseph. "Make sure you do not get too clever with Commander Titus! Don't try to escape by using him! You can trick him, but you won't get away from me!"

He gave Yoseph a hard look and walked off. The guards looked at each other, smiling secretly.

Caputo regained his composure and ordered the company to proceed. The closer they came to Titus's tent, the heavier security grew. Caputo was stopped every dozen meters, and each time had to explain his mission — bringing the prisoner to Titus. A heavily armed phalanx of Praetorians circled Titus's tent, and high-ranking tribunes and generals rushed in and out of its entrance.

A hundred meters from the tent, Caputo ordered his men to halt.

"Go back to your duties," he ordered.

They looked at each other in puzzlement, then marched off briskly, leaving Caputo and Yoseph suddenly alone. Yoseph sensed there was something on the Roman's mind.

Caputo sauntered towards one of the small stone buildings that dotted the camp. They were used for storing arms or securing dangerous prisoners. Yoseph followed him until they were partially concealed by a wall but could see anyone approaching. Caputo studied Yoseph's face closely, as though trying to read his mind.

"Levite, who are you?" he asked.

"What do you mean, who am I? You know who I am — a Levite, a musician, Titus's prisoner."

"Are you a sorcerer?"

Yoseph shook his head in disbelief. He fought to keep his voice down. "Sorcerer? Why do you keep on asking me this? Centurion, have you had too much Judean sun? You know who I am. I am a simple shepherd, a Levite who worships his God!"

But Caputo persisted. "You have a power — even Titus is afraid of you. That is why he confiscated your harp. Our troops are ready to enter the Temple, but he won't move forward until he talks to you."

"Then Titus is mad!"

Caputo glared at him. Had he been anyone else, Caputo would have dispatched him right there. Yoseph grew frightened, knowing he had been too outspoken.

"I mean, the idea is crazy! The notion that I am a sorcerer or have some powers — it's not true! I am just a simple, unlearned Judean shepherd — why doesn't anyone believe me?"

"Levite, last night I had a dream. Your grandfather came to me and told me that Titus would summon you today. No one knew that — even Titus did not decide to call you until this morning. Your grandfather warned me to watch over you and make certain that no harm befell you...."

Yoseph was suddenly intrigued. "How did he look, my grandfather?"

"He looked — like he was glowing. His face was a magnet that drew me to him. He told me to protect you — and then he was gone. Look, there is something weird going on here between you and Titus and that giant Rufus, and I am in the middle of it. I don't fancy it at all."

"It's not my doing," Yoseph defended himself. "Whatever it is, I am caught in the middle of it just like you."

Caputo shrugged and looked around to make sure there was no one listening.

"Look, any minute you are going to be summoned before Titus. He is in awe of you. Princess Berenice has convinced him that you have divine powers. Don't be a fool. Your whole life will be determined in the next hour. Titus is in a very high mood. We are at the edge of a tremendous triumph. It's just a matter of days before the Temple is ours. The Upper City may hold out a little longer, but who cares? It's the Temple that means victory. Levite, he will ask you questions — tell him what he wants to hear. He will do what he wants to do anyway. Tell him that he will be victorious. Don't be a martyr. If you answer him the right way, he will reward you unbelievably. Then you'll be able to help your own people."

"Why do you take such interest in my welfare?"

Caputo stared hard at Yoseph and shook his head in frustration: "You just don't understand, do you?"

"You mean — my grandfather?"

Caputo's head nodded almost imperceptibly. "Yes...your grandfather."

They proceeded to Titus's headquarters. There was an air of

celebration despite the stone-faced guards who surrounded his tent. Victory was in the air, triumph for Titus, celebration for Rome. The huge Roman army was poised at the gates of the Temple. There was no second front, no distractions.

It was already midday when Yoseph and Caputo reached the tent, but, much to Yoseph's surprise, they were told to sit down and await their summons. Titus was in no rush. Generals, tribunes, centurions, and commanders of auxiliary armies came and went. They all wore ceremonial uniforms, proudly showing their medals and badges in honor of Titus. They entered the tent in a high state of excitement and left beaming and jubilant.

Night fell finally, and torches were lit around the tent. The night was warm, and hot winds blew the dry earth into tiny dust swirls. A thin moon appeared briefly over the western hills and was soon gone.

Presently, a procession of regally dressed officers escorted a group of women towards Titus's headquarters. As they approached, the Praetorians saluted sharply, and the other dignitaries who waited on Titus stepped back and bowed in deference. In the center of the group, a company of slaves carried a sedan bearing an exquisitely dressed woman. Her coiffured hair was crowned with a crescent of precious stones. There was an excited stir in the crowd. Yoseph recognized her as Princess Berenice.

Berenice's royal chair was set down before the tent flap, and she climbed out carefully, assisted by her attendants. A carpet was rolled out so that her dress not touch the dusty ground, and she strode regally into Titus's tent.

Still more dignitaries came and went, and Yoseph continued to wait. Presently, a half-dozen high officers left the tent together, having ended a critical meeting. Titus's war plans had been finalized, and now only special guests were invited to celebrate the evening.

Yoseph grew more and more uneasy. Why was he here? What business did he have with these people? Presently, a Praetorian guard emerged and headed for Caputo. "You can bring in the prisoner now," he said.

Prisoner? Yoseph felt sick.

An officer held the entrance open, and Yoseph followed Caputo inside. The large tent was lit up by lamps and torches. A row of imperial standards stood impressively against the back wall. Servants carried drinks and delicacies around the room, and there was an atmosphere of victory in the air. Titus sat on a dais, Berenice next to him. They were both relaxed, laughing with the generals and commanders. Yoseph was surprised to see that Josephus was there, too — he had not seen him in almost three months.

Caputo stood at the edge of the group, discreetly awaiting orders. Titus continued his banter, ignoring their entrance. Yoseph stared at the harp that lay on Titus's table — his harp. When he lifted his head, he saw Princess Berenice's eyes on him. He looked away.

Casually, Titus rose from his chair. He ambled towards the table and scooped up the harp. He held it up, admiring its strings, then plucked a string and cocked his ear. His face lit up, and he lifted his head triumphantly.

"Whose instrument is this?" he asked theatrically. He did not look in Yoseph's direction at all. Caputo pinched Yoseph's arm discreetly, signaling him to remain silent and let Titus play out his game.

Titus held the harp aloft and waved it before his guests. "What, no one claims such a beautiful instrument? I promise you, it is very potent."

He paused, enjoying himself. "No one?" He turned towards Yoseph. "Levite, perhaps you wish it back? It is yours, if you will play just one song for me. One song for Titus Flavius — what do you say, a deal?"

Yoseph looked down. Then he looked up, straight at Caesar, and shook his head.

Titus's face hardened. Like a summer storm, his face quickly darkened, and amusement turned to fury. He turned to Caputo. "Centurion — you received this cursed thing. By the morning, smash it to a hundred pieces!"

Caputo stepped forward briskly and took the harp from Titus.

Titus turned to Yoseph. "Come forward, Jew! Stand here, right before me!"

Yoseph hesitated, and Caputo almost pushed him forward. Yoseph stood just a few steps from Titus. The Praetorian guards moved very close, lest Yoseph reach out to harm their commander.

Titus, meanwhile, had collected himself, and the smile returned to his face.

"Tell me, Levite, where did you get that harp?"

"I made it myself."

"Yourself? You did not acquire it at the Temple?"

"No. I am a poor shepherd of Tapuach, in Samaria. My ancestors were musicians before the holy altar in Jerusalem. I prepared myself for the holy task by making my own instrument. The wood came from a cedar tree, and the strings from the dried veins of sheep."

"I have never heard you play. It is not too late — will you not play for me, for Princess Berenice who has kept you safe until now? Play one song, and the harp is yours again — and you are a free man!"

Yoseph shook his head. "I made that harp to sing to my God. A holy man heard me play and gave me a string that he spun himself. The beauty of my song is the beauty of the Temple and the beauty of the holy altar. It is not for any man, not even Caesar,"

There was a great stillness in the room. Yoseph's words were spoken quietly but firmly, with utmost sincerity and dignity. Titus looked at him, and then turned to Berenice. "You are right — he is special."

Turning to Josephus, he exclaimed, "General, I congratulate you on finding this precious jewel, this Levite. It will go to your honor."

"I offer all my honors to the service of Titus," Josephus answered grandly.

Titus snorted. He looked at Yoseph. "You have answered well. Perhaps I shall return your harp to you anyway — we shall see. But you are a sensible young man. Tell me — you speak about your great God. You sing to Him, the All Powerful. Where is He?"

Titus warmed to his question, and, gesturing with his hands in true Roman fashion, he shouted: "Tell me, where is He? Why has He not stopped me? My men are at the doors of His holiest place!

Do you know what a slaughter is going to happen? Five thousand fools have run up to the Temple because they think some holy man is going to appear at the last moment. Do you know what we are doing? Our grindstones are turning red hot, preparing our swords for the slaughter. We fought, you fought — but the battle is over. The defenders have wasted away to skin and bones — or died! What we will do now is not fight, but butcher — right at the foot of your Temple!"

Titus raised his voice. "Where is your God? Why does He not send a lightning bolt to strike me down? Give me an answer!"

Yoseph looked down and remained silent.

"Answer me!" Titus shouted angrily. "Where is your God? Why doesn't He show Himself? Why does He let me commit this desecration — why does He not fight me? Can't some Jew answer me that?"

Yoseph raised his head, near tears. "Mighty General, I don't know! I am not a sage, I am a plain shepherd. I cannot answer. There are seventy wise men, the sages — ask them! But —"

"But what?"

Yoseph shook his head. "Nothing."

"Speak!"

"I am just a shepherd, a simple shepherd."

"No, you are a coward! You have something to say, so say it."

Yoseph looked directly at Titus. "Before my grandfather died, he taught me about our Mikdash — our Temple. There are two Temples. There is the Temple here on earth, filled with priests and Levites, Israelites and converts. That Temple is the Temple that you will enter — there you have the power, for it was built by man. Perhaps we were not worthy of keeping that Temple, for we defiled it by our actions, our divisions and hatreds.

"But there is a Temple above this Temple of Jerusalem. It is the Beit HaMikdash shel Ma'alah, and there the high priest is the archangel Michael, and the sacrifices are the souls of the righteous who you have slaughtered, and the ashes are the ashes of our forefather Isaac. That Temple you cannot touch with all your legions, and when the time comes we shall worship in that holy place, and we will be triumphant, and our enemies will be abashed."

"What, will you climb to the Heavens?"

"No, but Heaven and Earth will be one, and the Kingdom of God will fill the universe."

Titus listened, and then burst out: "Phooey! Phooey!"

He lifted his arm and splayed his fingers. "You see this thumb — I have more power of life and death in this thumb than your God has in all His universe. He does not fight because He cannot fight me!"

Yoseph lost his reserve. He clapped his hands over his ears, squeezed his eyes shut, and began shouting at Titus, "Don't say that! You must not say that! I am not allowed to hear this!"

The guards ran up to him, but Titus drove them away.

Opening his eyes, Yoseph pointed at Titus. "You are wrong, General! You are just flesh and blood! Our God lifted you up and if He wishes — He can bring you down!"

There was a shocked silence in the room. Titus stared hard at Yoseph but did not answer immediately. Finally he answered mockingly, "Then let Him beat my thumb — just my thumb!"

"My God has beaten your thumb many times over! You can kill by a wave of your thumb, but my God performs wonders with the whole hand!"

Yoseph lifted his index finger. "With this finger our high priest purifies the soul of Israel in the Holy of Holies, sprinkling heavenly light into great darkness." He stuck out his fourth finger. "With this finger he performs the tithing of the life-giving grains, drawing out the holy sparks from the earth and igniting them heavenwards on the altar...." He lifted his thumb boldly in front of Titus's face.

"You can kill a man with your thumb — but you cannot destroy his soul! You cannot touch his soul! Yet a drop of Temple blood on the thumb of a leper purifies his spirit and restores him to the holy nation!

"Commander Titus, we have the power of God, of the spirit! Our God is mighty, and your armies are just His playthings."

Titus smiled at Yoseph's words. He turned to his generals and tribunes.

"You hear, fellows? Our legions are God's playthings!"

There was a gale of laughter. Yoseph turned to Josephus for

help — but Josephus just shook his head in pity.

Titus was exuberant. "So — your Jewish fingers are stronger than our Roman thumbs. Very good! Let me see your beautiful hand."

Yoseph stood stock still, confused by Titus's request.

"Your hand," he ordered. "Let me see your hand that has all those holy, all-powerful fingers."

Self-consciously, Yoseph lifted his hand, spreading his fingers. Titus took it in his hands, squeezed it, and moved it up and down, measuring its weight.

"Yes, a good hand — fine, strong fingers. Too delicate for a shepherd, though. No, you have the hands of a philosopher, of a saint."

He turned to Caputo. "Centurion, come here."

Caputo approached Titus.

"Your hand," Titus ordered.

Caputo raised his hand, and now Titus held both hands in his, Yoseph's and Caputo's. He lifted them together, as if he was weighing one against the other. Then he lay Caputo's palm flat on the back of Yoseph's hand, finger to finger.

"Yes," he said, "they are about the same size, a fair match."

He dropped their hands and turned to Berenice. "So, my Jewish princess, you got your wish to see the Levite again. He is obstinate, you see that."

"He has so much faith, Titus," she answered. "That gives him his courage. Please do not punish him!"

"Punish? Who spoke of punishment? No, we will have a contest. Let us see how powerful his God — and his holy hand — is. Caputo — you will represent Rome. You, Levite, will represent what is holy to you, your Temple, your God — even your harp."

He turned to his guards. "Set two chairs on either side of the table."

The chairs were set, facing each other. A guard raced to the side of the room where the harp lay and brought it to Titus. Titus raised it high, showing it off to his guests.

He smiled and announced: "We shall see who has the power — the mighty God of the Jews, or one of the tiny 'playthings' of the Roman legions. The pagan thumb of Rome, or the hallowed fingers of Jerusalem."

Yoseph and Caputo sat down at the table. One of the Praetorians came forward and set their hands on each other, palm to palm. Awkwardly, Yoseph and Caputo set their elbows against the stone tabletop and grasped each other's hand tightly. They stared into each other's eyes, trying to understand. They were of enemy peoples, but they were mysteriously bonded — by Sabba. There could be no middle way — one would win, and one would lose. If Yoseph won, he would regain his harp, capable of defeating powerful enemies. If Caputo lost, he would be destroyed before Titus and disgrace the Roman legions.

I must win, thought Yoseph.

Their eyes locked, their fingers squeezed each other's tightly, and they struggled against each other's grip. Caputo's short tunic sleeve fell back, revealing muscles like iron. His face turned deep red as blood rushed to his head. Yoseph's arm was thinner and less developed, but still his years of shepherding had instilled it with considerable power. His face flushed, but he breathed deeply and evenly, and he could exert equal force on Caputo's hand.

Their arms were still upright, one bending for an instant and then regaining strength and bending the other. The rules forbade them from lifting their elbows off the table or rising from their seats to push with their weight. They struggled, emitting loud grunts when the other prevailed, barking loudly as they fought back. Titus clasped the harp to his chest and hovered above them like a referee. Princess Berenice rose from her chair in her excitement, and the other dignitaries forgot Titus's regal presence and crowded closer to watch the match.

Suddenly, both wrestlers knew that something had happened. Caputo looked up and met Yoseph's gaze. Yoseph knew also. Caputo's greater strength was beginning to overwhelm him. Yoseph held on desperately, but that was all he could do. He had no more strength to push back Caputo.

Slowly, inexorably, Yoseph's arm began bending backwards, downward. He pushed back with all his might, but all he could do was slow his defeat. Now, his face, too, was deep red, and a smile spread over Titus's face. The general ran his fingers in triumph over the harp strings, back and forth, back and forth.

The sound of his harp playing filled Yoseph's soul. It reminded him of the holy man's blessing, of Rachel, of the child waiting to be born. It was the sound of Tapuach, the scent of the apple tree, the song of the Levites, flooding down into his soul, into his body, into his arm, into his fierce grip.

Yoseph breathed deeply, and his face grew dark with intense rage. His arm turned into stone, and Caputo's advance was stopped cold. Yoseph took a deep breath and pushed upwards. Caputo fought back with all his might, but Yoseph's arm rose to the center, and then over the top to the other side. Caputo struggled, but now it was he who could only protect himself. There was no way Caputo could resist, but still, still he struggled. The expression on Titus's face turned to dismay. Yoseph glanced up to watch his foe's final collapse, and suddenly he saw his Sabba staring at him.

Sabba, why are you here? asked Yoseph.

Let him win, Sabba whispered.

But I am so close to beating him, beating our enemy!

Let him win, warned Sabba. *As Yaakov bowed to Eisav, let him win!*

But Israel must win, Sabba, we must win.

We will win, we will win — but now, bow before Eisav — let him win!

Suddenly, Yoseph's immense strength began seeping out of his hand. As suddenly as it had flowed to him, so now it ran out. Caputo, sensing the change, stared at Yoseph with bewilderment, fearing some trick. He pushed hard against Yoseph's hand, and, bereft of strength, Yoseph's hand collapsed back to the table.

Caputo stared at Yoseph in stunned disbelief, not comprehending his sudden victory. Titus was all over Caputo, embracing him, waving the harp triumphantly.

"We beat the Jewish God!" he shouted. "The fat Roman thumb beat the whole hand of the Jewish God!"

Yoseph sat, also in shock. Victory had been near, and it was snatched from him. Why? Why had Sabba done this to him? He looked around, but no one would look back. Behind him, Princess Berenice was crying.

That night, a new, stony-faced escort of Praetorians returned Yoseph to his tent. Caputo remained with Titus, to be feted and rewarded. For Yoseph, it was all over.

Chapter Eight

The Churban

Yoseph awoke the next morning to find himself alone. Where were Ezra and his grandsons? He washed his hands and wet his eyes. He recalled the events of the night before — arguing with the mighty Titus, wrestling with the centurion Caputo — had it all been a dream? Here he was back in his tent, and it all seemed so unreal.

He stepped outside the tent and knew at once that last night's memory was no dream. A half-dozen grim, unfamiliar Praetorian guards stood guard outside his tent. They did not acknowledge him in any way as he exited, but when he began walking to the synagogue, an escort of four guards followed silently at his heels. He was under special watch — by Titus's orders.

When he entered the synagogue, the men were already praying. He quickly donned his tallit and tefillin and found his place. No one acknowledged him, but as he prayed he saw the worshipers watching him furtively. *Something is going on here*, he thought. He forced himself to drive away outside thoughts and pray with *kavanah*. It was a test of his will, and he refused to fail.

"Ribbono shel Olam," he murmured, "I have done mine. Now You do Yours."

Shacharit ended, and Yoseph approached one of the men who had been at his tent the day before.

"Do you know where Ezra is?" he asked.

The man shrugged his shoulders and rushed off. The same happened with two other men he approached — they were afraid to speak to him. Finally, he approached the sage who had shown such gentle wisdom with Ezra.

"Master," he pleaded, "what happened to Ezra? Why is everyone running away from me?"

The scholar hesitated, then looked around furtively. "We are being watched," he whispered. "There is an informer in our midst watching you. That's why they are all afraid. The Romans took Ezra away in the middle of the night."

He rose and hurried out of the synagogue. Yoseph looked around. Who was the informer? How could a fellow Jew do this to him? It chilled him. There were still many men left in the synagogue, studying, reciting *Tehillim*. He had wanted to stay in their company, but the knowledge that a traitor was in their midst sickened him.

He returned to his own tent, dogged by the guards.

For the first time in months he was truly alone, bereft even of his harp. He chanted verses of *Tehillim*, but his lonely voice made the room seem emptier. He daydreamed of Rachel, of the baby. Was she alive? Was he a father? Would he die today?

He floated in a vacuum, not knowing anything. He rested his head against his hand and prayed to the God who knew everything. "Please, help me!"

He was trapped in a mood of fantastic speculation and fear, but at last, sick of himself, he broke free of it. He could not take this isolation. Better the company of the informer than the torture of his imagined fears. He washed himself, changed into a fresh tunic, and prepared to go back to the synagogue.

He was about to leave the tent when he heard a heavy fumbling at the tent flap. Someone was eager to enter. Was it Ezra returning? The tent flap burst open, and there was — Rufus! The giant rushed into the tent, filling it with his immense bulk. His face was flushed and he seemed very agitated. Yoseph actually welcomed him with a smile. Even the colossus was a welcome break from his loneliness.

"You've done it now, Levite."

"My name is Yoseph, Rufus, not Levite. What are you talking about?"

"You're the talk of the camp. What happened last night with you and the centurion?"

"We had an arm-wrestling match. I almost beat him, but he

won. What is the big deal?"

"And you insulted Commander Titus to his face?"

"I didn't insult anyone. He asked me questions, and I answered him truthfully. I told him there is a God in the world and that He will prevail."

"Well, couldn't you have said it in a way that didn't make Titus lose face in front of Princess Berenice and the rest?"

"I am not a politician. I am a simple shepherd, a musician."

Rufus lifted his great hand roughly so that Yoseph feared he was going to strike him. He looked at Yoseph with anger — and pity.

"You are a dead shepherd, a dead singer — that's what you are! I tried to protect you, Titus tried to honor you — and you could not listen to anyone! When you lost to Caputo, you broke the spell over Titus — and Berenice. You lost everything and now Titus is going to finish you off!"

The blood ran from Yoseph's face. "What do you mean?"

Rufus ran his thumb over his own neck.

"He's saving you for the last. The final assault against the Temple is coming in a few days. Titus himself will direct it. And when they get into the holiest place, Titus himself will slit your throat there!"

In his shock, Yoseph could hardly speak. "How — how do you know this?"

"One of the Praetorian officers told me. Titus wanted to kill you from the first time you were insolent, but Berenice and Josephus held him back. Josephus really admires you! But you — you know better than anyone! You have to open that big mouth. You can't keep anything under your tongue! You have to be a hero! Well, good-bye, Levite!"

"Is that why you have been so jealous about guarding me, because Josephus ordered you?"

"Josephus is my god! He has more brains than any ten men I know! Once one of my captains wanted to have me scourged because I slept on the job, and Josephus saved me. Someday, when I am done fighting, he is going to bestow me my own estate. When someone is loyal to me, I am ten times as loyal to them.

"But you, big mouth — you threw it all away! Now Titus has ordered me to keep watch over you!"

"Titus?"

"He knows all about me. He calls me the Colossus of Rome!" Rufus's chest swelled with pride momentarily, and then he returned to his original subject. "I tried, Levite, I tried. And now, pray hard — because you are going to your Jewish paradise any day!"

Yoseph could not answer for shock.

Rufus raised his massive arms, displaying their trunk-like thickness, and glared at Yoseph.

"Levite — Rufus is watching you. Don't try anything! You hear? When the time comes, I myself am going to carry you to Titus!"

He stormed towards the door.

"Rufus!" Yoseph cried out.

The giant stopped at the entrance, turned to Yoseph, smiled, and saluted briskly: "G-o-o-d-b-y-e-e-e, Yoseph!"

Yoseph stared at the closed tent flap. Calmly, he went back to the basin, washed his hands, and proceeded to the synagogue for *minchah*. He recited *Ashrei* and prayed the *Amidah* carefully, reciting each word distinctly. One of the scholars rose between *minchah* and *maariv* and taught a lesson on the laws of Sabbath. Yoseph listened intensely, happy that he understood more and more of the intricacies of the law. *Maariv* followed, and again Yoseph recited the Shema and his prayers with a calm, sharp clarity.

Only when he returned alone to his tent did it hit him — he was going to die, violently and soon.

He ran his fingers over his throat, and his face broke out in a sweat. He lay down on his bed, and thought and thought. He slept in dribs and drabs, waking up again and again with a start.

He was going to die. His body would be cast into the gutters like the thousands of others, utterly forgotten. He wept quietly to himself, so the guards outside should not hear. There was no escape, no hope.

Finally, in the early morning, he fell into a deep sleep. He would have slept late into the morning were it not for the clamor of Ezra being led back into the tent. Yoseph opened his eyes. The old *kohein* was holding on to his grandson Elazar, and two soldiers carried him to his couch. Yoseph jumped out of his bed and ran to help. They lowered the old man into his bed, and he turned towards Yoseph. Yoseph's mouth fell open in astonishment. Ezra's face was soot black, and his eyes red rimmed and tearful. Elazar's face was badly bruised, one eye almost swollen closed. The soldiers left.

Yoseph knelt before the old man. He poured some water and held it to his lips. Ezra took the cup and swallowed the water eagerly. Yoseph refilled the cup and passed it to Elazar.

"What happened, father?" he asked.

Ezra did not answer. He waved his hand in despair, unable to speak.

"They killed Nadav before our eyes," Elazar whispered hoarsely. "They tortured him, then killed him."

"Why? Who did it?" asked Yoseph.

"The same bunch that interrogated Sabba a few days ago. Then they were polite and respectful, now they were like beasts. They screamed that Sabba had lied to them — they knew everything he said was a lie. They are about to enter the Mikdash, and they wanted to know everything! Sabba was brave. He remembered what he told them last time and began repeating it.

"Then they began beating Nadav viciously. Even so, Sabba refused to retreat.

" 'It is the truth,' he kept saying.

"Finally, one of the Romans took out his knife and slit Nadav's throat wide open. That was it — in a second. Nadav opened his eyes wide with shock, and then fell down dead. They grabbed me next and began hitting me. They held the knife an inch from my throat.

" 'Is he next, grandfather?' they asked.

"Sabba started sobbing. The blood was pouring out of Nadav's body like a fountain.

" 'I'll tell you, I'll tell you everything!' he screamed. 'Please, spare this boy, he is all I have left of all my family.'

"The guard drew away his knife.

" 'Grandfather, tell the truth and we'll spare him. Play games with us and he's dead.'

"So Sabba started talking and talking. He told them everything."

Ezra groaned and rocked back and forth mournfully. Elazar held his bony hands in his, trying to comfort the old man.

"It is all right, Sabba. They would have found out anyway."

Elazar turned back to Yoseph, desperate to talk.

"He told them everything. They knew a lot anyway. Every room, every chamber, every secret doorway, every tunnel. He was afraid they would kill me if he lied. One of them made a large map and marked down everything."

Ezra rocked back and forth and began chanting mournfully, *"Ezri mei'im Hashem, osei shamayim va'aretz... Ezri mei'im Hashem, osei shamayim va'aretz...."*

Yoseph forgot his own worries and spent the whole day comforting Ezra and treating Elazar's ugly bruises. The Praetorians allowed no one to enter. No words were possible or necessary.

Yoseph and Elazar had come to the same conclusion — they were all doomed.

YET THE next morning brought a miraculous change. The determination that had carried the ancient *kohein* for a hundred years returned to him. The tears and weakness were gone.

"*Hashem natan v'Hashem lakach* — Hashem gave and Hashem took...." The words were on his lips the whole day. "*Yehi sheim Hashem mevorach* — May Hashem's great Name be blessed!"

He consoled Elazar and gave him heart. His cousin had died for *kiddush haShem*. It was forbidden to ask questions — that was what Hashem wanted, and it must be accepted with *simchah*. His faith was a mighty rock, and Yoseph found new courage.

He told Ezra about Rufus's warning that Titus planned to kill him in the Mikdash. The old man would not let Yoseph lose heart. Who said it was true? Did anyone know what would be tomorrow?

"Have *bitachon*! Have *bitachon*!" he repeated over and over.

The Praetorians still allowed Yoseph to go to synagogue, at Titus's orders. They followed him to the entrance and left spies to watch him inside. It did not disquiet him anymore. Who knew what caused some Jews to betray their own people? The other prisoners were great *talmidei chachamim*, men of stature. Yoseph watched them secretly as they prayed. He took heart from their very existence.

The threat to his life receded from his thoughts. Three halcyon days passed, and everything continued normally. There was a false lull. The Roman lion crouched, awaiting his moment.

ON THE morning of the sixth of Av, Yoseph knew the lull was over. There was an electric tension in the camp. Legionnaires who had idled in the camp for days were marshaled. Led by their ensigns, to the crash of drums and the blast of trumpets, they marched out of camp, beating their spears lustily against their shields. They smelled blood, and spirits ran high. Riders came and went, and from the distance Yoseph saw dispatches being sent every few minutes from Titus's camp.

Suddenly, Rufus's words flooded back into his consciousness. Yoseph broke into a sweat, and his face turned white. Perhaps Rufus saw him from a distance, for in a few minutes the giant headed briskly in his direction. He wore his crested helmet, and he swung his huge, razor-sharp spear.

Why can't he just go away and fight like the rest of them? Yoseph wondered to himself. *What does he want from me all the time?*

Rufus approached Yoseph, a big grin on his face. "We're ready! We're ready!" he shouted. "We're going in — tonight's the night."

Yoseph looked at him miserably, his sudden rush of fear rendering him speechless for a minute. Then, finding his tongue, "What — what is happening?"

"Just what I told you! There are three legions ready to storm into the Temple. They can go in any time — it'll be a slaughter."

A desperate idea flashed though Yoseph's mind. "Rufus — have you seen Josephus? Has he been in the camp?"

"Of course he's in the camp," Rufus answered. "They are all in there with Titus. Even your friend Caputo. He's Titus's favorite now — after he beat you."

"Rufus — do me a favor?"

The giant looked at him suspiciously. "What favor?"

"I want to see Josephus, talk to him."

The giant nodded calmly. "Oh, so that's it. There is no way."

"Why not? He is your patron, isn't he? We are friends, aren't we?"

"When did we become friends, Levite? I have my job to do, that's all."

"Rufus, it's my last chance. I don't want to die. Maybe Josephus can save me, speak to Titus...."

"And what do I gain from this?"

"Rufus, you know that I am innocent of anything. You see me. I have hurt no one. All I wanted — want — is to serve my God. I have been honest, truthful, with my brethren, even with my enemies. Do I deserve to die for that? Somewhere under all that muscle and armor there must be a heart. Rufus, I beg you — talk to Josephus."

Rufus pulled himself up to his massive height. No one had ever told him before that he had a heart —just brawn. He looked down at Yoseph and mumbled, almost to himself, "I'll see. I'll see what I can do."

Rufus marched off to keep his watch from a distance. But now their roles were reversed. It was Yoseph who watched Rufus like a hawk. He was almost always in sight, but from time to time he disappeared for a short while. To eat? To report to the Praetorians? To seek out Josephus?

Meanwhile, the drums of war grew louder, soldiers sprang up by the hundreds to join the attack, the roar of fighting echoed on the mountains, the battering rams beat a deafening knock of death against the Mikdash gates. Even from a distance, the shock waves of battle reached Titus's camp and the elite prisoners were thrown into dread and panic. As if by signal, all the prisoners ran to the synagogue and cried out for a miracle, reciting psalm after psalm beseeching Hashem's mercy. Yoseph set aside his own fear and joined the congregation to pray for the Mikdash.

The prisoners stayed in the synagogue late into the night, until one by one they dropped out from weariness. Some stayed all night. By the morning, the minyan had gathered again, and the reports came in. The Mikdash had been breached, the Romans had flooded in, and a terrible slaughter was taking place. From time to time, companies of Roman soldiers returned to the camp, singing drunkenly, their uniforms soaked in blood. Usually well disciplined, their officers let them loose. It was not a battle anymore, but a carnival of death, a festival of slaughter.

Up to now, the prisoners had been under a special royal protection. They were wanted for interrogation or to help convince the defenders to surrender. But now the protective shield was lifted. One by one, the prisoners were summoned and led away by guards — and they never returned. Word was that they were being brought to the Mikdash to be killed right on the altar. Yoseph prayed with all his heart for the Mikdash — and for himself.

In the afternoon, he could not keep his eyes open. The heat, the fasting, the endless prayers were taking their toll. He returned to his tent to sleep. When he entered, Rufus was sitting on his couch, waiting for him. He had made himself at home and was eating Yoseph's food. His helmet was laid aside, while Ezra and Elazar cowered in fright in their corner.

"What took you so long, Yoseph?" Rufus bellowed.

Yoseph could see that Rufus was in a good mood, because he had called him by his name. He raised his hand to his mouth and nodded towards the old *kohein*.

"Not so loud, Rufus. You are scaring the old man."

"I got you your interview." Rufus kept shouting, ignoring Yoseph's plea. "Josephus has agreed to see you. You can thank me."

"Did he say anything?" Yoseph pressed him.

"That's not my business, Levite. You wanted to see him; well, he'll see you. Come on!"

Yoseph wanted to wash up and change into a fresh tunic, but Rufus wouldn't hear of it. He rose to his great height, threw on his helmet, and approached Ezra, who looked up at him with utter fear. Rufus pointed a great finger at him and roared: "You behave yourself, hear!"

He roared with laughter and marched Yoseph out of the tent. The Praetorians had given up following Yoseph's every step, especially since they knew he was under Rufus's watch. Yoseph and Rufus crossed the camp, passing groups of celebrating soldiers, and approached a tent not far from Titus's own. The guard was very heavy, but they fell away before the massive Roman.

Keeping an eye on Yoseph, Rufus opened the flap to Josephus's tent and peered in. Yoseph recited the psalm *Mizmor LeDavid* and whispered a quick prayer. He knew his life hung in the balance. In a moment, Rufus reappeared.

"Go in and wait," he ordered.

Hesitantly, Yoseph entered. Josephus was conferring with some underlings. He glanced at Yoseph but did not acknowledge him. They were briefing him on the battle for the Mikdash. The officers were very animated, very excited, swinging their hands to indicate troop movement. Josephus listened intently, but said nothing.

Finally, Josephus seemed to have enough. He interrupted one of the officers in midsentence, thanking him for his time. They took the hint, saluted, and walked briskly past Yoseph to the tent's entrance. It was the first time that Yoseph and Josephus had been alone since he had shared the general's tent.

There was a heavy silence. Josephus stared at the table before him, saying nothing. He was tight faced, not the smooth cosmopolitan that Yoseph knew.

"*Shalom aleichem*, General," Yoseph said.

Josephus still did not look up.

"*Shalom aleichem*," Yoseph repeated.

There was a stone paperweight on the table. Josephus reached down and hurled it straight at Yoseph's head, missing him by inches.

" '*Shalom aleichem*,' that's all you can say?" he shouted furiously. "They are massacring, they are slaughtering, they are butchering our people by the thousands and you say '*Shalom aleichem*'?"

"What should I say?" responded Yoseph. "What can I do?"

Josephus glared at him. "What can you do? What can you do? Nothing, absolutely nothing! It is too late. Our Temple is doomed. But you could have done something! I gave you a chance! I gave you a chance to play before Titus, before Berenice — to please them, to flatter them, to bow and scrape before them — like I do! Maybe, maybe you could have pleaded, maybe you could have begged, maybe you could have saved something. Now, there is nothing! Where are your brains?"

Yoseph recalled the purpose of his visit. Josephus was in a bleak mood. He knew he must be silent.

"I am sorry," he said simply.

"What is it you want from me?" Josephus asked abruptly.

"I — I came to ask for my life...."

"What?"

"I came to ask you to speak to Titus. Rufus told me that I am going to be killed by Titus himself — in the Temple."

"For this you come to me? Didn't you tell me how holy it was to die for *kiddush haShem*? How the martyrs go to the highest seat in Heaven? And now you want to be spared?"

"When they captured my grandfather, I pleaded for his life. As long as we are alive, we have to try to save ourselves."

"So you are afraid after all —"

"The Torah teaches that we must live — as long as we can. We were once friends. I beg of you — can you not speak to Titus?"

Josephus almost smiled. "I don't understand you. You could have been Titus's chief musician. You could have saved hundreds of Jews. You threw it away — and now you want to spare your own life? Coward! Thousands are being slaughtered, and you'll be just another!"

"But —"

"Get out of here! At least die like a man! Don't come begging!"

"But —"

"Get out! Rufus!"

In a flash, the giant appeared. "Take him away! Bring him back to his tent! Don't let him out of your sight, you understand?"

"Trust Rufus, General." He grabbed Yoseph by his shoulder and spun him around harshly.

"Out!" he ordered.

Rufus hurried Yoseph back to his tent, prodding him roughly to quicken his pace. His jabs were painful, and Yoseph looked up at him in surprise and hurt. It was like looking at a stone statue. Rufus did not know him. When they reached his tent, Rufus shoved him roughly inside.

That night, Yoseph turned over and over, unable to sleep. Was Josephus right? Had he made a terrible mistake? It did not matter. It was too late.

IT WAS the morning of the eighth of Av.

Yoseph woke late, after a sleepless night. A strong wind had risen from the southeast, causing the walls of the tent to flap violently, as though the waves of suffering were beating against his door. Ezra sat on his couch swaying in prayer, Elazar tending to his every need. Yoseph washed his hands, went to the entrance, and peered out. The yard was deserted except for a pair of prisoners who hurried by from their prayers. They walked with their heads down, as though trying to escape the fierce stares of the Praetorians who were stationed in front of Yoseph's tent. He thought he heard a scream from the distance, as though someone was undergoing torture. The guard closest to the entrance saw him, rushed over, and pulled the flap closed in his face.

Yoseph placed his ear against the tent curtain, trying to hear what was happening. He thought he heard screams, but he could not be sure. The crack of the tent curtains flapping drowned out everything, as though the very tent sheets were angry at him. He looked to Ezra for comfort, donned his own tallit and tefillin, and prayed *shacharit*. He faced the Mikdash for the *Amidah*, but was full of agony. He wasn't facing holiness, but death — he was praying towards a killing field. How could so much suffering mix with so much *kedushah*?

He completed his prayers by midmorning. He knew that Ezra was fasting, and he himself had fasted the last two days. But it was too much for him — too much worry, too much sleeplessness, too much despair. He ate a little something and, like Ezra across the room, began reciting *Tehillim*.

Around midday, the tent flap parted, and a half-dozen soldiers flooded into the tent. Frightened, Yoseph jumped up. But they ignored him and went straight to Ezra's couch. They did not speak — they did not have to. The ancient *kohein* looked up at the captain, lifted his hands in resignation, and said: "So — it is time."

Neither he nor Elazar protested or pleaded. Death and execution were like forces of nature, inevitable as night following day. One of the Romans helped Ezra rise from the couch. They surrounded the old man and his grandson, and he shuffled slowly towards the exit. Yoseph rose and ran to stop him. One of the soldiers lifted his spear to knock him away.

Ezra cried out: "Wait, please! Let me share just a word! The Angel of Death will not run away!"

The captain nodded, and the soldiers made room for Yoseph. The old man took Yoseph's hands in his.

Yoseph began weeping. "Abba! Abba!" he cried.

Ezra consoled him. "Not to cry, not to cry, my son! There is nothing to fear. When a Jew goes willingly to die for *kiddush haShem*, he feels no pain. The knife blade is like a feather, and we are gone. When your time comes, be strong. Do not run, do not transgress by railing against your God. We will be apart just a little while. If you are summoned, I shall greet you soon in Gan Eden. *Chazak v'ematz!*"

"Enough!" the captain said. Yoseph was pushed aside, and the company continued on its mission. They pulled aside the flap, marched out, and closed the entrance tightly behind them.

Yoseph was alone, the tent walls flapping angrily at every side, screaming at him: "You're next! You're next! You're next!"

Yoseph prepared himself. He could not say any more Psalms — he was *Tehillim*ed out. He thought to himself, *how will I face kiddush haShem? Will I have faith? Will I weep? Will I keep my head high?* He thought of Sabba and how he had suffered — his death hadn't seemed painless at all. But Sabba could still say Shema at the last moment!

Yoseph expected a visit at any moment. But the Romans were not in a rush for him. He sat waiting, thinking, praying *minchah* as soon as it was past *chatzot*, reciting more *Tehillim*, sleeping a little, waking, waiting, waiting, waiting.

THE SUN set. It was the night of the ninth of Av — Tishah B'Av.

Outside, the wind had settled down. Yoseph approached the tent flap, but he was afraid to open the flap. He listened — he heard something, but what, he could not tell. He was very alone. How he wished he had his harp — his closest friend. He would hold it near his chest and sing to Hashem. But the harp, like Rachel — he hardly thought of Rachel — was from a different life, a different world. He was on earth, and they were somewhere up there, with the moon. He knew that every minute was precious, for he did not know what the next minute would bring.

He sat on Ezra's abandoned couch and leaned his elbows against the tzaddik's table. He felt warm, as though Ezra's *neshamah* was still there. He pressed his hands against the smooth marble tabletop as though he were holding the *kohein*'s hands. He felt comforted. He rested his head in his hands and recited the blessings of the Shema, slowly, intently. He lifted his hand to his eyes and pulled together his whole soul, every thought, every fear, every hope, every longing — and poured it into the six simple words:

Shema Yisrael Hashem Elokeinu Hashem echad.

He felt strengthened, encouraged. He rose and went to his prayer spot by the tent wall. He faced the Mikdash, not the tragedy but the holiness that shone Above and Below. God knew what He was doing — that was enough. He prayed with intensity, even with joy. Whatever happened, he would face it with *bitachon*.

He finished his prayers and returned to his couch. He waited — patiently. Even before he heard them, he felt the footsteps approaching. It was the third hour of the evening when the tent flap opened. At first there was nothing, and then the massive bulk of Rufus filled the tent. He leered at Yoseph without speaking, holding him in suspense. Then his face broke into a great smile.

"Time's up, Levite!" he bellowed. He pounded the end of his spear in the ground, like a magistrate passing judgment.

Yoseph rose slowly. He began walking towards the entrance. Rufus lowered his great spear in front of him, blocking his way.

"Wait — what's your rush?"

"What are we waiting for?" asked Yoseph.

"Caputo," answered Rufus.

They stood there silently, the great Roman giant looking pleased, his Jewish prisoner murmuring *Tehillim* frantically, trying to be brave.

The waiting continued and Rufus grew impatient. "Where is he?" he grumbled.

Presently, the flap opened again, and Caputo entered the tent. He glanced at Rufus, and the giant glared back. Although Caputo was of a much higher rank, no one looked at Rufus without a twinge of fear. Caputo approached Yoseph.

"Do you know where you're going?"

It was a strange question. Yoseph nodded, unable to speak. Caputo looked strange, out of control. Yoseph could smell the odor of strong drink on his breath, and his face twitched nervously. He looked haggard, like a man who had not slept well. He looked hard at Yoseph, as though trying to read his face. The last time they were together, they had wrestled for their lives — and Yoseph had let him win. Did he know that?

Caputo gestured towards the entrance. Hesitantly, Yoseph began the walk to his fate. The camp was deserted — even the Praetorians had been dismissed to share the final assault on the Temple. Rufus walked so close to him on the left that his huge spear rubbed against Yoseph's shoulder. Caputo marched to his right, carrying a torch. Yoseph heard a din in the distance, like a great crowd roaring. He listened closely. It was a deep howl, a howl of people crying out in fear and pain. An involuntary shiver coursed through his body. He was hearing his brothers and sisters being slaughtered in the Mikdash, their final screams. Although the Mikdash was on the side of Jerusalem, to the southeast, the screams carried far in the clear night air.

"Where are you taking me?" asked Yoseph.

At first, no one answered.

"Please — tell me."

"To the vault," answered Caputo. Rufus snickered loudly.

As they walked, the deserted campgrounds shone white from the silver moonlight that flooded down. Yoseph glanced up and saw the radiant face of the half-moon watching him, Rachel's face.

He whispered up to her: "Rachel, do not forget me! It was so sweet being your husband. I studied Torah as you asked. I shall miss you very much, and our baby.... You are so precious to me, and I shall whisper to you each night from way up high...."

They reached the end of the camp. Yoseph did not have to be told he had arrived. The vault was a grim stone structure, almost two stories high. It had no windows, just one massive wooden door, secured by huge iron latches. The walls were thick, and the structure looked like the sepulchre that wealthy Jerusalemites built for themselves. Perhaps it had once been a tomb. In the middle of the deserted camp, it stared down grimly like the entrance to the netherworld.

All this time, Caputo had remained absolutely silent. Yoseph glanced at him from time to time, hoping for some word, but the centurion seemed lost in his own universe. Rufus, though, was absolutely jaunty.

"Well, here's your new home," he said jovially, "until Titus is ready to —" He slid his great thumb across his neck and laughed.

Yoseph surveyed his new quarters, glanced up at the moon one last time, and sighed. Caputo extracted a long iron key from his tunic and undid the lock, raising the latches. He pulled the massive door partially open. It was a huge door, made of heavy timbers bolted together. Inside it was pitch black. Caputo handed his torch to Rufus.

"Go inside and inspect the cell," he ordered.

Rufus glared at him. "Inspect it for what? There's nothing in there."

"Are you disobeying my orders?" Caputo challenged. "The last thing I need is for the prisoner to find something to take his own life with. We'll both be crucified. Go inspect!"

Sullenly, Rufus lowered his head and climbed into the chamber. "Check the far wall," Caputo ordered.

The echo of Rufus's footsteps moving towards the back could be heard. Suddenly, to Yoseph's shock, Caputo leaped at the door and swung it shut. His hands shaking, he reached desperately for the huge bar and swiftly closed it over the latch. Then he sealed the two iron bars above and below. He took his great key and locked all the bars tight.

In a moment, they heard the faint sound of Rufus banging furiously against the door, the massive timbers muffling his blows.

Caputo looked around. "Come on," he whispered.

"What are you doing?" asked Yoseph, still stunned by his action.

"Can't you ever follow orders?" Caputo hissed angrily. "Just follow me."

He raced around the side of the vault. They were in the shadows now, between the high fortification wall and the building.

"Follow me along the wall," he whispered. "Don't run, don't make any noise." Caputo strode ahead. He made no attempt to hide. If he were stopped, he would be an officer charged with bringing a prisoner for execution. They followed the wall for a few minutes until they reached a corner tower.

"Stand next to me," he ordered. Yoseph moved closer, and Caputo grasped his arm painfully. They marched across the yard, a centurion with a prisoner in tow. The few soldiers standing on guard hardly took notice of them. They reached a small tent, and Caputo shoved him quickly inside. He saw a couch, a table, and a small lamp. In the corner, a uniform lay crumpled on the floor. Caputo raised his finger to his lips. He strode to the door and peered outside. Satisfied, he returned to the couch and took off his helmet, then signaled Yoseph to sit next to him.

"Don't talk louder than a whisper," he began. "We only have a few minutes and then we have to leave."

"Where am I going?" asked Yoseph.

"I am taking you out of here, out of Jerusalem — if you can make it," Caputo answered.

Yoseph look at Caputo in disbelief. He shook his head to see if this was a dream. "You're helping me escape — why?"

Caputo looked at him without speaking. His eyes had the same mad look as they had when he had come to collect him with Rufus. Finally, he raised his hand and pointed an accusing finger at Yoseph. "You — sent him to run after me, pursue me!"

Yoseph shook his head. "I sent? I sent who?"

"Your grandfather. He doesn't leave me alone. I see him day and night. I turn around and he's staring at me. I go to sleep and he is in my dreams. 'What do you want from me?' I asked.

" 'Help my grandson live!' he yelled. 'You killed me, but let him go free!'

" 'I can't do that,' I told him, 'they'll crucify me!'

" 'You must! He let you win in front of Titus. He could have disgraced you in front of all of Rome! Now you must help him go free!' "

Caputo's finger almost jabbed Yoseph's nose. "You sent him after me. You are a demon, a sorcerer! The old man doesn't let me live. He's everywhere, tormenting me. You sent him! I can't sleep, I can't think, I can't lead my men!"

Yoseph stared uncomprehendingly at the centurion. Was he a madman — or was Sabba really helping to save him? Who cared? It was Hashem's doing.

"Help me get free, and I will pray that he leaves you alone," said Yoseph. "But what about Rufus — when he comes after you?"

Caputo dismissed Rufus with a wave of his hand. "That Sicilian oaf? He'll never get out for days — not until I let him out. I'm the only one who has a key to those bars. No one will hear him, and if they do, they'll think it's some Jew. I'm in charge."

"But you'll have to let him out sometime."

Caputo snorted contemptuously. "I guess I'll have to. I'll say you overpowered me. He will be as guilty as I am for letting you get away. He'll shut up."

"And Titus — what will you tell him?"

"Titus? Titus is in the Temple with his armies. He probably forgot you ever existed. Now listen — there's no time. I brought you a Tenth Legionnaire's uniform. I am going to try to pass you off as a junior officer. At night they won't look too hard. Just keep your mouth closed. Hurry up!"

Climbing into a Roman uniform was awkward. Caputo had brought everything, the tunic, armor, breastplate — even a helmet. Yoseph shivered as he donned the enemy's uniform. When he was forced to wear a slave's badge, he had felt like a slave — he had become a slave. Now that he wore a Roman uniform, he was a part of the enemy. He felt ashamed — if his brother Shimon saw him, what would he say?

Is Shimon even alive? he wondered. *Where is Binyamin?*

But there was no time for guilt. Caputo inspected his appearance with a look of amused satisfaction.

He nodded. "You know, you could really pass for a Roman!"

Now that Yoseph was disguised, Caputo seemed less anxious. They left his tent and headed for the cavalry stalls. They walked by Roman guards, even Praetorians. Yoseph kept his head high, but avoided looking at anyone directly. Some of these soldiers may have guarded him as a prisoner. But they walked by, unmolested.

Caputo went to a stall and in a few minutes returned with his mount. He had saddled it previously, with an extra blanket for a passenger. The beautiful white mount was high-strung, and sniffed at Yoseph's neck suspiciously. Caputo, who had been so agitated earlier, had regained some of his authority. His face took on the demeanor of a Roman officer, and he ordered Yoseph to mount behind him.

"When we get to the gate, don't say anything. Let me do the talking."

Yoseph could not pray, not even in a whisper. He had been just a hair's breadth away from death. Now he was mounted on a Roman steed, on his way to freedom. He recited the twenty-third psalm in his head, hoping that a miracle would occur. They reached the heavily guarded gate, and Yoseph trembled, afraid one of the guards would recognize him. Someone may have seen him with Ezra, or wrestling Caputo. But the entrance was more like a party than a guard post. The guards were milling about, laughing, even drinking from mugs. Only a handful of Praetorians were truly at their posts. They approached Caputo, their spears pointed at his horse. "Who are you, and where are you going?" they challenged.

"Caputo, centurion of the fifteenth cohort, Tenth Legion. We are going to the Temple — at Titus's orders."

They turned to Yoseph. "Your name and rank?"

Yoseph did not answer. The guards approached closer. "Soldier — name and rank?"

He felt the stab of Caputo's elbow in his stomach. His silence had stirred the guard's interest.

"Josephus Leviticus, adjunct in Agrippa's forces, here to interrogate the prisoners. I am ordered back to my unit — there is no more need for my service."

The guard snorted. "You can't interrogate corpses. Proceed!"

Caputo slapped his reins and rode swiftly out of the camp into the darkness of the Jerusalem night.

I am out, thought Yoseph, *I am out!*

They rode eastward, traversing the New City, then south towards the Mishneh wall. In the distance, Yoseph saw a huge glow coming from the Mikdash, like the flow of the lamps of the Simchat Beit HaSho'eivah on Sukkot. The chorus of screams, the roar of soldiers cheering in triumph, and the crash of drums grew louder and more frightening. The streets of the New City were deserted except for bodies. The Jews were gone, and the Romans had all run to the Temple.

Yoseph knew he should be full of sadness, mourning, shame, but in truth he was happy — for his own escape. He had cried enough for others; now he had to look after himself.

The Roman siege wall cut through the neighborhoods of Jerusalem like a great, ugly wound, traversing the Second Wall into the Mishneh neighborhood and then to the Temple. Caputo crossed the siege wall and followed the Second Wall past the north gate. They rode deep in the shadow of the huge wall, concealed from the eyes of the moon. The wall met the edge of a craggy hillside.

Caputo dismounted, and Yoseph jumped off after him. A huge cave entrance loomed before them. Holding the horse's reins, the centurion approached the forbidding black entrance.

"Do you know this place?" he asked.

Yoseph shook his head.

"Your old priest told us it is the burial place of the kings. They quarried stones from here, and the tunnel goes right through the city underneath, as far as the Temple itself. No one goes here except for fugitives who are trying to hide — and that's you. The legion is too busy looting the Temple to look for a few Jews tonight. Go in there, as far in as you have the nerve. I hear it's pretty frightening at night. Tomorrow night, right after sundown, I'm going to rendezvous with you."

"Where, here?"

"No. I have to be with Titus tomorrow — in the Temple. You remember the Antonia Fortress, overlooking the Temple courtyard?"

"Yes...."

"It's rubble now. But part of the main tower is still there. Climb up tomorrow evening through the back pile. When you reach the tower, hide. There are still a few small rooms left. I'll come for you with a change of clothing and some supplies. I can get you out of the city — the rest is up to you."

Yoseph gazed at the tomb-like entrance, and a shiver went through him. It was like a great black mouth, ready to swallow him.

Caputo saw his hesitation. "Okay, Levite, is it yes or no? Make up your mind, or I'll leave you here on your own."

"Yes — we'll meet."

"This is the only safe place for you to hide," Caputo repeated. "I knew you would be scared. I would be also. There are bats and scorpions and who knows what else in there. But I brought you a companion —"

Caputo reached up to a saddlebag strapped along the horse's neck. He opened it, carefully extracted a leather pouch, and placed it in Yoseph's arms. It was his harp!

Yoseph stared at Caputo in shock and wonder. Was this the man who had been so cruel to his Sabba? Could evil turn into good?

"Go!" Caputo hissed. "Go before we are both caught!"

Clutching the harp under his arm, Yoseph turned and slipped into the mouth of the black cave.

THE TIME had come. In the afternoon the pains began. She and Leah stayed hidden in their little cave, protected from the sun by the olive branches they had laid over the entrance. Now the sun was about to set, and she begged Leah to stay by her side. Like a good sister, Leah vowed that she would be with her wherever she was.

Their little hiding place, a refuge from the relentless Roman searchers, was like a prisoner's cell. It was airless and small. Rachel wanted her baby to be born free, under the heavens, under Hashem's protection.

The sun was just at the treetops when she took Leah by the hand and led her to her secret hiding place by the apple tree. It was there that she had spoken her first words and had rediscovered her radiant smile. She took branches and leaves and made a soft bed. Leah dipped towels in the cool stream to wipe her brow. The sun set, and in the east the yellow moon of the ninth of Av showed its face over the mountains of Shomron. Rachel gazed up at its golden beams and knew that she was no longer alone.

Soon after, the moon rose higher and became the purest white, and her real labor began.

Her pains were very strong. They began intermittently, stopped, and started again. She had never given birth before. Leah had never attended a birth before. *We are the mothers of Egypt,* Rachel thought to herself, *and the angels will be our midwives.* When the pains came, Leah wiped her brow with the cool rags. When they desisted, Rachel lay back and laughed and dreamed of the joy ahead.

It was now the middle of the night, and the pains came quicker, more intense. Rachel cried out in anguish.

Leah tried to calm her, guide her, but she was just murmuring words of affection and encouragement. She did not know what to do. Before, there had been pauses, rests, but now they came one after the other, terrible, terrible birth pangs. Rachel cried out in pain, Be born, baby, be born, you are causing me such pain. But it was not yet time.

"Help me, Leah," she screamed in anguish. "Do something, I'm dying from the pain!"

Leah cooed and caressed her hair, but what else could she do?

IN A wood not far, the holy tzaddik Yaakov stood and recited *Tehillim* fervently. He heard her suffering, but he knew that there was nothing he could do — yet. It was not time yet. He felt her pains in his own body, they seared his soul. But it was not time — yet.

IT WAS the small hours of the night. Her screams were heartrending. "Help me, Hashem, help me! I cannot take it anymore." She looked straight up at the moon high above her and wept. She remembered Yoseph, she remembered his beautiful melodies, and she held on, held on.

Rachel grew strangely quiet. Leah put her face close to Rachel's and saw her staring up into the dark sky. Rachel turned to Leah. "Where is the moon?" she pleaded.

Leah reassured her, "The moon is going down. Look, Rachel, the beautiful morning star is rising. Soon it will be dawn. Hold on just a few more minutes, and the sun will rise. Be strong, my sister."

Rachel could not bear it any longer. She could not cry out, so great was the suffering. She looked at the lighting sky, and she knew this was the end.

HE STOOD there, watching the sky grow gray and then pink. He knew this was the day he dreaded, and the day he waited on, the day of the maelstrom, and the day of — revenge.

Soon, the sun would rise — *netz*. He waited, waited and prayed. Then he saw the first fiery shafts burst out of the womb of the eastern sky. His eyes glistened. Three times, he sang:

"*Or zarua latzaddik uleyishrei lev simchah!*

"*Or zarua latzaddik uleyishrei lev simchah!*

"*Or zarua latzaddik uleyishrei lev simchah!*

Sparks of the light, seeds of light, planted deep in the earth, ready to blossom forth for the righteous at the time of Redemption.

THE FINAL pains came like a great, powerful wave.

Leah cried, "Rachel, the baby is coming!"

And then, in a rush as strong as life itself — the baby was delivered.

Rachel's head fell back against the great stone that was her pillow. She closed her eyes and wept.

"*Baruch Hashem,*" she murmured over and over. "*Baruch Hashem*!"

Her eyes still closed, she called out: "Is he all right, Leah? Is everything all right?"

Leah did not answer immediately. Rachel opened her eyes.

"Leah, answer me — is my baby well?"

Leah held the child close, protecting him.

"Look, Rachel," she said finally, surrendering the baby.

She passed the child to his mother. Rachel stared at his beautiful face. The rising sun bathed his face in golden beams, so that it appeared that the shine came from his face and lit the sun. She looked at his head and caught her breath — his head was covered with flaming red curls, like a little crown of fire!

RUFUS SAW Caputo slam the door shut.

After sweeping the torch around the vault in a fool's errand, he turned just in time to see the centurion pushing at the door desperately. He ran back as fast as he could, but the bar was already scraping into its latch. He banged furiously against the wooden beams, but it was like hitting stone. Even his powerful fists couldn't make a dent.

For a second he was stunned. Why had Caputo done it? It wasn't the Levite — he had seen him standing back, rigid as a dummy. Had he known about it? It didn't look like it — he had been scared stiff the minute they began the march to the vault.

Why had Caputo done it? Was Josephus behind it? It could not be. It didn't make sense. He stood there, a great clumsy giant, trying to assimilate the shock and the shame. His shame turned to anger, and his anger to terrible fury. He had been played the fool, and soon the whole Praetorian Guard would hear about it, and he would be the joke of Rome. He breathed in deeply in his anger, but the smoke of the torch he still held in his hand filled his lungs, and he erupted with a great cough. Angrily, he threw down the torch and stomped on it to put out the flame. Now he could breathe, but he was cast into pitch blackness in the sealed vault.

There was a little stone bench along the back wall. Rufus sat down to think, still holding his great spear. Because he was so big, they thought he was dumb. He could not help having been born big. They thought he had no feelings, like a beast of the field. In front of him they shook, yet behind his back they laughed. He had feelings. He had a brain. But now he was locked in the stone vault, stuck like a fool, and everyone — everyone — would have a good laugh at his expense. Rufus seethed with anger.

As his eyes grew used to the dark, he saw a tiny point of light on the ground. Where was it coming from? He stood up and inspected it closely. It was moonlight, coming from above. The tiniest shaft of moonlight seeped down from the roof, like a tiny finger, beckoning him. How could there be moonlight coming through the impenetrable roof? The roof was not quite two stories high. No prisoner could ever reach it. But he was Rufus, who stood almost seven feet tall. He lunged at the source of the light with his raised spear. The point of the spear hit the roof with a thud.

The roof was thick and solid, made of layers of heavy timbers bolted together, with hardened clay sealing the gaps. But somehow, the winter rains had seeped through the wood. In his fury, Rufus lifted his great arms and smashed again. The slightest shower of wood dust fell across his face. He smiled.

Again, he held the spear between his hands and raised his arms like two mighty pistons straight at the beckoning moonlight. More dust fell, and a tiniest splinter. Again he struck, and yet again! He struck with every muscle in his arms and legs, with the force of the fury and shame he felt, with all the might of Rome and the sacred ensigns, with the vision of his father and mother urging him to bring honor to the family. He struck again and again, until the mighty wood, mighty but rotten to the core, began to crack under his terrible assault. He saw the face of Caputo, and each blow was a strike at his head. He saw the face of the Levite, the Levite he had been kind to, who had now run away like a rabbit — and he swore to catch him.

Rufus worked relentlessly all night. The roof was a powerful adversary. It was ten inches thick, and even in its weakness it gave way grudgingly. The moon that had beckoned him had disappeared, and for a few hours he hacked away in pitch darkness. At last he stopped to rest and to appraise his progress. He had made an opening the size of a hand through which the faintest gray light of dawn had begun seeping through. He knew that soon the guard would change, and fresh legionnaires would man the watchtowers.

He took a deep breath and, with some of his rage now vented, pounded steadily, chipping away at the sides of the wood, splinter by splinter. The sky above grew brighter. Rufus arched the spear behind his back and, with one great thrust, heaved the point against the side of the opening. There was a groaning sound, and then a shower of wood and stones came raining down on him. Rufus held his hands up to protect himself and then surveyed the fruit of his effort. Above him was a big opening, the size of a man. He was overjoyed at its sight, eager to be free of the prison. But there was no way to climb out. He could reach the roof with his spear, but there was no way he could lift up his hands and pull his huge bulk up there.

He held his spear high and passed it through the opening, raising and lowering it like a signal. "Hallo!" he bellowed. "Hallo! Can anyone see me? Hallo!"

He called again and again but received no answer. Where was everyone? Probably drunk. Maybe they were all in the Temple looting, while he was stuck in his hole. His face grew red from frustration. He was about to lift his spear one more time when suddenly the opening was blocked by a face. A legionnaire peered down at him.

"Who is that?" the legionnaire asked.

"It's me, Rufus!" the giant bellowed back. "Get me out of here!"

"Who?" The legionnaire squinted. He stood back to let the light fill the vault. "Is that you — the giant?"

"It's me!" Rufus answered roughly. "Don't just stand there! Get me out of here! Get help!"

The face disappeared. Rufus looked up at the brightening sky with disgust. But in a few minutes, not one but two faces peered down. Rufus recognized the second face. It was a captain of one of the companies. He looked down and grinned.

"Rufus, what are you doing in the vault?"

Rufus burned with anger at his pleasure. "I'll write you a letter.

Get me out of here — now!"

"Look," the captain said, "we can't open the door; it's locked. And we can't break it open, either. Wait a moment, we'll get you a ladder. You can climb out."

Rufus waited helplessly. He looked at his uniform. It was covered with powder, and his face was as black as a chimney sweep's. Presently, a face appeared and called down, "Step back — we're going to get you out!"

In a moment, a ladder appeared at the opening and was quickly lowered down. It was a tall, narrow ladder used to scale enemy walls, and it reached over the roof. A face peered down. "There's a few of us up here, Rufus. We'll try to help you."

The giant began climbing the ladder. Under his great weight it began buckling, and the men above struggled to pull it straight. He reached the opening and stuck his head out. He took his first breath of fresh air. The red ball of the sun was just rising over the camp wall.

Four men were on the roof to help him. On the ground, a dozen soldiers watched his progress, laughing and making jokes. Rufus was humiliated. He could not pass through the opening; his shoulders were too broad. He stepped down the ladder, raised his arms through the opening, and stuck his head out.

"Pull me out of here!" he roared.

The men on the roof grabbed his arms and began pulling. Inch by inch his great bulk emerged. For a moment he became stuck and could not move either in or out. The men below were beside themselves with laughter. He had been stupid — had he removed his clothing, he could have slipped right out.

Two more men clambered up to the roof and grabbed his arms.

"Pull!" the captain shouted. Rufus forced himself upward, the men tugged with all their strength, and with a mighty grunt Rufus was free.

The giant stood on the roof like a newly hatched chick, covered in gray dust. Wood chips hung from his disheveled locks. He raised his arms in fury and glared at the men below.

His angry gaze moved from man to man. "Who wants to laugh at me?" he roared. "You? You? Go on — you were laughing! Here I am! Now — who wants to laugh?"

No one smiled or looked at him straight. Rufus flexed his arms triumphantly, shook himself free of dust, and turned to his liberator.

"Where is the centurion?" he screamed. "Where is Caputo?"

CAPUTO AWOKE from a dreamless sleep and smiled. He had finally slept without the old man stalking him in his dreams, threatening him, filling him with a dread that pursued him every waking hour.

He had done it — the Levite was out of the camp. He would have a lot of explaining to do — to Titus for not appearing at the Temple last night and to the warden in charge of the prisoners. He had a story ready for both. The only shadow of worry was the great ox locked up in the vault. What would happen when he freed him? It was like letting a beast out of a pen. He would let him bake in the vault for a few days and then make up some story about the Levite overpowering him and taking away his key. If Rufus made trouble, he would lay the blame on him for the Levite's escape. There was no way Rufus would be believed against a centurion. The penalty for letting a prisoner escape was crucifixion.

He sat up in his bed. Titus was probably sleeping after a night of carousing at the Temple. He had just pulled on one sandal when the tent flap was torn open. Caputo looked up. The huge figure of Rufus towered over him, his legionnaire uniform in tatters, his face covered in gray soot.

Caputo had no time to react. In an instant, the giant sprang at him, throwing him back down onto the bed. He jumped atop him, dropping his great bulk on the centurion's chest. Caputo tried to cry out, but he couldn't breathe. Rufus glared down at him like a wild beast.

"Where is the Levite?" he roared.

Caputo tried to answer, but he was suffocated by Rufus' great weight. Rufus slapped the side of his face hard.

"Where is the Levite?" he repeated.

He lifted his palm to strike again. Caputo tried to answer, but all he could squeeze out was a thin cry. His eyes began rolling upward.

Rufus saw his distress, sneered, and lifted his great bulk a few inches up. Caputo drew in air furiously, like a drowning man. Rufus repeated: "Where is the Levite? You let him go free! Where did he go?"

Caputo shook his head. "I — I don't know."

Rufus dropped his great weight back onto Caputo's chest. With a great crash, the bed collapsed to the floor. Caputo struggled to escape from under the huge weight. Rufus saw his struggle and grasped his face in his massive paw. He squeezed hard. The centurion's eyes were wide open with fear.

"I don't know why you did it, but you did it! I saw you! You — you locked me in! He's gone! You've made me the laughingstock of the legion. Titus! Josephus! I'll give you one more chance, or I'll squeeze you until you croak! Where is the Levite?"

Caputo feebly raised his hand, begging Rufus to let him breathe. The giant released his grip, squatting over him like some great beast. Caputo could not speak. He gulped in air, his chest heaving. Finally, the color returned to his face.

"I had to do it, Rufus. He is a sorcerer. He sent his grandfather to haunt me, day and night. I had to set him free, that's why I did it. I had to lock you in — to let him escape —"

Rufus's face darkened. The centurion was admitting his guilt — he admitted that he had locked him in the vault, locked in to die of thirst, to roast like an animal. He stared angrily at Caputo. His voice lowered to a feral growl. "Where is he? Where is the Levite?"

"If I tell — if I tell you will you get off me?"

Rufus glared at him. "Tell me the truth and I'll get off you."

"He is hiding in one of the caves under the city. I'm supposed to meet him tonight."

"Where?"

"At the ruins of the Antonia Fortress. I was going to spirit him out of the city."

"And me? What were you going to do with me?"

"I was going to let you out. I swear! Once he was safely away, I would have let you out, told you everything, gotten you a commission, an estate...."

"Do you know what the heat is like in that vault, centurion? The stones burn like an oven. What would you have opened the door to, my ashes?"

"Rufus, I'm sorry.... The grandfather —"

The giant shook his head. "Centurion, I'm also sorry."

He held the centurion's face in his hands, peered into his terrified eyes, and gave his head one sharp, violent twist. Satisfied, he dropped Caputo onto the bed.

Rufus lifted his great bulk and rose. He stood at the side of the collapsed bed and gazed down at the centurion's body. "I kept my word, didn't I? I climbed off you, like I said!"

He saluted smartly. "Good-bye, Caputo!"

He stormed out of the tent, looking neither right nor left. The Praetorians saw him, but no one dared approach. Something bad had been done to the giant — Rufus had not locked himself into the vault. They kept their distance.

Rufus stormed into his own tent, which he shared with three other legionnaires. They were all gone, probably at the Temple. He pulled off his disheveled uniform and washed himself clean. His body was scraped raw from squeezing out of the vault. He anointed his wounds with oil, then reached into his kit for a clean uniform and a bright red tunic. He went to a corner and extracted his massive bronze breastplate, the one that the Levite could not even lift, and drew it over his great chest. He donned his great iron helmet, topped by a flaming red crest that almost reached the roof. He tested his visor, dropping and lifting it over his face. He could see the frightened eyes of the enemy, but they could not see him. He had never yet used his great polished oak spear, with its razor-sharp hooked iron spike that tore to bloody shreds wherever it struck. When he fell upon his enemy, he would be an invincible engine of death.

Rufus smiled and raised his great arms. He roared a great shout of joy, like a lion of the field.

Rufus was back!

Caputo, who had tried to trap him, was dead!

And now he would find the Levite and carry his shredded body back to Titus as a trophy!

IT WAS midnight when Yoseph entered the yawning cave entrance. Somewhere deep inside lay the bones of the kings of Judah, but that did not frighten him. But as he proceeded deeper into the tunnel, the faint glow of moonlight disappeared, and he was in utter blackness. He stuck out his arms like a blind man, not knowing where he was going, why he was going. He scented the musty moisture around him and knew that the walls were closing in on him. He heard the echo of his own footsteps. Caputo said there was a way out at the other end. How far was it? The ground was carpeted with stones, and he almost tripped. He walked slowly, like an old, blind man.

He had walked a half-*mil* when his eyes began growing accustomed to the darkness. He suddenly realized that he was not alone. There were other people here. First he felt the heat of bodies, then he heard the slightest sound of breathing. From time to time, his boot brushed against something that was not a stone, but a foot. Yet everything was totally still. This was the last refuge for the terrified Jews of Yerushalayim. This was the last place where they could escape the terrible slaughter above, like fish descending to the depths of the sea while a storm raged above.

The deeper he proceeded, the more he felt the presence of others. The cave, which had been cool and wet, now grew warm from living human bodies. Suddenly, someone reached out and grabbed him by the ankle. He tried to pull free, but whoever it was wouldn't let him go.

"Sit! Sit!" the voice hissed in Aramaic.

Yoseph fell to the ground alongside his captor, angry that he had been snared. He reached out to feel the other man's face, and his hand fell on a beard and *pei'ot.*

The man placed his mouth near Yoseph's ear. He spoke in the faintest of whispers.

"You have just come here?"

"Yes."

"What is above?"

Yoseph did not want to answer.

"So awful?"

"They have overrun the Mikdash."

The man did not respond, but Yoseph felt his shoulders heave with grief. Yoseph lifted his hand and placed it on the unseen shoulder, trying to console him.

After a few minutes, the stranger stirred himself.

"Why are you here?" he asked. "There are many others hiding in the cave, but they have not come so deep inside. Where were you going?"

Yoseph did not know how much to tell him. But he thought to himself: *I am in this tomb, blind, helpless, and starving — what more can I lose?*

"I was told that there are other exits from this cave. I am supposed to meet someone at the Antonia Fortress. Do you know where that exit is?"

"Shhh!" the man warned. "You are speaking too loudly. The Romans may hear us. Listen — they quarried these caves for many years. It is like a bee's hive. There are little tunnels that run everywhere. Some have steps that reach up to the outside. You must find your own way. Hashem must guide you!"

He grew silent and dropped his head, returning to his misery. Yoseph could not bear to just sit and hope. If he moved on, he might come across a shaft that led outside. He grabbed the stranger's arm.

"Who are you?" he asked.

"What's the difference who I am?" the man answered bitterly. "Ask better who I might have been!"

Yoseph blessed him, and the stranger squeezed his hand in gratitude.

Yoseph rose and began making his way deeper into the tunnel. For a moment he was afraid he had lost his direction and was going back the way he came, but the air grew lighter, and the cave ceiling began to rise. Fresh air was seeping in from somewhere, giving him hope. But he still groped in darkness.

He estimated day would soon break. So much had happened in so few hours — his death march, his escape, his midnight ride through Jerusalem, and now the underground walk beneath the city. He had not eaten or drunk since yesterday afternoon. Thirst and exhaustion gnawed at him. He walked and walked, but to where — and for how long?

He came to a crossroads in the underground labyrinth. The tunnel divided into three directions, straight ahead, right, and left. During his walk, the tunnel had made many twists and turns. He had no idea where he was or which direction he faced. But he remembered the maxim of the Mikdash:

"*Kol pinot she'atah poneh eino elah layemin* — always turn right."

He placed his faith in Providence and turned right, descending a narrow tunnel that sloped downwards into the very bowels of the earth. And yet he felt a freshening breeze, so he knew there was an opening somewhere. Here there were no more refugees hiding — it was too cramped. And yet the fresh air that blew in smelled sweet. It smelled familiar.

Yoseph stopped and breathed in deeply, and the hair on his neck stood on end. He knew that scent! It was the smell of the *besamim* wafting down into the shaft. Even now, the fragrance flowed softly over the narrow, limestone walls.

I am under the Mikdash. The Mikdash is right here, right above me!

He stopped and wept, clasping his harp close to his chest. *Kinor, kinor, we made it! From under the apple tree to the foundation of the Mikdash, we made it!*

He did not want to go further. He was happy to die right there. But he knew that he had no right to stop. He must try to survive, to live. He inhaled the intoxicating smell of the *besamim* and lay his head down against the stone, tucking the harp next to him like a child would a pillow. For the first time — for the first time in many months, he was at peace!

He closed his eyes and fell into deep, deep slumber....

YOSEPH WALKED in a garden of *tzari* and *tziporen*, frankincense and myrrh, spikenard and saffron, and all the beautiful spices of Eden. A smooth path of asphalt stones marked the way, and he picked here and there a flower, a spice, a fruit. He came upon a cool brook that bubbled across the path and took a deep drink.

Suddenly the branches fell away and Yoseph stopped in awe and fright. Way above him was a huge mountain...more than a mountain, a colossus that rose from a massive base and rose and rose — into the very sky itself, past the moon. Its base was deep black coal, its middle was lustrous silver, and high above was a blinding peak of the purest gold. His whole body shook at its awesome size.

"What is it?" he asked Sabba, who stood near him, smiling.

"Aha!" said Sabba, "you see what we have accomplished! It is our mountain!"

"Our mountain?"

"The mountain of Israel! Our *tefillot*, day after day, night after night, soul after soul pouring its heart out to God. We thought we were accomplishing nothing — that our prayers were in vain. But the prayers created a holy mountain whose peak reaches right under the *Kisei HaKavod*!"

"Why is its bottom coal black?" Yoseph asked.

"Those are the *machshavot chitzoniyot*, the outside thoughts that were mixed into the prayers. They also became part of the mountain, but fell down to the base and turned to coal."

"And what is the silver?"

"Those are the prayers that were said with full heart and full *kavanah* for the needs of our holy people!"

"And what is that blinding gold that reaches right up to the Heavenly Throne?"

"Those are the prayers of tzaddikim who prayed for the *Shechinah* to be united with its Source above...."

Yoseph walked in a wide meadow beside the mountain, taking in the many beautiful grasses and flowers. He walked through pastures where cows grazed at peace and over hills covered with sheep like waves of white snow.... Then the ground trembled and a great shadow appeared. It grew darker and darker, and as the footsteps grew nearer it became as dark as night. A huge ox approached, larger than a mountain. He had great horns and tossed his head from side to side. But he was not angry, just so huge that he blotted out the sun.

Sabba smiled at the sight of the huge beast.

"Sabba, what is that great ox?" asked Yoseph.

"It is the Shor HaBor, the Great Ox, and it is ready to be slaughtered for the Feast of the Mashiach. Look how he bows down and stretches his neck for the *shochet.*"

The *shochet* waved his great *chalif*, and the Ox bowed before him, stretching out his neck — one, two, three, and the Ox was done, ready....

Yoseph walked along the seashore and saw the huge sea birds circling above. The sands were golden, and out in the distance fish frolicked and jumped in and out of the water. The sun was warm, and the air so clear. Suddenly, waves began rising from the sea, washing up farther on the beach. Yoseph ran back from the sea, but still the waves rose higher and crashed deeper. In fright, Yoseph ran up to the hill, and the sea grew taller, taller than a mountain.

Sabba smiled merrily. "Oh, we are going to have a beautiful feast!"

"Why is the sea churning, Sabba?" Yoseph asked.

"It is the Livyatan approaching, the great Leviathan, king of the sea. He is coming to be caught by the fishermen — look, here he is approaching!"

Like a huge ship, the black shape of the Livyatan approached from the far sea, churning white water and raising great blue waves. He swam straight for the shore, and Yoseph was afraid he would strike high upon land. But a hundred fishermen stood with their nets ready. At the last minute the great Leviathan raised his huge head to the sky, stared down with his two enormous white eyes, and bowed his head to be caught. In a moment, the fishermen tangled him in their nets, and he did not struggle.

Flowing through the tunnel walls was the fragrance of the holy *ketoret* and the Ineffable *kavanot* of the high priests in the Holy of Holies. They seeped through the hot, intoxicating air. Yoseph breathed in, breathed out the Mikdash, the Mikdash Below and Mikdash Above, and he slumbered on, deeper and deeper....

He sat among tens of thousands, among millions and millions, at golden tables with crystal plates and golden cups, and wine flowing from jasmine jugs. Above them stretched the *or halivyatan*, the skin of the Leviathan, like a great rainbow canopy, glistening so much that there was no need for lamps, although it was the middle of the night, and the red moon rose below. Servants in purple Roman robes brought platters of meat and set a golden dish before each person. Yoseph tasted the flesh, and it melted like honey in his mouth. His eyes lit up.

"Sabba, what is this food?"

"Aha!" laughed Sabba, "it is the flesh of the Great Ox, and it has the taste of Gan Eden. For it is time for Mashiach to arrive, and this is his great feast. Listen to the singing, listen to the Torah, listen to the rejoicing!"

The sound of Torah and *zemirot* filled the earth.

"Get ready," Sabba warned. "Any minute now, he will arrive, redemption will be here!"

His whole being shaking, Yoseph waited. He ate, he drank, he sang, he imbibed.

Suddenly, there was a great clap for silence from the front of the hall.

"*Rabbotai*! Stand up! The Mashiach has arrived!"

There was a great hush in the hall. Millions stood up. Not a sound was heard. Not a peep. Everyone stood, stood. They waited five minutes, ten minutes, a half-hour.

At last the announcer came back into the hall. "*Rabbotai*! Not yet! He is coming soon! In a short while! Let us rejoice!"

In a second, everyone sat down. They returned to their celebrations, to their rejoicing, to the *sitrei Torah*, the hidden secrets of the Torah that poured out from every side.

Yoseph turned to his grandfather, disappointed. "When, Sabba?"

Sabba smiled. "Not to worry! They said he is here! Soon! Soon!"

Suddenly, there was a tremendous burst of excitement in the front of the great hall. Those at the head began rising, and the announcer ran to the front again: "*Rabbotai*! Stand up! He has arrived! The Mashiach has arrived!"

Millions and millions rose like one. They stood, eyes glued to the side door where he would appear. Not a word, not a sound. Yoseph held his breath. They waited. Ten minutes. A half-hour. Where was he?

In a few minutes, the announcer reappeared from the side

door. He stood in the middle of the floor. "*Rabbotai*! I am sorry to inconvenience you for nothing! I am assured he is on the way! Just a few more minutes! Let us rejoice — he on his way!"

"You hear?" one cried to another. "He was late just two times. It means he is coming closer. Every delay means he is closer! Soon, soon!"

As if to compensate the guests for their disappointment, the servants returned with even more platters of the meat of the Shor HaBor, and jugs filled with wine from the Seven Days of Creation. Soon the disappointment was forgotten, and the *zemirot* resumed at a higher pitch than before.

Yoseph turned to his grandfather. "When, Sabba, when?"

Sabba smiled joyfully. "Can't you tell, he is very near. Look!"

Sure enough, the announcer returned to the center of the floor. "*Rabbotai*! Stand up! It is no mistake this time! I have received the news. The Mashiach is here! Stand up! Be ready! Not a word when he walks in! The Mashiach, he is really here!"

The announcer ran again to the side door. He disappeared for the longest time. No one spoke. No one breathed. No one looked away from the door, waiting for the first glimpse of the Mashiach. Suddenly, the door was flung open. The announcer raced to the middle of the floor. He screamed out:

"*Rabbotai*! I have made a terrible mistake! It is not the Mashiach! It is the *chevlei haMashiach*! The time of the birth pangs of the Mashiach has arrived! Run! Hide for your lives! It is the birth pangs of the Messiah!"

A great fright possessed the guests. A cry of anguish and fear rose from their throats. People began running hither and yon. The ground shook underneath, shaking like an earthquake. Yoseph turned to grab his grandfather, but he had vanished. People ran everywhere, and there was a great commotion. Yoseph looked up, and the sky had turned into a great fiery ball, and there was chaos.

He began weeping. Where could he run? Where could he hide? The sky was on fire! The earth was trembling!

"Come, come into my sukkah," a friendly voice beckoned.

Yoseph looked hard. That sweet, homely smile — he recognized it. "Sabba Zerach, what are you doing here?"

"Don't be afraid," he welcomed Yoseph. "Come, come under my sukkah and you will be safe from the fiery sky and the trembling earth."

It was such small, flimsy sukkah, with only a few branches. But here he was safe, and it was peaceful.

In his sleep, Yoseph began crying like a baby, crying, crying, crying until...

...HE AWOKE, and he was in a coal-black tunnel deep in the womb of the earth.

His throat was parched. The heat of the cave had dried up whatever moisture his body retained. He had no idea what time it was, whether it was day or night. He had no idea where he was, which way to proceed, or how to escape. For a moment, he was struck with panic. The whole weight of the Mikdash lay atop him, and he felt its walls crushing him. He jumped up, scraping his head. It was a narrow, low shaft. He felt a breeze blowing from one end, and on the breeze, a whiff of spices. It was not his imagination. The fragrance of the Mikdash *ketoret* could be felt as far as Yericho and its sweetness still lingered in the air.

But that meant danger. If he followed his nose, he would be led straight to the Mikdash. He would be caught in the Roman slaughter. He dared not panic. He retraced his steps from his hiding place to the main cave. He was back at the crossroads.

"*B'yadcha afkid ruchi*.... In Your hands I place my spirit..." he murmured.

He marched straight ahead, determined to follow the main cave wherever it led him.

He had walked about another half-*mil* when he sensed that the cave floor was beginning to slope upwards. Heartened, he quickened his pace. He perceived the faintest glimmer of sunlight in the distance. With his eyes accustomed to the pitch darkness, the sunlight shone like a beam, although it was just a tiny shaft. He was so overjoyed to see the daylight again that he wanted to run as fast as he could. But as the light grew stronger, he saw that the floor was strewn with stones, and he had to step carefully over them. There was no question now. The cave grew narrower but was sloping sharply up towards an opening. He craved the light as much as food or drink.

The last few feet were very steep, with rough steps hewn into the wall. There was a small, narrow entrance, like an escape hole someone had cut. He climbed the steps and peered out. All around were mounds of rubble, half-burnt houses, and corpses littering the street. Nobody was about, but the deserted walls echoed with the chilling sound of a great assault taking place nearby. Should he exit? He felt his grimy face and looked at his disheveled Roman uniform. He looked like a legionnaire who had fought a tough battle. What more did he have to lose?

He stepped out of the opening and looked around. On one side was the great northwest corner of the Temple wall. And there, beyond the rubble, was the back of a great tower — Antonia! Caputo had told the truth — he was right at the fortress!

The fortress stood like a mighty testimony to the great battles that had taken place. Much of it lay in ruins, a mountain of rubble that climbed up to the one remaining tower. That was where he was to meet Caputo. Should he wait for nightfall to climb up? No. He was drawn to climb now. Overhead, the sun was well to the west. He must have slept through the whole day. He heard the sounds of battle, the sound of shrieks mixed with roars of triumph, the booming of drums, and the blasting of trumpets. He suddenly realized that he was still grasping his harp to his chest. He hadn't even realized he was holding it. The sky grew dimmer as dusk began to fall.

"Come, *kinor*," he whispered. "We will gaze again upon the holy Mikdash."

Half-climbing, half-crawling on all fours, he scaled the steep slope of rubble. It twisted north, behind the one standing tower, so that he could not see the Temple courtyard until he ascended to the top. Above, the red ball of the setting sun warmed his side. He reached the top of the pile and jumped over to a walkway that hung out from one of the towers. He wiped the sweat from his eyes and turned to look down on the Mikdash.

The Temple stretched like a great, wretched canvas below him. Great fires burned along the walls and balconies of the courtyards round about, framing the Mikdash in a curtain of black smoke. *Dam va'eish v'timrot ashan* — blood and fire and pillars of smoke. The Temple grounds were packed like they were on Yom Kippur, legion after legion pouring onto the holy grounds, swords slashing right and left, spears and daggers slaughtering thousands of Jews trapped among them. There was no battle, no defense. There was not even ground to walk. The shrieks of the dying and soon to be dead, the pleas for mercy, the last desperate rattle of resistance.... The walls, the courtyards, the towers, the roof of the Heichal, the gates, were packed with the executioners and their victims.... Blood, blood everywhere, and corpses without number.

He stared at the altar in horror. It was covered with legionnaires and their helpless victims, like the carcass of a lion swarming with black ants. One at a time, Jews were being led up the *kevesh* ramp to have their throats slit atop the altar. Some of the victims walked to their fate calmly, reciting Shema, while others were crying and struggling and had to be held tight by burly legionnaires until the slaughter. The *kevesh* ramp was awash in blood, blood running down it like a stream. Piles of bodies lay all around the altar.

In the midst of the horror, there was great celebration. More and more Roman cohorts entered with their proud banners and ensigns, from the Fifth, from the Tenth, from the Fifteenth, from the auxiliaries, from Gaul and Spain, Arabia and Dacea, Greece and Africa, their trumpets blaring, their soldiers roaring like victors in a gladiatorial contest. How could the enemy fit in even more? But they came, rushing in for the slaughter, for the plunder, for the victory, for more slaughter, the slaughter of the hated Jews. The roar of the dying and of the victorious, the babble of every tongue, reached to the heavens.

Legionnaires plundered everywhere, forcing open every chamber and window, violating the most sacred precincts. Nothing escaped their grasp. The Lishkat HaGazit, the Beit HaMoked, the chamber of the shekalim, the chamber of the gold and silver vessels, even the very gold paint on the walls was peeled off. They stripped all like locusts, grabbing what they could hold, wallowing in the riches of the Mikdash. They found the hidden chests of silver shekalim, tens of thousands of silver coins, and showered down their treasure like candy.

Dam, va'eish, v'timrot ashan! Blood, blood everywhere, and flames forming a map of fire, outlining the outer walls and balconies of the Temple. Plumes of inky smoke mushroomed upward like a great black beast. The Mikdash was a maelstrom of death and holocaust.

Amidst the chaos and the thunder, an even more jubilant roar suddenly rose from the Romans. They all turned to the entrance of the Heichal, which was out of Yoseph's sight from his vantage point in the northwest corner. Even the butchers on the altar stopped their bloody work and raised their arms in salute.

Then Yoseph saw the object of their cheers. Titus himself descended the steps of the Heichal, followed by his legion commanders. Behind him, soldiers bore a heavy, swollen blanket. It was the beautiful *parochet* itself, rolled up, engorged like a great serpent with the sacred Heichal vessels that it had swallowed whole. Titus marched through the Temple ground, through the bloody streams that ran down the *kevesh*. He saluted, beaming, and his generals at his heels were stern and triumphant. Along the east wall, the sacred Roman ensigns were raised in salute!

The drums boomed, the trumpets and horns struck a victory march, and the slaughterers went back to their bloody task.

Was this the place where Avraham had bound up Yitzchak for the *akeidah*?

Where was an angel to scream, "Let the lad live!"

Yoseph collapsed to the ground and held the harp to his face, like one comforts a newborn baby. He kissed it and pressed it to his bosom, running his fingers slowly over the strings.

Together they wept for the *churban* happening before their very eyes:

> *Ehli Tziyon v'areha kemo ishah v'tzireha, v'chivtulah chagurat sak al ba'al ne'ureha!* — Wail, O Zion, and her cities, like a woman suffering from birth travail, and like a maiden girded in sackcloth, lamenting the husband of her youth!

RUFUS PEERED out from his hiding place and saw a legionnaire standing in the fortress above, watching the battle. Why was he not there fighting like the rest? Where was his unit? Then he saw him fall to the ground and draw a harp up to his face. Then he knew — the Levite! He fondled the long shaft of his spear and it grew warm from the stroke of his hand.

From where had he gotten that legion uniform? Caputo, probably. It was filthy, like he had crawled through a hole in the ground.

There was no rush. There was plenty of time to relish the strike. Rufus surveyed the tower in the setting sun. There was no place for the Levite to run, no other exit, unless he jumped off the tower to the flames below. But he, Rufus, wanted him for himself! He felt the honed head of his spear. He wanted the Levite hanging from that head! He went back to observing him. The Levite was playing his harp! He was singing to his God while his people were being killed in front of him! He was strange, that Levite! Rufus observed him closely, with studied curiosity, like a cat inspects a mouse before he chews him up.

He admired the Levite — but he hated him.

Rufus had the spear, but he had the harp — not just the harp, but also the voice, the living God, the soul that would never die....

All Rufus had was his huge hand wrapped around the shaft of his spear. All he had was the sting of death.

Something warned him: *Kill him or he is going to kill you!*

RUFUS LOWERED his mask, lifted his spear, and silently climbed from his hiding place. Yoseph did not even notice him, so lost was he in his prayers. Rufus lowered the spear chest high and twirled it around like a plaything, weighing its heft, measuring distances.

Hearing footsteps, Yoseph looked up, expecting Caputo, and there loomed Rufus. Crouching on the ground, his harp clasped to his chest, Yoseph stared at the giant, his eyes wide with shock. Rufus stood like a huge robot, faceless but watching, the deadly barb of his spear aimed at Yoseph's heart. No more than thirty feet separated them.

The Malach HaMavet is here, Yoseph knew.

Yoseph jumped up instinctively, holding his harp like a shield. Still the giant said nothing, just stared. In his massive breastplate, his crested helmet which seemed to brush the sky itself, he looked like something unworldly. The silence added to the feeling of unreality.

"Rufus," Yoseph asked finally, just to hear a voice, "how did you get out of the vault?"

The giant broke his ominous silence with a short, bitter laugh. "It was the moonlight, Levite. The moonlight was the angel that showed me how to hack my way out."

Moonlight? It could not be, thought Yoseph. *Would my beloved Rachel show him the way to escape?*

"Where is Caputo?"

Again, he laughed. "You were expecting him to help you? I snapped his neck with these two hands — look!" He put his spear into his elbow and lifted his hands, squeezing his fingers.

Again, there was a brooding silence, the silence of imminent death.

Yoseph turned and looked behind him. The walkway ended in thin air. The way he had come was blocked by Rufus. There was nowhere to run. He could feel the heat of the flames along the bottom of the tower. There was no escape.

"Rufus, what is going to happen?"

Silently, the giant lowered his spear and aimed it at Yoseph's middle. In a display of skill, he twirled the spear swiftly like a top, so that the winged barb whirred like a drill. He twirled and paused, twirled and paused, over and over. Rufus was enjoying himself. The cat was playing with the mouse before eating him.

Yoseph glanced heavenward and silently begged Hashem for help. He held his beloved harp over his heart. Out of the corner of his eye he saw small puffs of smoke rising out of the Heichal's golden windows. The setting sun bathed everything in a crimson light, as if the air itself had turned to blood.

"Rufus, can we just talk for a moment, before...."

The giant lifted his spear casually. "I am in no rush. You're not going anywhere."

"Yes, but I want to talk to you, my old friend Rufus, not to an iron mask. Can't you lift your visor?"

The giant hesitated, then reached with his left hand and lifted the visor. The setting sun shone on his face, painting it blood red. He stared grimly at Yoseph.

Now he was no longer a machine, but a man. Yoseph looked Rufus straight in the eye. "Are you going to kill me, just like that?" he asked.

Rufus twirled the spear playfully in his hands. "No, Levite, not just like that. I am going to ram this spear right through you, give it a good spin, and then present your leftovers as a personal gift to Titus."

"But Rufus — what did I do that I should die? What is my crime? Did I kill your father, your mother? I never harmed anyone in my life."

"You die because Rome says you must die! Because Titus has ordered your execution, you and all the other Jews who are resisting!"

"Resisting? Rufus — this is our land! This is our city! Jerusalem is our heart! The Temple Mount has been ours since Abraham! What business do strangers have in our land?"

Rufus stamped the spear on the ground angrily. "Don't start debating with me, Levite! I am Rome! You are Jerusalem! Either we rule or you rule — and our gods say that we rule, and you die!"

He lowered his spear and took a step forward, the spear pointed straight at Yoseph's neck. Yoseph stepped back instinctively, holding the harp in front of him like a shield. Rufus saw his pathetic attempt to defend himself and grinned.

Yoseph lifted his hand, declaring a time-out on his execution.

"Just know, Rufus, that we have a God of justice. This harp I am holding is very powerful. If you kill me, I will come after you like a demon in your dreams! I will pursue you all the way home to Sicily!"

The mention of his Sicilian home infuriated the giant because it was always used to mock him. He lifted his huge spear and with one terrible blow knocked the harp out of Yoseph's hands and smashed it to the ground. Yoseph looked down in horror. The poor harp's frame was broken and its strings were twisted. His beautiful, holy harp was destroyed!

He turned to the great giant in front of him and screamed in pain and fury, "You big ox! You broke my beautiful harp! You smashed it! You are not a Rufus — you are an Esau!"

"A what?"

"An Esau! You are the angel of Esau! You are horrible! You were born to destroy."

"I am Rufus," the giant roared back furiously. "I am not Esau!"

"Esau!"

"Rufus! I am Rufus!"

Yoseph's words had struck him to the quick. His face turned dark, and his eyes burned with maniacal fury.

"Enough!" he screamed.

He lowered his visor, revealing his death mask. He took a great breath, raised himself erect, and then lunged forward, his huge spear clenched tightly in his hand.

Unconsciously, Yoseph backed away, but there was nowhere to go.

"Don't move!" his grandfather whispered. "Stand still!"

Rufus gained speed, building momentum like a charging bull. He closed the gap between himself and Yoseph and then, blinded by his visor, he stepped right onto Yoseph's harp. The harp jumped up like a little animal, snared his boot, and held fast. The giant stumbled, then pushed forward with a terrible grunt, unintentionally digging his spear deep into a crevice. Swept up by his own momentum, he suddenly shot upwards, high over Yoseph. Rufus screamed in shock as the spear lifted him over the tower wall so that he hung precariously over the abyss below.

Yoseph stared in disbelief. Rufus's spear bent and swayed like a straw. His visor flew open and he gazed down, wide eyed, at Yoseph, speechless with terror. Suddenly, with a terrible crack, the pole broke cleanly in half, dropping Rufus silently over the wall like a stone. Yoseph ran to the edge of the tower and looked down. The great form of Rufus lay across the flaming pyre below, his armor already beginning to melt around him.

Yoseph stood up in shock. He was so resigned to death that he expected to see Rufus still standing on the walkway, his spear pointed at him. But he was gone! Rufus was gone! Numb, Yoseph ran to his harp and lifted it, stretching its burst strings. He inspected it closely. One string had survived, the string that had tripped Rufus! Rabbi Yaakov's string!

NIGHT FELL, but the great Temple courtyard was as lit up as day.

Yoseph gazed at the multitude below, all staring at the Heichal. The Heichal was in flames, burning like a great candle. From every window sprouted huge tongues of orange flame, and a thick cloud of black smoke formed a crown over the Temple's golden head. A world was coming to an end, and even the Romans were awestruck by the disaster they had wrought. The Jews being led to slaughter wept.

Yoseph gazed one last time, at the vast multitudes, at the doomed Mikdash, at the thousands of faces bathed in the red and orange glow of the conflagration, and it seared into the deepest chambers of his soul.

I am the witness of my people, he thought.

He backed slowly away from the doomed Mikdash, climbed past the tower and out of view.

I must run. I must hide. I must survive.

He turned and scrambled wildly down the hill of rubble. He glanced once at the rising moon, veiled behind the mushrooming clouds, and escaped silently into the refuge of darkness.

EPILOGUE

The Fifteenth of Av

Nachamu nachamu ami.... Comfort, comfort, My people, says your God.

Speak to the heart of Jerusalem and proclaim to her that her time of exile has been fulfilled, that her iniquity has been conciliated, for she has received from the hand of Hashem double for all her sins!

A voice calls in the wilderness: "Clear the way of Hashem; make a straight road on the plain, a highway for our God!"

Every valley shall be raised, and every mountain and hill shall be made low, the crooked shall be straight, and the rugged a level low land!

Behold, my Lord Hashem shall come with strength, and His arm will rule for Him; behold His recompense is with Him, and His wage is before Him. Like a shepherd who grazes his flock, who gathers his lambs and carries them in his bosom, who leads his nurslings!

She stood under the full moon of the Fifteenth of Av. Night shone like day as the huge celestial sphere rose higher and higher, turning every leaden rock into gleaming silver. Was this the day on which the mountains had rung with the voices of maidens rejoicing in their beauty and holiness, dancing in great circles with garlands in their hair, wearing snow-white dresses to show the pureness of their dreams and hopes? Where were the fair maidens now? They had been snatched away by wicked soldiers, never to see their fathers or mothers again. The hills were silent, and only she and Leah survived by hiding, hiding like beasts of the field.

She was alone except for the tiny baby she clasped to her heart. She gazed down at his little face. The white moonlight lit up his features. He had a tiny smile. Maybe he recognized the face of his *abba* up in the moon.

She had told Leah to stay in their hiding place and had gone alone to stand in the hollow near the brook. The branches of the apple tree spread over her like a fragrant canopy, and she called up to Yoseph, "Abba, Abba, how we miss you! Shine your countenance down upon us! Look how round and bright you are tonight! Does that mean that you are close? This is the first night that I have been strong enough to leave my hiding place and show you our baby. Look! I gave birth to him right here, under the apple tree. The branches were my protection!

"How alone I have been, even with Leah! How I have counted the days! I sent you to study Torah. Does that mean I shall only speak to you on the moon? Have you forgotten me, my Yoseph?"

She stared up at the great white orb, and a tear formed in her eye.

"I have not forgotten you," his voice whispered.

She continued staring upward, not moving.

"Have you longed for me as I longed for you? I longed for you through fire and earth, air and water, in the bowels of the earth, and walking among princes and rulers. Rachel, I am back."

Slowly, she turned and looked. Yoseph stood at the gnarled trunk of the apple tree. Bathed in white moonlight, he looked like a spirit, not a man. Was it really he? Was it his spirit? Perhaps her wild imagination had conjured him up? He smiled and took a step towards her. Frightened, she ran away.

"Rachel, I fled all the way from Yerushalayim to be with you, and now you run away?"

She gasped. "I don't know if it is really you — or an impure spirit of the forest...."

"Would a demon carry this?" He reached down and lifted a harp. "Do you recognize it?" he asked.

"Yoseph's harp — your harp!" Her eyes widened, and her face contorted with joy. "Is it you — is it really you? You look so thin! And your harp, what happened? Look, every string is burst —"

Yoseph smiled. "No — there is one string left. It is the string given me by the tzaddik, Rabbi Yaakov. Even Rufus could not destroy it."

"Who is Rufus?"

"It does not matter! But listen to this one string!" He lifted his hand for quiet.

He stood in the dappled moonlit shadow of the branches and plucked the string. It trembled and vibrated like a firefly, and out flowed a melody so sweet it could have come from a ten-stringed harp. He stopped and grinned. "You hear the miracle? Rabbi Yaakov poured all pitches and chords of the other strings into this one string! It receives from all and pours out all."

Rachel gazed at Yoseph without speaking. Yes, it was he — he was back! But now she was shy of him. She had spoken for months to Yoseph on the moon, but now, after all these months, this magnificent young man was almost a stranger to her!

She took a deep breath. "Come — don't you want to see your baby?"

Yoseph approached cautiously. He, too, was shy — he had forgotten how to be a husband. Yet the closer he drew to her, the more their shyness melted. They were husband and wife, and this was their child.

She drew back the baby's blanket, and he peered into his little face. It shone in the moonlight. He was beautiful. Yoseph closed his eyes and pronounced a blessing over his new son.

She looked up at Yoseph. "What shall we call him?"

Yoseph was about to answer when he heard footsteps. He lifted his finger to his lips and listened closely. Rachel heard the footsteps, too. They were not coming from her hideout — it could not be Leah.

The steps grew more distinct — it was a man, or men.

Yoseph's face grew dark with fury. He had run all the way to here to escape from the Romans, had finally found his wife and baby — and now the nightmare was back. The Romans were relentless in their hunt. He set down his harp and found a thick branch that had fallen from the tree. It was the only weapon he had. He would not plead this time — he would fight them. He kept his finger to his lips, gazed at Rachel one last time, and faced the approaching footsteps.

Whoever it was was coming from a dark copse of pines that bordered the hill. Yoseph and Rachel stepped back silently, seeking whatever concealment they could find under the tree. They had a clear view of whoever was approaching. Suddenly their intruder was in clear view, bathed in the purity of moonlight.

It was the tzaddik, Yaakov.

He stood there and gazed down at them. Yoseph stared in disbelief. Yaakov looked at them and smiled. He spoke so softly that Yoseph could not hear him, but he could read his lips: "*Baruch Hashem*!"

Yoseph dropped his stick and raced up the hill to the old man. They embraced, and then Yoseph helped him down to the apple tree. He did not need much help — despite his age, he walked with the step of a youth. Yaakov's eyes were fixed on the little bundle in Rachel's arms.

They huddled in the dappled moonlight under the tree. "How did you know where we were, that I had returned?" asked Yoseph.

Yaakov smiled at the question. "How did I know? My heart never parted from you for a second — or from Rachel!"

"Come, Father Yaakov," Rachel invited, "come see our baby!"

Proudly, she drew back the blanket. Yaakov studied the baby

closely, but said nothing.

"Is it bad that he has such red, red hair?" Yoseph asked.

"King David also had red hair," Yaakov answered.

"But Eisav was Edom, red of red...."

The holy man shook his head. "*Ha'adom, ha'adom!* If Eisav had chosen to be a tzaddik, he could have been a thousand times greater than his brother! He could have attained the *neshamah* of Mashiach, from the highest realms!"

They stood there, savoring the moment of peace, the beauty of the light, the miracle of the baby.

"What shall we name him, Father Yaakov?" asked Rachel.

"What do you wish to call him?" he responded.

"Shall we not call him David, for his red curls?"

Yaakov shook his head. "No — it is not time yet for David. David is for the future, for the Redemption. Call him —"

He paused and concentrated. He opened his eyes and sighed deeply, trying to control the tears.

"Call him — Menachem Tzion — the Comforter of Zion, for he will comfort us from our terrible destruction."

"Did you see the Mikdash burning?"

Yaakov nodded. "Yes, I saw them burning."

Rachel turned to the old man. "Holy tzaddik, what shall happen to us — to Yoseph and me, the baby, my sister Leah?"

"You must go into Exile — you must leave the Holy Land," he declared.

Yoseph struggled to contain himself. "Leave Eretz Yisrael? Leave this holy land? How can we?"

Yaakov nodded emphatically. "Look up. Do you not see?"

He pointed to the white moon, sailing like a lonely bride across the star-filled night.

"See — the Holy *Shechinah* is going into exile! Look how she weeps, like Mother Rachel, for her children! She has seen the suffering of her people, and now you must flee with them...."

"Why must we suffer so?" cried Yoseph. "For how long, Father Yaakov?"

"These are the *chevlei haMashiach*, the birth pangs of the Messiah. Be strong! Have faith! Push, push like a baby pushing to be born from its mother's womb, so push for the Redemption to be born.

" '*Ateret tiferet l'amusei vaten* — a crown of splendor for those born by Him from the womb who are destined to renew themselves like it...."

"*Chazak v'ematz*! Be strong and courageous — for you shall live, and you shall return, and you shall build, and you shall ascend the Holy Mountain!"

Yoseph and Rachel stood there with tears in their eyes.

"I must go now." Yaakov turned and began walking up the rise, back into the dark woods.

Yoseph ran after him and laid his hand upon his shoulder. "Wait, Father Yaakov!"

The old man stopped and turned. Yoseph ran back to the apple tree. He lifted the harp from the ground and raced back to Yaakov.

"This harp saved my life — please take it as a gift."

"It is yours, I cannot take it."

"Please," Yoseph pleaded. But the old man shook his head firmly.

"Father Yaakov, we must go into Exile now. I beg of you — keep watch over this harp until we return and reclaim it in the name of all Israel."

Yaakov lifted his great brows: "*B'sheim kol Yisrael* — for all Israel? That is different!"

He took the harp like a bride accepting a *ketubah*, a guarantee, a security. They embraced, and Yaakov turned quickly up the hill and disappeared among the pines.

Yoseph returned to Rachel. Even in the darkness of the night, Menachem Tzion's face shone like daylight, and his bright red locks were a garland of fire.

"Come," Rachel whispered to her husband, "we shall set upon our journey...a journey that will lead us back to Jerusalem."

"And there," answered Yoseph, "we shall reclaim our harp in the name of all Israel!"

Brach dodi u'dmei lecha letzvi o l'ofer ayalim, al harei vesamim... Flee, my beloved, and be like a gazelle or a young hart on the mountain of spices....

A NOTE FROM THE AUTHOR

The Harp is a work of the imagination which came to me each Tishah B'Av, begging to be written. The fictional characters are real — for they are the *neshamah* of every Jew seeking to ascend to Yerushalayim, to enter the courtyards of the Mikdash, to bask in the holy presence of the *Shechinah*.

There are a number of historical characters who appear in *The Harp*. This writer is not a professional historian, but I will try to briefly describe their place in history.

- Josephus, or Flavius Josephus, was born in Jerusalem about 38 C.E. He was a *kohein* and a Jewish general who eventually went over to the Romans. During the battle for Yerushalayim, he tried to convince the besieged Jews to surrender and was struck by a rock hurtled from the walls. He wrote *The War of the Jews*, from which the descriptions of the battles in this book were culled.

- Agrippa II was the great-grandson of Herod and the last "King of Judea." He aided the Romans and led an army of three thousand against the besieged city.
- Princess Berenice was the sister of King Agrippa II and renowned for her beauty. She met Titus in Alexandria and, together with her relative, General Tiberius Alexander, supported Vespasian in his bid to become Emperor of Rome. (It should be noted that Rome was in the throes of a civil war, with different generals vying to become emperor. Vespasian won.) She later became Titus's consort.
- Rabbi Tzaddok was a great *Tanna* who is mentioned in the Talmud as having fasted for forty years to save the Mikdash from destruction. Rabbi Yochanan begged Vespasian for a doctor to help Rabbi Tzaddok recover from his terrible fasting. (The few words that Rabbi Tzaddok utters to Yoseph are adapted from the Chafetz Chaim's *Introduction to Lekutei Halachos* on *Zevachim, Zeicher Chanoch* edition.)

I thank the Almighty that He allowed me to write *The Harp*. May you and I and all Israel soon see the coming of the Messiah and the rebuilding of the Holy Mikdash, where we will worship in joy *kimei olam uch'shanim kadmoniyos* — as in days of old and in former years, *amen selah*!

M.U.G.

GLOSSARY

Abba — Father

achat — one

achat ushtayim — one and two

achat vasheish — one and six

achat vasheva — one and seven

achat ve'achat — one and one

achat ve'arba — one and four

achat vechameish — one and five

achat veshalosh — one and three

Aleinu — prayer recited at the end of the three daily prayers (after *Shemoneh Esrei*)

aliyat haregel — pilgrimage to Jerusalem for the three holidays of Passover, Shavuot, and Sukkot

am Hashem — the nation of God

Amein — Amen

Amidah — the prayer recited thrice daily (also called *Shemoneh Esrei*)

amud — where the chazzan stands to lead the prayers

aron kodesh — holy ark

avodah — service

avodat Hashem — service of God

ayin hara — evil eye

azarah — the courtyard of the Temple

badchanim — merrymakers at a wedding

barkai — the morning star, the announcement of dawn

Barechu — lit. "Blessed is He," a prayer recited before Shema

baruch Dayan ha'emet — blessed is the True Judge (said when one hears of a death)

baruch Hashem — thank God

bayit — home

begadim — clothing

Beit HaMikdash — the Holy Temple

Beit HaMitbachayim — the Temple slaughtering house

Beit HaMoked — a central hall on the north side of the Temple

Beit HaMikdash shel Ma'alah — the spiritual equivalent of the Holy Temple in the Heavens

beit midrash — study hall

ben Torah — Torah scholar

besamim — spices

bikkurim — the first ripening fruits of the season, which are brought to the Temple

bitachon — trust (in God)

bli neder — without a vow

chag — holiday

chalif — ritual slaughtering knife

chas veshalom — Heaven forbid

chatan — groom

chatat — sin offering

chatzot — noon or midnight

chazak v'ematz — be strong and courageous

cheirut — freedom

chesed — kindness; also a reference to one of the seven Divine attributes through which God sustains the world *chevrah* — group of friends

chodesh tov — have a good month

chupah — wedding canopy

Churban — the destruction of the Holy Temple (literally, a destruction)

chutz limkomo — intent to put the blood of a sacrifice in the wrong place

derech ha'avot — in the pathway of the fathers

deshen — ashes

duchan — the dais in the Temple

Ein Sof — the Infinite (God)

emunah — faith

erev Pesach — the day before Passover

eirusin — engagement

Essenes — a sect of Jews that separated itself from the mainstream and adopted many foreign practices

eved Hashem — servant of God

Gan Eden — the Garden of Eden

gevurah — strength; also a reference to one of the seven Divine attributes through which God sustains the world

Hallel — verses from Psalms recited on holidays in praise of God

Hallelukah — praise God

Hashem li velo ira — Hashem is with me, I shall not fear

Heichal — the inner chamber of the Temple (which contained the *shulchan*, the *menorah*, and the golden *mizbei'ach*)

hod — splendor, one of the seven Divine attributes through which God sustains the world

Hodu laShem ki tov — Give thanks to Hashem, for He is good

kallah — bride

kameah — an amulet

kavanah — concentration

kedushah — holiness

ketoret — incense offering

ketubah — marital contract

kevesh — ramp

kibbud av — honoring one's father

kiddush haShem — sanctification of God's name

kinor — harp

kippah — skullcap

Kisei HaKavod — the Throne of Glory (God's Throne)

kiyor — basin

Klal Yisrael — the congregation of Israel

kodashim — sacrifices

Kodesh HaKodashim — Holy of Holies in the Temple

kohein (pl. *kohanim*) — priest

korban Pesach — Paschal sacrifice

korbanot — sacrifices

l'chayim — a toast; literally, "to life"

lishkah — chamber

Lishkat HaEitz — the chamber of the wood

Lishkat HaGazit — the chamber of the Sanhedrin on the Temple Mount

ma'arachah — pile of wood on the outer *mizbei'ach*

maariv — evening prayers

machatzit hashekel — half-shekel collected yearly from every Jewish male

machshavah l'haniach — intent to put down the blood of a sacrifice

malach — angel

Malach HaMavet — the Angel of Death

malchut — royalty, one of the seven Divine attributes through which God sustains the world

maror — bitter herbs

matzot mitzvah — matzah baked especially for the mitzvah of eating on the night of seder

mazal (*mazla* in Aramaic) — fortune

mazal tov — congratulations

mechutan — one who is related by marriage

mekomo — the correct place for the blood of a sacrificial offering

melamed (pl. *melamdim*) — teacher

menachot — flour offerings

mesirut nefesh — self-sacrifice

meturgeman — a person who transmitted a Torah scholar's teachings (literally, a translator)

metzora — one afflicted with *tzara'at*, a disease similar to leprosy

meyuchas — one of good lineage

middot — character traits

Mikdash — the Sanctuary

mikveh — ritual immersion pool

mil — a measure of distance, approximately a kilometer

minchah — afternoon prayers

minchah gedolah — the earliest time one can daven *minchah*

mishmar — a group of *kohanim* in charge of a week of Temple service

mishnah (pl. *mishnayot*) — a halachic teaching transmitted orally until the days of Rabbi Yehudah HaNasi and codified in the body of law called the Mishnah

mizbei'ach — altar

Mori — my teacher

neshamah — soul

netzach — eternity, one of the seven Divine attributes through which God sustains the world

nissuin — marriage

olei regel — those coming to Jerusalem for a festival

parnasah — livelihood

pasuk — verse

pei'ot — locks of hair on the side of a man's head which may not by cut by a razor *perutah* — penny

Perushi (pl. Perushim) — Pharisees; the sages and their followers, who adhered strictly to mitzvah observance

Pesach — Passover

pesiah — step

Pesukei D'Zimrah — verses of praise recited daily as part of the morning prayers

pigul — a sacrifice which was carried out with improper intentions

rabbotai — my masters

Ribbono shel Olam — Master of the Universe

Rosh Chodesh — the beginning of a new month

Sabba — Grandfather

Sanhedrin — High Court in Jewish law

sefirah — one of the seven Divine attributes through which God sustains the world

sela — an ancient monetary unit

seudah — meal

seudat hodaah — meal of thanksgiving

Shabbat — Sabbath

shaliach tzibbur — prayer leader

shalom aleichem — peace be unto you

Shamayim — Heaven

shammash — the flame in a menorah used to kindle the rest of the lights

Shechinah — the Divine Presence

shirah — song

shiur — Torah lesson

shloshet y'mei hahagbalah — the three days before Shavuot

shochet — slaughterer

sicarii (Latin) — criminals

simchah — joy

simchah shel mitzvah — joy of doing a mitzvah

Simchat Beit HaSho'eivah — the celebration of water drawing, a ritual performed in the Temple on Sukkot *sinah* — hatred

sukkah — a booth

talmid chacham (pl. *talmidei chachamim*) — Torah scholar

tamid (pl. *temidim*) — daily offering

Tanna — a Sage of the days of the Mishnah

tefachim — handbreadths

tefillah (pl. *tefillot*) — prayer

Tehillim — Psalms

tena'im — prenuptial agreement

tiferet — glory, one of the seven Divine attributes through which God sustains the world

tishbachot — praises

tzaddik — righteous man

tzitzit — fringes that the Torah commands us to wear on a four-cornered garment

tzurvah d'rabbanan — a young Torah scholar

ulam — the hallway that separated the outer court of the Temple from the Heichal

Ve'emunah kol zot — the opening of the third blessing of Shema in *maariv*

Yaaleh V'Yavo — additional prayer recited on Rosh Chodesh

yegiah baTorah — toiling in Torah

yesod — foundation, one of the seven Divine attributes through which God sustains the world

zemirot — *songs*

zerikah — throwing the blood of a sacrifice

zivug — mate

Made in the USA
Middletown, DE
31 July 2025